OUR OWN WAY
by Misty Vixen

D1528764

CHAPTER ONE

Freedom did not feel like it was supposed to.

As he drove down the rain-slicked streets of his city, beneath a fading October sunset and slate gray skies, Gabe Harris reflected on what exactly it was 'supposed' to feel like.

Words came to him.

Liberation.

Exaltation.

He would have settled for joy.

Up ahead, the light turned red and he rolled to a stop at a vacant intersection. He glanced at the clock mounted in his dash and saw that it wasn't even six in the afternoon yet. Looking up through the saturated windshield, he could see that there was perhaps half an hour of daylight left.

And then the city would be shrouded in darkness.

Maybe it was just the gloomy atmosphere sapping him of his serenity.

The light turned green.

He resumed driving, looking forward to ending this process of moving all his crap from one location to another. If nothing else, the day had been taxing and he just wanted to lock himself behind a door and turn his brain off.

That was possible now.

That gave him a flicker of excitement, and something like hope.

Yes, he could go to his new apartment, walk inside, close and lock the door, and no one could come in if he didn't want them to.

Well, that wasn't *completely* true, but on a social level, he could tell everyone to screw off and they'd have to abide by it.

And he was in a mood to after the past…

Gabe tried looking for a suitable stopping point in his past.

The past six months? No, longer.

The past year? Certainly longer than that.

Decade would have to do.

"Damn," he muttered as he almost missed the turn into his new parking lot.

Pulling in, he found a spot as close to his new apartment as possible and parked. Killing the engine, he popped the trunk and got out.

The rain had stopped.

Though the distant thunder that still rumbled occasionally meant more was coming. For a moment, Gabe looked up at the intense clouds that defined the sky above him. It wouldn't have been out of place in some dramatic painting. He knew his predilection for storms meant that the far off thunder was more promise than threat.

As he began gathering the last of his things from the trunk, (just two boxes that, despite every effort simply would *not* fit during the previous trip back from his old place), Gabe was forced to admit that while freedom may not feel like how he had hoped, it *did* feel like something.

And that something felt a hell of a lot better than the past several years.

Balancing the boxes against his leg while resting it on the bumper, he slammed the trunk shut, then gripped them and headed towards his new apartment building.

Shouldering his way through the door and into the dimly lit interior, he was glad to find the stairwell and, as far as he could tell, hallways above and below, vacant. As a broke twenty-something attempting to do something probably really stupid with his life, he'd been forced to live in a not great part of town and already had been stared down by a few guys.

Heading downstairs, Gabe got into his basement apartment and, setting the boxes on the floor, he shut and locked the door against the world.

Finally. Alone.

He was alone.

For a long moment, he simply stood there and looked around the apartment. He had always been forced to live with at least one other person until this very moment. His family, his 'friends', coworkers, random roommates.

But here? Here was isolation.

And as an introvert living a life of forced interaction day in, day out, isolation was a gift.

Or was it?

Gabe sighed softly as he picked the boxes back up and moved them deeper into the studio apartment, knowing that if he didn't do it now, he would leave it until tomorrow. Moving around the TV stand that was the only thing serving as a wall between the 'living room' and the 'bedroom' of his squalid home, he set the boxes on the dresser and started unpacking.

There wasn't a whole lot there.

Books, mostly.

A small lamp.

A few games that hadn't made it over during the previous trip.

Some clothes.

Most significant was his sound system. He set that up with great care. It might be little more than a docking port for an MP3 player and a pair of speakers, but when he'd finally bought it a year ago it had become invaluable to the preservation of his sanity.

Getting it plugged in behind the dresser, Gabe set it up, selected the first lo-fi playlist available, and let it play.

He actually felt himself relax, his entire body, as the music began.

After he finished unpacking the boxes and putting everything away, he broke them down and pushed them into the trashcan, then walked over and collapsed onto his sofa. It was more of a loveseat than a sofa, really.

He found himself making little mental amendments like that in his life all the time, almost as if he himself should come with an asterisk.

He had a car, but it was a shitty hatchback with little room.

He had a laptop, but it was eight years old.

He had a bank account, but it was in the red.

He had a phone, but...

Gabe pulled his phone out of his pocket and started at the glossy black rectangle bitterly.

But it had cost him goddamned six hundred dollars.

He was still regretting that one, even though he knew it was unreasonable. He was so sick and tired of having a crap phone, having crap *everything*, but when his phone had broke it was either get another crap one or actually upgrade.

And he'd finally had a little bit of money, so...

But the money was already gone. All gone now, in such a ridiculous gamble.

His mind swirled as he sat there on his loveseat, staring at his phone. Well, really staring at his reflection in it. Unhappy with that particular sight, he activated the screen. He laughed softly as he saw the date.

October 19th, 2023.

Today was supposed to be the first day in the next chapter of his life. The day he turned over a new leaf. The day he buckled down, got his shit together, and stopped being such a failure. The day it all changed.

It was a Thursday.

Somehow, it didn't feel right. Who the hell revolutionized their life on a Thursday? In October, no less?

With a sigh, he unlocked the screen and called up the contacts, then stopped.

Why was he checking out his contacts?

Gabe looked around his apartment. It felt barren, and not just because he was poor and didn't have a lot of furniture or stuff, nor that even if he wasn't, he preferred a more minimalist style of living. It was another thing entirely.

He was lonely.

Isolation was a gift, but he was lonely.

He'd lived with people for his entire life, but he had often been alone.

With a weary sigh he began scanning the list. There were just about three dozen names there. For some reason his parents were still in there, and his brother. His last several roommates. A scattering of coworkers from the past several jobs he'd had.

Every name he looked at gave him a bad feeling in his stomach.

He wouldn't call Jeremy, the guy had stolen from him.

He refused to call Peter, the guy was a psycho

who couldn't go out in public without starting a fight.

He definitely wasn't looking to hang out with Lisa, not after that absolutely miserable single date they'd gone on.

God, what did he even still *have* Nick's number!?

Gabe went through the list twice before realizing that there wasn't even a single person he wanted to see. Was he that much of an antisocial introvert? It was possible, but as he began running through the list a third time, growing almost desperate in his bid for some kind of human contact, he kept coming up with memories, bad ones.

Memories of things he had decided he would no longer tolerate.

Abruptly, the screen cleared to show an incoming call from an unknown number.

For a moment, he stared at it, almost automatically deactivating the screen, because scam calls were out of control now, no matter how many times he blocked them. And declining the call told them there was a human being on the other end, so he'd just taken to deactivating the screen to shut his phone up and let it go to voicemail.

They didn't even bother with automated messages anymore, not that he was complaining.

Except this number didn't come with a tag that said **SCAM** or **POLITICAL CALL** or **MARKETING CALL**.

It came with no tag, and now that he was thinking about it, he actually recognized the number. Not enough to know who it was, but to know that he had once had this number in his memory. But who in the name of God could it be that he'd actually gone to the trouble of deleting?

Curiosity, and the crushing burden of loneliness,

forced his hand.

He answered the call.

"Hello?"

A long pause came that made him start to think it was indeed a scam call, it had just slipped the net. Only...no, he could hear breathing and the faint sounds of traffic on the other end.

"...Gabe?"

A woman's voice. Familiar, dauntingly familiar, but for a moment he grappled helplessly with his memories, trying to put a name to the voice.

It was a coworker, a former coworker, it had to be. He was sure of it.

Someone he'd talked with many times, but the only woman he really remembered talking with frequently was–

"Ellen?"

"Yeah, it's Ellen. Um. Hi...this *is* you, right?" she asked uncertainly.

"Yeah. Yes. Sorry. It's Gabe. I, uh, almost didn't recognize your number." He waited and another uncomfortable pause went by. He had the sense that something was wrong, he could hear it in her voice. "Are you okay?"

"Not really," she murmured. Then, more resolutely: "No, I'm not okay."

He felt a stab of icy panic grip him. "Are you hurt? Or is someone after you?"

"No, nothing like that. Sorry, I didn't mean to freak you out. I'm, um, I'm safe. I'm not hurt. Just...I'm in a bad spot." She paused again.

It sounded so alien, hearing her like this, especially when he became convinced that she had been crying. He wasn't sure how he knew, but he felt confident this was the truth.

Something in her tone.

"Can I help?" he asked finally.

She'd obviously called him for a reason.

"Yes." Another uncomfortable hesitation. "Can I come to your place? I need a place to go. I need someone to talk to."

"You can come over," he replied.

"Thank you. I still remember where your place is, I shouldn't be too far away."

"I've just moved, actually. Well, I've moved like three times since the last time we spoke, but I've just moved again–let me text you my address."

"That'd be great. Also...thanks."

"Not a problem," he replied.

"See you soon."

"Yep."

They said goodbye and he hung up and fired off a text with his address in it.

Half a minute later he got a response: *Thanks again. I'll be there in about twenty minutes.*

Gabe stared at the screen for a long moment, a strange sense of unreality settling over him like a smothering cloak.

Shit.

CHAPTER TWO

The biggest thing that allowed him to successfully clean his entire apartment in less than twenty minutes was that he was a little obsessive about some things, and had already organized and cleaned most of it by this point.

Gabe had, at some point, been hoping to have a girl over to his place. Now that he had a home that was *his* place, in that he didn't have to share it with anyone else.

But definitely not so soon. Certainly not the actual first day.

As he worked, he thought of everything he knew about Ellen.

She was tall. She was beautiful. She was smart.

She was one of *those* women.

Most guys occasionally ran into a woman that left a deep impression, whether of romantic attraction or pure lust, sometimes both. Such a deep impression that they found themselves thinking of her even years later.

Ellen might actually be *the* woman in that regard.

Almost four years ago, they had gotten to know each other over the course of three months in what struck him as an extremely unlikely situation. For the most part, up until nine months ago, he'd spent the past few years working at a grocery store called Becky's. Not long after he'd started working there back in late 2019, Ellen had taken on the job of accountant.

Due to luck, they both tended to work similar shifts and ended up sharing the break room more often than not. After a few awkward silences, Ellen had actually struck up a conversation with him and he'd found her easy to talk to.

What surprised him the most was that she found *him* easy to talk to.

They'd spoken dozens of times, had a lot of great and natural conversations that he remembered enjoying immensely.

And then, one day in December, she'd quit.

He had known it was coming. It had quickly become obvious that she was vastly overqualified for the position, and had taken it out of a sense of desperation after being let go from her previous accounting job.

She was clearly smart, sharp, and tenacious enough that he knew she wouldn't be with them for that long.

Honestly, he was surprised it took as long as it had.

Why did she even have his number? He was thinking about that as he took a leak and then quickly washed his hands and face.

Oh right, his car had broken down and for a few weeks there she had occasionally given him rides to or from work as their schedule aligned, and it was easiest to coordinate via text. And now he remembered why he'd deleted her number.

Despite the fact that they'd actually got as far as finding each other on social media and talking more often than seemed likely, he felt there were too many differences between them to be real friends outside of work, and that he would never, in a million years, successfully ask her out.

To hold onto her number for that reason seemed futile.

And not just because she had been with someone

else at the time.

She wasn't just out of his league, she was out of his galaxy.

He might as well approach a movie star.

Gabe paused in drying his face as he thought he heard a car door shut somewhere nearby. He quickly finished up, then moved to the living room. Well, 'living room'. It was all kind of the same in a studio apartment.

For just a moment, he wondered if he'd misheard, or if it was someone else.

Then he heard footsteps in the hallway outside and then a sharp knock on the door.

Stepping up to it, he looked through the peephole and saw a familiar knockout blonde waiting unhappily.

What could have happened to her?

He opened up the door and stepped back. "Hi."

"Hello, Gabe," she said, pausing briefly as she looked at him, a look of surprise passing over her face. "You look...different."

"Do I?" he replied, looking down at himself reflexively.

"Uh, yeah. I mean, it's a good different."

She came in and he closed the door behind her. He found himself thinking something similar, though he didn't voice it at all. She looked miserable, her eyes red and puffy, almost certainly from crying, her face very pale.

And she definitely had put on some weight, but certainly not in a bad way.

She really filled out her jeans even more...

Needed to focus. She was upset, a bad thing had happened to her, and she, for whatever reason, had decided to come to him for help.

And he was going to help her.

"I'm not sure what it is," he replied. "I guess I stopped clean-shaving, so I don't look so freaking young anymore. I think."

"Yeah, that definitely is some of it," she murmured, standing there staring at him. "You've lost some weight, and...I think it's the t-shirt, too. I can't remember ever seeing you *not* in a button-down and that fucking apron they made everyone wear. The shirt looks good on you."

Was she hitting on him?

No, couldn't be, she was just being nice.

"Thanks," he murmured. "Uh...what happened?"

Whatever small smile had been building on her face collapsed and a look of anger mixed with abject misery swept across her beautiful, pale features.

"My life collapsed. Again," she replied, walking over to his loveseat and sitting down heavily.

"I'm sorry," he said, sitting beside her.

"Yeah, so am I...fuck. Where do I even begin? My fiance–" she paused, grimaced, glanced down briefly at her bare left ring finger, "–*ex*-fiance, cheated on me."

"Holy shit. I'm sorry, Ellen."

"Yeah. Fucking fucker." She reached up and pushed her long, pale blonde hair back, then suddenly heaved an irritated sigh. "Hold on," she muttered, going into her purse and coming out with a hair-tie. Gathering up her hair, she put it into a ponytail.

"There," she said. Ellen opened her mouth again, but no words came out. She looked at him suddenly. "Is this too weird?" she asked suddenly. "I know we haven't actually spoken in, what...God, three, no Christ, *four* years now?"

"Just about, yeah," he replied. "And no, it's not

too weird."

"I'm sorry we stopped talking. I'm just...bad at social media, and things got really busy with my new job—"

"It's really fine, Ellen."

She seemed to relax after studying him briefly and apparently determining he wasn't lying. "Thanks," she said. "Uh...so yeah, I, shit, where do I start? Sorry, I'm a goddamned mess right now. Just—shit." She rubbed her eyes.

"Take your time," Gabe replied, finding himself thinking '*how in the name of God could anyone cheat on her!?*'.

"Thanks," she said softly. Taking a deep breath, she held it for a few seconds, then exhaled slowly. "Okay. I began suspecting something was up like a month ago. I've been cheated on before, so this time around, the signs became more obvious. He was more distant, he wanted to go out on his own more often and was evasive about what was doing, where he'd been, who he'd seen. And I didn't want to be *that* woman—the one who gets all paranoid and jealous and clingy—so I told myself I *was* just being paranoid…

"Only I wasn't. Two weeks ago, after a lot of bullshit I finally successfully lobbied my workplace to let me go back to work-from-home. Which is a whole other thing I need rant about. I thought Blake would be happy, more time together, less time spent commuting to work, pissing away money on gas, all that shit. But he was annoyed, he was practically mad at me when I told him, but he wouldn't really say why."

She paused, frowning intensely, looking off to the side as her eyes unfocused briefly. Then she blinked a few times and returned her attention to him.

"I kept getting more paranoid and finally, well, he left his phone at the condo today. And I knew his code, I'd seen him punch it in a few times, and *yes,* I became *that* woman who goes through her fiance's phone. But I was *right,* goddamnit. I was *right* he was *seeing some fucking slut*–I found all these sexts and nudes from this one girl. Some fucking college bitch–"

Ellen broke off again, hugging herself suddenly and leaning forward, clenching her teeth. "I found a video of them fucking in *our* fucking bed! I was so angry I vomited. Barely made it to the kitchen sink. I just–I grabbed some of my shit and threw it in my car and started driving. I didn't even know where the hell I was going. Just...*away.* I had this plan, I figured he'd call me. He'd realize his phone wasn't on him and come back home, see I wasn't there, get paranoid, because *he* was getting paranoid, projecting, that cheating fuck!"

She clenched her hands into fists and a tremor of fury ran through her.

"Ellen, do you want a hug?" he asked suddenly.

He couldn't stand to see her this miserable and felt severely ill-equipped to handle it, but he wasn't going to just not try.

She looked at him, the surprise plain on her face, and then her expression resolved. "You know what? *Yes,* I *do* want a hug. Badly."

She scooted closer to him on the loveseat and they embraced, hugging. Tightly, actually. She ended up squeezing him so hard it hurt, but he didn't say anything.

Even when she suddenly started crying.

"Fuck, I'm sorry," she managed, tried to say something else, then let out another sob.

Gabe felt like he'd been tossed into a situation he had very little prep for or knowledge on how to handle. So he just went with it, doing what made sense, rubbing her back as she squeezed him and cried on his shoulder.

"It'll be okay, Ellen," he said, not even sure if that was true, but he knew, on some deep level, that it was the kind of thing she needed to hear in that moment. "You'll be okay. I'm here for you."

He kept rubbing her back, trying to ignore the fact that her breasts were pressed against his chest. This was about the absolute worst time to be having sexual thoughts, and he was glad to find that it was actually surprisingly easy to push those thoughts away.

She cried for another few moments, and then fell silent.

Finally, she sniffed heavily and released him, sitting back up. "Thank you," she murmured, wiping at her eyes. "Ugh, God, I thought I was already cried out, now I'm all gross again. Um, can I use your bathroom?"

"Of course," he said, pointing deeper into the apartment. "Last door in the row."

"Thanks," she murmured, standing.

She disappeared into the bathroom and he heard her blow her nose, then running water, and finally a moment later she reappeared, her face washed, leaving her looking a little more refreshed. She sat back down beside him.

"Uh...that was embarrassing," she muttered. "I'm sorry. Shit. I'm realizing that I'm just showing up on your doorstep basically out of the blue after years of no contact, ranting and raving about my pathetic life, and now I'm crying all over you…"

"Ellen, it's fine. I'm here to listen, to help if I can. I *want* to help you."

She looked at him when he said that, he expression changing, like she was somehow appraising him. Finally, she just gave her head a small shake, like she was trying to dislodge a thought.

"I appreciate it," she said. "I guess I should finish my story. I was driving around, trying to cool off, failing, crying. He called, and this calm came over me. I was going to play it cool, try to get him to maybe admit to it, but as soon as I heard his voice–it was like seeing red. I lost it, screaming at him. He tried to deny it, briefly, but it was pretty obvious he was fucked. He was found out. Tried to defend himself, told me it was my fault, pulling out all the stops. I sucked in bed, I'm getting fat, I'm awful at giving head, just everything he could think of."

"Jesus fucking Christ, that's awful," Gabe said.

"Yeah. I told him to fuck off, it's over, hung up, drove around for a while longer and then just...cried my fucking eyes out. And then, eventually, I was cried out, or so I thought, and I started thinking of people I could call on, places I could go, because I had to go *somewhere*."

"And you chose...me?" he asked.

"Yeah. I did," she murmured. She began to say something else, but her stomach growled. Rather loudly. "God, I'm fucking *starving*. I had breakfast, and then...I vomited. And then I haven't eaten anything since then."

Gabe stood up. "I'll put something...aw dammit."

"What?" she asked.

"I don't have any food."

"Wait, like, literally no food?" she asked.

"Basically. I just moved in."

She looked around. "Seriously?"

"Yeah."

"Oh, wow. Now I feel bad for just showing up while you're in the middle of getting settled."

"Don't feel bad," he replied.

Her stomach growled again. "How about I order a big, giant pizza, and wings, and soda, and we enjoy *that* for dinner? Because I could *use that* after today. And I'll pay."

He hesitated, but only briefly. What choice did he have? There was really no food here, and he was negative in the bank. "I accept."

She laughed. "Okay then."

Ellen pulled out her phone.

CHAPTER THREE

"Okay, order's in," she said, setting her phone on the coffee table. "And now I feel kind of bad for just dumping all this stuff in your lap out of nowhere. Tell me about what's been happening with you."

"I...are you sure?" he replied as he sat back down.

She suddenly seemed more composed, and that easy, charismatic confidence he remembered so clearly from their previous conversations shined through, even now in her dismal state. "I'm sure. Catch me up. What's the pandemic been like for you?"

He sighed. "Surprisingly normal. Just a lot more irritating...well, until recently."

"Why's that? What happened after we parted ways?" she asked, and damned if she didn't seem genuinely interested.

He actually felt bad. Here her life was falling apart, to the point where she was crying on a relative stranger's shoulder, and she felt she had to ask him about himself.

But it felt weird to try and rebuff her efforts, and Gabe had to admit, he was desperately lonely. Having anyone, let alone Ellen, asking after him, was almost intoxicating.

That was probably pathetic, but it was the truth.

He couldn't even remember the last time it had happened.

"Well, we parted ways...what, December 2019? I kept working at Becky's for another two months or so and decided I wanted out. Managed to land a job waiting tables near the middle of February and then the lockdowns started hitting. I lasted about two months, then spent two months desperately searching for a job. I somehow managed to survive until getting my job at Becky's back in June, and...there I stayed until early this year."

"Oh...jeez. That had to suck," Ellen muttered. "That place wasn't particularly good to work at."

"No," he agreed, "it was not. Especially..." He hesitated, an extremely unpleasant memory coming back to him. He pushed it aside. "Anyway. Against all odds, we stayed open, and I struggled along until finally getting a job at a gas station. It was another dollar an hour, but it only lasted about five months. I got let go in July."

"But you've obviously got *something* going," Ellen said, looking around. "You've got your own place now. Which, can I just say: thank fucking God. The few stories you told me about your roommates, just..." she shuddered. "It sounded awful."

"It never got better. I moved four times since then. The last place was this awful fucking apartment where this guy had three cats and everything smelled like cat piss. And then he got a dog. Who shit everywhere. And he never did the dishes."

"I'm so sorry," Ellen replied.

He laughed bitterly. "Yeah, me too. Anyway, I had this...I guess you could call it an epiphany? I don't know, maybe that isn't the right word. Revelation sounds too dramatic. Realization, maybe. I had a realization a few days after I got fired."

"What was it?" she asked.

"I was sitting there in my room, at my desk. It was one in the morning. I was just...staring at my laptop. Smelling cat piss." He sighed heavily. "I don't have anything against cats, I love them, actually, but...God, that smell."

"I can imagine," she murmured.

"Yeah. So, uh, I'm sitting there and I don't know, it was like...looking down the barrel of a gun? Only into the future. Like it just hit: this is it. This is my life, isn't it? It's never going to get any better. My life is just going to be shitty minimum wage job after shitty minimum wage job, barely being able to pay the bills, let alone actually *live* my life or enjoy anything, living in crappy apartments with people who are irritating or insane or assholes because I can't afford to live on my own, and I'm never going to be a fucking writer...

"Unless I *do* something about it. And this really weird feeling came down over me like a hammer. Just...*so* intense. I think I lost my mind temporarily, but like, in a good way? I don't know. I saw all that stretched out before me and I just knew I had to do *something*. Anything. Every month or so I'd do some research on writing and jobs related to writing, so I knew of a few places I could hit up, but I never wanted to before, it felt...I don't know. Wrong."

"What kind of jobs?" Ellen asked.

He paused, surprised both by how invested she seemed in what he was saying, but also how smoothly it felt like they were slipping back into their old conversations.

"Well, not exactly entirely ethical stuff. There's a shitload of people out there who want someone to basically write their college papers for them, term papers, assignments, stuff like that. But then there's sites that want blog posts smashed out. And then there was stuff like contests. Short story contests, flash fiction, poetry. And also commissions. People would pay five, ten, twenty bucks for scenes or short stories.

"And I...tried it all. I stayed up the entire night, all the next day, and most of the next night. I left the room to piss and grab a sandwich and some sodas. Once I ran down the street to grab some energy drinks. I started hitting up all these sites, figuring out which ones were bullshit, which ones were legit. I was desperate, I mean fucking *desperate.*

"Not just because of the future thing but also, I didn't have a lot of money left, and all at once the idea of getting another shit job...well, let's just say that the notion of hustling hard and grinding my ass off suddenly looked so much better."

"So...it worked?" she asked, looking around. "This place looks, well, uh...I don't mean to come off like a stuck-up bitch, but it looks a lot nicer inside than I thought it was going to. You have a really nice, clean apartment."

"Thanks," he replied awkwardly. "I actually just moved in today, and–"

"Wait, like, *literally* today?"

"Yeah."

"Oh wow, I really did pick a bad time for this. Shit, I'm sorry."

"It's not like you actually *picked* this, and it's really fine. Like you aren't interrupting anything. Actually...I was trying to think of someone to try and hang out with and I couldn't think of even a single person."

"Really? Who helped you move?" she asked.

"No one. I did it by myself."

"You–" She paused and stood suddenly, looking over the top of the TV at the bedroom area, then sat back down. "–you moved *all* this by yourself? Seriously?" He nodded. "*How?* In one day? Alone?"

"Alone, one day. I had a dolly and that helped. I

mean, it was a *huge* pain in the ass. But I managed it. Really it was a lot of shoving, and I rented a van."

"Impressive. Okay, so what *happened?* With the writing?"

He laughed awkwardly. "Well, for weeks and weeks there it was just hustle and grind. I was writing basically everything that paid. Even if it was five bucks. For the last week of July and all of August and some of September it just felt like I wasn't getting anywhere. I mean, I was making money, but not enough. I had enough to pay the bills in August, but in September I didn't make enough and I went negative paying the bills. And I thought it'd just get worse, but then...I felt like I crashed through some sort of barrier."

"How so?" she asked, leaning forward.

Gabe fought the sudden, insane, and nearly irresistible urge to look down her shirt. She was wearing a t-shirt and her large breasts were showcased nicely by it.

"The commissions I got, they just aligned with what I was wanting to write more often, and they paid better, and things just seemed to get easier. And I managed to get out of the red at the beginning of the month again, and then I hit a *real* break. Some guy had read a short story I'd written somewhere, tracked me down, and asked me to ghost write a novel. He'd pay me a grand to do it, if I could bang it out in a week."

Ellen's eyes widened. "A *novel* in a *week?* How? That...doesn't seem possible."

"I wasn't so sure myself, although I felt a lot more confident given the sheer amount I'd been writing. And he had an outline, pretty detailed, and he really just needed the bones of the novel. About sixty thousand words. So roughly eighty six hundred words a day. That was what I set for myself. And I did it. It was a close call. I started burning out on day four. By day six I was just...dying. On the last day, I worked so fucking hard. And I got it in. And then I took a short break and started working on my next big project, something I'd discovered."

"What?" she asked.

He shifted uncomfortably on the couch, unsure of how he was going to put this. So far, no one knew.

Literally no one.

"I...learned of a certain thing I could write, and self-publish, on Ignition, that huge self-publishing website that's everywhere now?"

"Yeah, I know about it. I actually have the app on my phone and I read some stuff...so you're self-publishing stories?"

"Yes. And they're starting to sell. Nothing crazy, and it'll be a bit before I see the actual income, because they pay out monthly, so I'm still running the other jobs, but it seems to be working, and I'm hoping to scale up now."

"What is it you're writing?" she asked.

"Uh...well..."

He paused for too long, trying to come up with a good lie or diversion.

But he had nothing.

His brain was fried, and this whole situation was so surreal that he was having a hard time putting his mental faculties to use.

A knowing smile suddenly began spreading across Ellen's face.

"Wait..." she said, the smile becoming a smirk. "Is it smut? Are you writing smut?" He didn't even get a chance to answer before her face lit up, her eyes widening. "Oh my God, it is! You are!"

"Technically, it's called erotica," Gabe replied, not looking at her.

"You're blushing! Oh my God! This is amazing!" He sighed uncomfortably and she seemed to rein it in suddenly. "I'm sorry, to be clear: I'm not making fun of you. Not at all. I just think–I mean, it's funny. But not in a bad way! Just...amusing! It's amusing!"

"Why?" he asked.

"I don't know! Just...I never imagined you writing smut. Uh, erotica. All the stuff we talked about in the break room. The sci-fi, the fantasy, the horror. You were into horror, I remember that. And cyberpunk? But never any hint of anything sexy or romantic at all. You're blushing!"

He sighed again. "I'm not making fun of you, Gabe, I swear to God. I think it's cool, and just...different! And a little funny, but not in a bad way! I'm sorry."

"No, it's fine, I believe you, actually." He paused as something that had been bugging him ever since he'd hung up the phone came back to him. "I had a question for you."

"Yeah?"

"Why me?"

"What?"

"Why'd you call *me?* Why'd you come to me? I mean, I'm not complaining. I'm actually really glad you're here. But...surely you had someone else more, um...suited? To helping you feel better about this mess?"

Ellen's expression slowly grew more serious, as though she were really considering his question.

"I really don't," she replied quietly, all humor

gone now. "After I cried my eyes out and drove around for a while and started realizing I needed to figure something out, I started thinking about everyone I knew. My family, my 'friends', and all I could think was what they'd tell me. That I was being stupid. That Blake was just 'so great', and so what if he cheated on me? He loves me! Every guy slips up every now and then! I'm being selfish!"

"Jesus fucking hell, Ellen, would they really say that?" he asked, horrified.

"Yes, actually, because this has happened before. This was going to be my third time getting married. Ugh, Christ," she muttered, hugging herself again, frowning deeply. "Thirty four, twice divorced, almost three times if the pandemic hadn't fucked up our wedding date. Thank God for that, apparently. Fuck." She paused for a long moment, looking lost. "Fucking fuck," she whispered finally, hanging her head.

"I...am really sorry," he said, feeling just as lost again. "I wish I had more to offer. You're suffering and I can't help—"

"No," she said, her head coming back up suddenly. "No, Gabe. This is helping. You are helping. You're right, that I'm suffering. I am, by God. But I already feel, just, *so* much better. Or, at least, less miserable. A lot less miserable. I feel..."

She looked around his place, as if realizing something, then settled her bright blue gaze back on him. "Safe. I feel safe here. And that means a lot. A *lot*."

"All right," he replied when her gaze turned a little insistent. "I, um, I'm glad. That you feel safe. And that I'm helping. You're a great person, and you were always so nice to me, and pretty much no one else was."

"No one was nice to you at the store?" she asked.

"Well...maybe that paints too bleak a picture. Everyone else was either, yeah, a jerk, or neutral. Which I can't really complain about, it's just…"

"Just what?" she asked.

"I don't know."

Ellen frowned, focusing in on him even more now. "No. You know. I can tell you know, you're just holding something back. Don't hold it back."

"I, uh...fine. Everyone was nice to you."

She looked down for a moment, lost in memory. "Were they?" she murmured. "I feel like I'd describe everyone as being mostly neutral towards me."

"No, Ellen. Everyone was nice to you."

She began to respond, and then there was a knock at the door, derailing the conversation.

"Must be the pizza," he said, getting up, grateful for the distraction.

CHAPTER FOUR

It was the pizza, and the conversation was mercifully derailed.

He set it all up on the coffee table in front of him.

"Can we watch something?" Ellen asked as she poured some soda from the 2-liter they'd ordered.

"Yeah, definitely. What do you want?"

She paused for just a moment, then sighed and shook her head. "You choose. I can't...think right now. I keep going back to...darkness."

"Okay," he said, turning on the TV and then the console he had hooked up to it.

He felt a moment of anxiety as he did that. So far, in his experience, him playing video games and the few women who ended up going on dates with him hadn't mixed. It felt bizarrely antiquated, given how many women gamed, and gamed hard across all genres, nowadays, but somehow he kept finding women who thought playing video games was a sign of immaturity.

He didn't know where Ellen stood on that issue, but it was too late now.

And besides, he reminded himself, it wasn't like he had a chance with her. And even then, she'd just got cheated on.

Not really a good time to be looking for a new boyfriend.

It wasn't like it mattered, though. Besides his laptop, it was the only way he had of watching anything. He tried to remember what she liked as he fired up the only video app he had a subscription to, kept only out of desperation for sanity as he'd chopped away at his spending habits over the past year.

Finally, it came to him: she liked fantasy.

He remembered seeing something about an adaptation of some big fantasy series that he hadn't had a chance to read but seemed up her alley.

"How about this?" he asked, selecting it.

"Oh! I've been meaning to watch this, yes! Really good pick," she said.

"I remembered you like fantasy," he replied.

She looked over at him. "You actually remembered that?"

"Yeah. I mean you remembered I like horror."

"Yeah, just...nevermind. Let's do this."

He fired it up and they settled in to watch.

...

"That was...well, it was all right," Ellen murmured as they finished the first season.

It was a relatively short one, eight episodes divided across about four hours. They'd finished off their meal and had pretty much just been vegging out.

"I liked it," Gabe replied.

"Yeah, it's just...I don't know. There was a lot in the book that they just kinda glossed over for the adaptation." She paused, and a look of horror came onto her face. "Holy shit. I just-oh shit. I just ate five hours of your time without even thinking about it. You were telling me you've been so busy with writing-do you need to be doing something else? I absolutely can entertain myself."

"No, it's fine," he replied. "This has been fun."

Ellen sat up straighter and looked more firmly at him, not looking mollified at all. "Gabe, I want you to tell me if I'm imposing on you."

"You aren't," he replied, a little surprised by how intense she was turning.

"Okay, but-I just, I have this way of sort of bulldozing people. And I know I've got this way about me, I-" she sighed, "-as arrogant as it sounds, I know I intimidate people. I've been trying to be better about it, but, I just wanted to say: if I'm bothering you, or doing something that's pissing you off, or imposing on you, can you just tell me to my face? I promise I won't get mad."

He could tell this was a serious matter to her. "I will tell you, Ellen. I promise."

"Thanks...sorry. I just-my emotions are at fucking ten right now. Everything's a mess..." she sighed heavily and leaned back against the loveseat, running one hand down her face.

"I understand," he replied. "And really, I wasn't planning on writing tonight. I was actually very intentionally taking the rest of the day off from writing. And like I said before, I was actually trying to find someone to come hang out when you called."

"Yeah, that's true." She pursed her lips. "We really struck out for friends, huh?"

"Apparently. On the other hand, we did find each other."

She smiled at that. "Yeah, we did."

He got up and began cleaning away the remains of their meal. Ellen sat on the loveseat and looked at nothing in particular, lost in thought.

His mind was working as he cleaned up. He *was* going to have to get back to the grind tomorrow, though. There were a lot of orders he had to fill, a few of them due at midnight tomorrow, and he wanted to get more progress done on his erotica.

Where was he going to write, though?

He had his desk, but this whole apartment was basically one big room. He had headphones, though they weren't very high quality. That could work, he'd just have to be quiet if he got up before Ellen, because–

"Oh...fuck," he whispered as something abruptly occurred to him with all the force of a bullet.

"What? What's wrong?" Ellen asked.

"I, uh…" He looked around for a moment, seeing if he was missing anything. Gabe quickly concluded that he was not. "I don't know where you're going to sleep...I guess the bed. There's just no way the loveseat would work. I'm not sure I could sleep on it...I guess I could sleep on the floor? Or put my feet up on the coffee table?"

"Gabe," she said, interrupting him. He looked at her. "We can just share the bed."

He looked at her for a long moment. "...are you sure?"

"Yes. I trust you. We're adults. I'm not letting you sleep on the floor of your own apartment, or this loveseat. I'm just not. But, if it's too weird, I will go get a hotel room. And I don't want you to feel guilty about that. I'll do it without resentment, okay?"

He considered it for a long moment.

Would it be too weird? Would *he* be weird about it?

No, he wouldn't be. He knew he wouldn't actually do anything intentionally to make her uncomfortable or to try and take advantage of her. But he'd never been in a situation where he was sleeping in a bed with a woman he wasn't trying to fuck, or had already.

He couldn't really see any other alternative, though.

Either he and Ellen shared a bed, or she would go get a hotel room, and he didn't want that.

"All right," he said. "We'll share."

"Good." She smiled. "I'm glad. Now, what time do you need to wake up? Or do you? Because I have to at a certain point...oh." She lost her smile.

"What?" he asked.

"Just...remember how I said my entire life was collapsing? The whole cheating thing was only part of it. I'm also getting fired."

"You-what? Seriously? How? You're the hardest worker I know!"

She laughed sardonically. "I am, but I'm also an extremely stubborn bitch when I want to be."

Gabe walked over and sat back down beside her. "You want to tell me about it?"

"I do, actually, because it's fucking bullshit. It's supreme bullshit. So, my company was a holdout for the whole work-from-home thing, but eventually they switched us over to it when things got serious enough. Or at least when they were forced to actually pretend to give a fuck about us. At first I was kind of worried I might lose my mind a little from being home all the time but...holy shit. It was the opposite. I fucking loved it."

"Yeah, it certainly worked out better for me...except for the whole fired thing," Gabe said.

"Exactly. It was great. I was saving time, saving money, feeling saner. I mean eventually it started to wear on me, being apart from people, but I could be with people *without* going to work. I managed it for a whole year and I legitimately believed that it was just my new life. I mean, it made *way* more sense. I was more productive, I actually got more work done, and in less time...and then, all of a sudden, they called me back."

"To the office?"

"Yes. At first it was just one day a week, for meetings and pointless shit like that. I actually kind of liked it, because it was sort of like getting a *really* long weekend. I still got the part of my old life where I went to work and saw people. And that stayed when they shifted us to two days a week, and then it began falling apart a little when we got bumped up to three days. That was about the time I began trying to pump the breaks."

"Where do you actually work? I just realized that if I ever knew, I've forgotten."

"Oh, an accounting firm downtown. We pretty much crunch numbers for other corporations. Or, in other words, we find out how to help them fuck their workers over as much as possible while also hiding as much money from taxes as possible. So, a shit job. But it's what I'm good at, evidently."

"Huh...all right, go on. I imagine it didn't go well."

"No. I started out light, sort of asking what was keeping us from just keeping it at two or three days in the week, and pretty much got stonewalled. They fed us some meaningless bullshit excuses that just didn't hold up to scrutiny, and for a while I tolerated it. But then when they moved us back to four days a week, with the promise of a full return to how it was before, I started actively hitting the breaks. I fought back.

"And that, as you say, did not go well. I mean, at first it did. Although I had only been with the company about eighteen months at that point, I had built up a lot of rep. I'm a hard worker *and* a smart work. I turned in more, and better, work than basically anyone else in my department. In the whole fucking building. So they were willing to work with me and I got to get stuck at three days a week at work."

"I'm guessing it didn't last."

She sighed and shook her head. "Nope. I *thought* we had stabilized, although honestly at that point I was going to try and petition them for more work-from-home days. Because there was no *reason* I needed to be in the office. But it was a nice equilibrium. I cruised through last year like that. And then, near the beginning of this year, they sort of just told me they needed me back in the office all five days. And there was nothing I could do to stop it."

Ellen clenched her fists suddenly and her body went rigid. He could see fire in her eyes. "It was such fucking *bullshit*. I raged for a while but they were pretty much just like 'no'. And it makes no fucking sense! *Everything* about work-from-home was fucking better, on *both* our ends. I was happier, my mental health was better, my work-life balance. Not that they gave a single fuck about any of those things, but I was saving *them* money, *and* fucking *making* more money! I was literally more productive at home than at work–"

She stopped herself, took a deep breath, let it out slowly. "Sorry, I'm ranting. This has been in my head all fucking year long. Anyway. When I went back to work full time, I slowly began realizing that I fucking hated it there. Any of the things that I thought I missed, I realized were either not that great or actually kind of annoying. And the things I tolerated became intolerable. I just kept getting more and more pissed off...I sound like a bitch, don't I? Like an entitled bitch?"

"No," he replied.

"You can tell me if I am. I know your situation sucked shit."

"No, I really don't think you are. It sounds like bullshit. But, then again, most of the world is bullshit," he replied.

She pointed at him suddenly. "I think that's a key," she said with a stark intensity. "A lot of people seemed to lose their minds after the lockdowns lifted. Like, there was this huge surge in unreasonable, ridiculous, and even violent behavior across the board, over the pettiest shit, and it's for a number of reasons—I'm sure the sociologists will be parsing it for years to come—but I think one key is that they told us for *decades* that working from home was completely unfeasible. Couldn't be done. Impossible.

"But then one pandemic happens and not only do they do it, they do it *with fucking ease.* I get that there are tons of industries out there who couldn't, but there are tons more that could. It was like flicking a goddamned switch for them! They had been fucking lying to us for *years!* How many other things they claim are impossible are actually *completely possible,* they're just too fucking greedy or lazy or both to actually do it?"

She stopped herself once more. "Fuck. I'm ranting. Again."

"I mean, it's a really valid rant," he replied.

"I know, just...anyway. Why I'm getting fired. Sorry, I keep getting derailed. I'm so fucking worked up and angry right now. My mental health was degrading like never before and my work was suffering, everything was just suffering and misery. I finally put my foot down. I put together a research presentation, like with actual facts and figures, on why we should be given the option to work at home.

And then I presented it to my boss."

"He was a complete asshole about it?" Gabe asked.

"Yes. And worse than I thought, too. Like, he was genuinely angry about it. We had a long argument about it. I knew it was stupid, I should've just given up, but then I realized something, and it made me snap a little. I figured out *why* they were doing it. Why, specifically, my boss was *so* goddamned intent on having us physically there at the office: control. When it hit me that they were willing to lose money, the thing that they pretty much will almost literally sacrifice human lives for, just for the feeling of petty power over other people…"

She shook her head slowly. "That was too much. It was already bad enough, the way they obsessively squeeze every last possible penny out of us, working us as long and as hard as they can, but when I learned that the only thing they truly gave a shit about more than money was literally just bossing people around and 'dominating' them…that was a bridge too far."

"So what happened? You obvious walked out of that meeting without being fired, unless I missed something," he asked.

"I finally told him I was going to go over his head and that seemed to change something. He relented, a little, and said he'd talk with his own boss about it, and sent me out. Then he called me back in, and just…the smile on his face. The shit-eating grin. I thought he'd gotten permission to fire me on the spot, but he told me that his boss had agreed to my request, and I could work from home five days a week now.

"And there was just something in his reaction to it…like he'd won a victory. I put together pretty quickly what it was. He *had* gotten permission to fire me, but only after I'd been replaced. And I've been proven right. They're siphoning off my workload. This was three weeks ago. I do less than half the work I used to before that meeting. They're basically winding me down so that when they fire me, it'll be a smooth transition.

"And that just blows my fucking mind. I'm the best worker they have. Again, I know that's an arrogant statement, but I also know my own abilities, and those of everyone else around me. Everyone has strengths and weaknesses, but I am definitely the hardest and smartest worker. They are fully willing to lose me simply because I want to work in a different building."

"No," Gabe said, and she looked at him. "They are willing to lose you because you won't submit to them. In my experience, most jobs are about power. Petty power plays. Micromanaging. Bullshit. It's like people always say: workers don't leave bad jobs, they leave bad bosses."

"Very true in my experience," she replied. "So...yeah. That's it. That's why I'm getting fired." She yawned suddenly. "God, I'm *tired.*"

"You've been through a lot," Gabe said.

"Hardly. I just got cheated on and am going to lose my job. I don't have cancer or–"

"Oh come on, Ellen. Don't go down that road. You've suffered. You're miserable, and for very valid reasons. Jesus, I can't imagine someone actually choosing to cheat on you." He yawned suddenly. "I guess I'm tired, too."

"We should sleep," she said, standing. "And I need a shower. If you don't mind."

"What? No. Use away. My stuff is your stuff."

She grinned. "You're awfully giving."

"Well...like you said: I trust you."

"Good. I am, in fact, very trustworthy. Now, um, I'm going to go take a shower. I'll try not to use up all the hot water."

"Oh, use away. I've already had one today, I'm good."

"Well, in that case, thank you. I could use a long, hot shower."

He watched her go as she grabbed her suitcase and headed into his bathroom. She closed the door and, a moment later, he heard the shower start up.

Gabe sat there on his loveseat for a while, thinking of many things.

But it all felt like too much. Just too much right now.

He needed sleep.

There were things to do, decisions to make, but he had slowly been learning his limits over the past several months, and knew the value of a good sleep reset.

He began winding down the apartment.

CHAPTER FIVE

Ellen emerged from the bathroom in a big t-shirt and some loose-fitting shorts, her pale blonde hair down and still a bit wet.

She looked around. The only light in the apartment now came from a small lamp he had on his bedside table. Gabe stood at his dresser, fiddling with his MP3 player.

"Hey, uh...I was just curious," he said, "would it bother you if I played some light music while we slept?"

She looked at him, again seeming amused. "What kind of music?" she asked finally.

"Lo-fi."

"What's that? I've never heard of that."

"Really? I'm a little surprised you managed to evade it. Here, let me show you. It's really chill, very low-key, calm. Atmospheric."

"Okay, yeah, show me," she replied.

He fired up one of his curated sleep playlists, adjusted the volume, and then stepped back, looking at her to see her reaction. She looked focused at first, listening intently, and then slowly a smile spread across her face.

"That *is* chill," she murmured. Her smile widened a little more. "I like it, yeah."

"Think you can sleep with it going?" he asked.

"I can."

"Okay. Let me know if it's interfering with your sleep," he replied, adjusting the volume once more, then moving over to the bed.

He'd felt caught for a bit about what to wear to bed. Boxers felt like too little, given the circumstances, but a t-shirt and boxers didn't feel like enough, but pulling his pants back on seemed like too much.

He wished he had sweatpants, but he didn't. So now he just had a t-shirt and boxers.

Ellen didn't seem uncomfortable, at least, as they pulled back the blanket and got in under it.

"Uh...sorry I don't have anything bigger than a full," he muttered as they got settled.

She laughed. "Well, Gabe, it's not like you could predict you'd end up with a six foot five blonde in your bed."

"No, but I'd always hoped," he replied. Then paused. "Sorry, that was weird—"

She snorted. "No, it was funny. You're funny, Gabe."

"I'll...take your word for it," he replied.

"Good. And, uh, goodnight."

"Goodnight, Ellen."

He rolled over, facing away from her, and got settled.

He wondered if he'd have trouble sleeping.

...

Gabe came awake in a haze of confusion.

Someone was in his bed. Someone large. Laying against him.

Soft and warm.

Ellen, he realized in a flash. The previous night came back to him and suddenly he found himself in a very awkward position.

Besides the fact that she was currently curled up against him in her sleep, he also had a hard-on. A bad one.

As he was deciding how to extract himself from the situation, she suddenly came awake. For a moment she simply stared at him, and he back at her.

"Oh, shit, sorry," she muttered, retreating.

"It's fine," he replied. "You okay?"

She looked a little freaked, or confused maybe. She stood up suddenly and grabbed her suitcase.

"Yeah, I'm fine. Just...uh...gotta pee," she replied, hurrying off to the bathroom.

She almost slammed the door shut, leaving him confused and more than a little anxious. Had he pissed her off or upset her? He hadn't done a damn thing all night. The last thing he remembered, he was trying to sleep and then the night had passed.

Reluctantly, he put it off, telling himself it was probably something else. Maybe she'd had a nightmare or something.

Wouldn't be unreasonable, given all the shit that had happened to her.

For a moment, he wasn't sure what he should be doing. He wasn't particularly good in the mornings. He heard the toilet flush and then the shower start up. He considered going back to sleep. It felt early, the quality of light coming in through the windows high in his walls telling him it might be only an hour or two past dawn.

But he felt awake, if a bit out of sorts.

No, he should get up. Get to work.

There was a lot to do, and he was in the red.

Gabe got to his feet and began to head for the bathroom, then stopped himself as he remembered abruptly that it was occupied. He shook his head and then rubbed at his eyes. Man, he was tired. Thinking was hard this early in the morning.

Speaking of that, how early was it?

Gabe grabbed his phone and checked the time, finding it was a little past seven. Definitely earlier than he was used to getting up. Then again, he'd gone to bed kind of early last night, and it had actually worked, given how exhausted he'd been from all of yesterday's work.

For a moment, he was stymied.

He couldn't start making breakfast, there was no food.

He couldn't go brush his teeth or take a shower, Ellen was in there.

Finally, he walked out of the bedroom area and around to his desk, tucked up against the wall beside the kitchen section. Taking a seat, he fired up his laptop, or tried to. It took a while to actually boot up.

Gabe looked resentfully at his phone, and then at his reflection in the phone.

Why had he fucking spent this much money on a phone but not a new laptop?

At the time, when he'd actually had the money to spend, he had justified it by reasoning that he shouldn't get himself a new laptop because if he did, he'd be tempted to get a fancy new laptop. And that meant access to newer games.

And that meant more temptation to do anything on his laptop but write.

The issue had been forced when his phone had broken.

But now it was looking like a stupid decision.

He sighed and shook his head, checking out his e-mails and social media for the day. Everything in his work life had been shunted into two different categories now. The first was what he called the grind, the second he called erotica.

Because Gabe was a simple man at heart.

Right now, that first column constituted roughly ninety percent of everything. He pulled up the actual document, seeing a big bulleted list, divided up by dates. There were three due today, with a fourth marked for bonus if he got it done today.

They were all relatively small. The first three were term papers and were, thankfully, the final ones. He'd decided recently to just stop taking those assignments. Besides their ethical ambiguity, they just sucked.

He hated writing them and they seemed to be taking more and more time to do.

After that were mostly just short stories or novella commissions or ghost writing. Those were a lot better, but usually ranged between 'this is kinda fun' to 'I fucking hate this'.

He frowned as he looked over at the other column.

It was a bit barren, but that was largely because he hadn't really fleshed out his newer ideas.

Gabe had been writing erotica for approaching six weeks now. He'd managed to push out a dozen short stories by this point. It had taken some time to learn how to make cover art, (and even the stuff he'd managed to cobble together by now barely did the job), and how to format to make it look passable on the Ignition eReader, but he found that banging out these shorts was surprisingly easy.

He did wonder how long that would last.

Most things were really fun and easy when you were first getting into them and lost in how awesome it was.

Then you started getting better, started taking it more seriously, and the shine began to wear off.

At the moment he was working on a new series.

In the beginning he'd just done stand alones, but then he'd had an idea for a sequel, and that had actually sold more than he thought it would, so that became a trilogy, and then the next a quadrilogy.

Gabe felt a cold stone settle into his gut abruptly as he thought of that current project.

When he had started working on it, he'd very obviously based the story and the character off of Ellen. What if she wanted to read some of his work? What if she found that particular story? Would she be offended? Flattered? Confused?

He sighed softly. Just another problem.

Gabe cleared his head and opened up the first of the term papers. He quickly refreshed himself on the information and laughed bitterly as he started writing, picking back up where he'd left off two nights ago.

He had never gone to college, and one of the things he listed as a positive on that was that he would never again have to write fucking assignment papers.

Yet here he was.

At least it'd be over after today. Presumably.

If he got desperate enough again, he could see himself turning back to them. There were always more that needed to be written.

He shook his head and got to work.

Something that Gabe had been surprised the learn was that he could slip into a focused work mode with shocking ease once he'd practiced up a little. He blocked everything else out and wrote according to the notes given to him.

Once he was finished with the writing, he gave it a once-over for basic edits and, confident he'd done his duty, fired the file off to his client.

He checked the time and realized he'd been

working for nearly half an hour. He could no longer hear the shower, but when he stood up and peered around the corner into the bedroom area, Gabe saw that the door was still closed.

For a moment, he stood there, unsure of what to do.

Was she just taking a long time or was something wrong?

Would it be weird for him to ask?

As he was deciding what to do, the door opened up and she stepped out, holding her suitcase and looking a little…

He wasn't sure how to interpret that look.

"Hey," she said, looking over at him, "uh...do you have a washing machine?"

"Yeah," he replied, pointing. "Door next to you there. Washer and dryer. Cheap but it works."

"Awesome. Do you mind if I use it?"

"Like I said, use what you need," he replied.

"Thank you. I appreciate it. Also, uh, sorry for taking so long in the bathroom. I, uh–" She looked over, startled, as her phone began emitting an alarm. "Shit," she muttered.

Walking over, she quickly turned it off, then marched over to the middle door in the row of three along his bedroom wall and opened it up. She began putting her clothes hurriedly into the washing machine.

"Uh...I don't see any detergent," she murmured.

"Oh...fuck," he replied. "I, uh...was gonna go shopping last night and completely forgot. I don't have, like, anything."

"Oh. Well, that's fine. Maybe we could do that later today."

He thought about his negative bank account.

Well, he couldn't just not get stuff. His next payment from his erotica was still damn near a month away. Even if he pushed really hard, he could maybe scrape together a hundred bucks today from these jobs.

Not enough to pull him out of the red, let alone buy gas and groceries.

"Yeah," he replied.

"I gotta get to work," she said as she finished. "Uh...I guess, do you care if I work in your bed?"

"Go for it."

"Sweet, thanks."

While she fished her laptop out of the case, he struggled not to look at her huge ass with her pink and surprisingly revealing and small short stretched across it, and...

God, her ass was pointed right at him.

And she was taking a while to get that laptop out.

He was suddenly struck by the idea that she was doing it on purpose.

Gabe shook his head and moved over to his dresser. He was just lonely and horny and tired and imagining things.

Gathering up a fresh set of clothes, he headed into the bathroom.

He took a long piss and then brushed his teeth. As he started up the shower and began stripping, Gabe immediately found his thoughts straying to Ellen and her immense beauty and tall...generous body, and the fact that she was actually *here* and that he'd slept in a bed with her last night.

He sighed heavily as he slipped into the shower.

This was going to be a difficult day.

CHAPTER SIX

"Hey, Gabe...is now a bad time?" Ellen asked.

He'd just let out a long sigh and sat back in his chair. "Uh...no. What's up?" he replied, running his fingers through his hair, trying to calm down.

"You look stressed."

"I just, uh...so I started working on one of my commissions after my shower. And I did what I thought was pretty good work. It was harder than usual, but I fucking got it done. And then I sent it off for the guy to check it over and send me my payment, and then I got to work on the next one. But then the guy started arguing with me, claiming I did a bad job, even though I'd done exactly what he specified. It's just a fucking power play, though."

"Oh...that's what that muttering was about earlier. Shit, I'm sorry," she replied.

"Was I muttering?...but yeah, we argued and I've spent the past fucking hour making changes, and then arguing some more, and *finally* got him to give me the fucking cash." He groaned and ran a hand down his face. "All this for fucking twenty bucks, this has to seem pathetic."

"You're working hard, that's not pathetic," Ellen replied. "*I* am pathetic, working for a company I fucking hate, doing work I fucking hate, for people I can't stand. Helping the rich get richer."

"You found something you're good at and you're making money," he replied.

She laughed, a little cynically. "Maybe. Doesn't matter anymore, I guess. Um...I was gonna ask: do you want to get lunch and go shopping?"

"Uh…" He looked at his screen for a long

moment.

He'd only made a bit of progress on his third project before having to stop. He knew he should keep going, but...

He was fucking starving.

"Yeah. Let's do that. Let me just take a piss."

"Okay, I'll get ready."

He went into the bathroom and relieved himself, washed his hands, then headed back out and pulled his shoes on.

As she put her laptop away and then changed into a pair of bluejeans and another low-cut t-shirt, it suddenly occurred to him that something was different about her. He wasn't completely sure what, only that she was acting distinctly differently from last night.

"Hey, Ellen...how are you feeling?" he asked as they finished getting ready.

"Less shitty," she replied with a smile that was surprisingly playful. "Okay, I *am* feeling better, actually. Sleep and a few showers and clean clothes have helped. Although we gotta get some food soon or I'll turn into a bitch."

"There's a grocery store a few blocks away I noticed while I was moving, it said it's got a deli. We could grab something to eat there?" he suggested.

"Sounds good to me." She paused, and he suddenly had the impression she was somehow measuring him. "Can I drive?"

"Yeah, sure," he replied.

She smiled a bit wider and grabbed her purse. "All right, let's go."

...

Yeah, he decided, something was definitely different about her today.

She was smiling more, but it didn't quite seem like it was because she was happy. It was more like...she was trying to tell him something without spelling it out.

Like she was waiting for him to notice something, or acting like someone who was planning a surprise party.

Unless he was projecting again, and she was just experiencing some emotional whiplash given what had happened to her.

Her car was nice. It looked new, and he felt a temporary anxiety from looking at it. It looked a little too nice for the neighborhood.

Okay, more than a little.

"This thing have an alarm?" he asked as they got in.

"Oh yeah, don't worry about that," she replied, starting the engine. "Where to?"

He gave her some quick instructions and she pulled out of the parking lot.

"So it'll be cool? You just...leaving your work for however long we'll be gone?" he asked.

"Yeah. Like I said, they've been siphoning off my workload. I'm basically done for the day. But even that aside, I've got an hour for lunch."

"Nice."

A moment of silence went by. Ellen seemed to be pondering something.

"So..." she said finally.

"Yeah?"

"I was just curious about your erotica." He sighed a little, he couldn't help it. "If you don't want to talk about it, that's fine. But...I really would like to know about it."

"It isn't, like...a joke. I'm not writing stuff like 'and then he crammed his giant tool into her wet womanhood'. For the record."

She immediately started laughing. "Oh my God, that's...okay, yeah. I get it now. I get why you'd be sensitive about it. Beyond the obvious reason of why people might be sensitive about it," she replied.

"Yeah. I haven't told anyone. Like, literally anyone. You are the first person to know this about me."

"Well I'm honored," she replied. She frowned. "That sounded sarcastic but it wasn't. I'm really honored you trust me with this."

"Thanks," he said. "Uh...I mean, what do you want to know about it?"

"What's it about? What's it like?"

"Right now? Short stories. The first five were stand alone pieces. Just short stories about, you know, regular people meeting somewhere, hitting it off, hooking up. Then I had an idea for a sequel and it was fun to write and people actually liked it. And it taught me something."

"What?"

"Writing a sequel will likely generate further interest in the initial story. I saw a spike in sales for the first one."

"That makes sense. New people come across the sequel, were interested, realize it was a sequel, so they decided to go back and read the first one."

"Yeah, exactly. So I had enough of an idea for a third one. And then after that I wrote another trilogy. Still shorts. And that sold better, but still not amazing or anything. That was about, uh, a couple on vacation."

"...and?"

"I mean, you know. They fuck. And find another woman to hook up with-this feels really weird to talk with you about."

"Why? We talked about just about everything back in the break room. I mean, I know it's been a few years, but...honestly I feel like we've kind of just slipped right back into it. Unless I'm mistaken there and I'm just...feeling something by myself?"

He glanced at her. There was something bizarrely suggestive about the way she'd said that.

"No," he replied, "I'd say, uh, I'm feeling it, too."

She smiled and briefly reached out and gave his hand a little squeeze. "Good. I'm glad we're both...feeling something."

Ellen pulled her had back slowly and he couldn't deny that he felt a jolt she'd touched him and smiled at him.

"It's just weird to talk about, it isn't you," he said, clearing his throat. "Uh...there's the place."

She pulled off the street into the parking lot and parked near the front entrance. The grocery store, which was a lot like Becky's, if a little more rundown. It was a low tide period of the day, around eleven, before the lunch rush.

They walked inside and over to the deli counter, where a bored-looking middle-aged man took their order. Ellen got a sub sandwich and he got meatloaf and mashed potatoes. Once they got some sodas, Ellen led him back outside to some tables they had set up along a sheltered walkway that ran the length of the store.

It was heading into late October now, but it was still decently warm out most days, and at the moment it wasn't even hoodie weather.

Which he privately lamented. The sun had come out this morning, replacing the rain clouds, shining brilliantly.

But he could see more dark gray clouds looming on the horizon, and they were a lot closer now. More rain was coming.

"Okay, so spill," Ellen said after eating her first bite.

"Uh…" He looked around.

"We're alone. Although again, if you don't want to talk about it, totally cool."

"I, uh, guess I could…actually, now that I think about it, I *would* like someone to talk to about this stuff. Although I'm also worried it's going to be embarrassing as hell."

"Don't worry, I won't laugh at you," she replied.

"You already did."

"That wasn't-I wasn't laughing *at* you, Gabe."

"I know, I was just teasing you."

She laughed and rolled her eyes, and he felt her foot brush his own below the table. A moment passed, and she just looked at him, waiting.

He finally decided not to say anything about it and continued. "The first trilogy isn't really anything special. Two people hook up and have hot sex all night, and then spend the next few days together getting to know each other and decide to keep it going. The next trilogy was a bit different. A couple on vacation decide to get experimental and fuck a few women."

"Very hot," Ellen murmured, leaning forward.

Fuck, her shirt was low-cut, and she had *huge* tits.

Was she doing that on purpose?!

It was still a struggle not to look. He maintained focus on her face.

"That's what I was hoping," he replied, and began eating his meal.

They ate for a bit in silence, Ellen not completely losing her little smile. At some point, she brushed his foot again with her own.

His heart fluttered in his chest as she did. He almost said something, but again maintained his silence. It was entirely possible she was doing it without realizing it, even if his instincts were telling him that wasn't the case.

"So what are you working on now? You made it sound like the vacation sex trilogy is finished."

"Oh. Uh. Yeah." He shifted uncomfortably. "It's, uh...I just started it. And it feels weird to talk about it while I'm still, you know, working on it."

Ellen stared at him for a moment, pursing her lips, and he waited tensely to see if she'd challenge that admittedly flimsy logic.

"Okay," she said, "I don't want to mess up your workflow." She glanced at the store beside them. "I guess we should go shopping now. Also...will you let me cover groceries?"

Gabe felt himself tense up a little, and felt an immediate urge to decline the offer. She'd already paid for the pizza last night, and this meal they'd just eaten.

But...

He was less than broke, he was in debt.

"I know it's a whole...thing, but you're letting me stay at your place after I had an emergency. And as chaotic and unstable as my life seems, I *do* have a surplus of cash right now, and suddenly have almost no bills. This is a real offer, it's not like some kind of weird test."

Gabe continued considering it for a few seconds longer.

There was definitely a part of him that was saying he needed to just fucking man up and go further into debt and not let her pay for anything else. To just suffer the consequences of it. But...

Why?

That sounded really stupid when he actually thought about it.

And he did trust her. He believed her. More than that, he was very confident that an insistence to pay on his part would not just go over poorly with her, but she might be, in some way, insulted by it.

"If you're offering, I'll accept," he replied.

She seemed to relax as he said that, and he hadn't realized she'd been tensing a little. She regained her smile. "Good. I'm glad. Come on."

They got up and threw away the remains of their meal, then grabbed a shopping cart and began making their way through the store. As they began making for the first aisle, he noticed a few heads turn their way.

Ellen didn't seem to. It occurred to him, suddenly, that it must be normal for her. And now that he thought about it, it did seem to happen a lot back when they worked together during the rare occasions where she came out of the back while he was working a register.

A nearly six and a half foot tall knockout platinum blonde was quite the head turner, he surmised.

"Oh hey, I love this," she said, stopping and walking around to the front of the cart.

She crouched down and grabbed a box of cereal off the bottom shelf and her breasts nearly tumbled out of her shirt as she did so. Without adjusting herself at all, except to actually lean *forward* a little bit, she looked up at him.

"What do you think, Gabe? Are they great or what?" she asked.

"...what?" he managed.

She smirked. "Marshmallow Bit Bites," she said, shaking the box a little...and making her breasts sway in her shirt. "What did you think I meant?"

He looked into her sparking blue eyes and she stared back at him.

Something shifted inside of him. He wasn't sure if it was a realization, a decision, or both, but all at once he was utterly convinced that she was doing this on purpose. But the real question was: was she doing this on purpose to fuck with him, or was she actually hitting on him?

His head told him 'no', that it was something else. Either he was misinterpreting, or she was fucking with him, teasing him.

But his heart told him 'yes', she was hitting on him. Because it was just too obvious to be misinterpreting, and her fucking with him, it just...

It didn't feel like Ellen.

They had been apart for nearly four years, and they had only known each other by way of break room conversations over the course of a few months.

But in those few months, he had gotten to know her so well. Not just her history, but who she was as a person.

And Ellen was a very kind, very authentic person.

And, he had always suspected, very flirtatious with the right person.

In that moment, perhaps he was the right person.

But the decision he came to, all at once, was: *You know what? I've been trying to be more confident and decisive since starting my 'new life'.*

So I'm going to be.

And two can play at this game.

He grinned back at her. "I just got a little distracted," he replied, "that's such a great shirt."

Her smirk broadened. "Is it now?"

"Yep."

"Well...I'm glad you think so." She stood up and tossed the box into the cart, then came back around to the rear of it and began walking forward.

She leaned on it, bending over a bit, and he realized that she had worn some jeans that seemed perfectly suited to showcase her fantastically fat ass.

She was swaying her hips just a little more than was natural as she walked.

He followed in her wake.

Oh yeah, this was going to be interesting.

CHAPTER SEVEN

Gabe felt like he had slipped through a hole in reality.

He had fallen out of his universe and into another one where Ellen Campbell was spending time with him and he was hitting on her and she liked it.

Ever since Ellen had called him up, everything had seemed different. It was already weird and off-kilter, him having just moved to a brand new place.

But her showing up and everything that had followed…

And now this?!

He was shopping, with Ellen, and flirting.

With Ellen.

They were moving up and down the aisles, and he was at least making a real effort to grab food that made sense.

But she was making it so fucking difficult.

At one point he saw her pick up a sausage and before he even really thought about it, the words "Are you sure you can handle that?" were out of his mouth.

She turned to look at him with that same knowing smirk she'd been wearing practically the whole time.

"Gabe," she replied calmly, "I think you would be *amazed* at what my mouth can do."

He felt his heart start hammering harder as she stared directly into his eyes as she said that. He had a steel hard-on at this point and he was just hoping it wasn't too obvious.

"I'd really like to see that," he heard himself say.

She let out a little laugh. "Would you now?"

"Yes."

"Hmm."

She turned back to the cold case, seemed to judge the sausage for a moment, then put it back. She moved a little farther and grabbed a tube of ground beef.

"I think we'd do better making tacos," she said, tossing it into the cart.

"I love fucking tacos," he said, then paused. "I mean, I fucking love tacos...eating tacos."

She didn't turn to look at him, and for a moment he thought something might've gone wrong with their little game. Then he realized that she was trying very hard not to laugh. She cleared her throat and resumed walking.

Well...

That was a good thing, right?

There was a lot of wisdom that said that being able to make women laugh had a rather direct correlation with hooking up.

Unless that was just wishful thinking.

Then he thought of some of the more famous comedians he knew, and the woman they had been known to date...

Yeah, maybe there was something there.

But was he *actually* going to hook up with Ellen? That still seemed somehow impossible. Why wasn't he freaking out more? Maybe it was because some part of him didn't believe this was actually going to happen, that he had no chance in hell with her.

On the other hand...

Maybe he did.

Looking back on it, he always felt there was a kind of spark there between them during all those conversations. At the time, and ever since honestly, he'd thought it was just wishful thinking. But viewing it as objectively as he could, maybe it wasn't.

Who was to say she wouldn't have asked him out if she'd been single?

Crazier relationships had happened.

He felt reality breaking a little as they put in a jug of milk and he looked at the growing grocery pile.

"Ellen, are you sure you're cool to buy all this?" he asked.

Ellen, however, didn't miss a beat. "What, you've never had a sugar mama before?"

"No, actually," he replied. "...is what you are?"

"Maybe I am. Is that what you'd like?" she asked, still with that fucking smile of hers.

She was the most confident woman he'd ever met, and she had every reason to be.

Gabe felt his composure slip. "Uh...I mean...I wouldn't say no," he murmured awkwardly.

She laughed. "Don't worry, Gabe, you aren't going to break my back...bank."

Had that been a genuine slip up, or not? He couldn't see her face so he couldn't tell.

Even if he could see her face, would that help? She had an amazing poker face, from what he remembered.

"You sure about that?" he replied.

She paused and glanced back over her shoulder at him. "...pretty sure," she replied. "But then again, you do seem like you have a really strong...appetite."

"I do," he said.

Her smirk widened just a bit more and she kept walking.

There was a part of him that desperately wanted to throw aside the innuendo and ask her flat out what was going on. If she was seriously flirting with him with intent to fuck. Because this had gone beyond simple teasing.

But he held back, because somehow he knew that would break the fragile surface tension of...whatever it was they had going on right now.

Would she toss aside the word games when they got behind a closed door?

He'd made himself live without sex, without contact of any kind really, for months now. Over half a year. Longer. Too long.

Way too fucking long.

As they finished up by grabbing some bread, she began guiding them towards the front again, and he struggled to focus.

"I think that's everything," she murmured. "I haven't had to do a run like this in forever. Eggs. Bacon. Milk. Bread. Cheese. Turkey. And...snacks. Maybe too many of those, but whatever. I could use it after my week."

She paused as they approached the self-checkout lane. "Did we forget anything?...Gabe? Earth to Gabe..." she murmured, then giggled.

"What? Uh. Yeah. No. No we didn't forget anything. That's everything," he replied.

"All right, I'll take your word for it, handsome."

Had she ever called him that before?

He genuinely couldn't remember as they headed into the checkout lane and ran through the process of scanning and bagging everything. He nearly had a heart attack when he saw that the price was over a hundred and fifty bucks.

Ellen noticed his expression and she grew serious for a moment. "Gabe...for real, don't worry about it. I really don't mind doing this. Okay?"

"I, uh...yeah, okay," he replied.

They put the bags into the cart after she paid and

headed back outside.

The pair made it back to the car and loaded the bags into the trunk, and then he put the cart away and a moment later found himself sitting beside her once more. She pulled out of the parking lot and began driving them back home.

Home.

Was it...it sort of was their home, for now at least. She was staying with him. Crashing at his place, technically.

But...

They had slept in the same bed last night.

Though out of necessity. Not that she seemed to mind at all.

Gabe was very grateful that he wasn't driving, because his mind was shifting like lightning here, there, and everywhere.

Ellen wasn't like anyone else he had ever known before.

He didn't really have a comparison to how he felt about her, sexually or romantically.

This wasn't a high school crush, this wasn't even like somehow scoring a date with a cheerleader. This wasn't even going home with the hottest girl in school.

Ellen was beyond that.

He had absolutely put her on a pedestal, but he couldn't help it.

It wasn't just that she was exceptionally attractive, nor that she was extremely tall. (She really was the tallest woman he'd ever met in real life by far).

Though those two things certainly helped.

That she was almost a decade older than him also played heavily into it. But she was just...so amazingly confident in everything she did. She was so powerful. That was a word for her: powerful. In his mind, in the world of women he wanted to take on a date, get into bed with, or both, Ellen Campbell was an apex predator.

It was like she had rolled high for *every* stat.

She was smart, she was kind, she was sexy, she was funny, she was witty.

And apparently, flirting with her was very much akin to doing drugs or drinking booze, because he absolutely had a buzz going on right now.

As they headed back to the apartment, Gabe kept telling himself to temper his expectations. It was still possible that this wasn't going to go the way he wanted it to, and if it did, he didn't want to fuck up his friendship with Ellen, not when it was being rekindled.

Although he admittedly would be very frustrated if she was stringing him along. He had a lot of slack to cut someone who'd just been cheated on, but he still knew where to draw the line.

That was another thing he'd promised himself sometime last year: no more bullshit.

Not from anyone in his life.

They pulled into the parking lot.

"You doing okay over there?" Ellen murmured.

"What? Yeah, just, uh...thinking," he replied.

"Oh yeah? What about?"

"You know. Um. Writing stuff."

"Writing stuff, huh? So...sexy things, then?"

He looked over at her and was frustrated to feel his cheeks heating up. "Yeah, you could say that," he managed.

She laughed. "Well, that's pleasant enough to think about. Let's get the groceries in."

"Yeah."

She popped the trunk and they got out. As they gathered up the bags, she looked up at the gray skies overhead.

"I'm pretty sure it's gonna storm hard tonight," she murmured.

"I hope so," he replied.

She looked down at him, a more authentic and less coy smile on her face. "You like rain."

"I do. A lot. And gray days."

"So do I. Everyone thinks I'm weird. But I guess it's just one of those things you either get or you don't. I can't really describe it."

"I know exactly how you feel. I think that there's just, like, switches in our brain. There's just some things we like and some we don't, with no real obvious reason why, and you can't properly articulate why that is."

"That makes a lot of sense."

She closed the trunk as they grabbed the last of the groceries and headed inside, down to his little crappy basement apartment. Though he did realize, as they headed inside and began putting groceries away, it seemed less crappy with her here.

As they filled the fridge and freezer and cabinets, it occurred to Gabe that the sexual tension between then had lapsed for a few moments. The way he was able to parse this was because of the fact that when Ellen brushed up against him in a very intentional way, it was like tossing a flare into a pool of gasoline.

The tension came back with a snap.

But he was ready. He'd been thinking on the way home of how to do this. He didn't want to just straight up ask her 'hey, do you want to fuck?'.

There was some sort of...game wasn't quite the

right word, because it felt more serious than that, but they were playing at something, with subtle rules, and he had only the barest grasp of them. But he knew it wouldn't be right to just outright ask.

Even if that's what he'd prefer.

But no, he had a plan.

As they finished up, Ellen turned to face him with an expectant look on her face.

"So...what do you wanna do?" she asked.

"I was thinking, how would you like back rub?" he replied.

She looked a little caught off guard by it. Had she expected him to just come right out with it? But she recovered quickly with a beautiful and inviting smile.

"I would *love* a back rub! I haven't had one of those in so goddamned long."

"I imagine you must be tense," he said.

"Yes...where's the best place, do you think?" she asked, looking around the apartment.

"The bed," he replied.

"That sounds like a great idea."

He tried not to sigh in relief. As much as he was committing to this, and as much as he thought she was practically rolling out the red carpet for him, there was still that part of him that was worried he'd missed something crucial, and each step he took closer to actually initiating sex with her might reveal whatever it was he'd missed.

She reached out while he was thinking about all this and took his hand, then guided him over to the bed. Her touch was electrifying.

"How do you want me?" she asked as they came to stand by the bed.

"Uh, I guess just, uh, sit in the middle there, facing the wall."

"All right."

She sat down cross-legged, facing away from him, and he kicked off his shoes and got onto the bed behind her on his knees.

Fuck, she was so tall.

He rested his hands on her shoulders and began massaging. She exhaled slowly and a shudder ran through her as he did.

"You all right?" he asked.

"Yeah. I am, actually. Very all right," she murmured. "I just...it's been a long time since I've actually been touched in a meaningful way. And know I fucking know why–" She stopped herself, giving her head a little shake. "Mmm-mmm. Nope. Not going there. Not today." She sighed. "Sorry."

"It's all right," he replied.

After a moment, she said, "Don't be afraid to, you know, go hard."

"Okay."

He started going harder, digging into her muscles, what they called deep tissue massage, and she let out a moan of satisfaction.

"Ah yeah, right...yeah, there. That's good," she murmured.

"I'm glad you like it," he replied.

"Like is a weak word for it...you know, I would very much appreciate you going much lower. This is fantastic, but if I'm being honest, my lower back could use a good, hard rub. Having huge tits has its benefits, but it certainly has its drawbacks, too."

He laughed. "That makes sense."

Gabe sat down behind her and lifted her t-shirt up a bit, revealing her lower back. And dear God, her pants were riding low, revealing the top of her amazing ass.

He placed his thumbs on either side of her spine as low as he dared, as he knew which muscles were likely giving her trouble. Finding them, he began kneading them.

"Ah! Oh shit! Yes! Fuck!" she groaned, stretching. "That's...oh man."

"Too hard?" he asked.

"No! No, not too hard. Go harder," she said. "I can take it."

As he kept going, pressing deeper and harder with his thumbs, bringing them up in a rising pattern on either side of her spine several inches then starting back at the bottom, he decided to go for his next move.

"This would be easier with your shirt off," he murmured.

"It...would," she agreed, but there was some reluctance in her voice.

"I can also manage just fine like this, if you aren't comfortable with that," he added.

"I appreciate that," she said after a pause. She sounded a little surprised. "But...I want to take my shirt off." She began shifting, then paused.

When she spoke again, he could almost hear the smile in her voice.

"You take it off for me."

CHAPTER EIGHT

Gabe took her shirt off, or tried to. It got caught on her bra.

He sighed as he adjusted it.

She giggled. "First time taking a girl's shirt off?" she teased.

"No, but it *has* been a while. At least in this context," he muttered.

She lifted her arms. "What context is that, exactly?"

"I guess we'll find out, won't we?"

"I guess we will," she agreed, the teasing note still in her voice.

He got her t-shirt off and tossed it aside. Now there was just her bra. He thought she might be wearing a sports bra but it was hooked in the back. He was extraordinarily tempted to start undoing those hooks.

Instead, he ran his hands over the lower portion her back. She inhaled deeply and let out a low moan of pleasure that definitely sounded sexual.

"That's...I fucking love that," she whispered. "Your hands are very nice."

"Thank you," he replied.

He stopped with the soft rubbing after a moment and began going harder again. Touching her was amazing, intoxicating. He shifted up higher, taking a moment to move her hair, then rubbing hard in between her shoulder blades.

"Your hair is the most amazing color," he said.

"It's natural," she murmured. "I hated it when I was younger. I wanted to be a redhead, and then later I wanted to be a 'normal' blonde. I used to dye it, but

I gave that up."

"I've always really liked it. That pale blonde looks so right on you," he replied.

"Huh...pale blonde. I don't think I've heard that before. It was always platinum blonde or bleach blonde. I like it." She laughed softly. "I guess I shouldn't be surprised, you *are* a writer."

He wasn't sure what to say to that, so he just moved down again, to her lower back. He kept working it until suddenly he leaned into, pressing hard on one specific spot, and something popped loudly.

"Aw! Fuck!" she cried.

"Sorry. Too rough?" he asked.

She laughed. "You fucker...no, actually." She shifted a little. "That's actually better. So much better. What the hell did you *do?*"

"Worked out a knot," he replied.

"Shit, man. Are you a professional?"

"No. Just good at it, I guess." He took a measured breath and prepared to dance along the razor's edge. "You know what would make this even easier?"

"What's that?" she murmured.

"If I could unhook your bra," he said.

"That does make sense," she agreed. "Unhook away."

Gabe could feel his heart hammering in his chest now as he reached up and undid the two hooks holding the bra together. He almost felt sick to his stomach, he was so aroused and excited. He hoped it wouldn't make him say something stupid.

He got the bra unhooked and it almost fell down her arms.

"Ahhh...yeah. That's better. I fucking hate bras,"

she muttered, and then, without missing a beat, she slid it down her arms and tossed it onto the bed.

Fuck.

He had Ellen topless in his apartment, *on his bed*. And he was massaging her.

Massaging her, right. He realized that he'd stopped. He resumed, sticking to the lower back, because he could feel a lot of tension there, though it had been releasing.

"You good for me to do another knot?" he asked.

"Yeah, just warn me this time," she replied.

He kept working her back, softening up the area around the knot of tension for another few moments. In his mind, Gabe could see her enormous breasts shifting and swaying subtly with his movements as he massaged her back.

He realized he was breathing heavily, his heart still thundering in his chest, but he couldn't seem to control it. It or the raging hard-on he had. It had mostly gone away in the car but now it was back with a vengeance.

"Okay, get ready," he said.

"I'm ready," she murmured.

He massaged it for a bit longer, then pressed, deep and hard, into it. Something popped loudly and she cried out again.

"Ah *yeah*..." she moaned, shifting around and rolling her shoulders. "My God, that's amazing. I didn't know massages could do this..." She was silent for a moment, then something new entered her voice. "Don't be afraid to massage in other places. If the mood the strikes you."

"Other places?" he replied, his heart hammering harder.

That *had* to be an invitation.

Right?

Well, time to go big or go home.

"You know, whatever you feel like touching and massaging," she replied, and again he could fucking *hear* the smile in her slightly teasing voice.

Gabe leaned forward, getting closer to her, and put his lips close to her ear. Close enough that when he spoke he knew his breath would be felt.

"I'm going to take you at your word, Ellen," he said quietly.

She exhaled hard and shuddered a bit more violently this time. "Good," she whispered.

Gabe went for it.

He reached around to the front of her and cupped her huge, bare breasts in his hands. There was a second there that seemed to last for an eternity. Because this was crossing the threshold. There was no more subtle interplay, no teasing innuendo that could be interpreted as highly sexual or as innocent words.

This was overt, and there was no going back from having done it.

But there was no bad reaction from Ellen. She said nothing, and her body language seemed to be more inviting than ever.

Even then, he tried not to go too fast. Gabe didn't have a great deal of experience with women and sex so far, but he at least knew some things. And he knew that something most women tended to really like was when you went slow and built it up.

And this was *Ellen*.

He had every intention of making her feel as good as he possibly could if she was actually going to allow him inside of her.

And her breasts.

Good. Fucking. Lord.

Her breasts.

That moment in time stretched out in a completely different way. It wasn't torment but paradise. He'd literally lain awake at night thinking about her huge tits. And now he had them in his hands, and he was gently massaging them.

"Your hands are very warm," she murmured quietly.

"And your tits...are huge," he managed.

Ellen giggled. "I'm glad you're enjoying yourself. You sound a little drunk."

"I feel a little drunk," he replied.

She giggled again and fell silent, letting him do whatever he wanted. As he continued massaging her big breasts, he leaned into the situation, and pressed his lips to the side of her neck. She gasped softly and tilted her head away from him, to give him better access. He kissed along the side of her neck, slowly, carefully, moving his way around to the back.

"Ah!" she gasped when he kissed against the back of her neck, just below her hairline.

"Good ah?" he murmured.

"Yes...*so* sensitive. Don't stop," she replied, panting a little now.

"You want more?" he murmured.

"Yes!"

He continued kissing the back of her neck and then he let go of her breasts and ran his fingers across her nipples. She groaned and shuddered harder, shifting around against him. He began using his tongue a little as he made circles around her nipples with his fingertips.

"Gabe…" she moaned, and that single word was more invigorating than anything else.

Hearing her moan that in sexual pleasure was amazing.

He felt emboldened and moved over to her other side, kissing along her neck, until his lips were beside her other ear.

"Take your pants off, Ellen," he whispered.

She made a sound that tried to be a word but failed, then seemed to get herself under control again. "You do it," she whispered. "Here, let me…"

She began move but she stopped suddenly, and her body language changed.

"What's wrong?" he asked.

"I…" She hesitated further.

"Whatever it is, Ellen, you can tell me. You know you can trust me. If you want to stop, I won't be angry–"

"I don't want to stop," she interrupted. "…you really wouldn't be angry?"

"I'd be *really* disappointed and sexually frustrated, but it's your right, Ellen."

"It isn't that. I just…maybe I could put my shirt back on," she murmured.

"What? No. I mean, if you really want to, but why? Are you really going to stop me from seeing your amazing breasts?" he asked.

She laughed, the kind of laugh that seemed to catch a person off guard. "No, I just…mmm. Shit."

"Come on, whatever it is, you can tell me."

She seemed to gather her courage. "I got fat, Gabe. I actually like what it's done for my thighs, my hips, even my ass, but my stomach…"

"Is *that* it? Ellen, listen," he fully let go of her breasts now and hugged her from the back, resting his head against the side of hers, embracing her, "I can't emphasize this enough: you are a fucking *goddess* to me, okay? I know that sounds ridiculous, but I'm completely serious. You are *so* fucking hot. You're a fucking eleven, okay? And I don't want you to be uncomfortable for this, but I also want you to know that I *really* want to see you naked."

She was silent for a long moment. "Well...I definitely believe you," she murmured. "You're sure?" she added quietly.

"I'm utterly positive. Turn around, lay on your back," he replied.

"Mmm...yes, sir," she murmured, sultriness creeping back into her voice.

He released her and she turned around, and he got a look at her topless from the front for the first time, and it was fucking amazing.

Her breasts looked so perfect to him. So huge, smooth and pale, with perfect, pink nipples. They swayed with her movements as she laid down slowly on her back. He looked up at her, and she looked back at him, chewing gently on her lower lip.

She looked more vulnerable than he ever thought possible.

"Ellen," he said.

"Yeah?" she murmured.

"You are so beautiful. And hot. Seriously, if this were a thousand years ago, there would be statues of you. There should be now."

She laughed. "Gabe!"

"I'm telling the truth."

"Your truth, maybe," she murmured. "But...thank you."

He reached out and unbuttoned her jeans, then unzipped them, then began pulling them down. She raised her hips, and as he pulled them down her legs, he realized she'd not worn any panties today. He found himself staring at her glorious, immense, pale thighs and her broad hips, and between them, her smooth, perfect pussy.

"You shaved this morning?" he murmured, still staring at it as he got her jeans off and tossed them aside.

She laughed. "No, Gabe. I got it lasered off a while ago. It was a bitch, the hair was too pale initially for the laser to work, but they got some new technique-whatever. It's gonna remain smooth," she said.

"Fine by me," he replied.

As he stared at her pussy and thought about what it was going to be like to be inside of her, a new thought came to him like a shock of cold water.

"Oh fuck," he whispered.

"What? What's wrong?" she asked.

"I...don't have any condoms."

"Oh." She looked at him for a long moment, then slowly smiled. "Well...I don't care if you don't."

"Seriously?" he asked.

"Do you have any STDs?" she asked.

"No. I got tested after my last girlfriend went psycho on me. I know, I know, all guys say that, but she really did go psycho on me. She tried to stab me."

"Holy shit! You gotta tell me that story...but later. Okay, so, here's the deal: I trust you, Gabe. Maybe it's stupid, but I trust you. And if you trust me, then...I don't have any either. I got tested, too. After I got suspicious, I got tested. I'm in the clear. And I've got a birth control implant. It actually got renewed like six months ago so it's good. So...you can totally fuck me raw, and come in my pussy, if you want to."

He stared at her for a moment, trying to generate a response to that. "Of course I want to," he managed finally. "But, I just-you're really cool with that?"

"Yes. I am."

"Holy shit. Okay. Um, well, in that case."

He took off his shirt and tossed it aside, then began undoing his jeans. She laughed as he flopped around for a moment, trying to get them and his boxers off. As soon as they did come off, though, he immediately felt fear shoot through him at being exposed.

This was always the hardest part: showing his bare cock to a woman for the first time.

Would she laugh? Would she be disappointed? Would she–

"Gabe," Ellen said, reaching out and laying a hand on his leg. "It's okay. Your dick is fine. I know it's a whole thing for guys, but...it's fine. Okay? Let's keep going."

He nodded and then slowly eased himself down next to her. She looked over at him, a small smile on her face, her eyes flashing with desire. As he looked at her, into her eyes, Gabe realized that a worrying amount of the excitement jolting through his body wasn't lust, but anxiety.

How many times had he fantasized about this exact situation?

Quite *literally* this? Having Ellen, completely naked, in his bed, wanting him to fuck her.

What if he sucked in bed? What if he couldn't satisfy her? She was, like, an entire half a foot taller than he was, and what if–

"Gabe," she said.

"What?" he replied.

"You're freaking out a little right now," she murmured, and then reached out and put one hand against his cheek. "But you don't have to. I'm fucking wet as *hell* right now, Gabe. And this is the important part: I'm wet *for you.* Okay? This isn't some lay of convenience because you're the nearest hard cock, okay? You fucking turn me on. A lot. I want to fuck you *so* bad."

He stared at her for a moment, finding that, shockingly, he actually believed her.

And, goddamnit, wasn't he choosing to be more confident now? Especially when it came to the women he tried to date, or sleep with.

"Good," he said, "because I'm going to make you orgasm so fucking hard."

The look that came onto her face was one of surprise, lust, and joy, and then he leaned in and pressed his lips against her luscious red lips.

Finally.

Finally.

He had dreamed of kissing Ellen Campbell for four long years now, and it was finally happening. She moaned as their lips met, and immediately deepened the kiss. She took his hand and brought it back to one of her big breasts, and a fresh jolt of lust hit him as he got a handful. He continued massaging her breast as they deepened the kiss.

Then she parted his lips with her own and slipped her tongue into his mouth, and her taste came on heavy and strong.

She moaned as she pressed against him harder, her hand slipping down to wrap around his erection. He broke the kiss as he exhaled hard.

"Oh my," she murmured, "that hard of a reaction from just touching your dick?"

"Like I said, been a while," he replied. "And you are...well, *you.*"

"Don't worry, I'm going to take *good* care of

you, handsome," she said, her voice huskier now.

"What are you gonna do to me?" he asked quietly.

"You'll know what I'm going to do to you soon enough," she murmured. "If you'd like, I can show you right now, though."

"Give a few minutes more."

"Got something specific in mind?"

"I do, actually."

He grinned into their kiss and stopped groping her big breast and instead slipped his hand down to her lower belly. She shivered as he touched her, and then he moved his hand over her hip, then down her thigh, enjoying the simple yet intense pleasure of skin-on-skin contact with her.

"Your thighs…" he whispered, and then was unable to finish that sentence.

She giggled. "You like them, huh?"

"Not nearly a strong enough word," he replied, running his hand up and down her thick, well-padded, pale thigh.

Carefully, he worked his fingers in between her thighs, and she took his meaning and parted them for him, spreading her incredibly long legs. He took a look at her smooth pussy, then ran his fingertips along the skin around it.

Ellen gasped again and he loved feeling her shiver against him. He slipped a finger in between the lips of her pussy and found her clit easily enough. She moaned as he made contact, then moaned again, much louder, as he applied pressure and began to gently rub it.

"Aw shit, Gabe…" she moaned. "You take your time, don't you?"

"Yes. I've heard that women like that," he

replied.

"You heard right." She gasped again and her hips bucked slightly. "Too long," she whispered, then closed her eyes and pressed her head down into his pillow.

He lowered his own head and began doing something he'd wanted to do for a very long time. Sticking out his tongue, he licked across one big, pale breast, and then over her pale pink nipple. She continued moaning and twitching as he lavished her with pleasure.

He sealed his lips around one of her nipples and began sucking on it. At the same time, he began rubbing her clit a bit faster, pressing down just a bit harder. He'd thought that it would be difficult to coordinate because of how anxious he was now that he actually had her naked and horny, but this mercifully was not the case at all.

Sucking on her big breasts was as satisfying and absurdly arousing as he'd always thought it would be. He switched to her other one and then slipped a finger inside of her.

Inside she was so slick and hot.

"Oh, *Gabe!*" she cried as he pressed up into her most sensitive spot.

Her hips bucked and he did it a few more times, getting loud moans of pleasure from her.

"You like that?" he asked.

"Fucking *yes!*" she replied, panting. "Two fingers," she added hastily.

He slipped a second finger into her and began pressing up, hard and fast. She let out a strange, almost strangled noise, now gripping the blanket they laid on, and her whole body seemed to thrum and pulse with sexual energy.

When her orgasm came, it surprised him, both with its abruptness and its intensity.

Ellen let out a loud cry of passion and pleasure as her hips jerked hard. He felt her slick inner muscles contract and flutter around his fingers, now deep inside her, and then abruptly a hot gush of feminine liquids escaped her.

"*Gabe!*" she cried.

He kept going, trying to help her ride the wave of the climax that he'd brought her to, and it seemed to go on for a good while.

And then, abruptly, it was over, and she flopped back against the bed, panting furiously, a fine sheen of sweat glistening on her long, pale body.

"Oh my fucking God," she whispered, staring at the ceiling with wide eyes. "Seriously, that was-holy fuck, man. I..." She raised her head. "Oh lord, I made a hell of a mess. I guess I should've put a towel down after all."

"Oh...yeah. That would've made sense," Gabe murmured.

"I didn't think I'd need one. I was debating telling you, but I didn't want to freak you out."

"What?" he asked.

"It's...kinda hard to make me orgasm. I was going to tell you, but then I was worried you might try to overcompensate and go too hard, or get really pissed if it didn't work out, just...it's a me thing. But, uh, apparently it's not a problem right now."

"Evidently," he replied, looking at the large, dark spot on the blanket.

"Here, up," she said, getting up herself.

They both stood and she grabbed the blanket and brought it over to the washing machine. There, she switched her laundry that she'd put in earlier (and had forgotten about) over to the dryer, then put the blanket in and started it going.

"Okay," she said, turning and looking at him with something almost predatory in her gaze. She pointed to the bed. "Sit down. It's your turn."

CHAPTER NINE

"So, this is what I meant when I said you would be absolutely shocked by what my mouth can do," Ellen said as she crouched before him at the foot of the bed.

He tried to think of something clever to say back to her, but nothing was coming to mind. She looked up at him with that confident smirk of hers, then pushed the hair back out of her face, then sighed suddenly.

"Hold on," she muttered, getting up and walking away.

He would have been a little concerned by the abrupt development, but it afforded him a really perfect view of her spectacularly large and shapely ass.

She found her purse and rooted around in it for a moment, then came up with another hair tie. Gathering up her long, pale blonde hair, she put it into a ponytail as she walked back over to him and got back down on her knees.

"There we go," she said.

There were questions he wanted to ask her, things he wanted to say to her, but all that went right out of his skull as she leaned forward and stuck her tongue out while exhaling slowly. A hot burst of air brushed across his erection and then her tongue made contact with his head.

He exhaled sharply and leaned back, propping himself up on the heels of his palms. Staring down at her, he watched as she wrapped two fingers and a thumb around his shaft and began to lick across his tip of his cock.

"Oh fuck, Ellen," he whispered, breathing hard already.

She let out a little laugh and kept going, tilting her head as she covered the tip in her saliva. After a moment of this, she tilted her head mostly to the side and pressed her lips against the base of his head, and then she began sucking on it, and he discovered just how sensitive that specific part of his anatomy was.

"Holy fucking shit," he gasped.

She laughed again, seemingly satisfied with herself, and kept it up for a bit longer. Then she straightened back up, opened her mouth, and took his entire cock into it. He groaned as she wrapped her lips around the base of his erection, his head hitting the back of her throat. Then she pressed harder, pushing the head just a bit down her throat.

She swallowed.

Gabe groaned loudly as all those tight, slick muscles contracted around his head, sending a shock of total pleasure through him. She did it twice more, then pulled back, breathing a bit more heavily through her nose as she began sucking him off.

Ellen moved with as much confidence now as he saw her use in all other aspects of her life. She looked up at him with those stunning, bright blue eyes of hers as she moved her lips up and down his erection.

At first she moved slowly, moving especially slow as her lips came up and then down over his head, which sent exquisite bursts of sheer ecstasy into him and made him groan loudly. Then she went faster.

He put his hand over the back of her head.

"I'm going to fucking come, Ellen," he gasped.

She made a sound that might have been the word 'good' and shrugged without stopping. Okay, so, she wanted a load in her mouth. Or at least she was willing to take one. Well, that was fine by him. He gripped her head a little more tightly, guiding her, and she let him.

He was just beginning to appreciate this fact when it happened.

His orgasm triggered and suddenly his dick was jerking hard, sending pulses of raw, perfect bliss screaming wildly through his body as he began pumping his seed out as hard and fast as he could. He groaned her name several times as she sucked him dry, her head no longer moving, her lips forming a perfect seal just a bit below the head.

He could feel those two fingers and that thumb still going, stroking smoothly up and down his shaft, working his cock to get everything out of him.

His whole body felt like it was aflame with the passion and pleasure of this orgasm she had given him. Ellen kept sucking his dick until he had nothing left to give, and then she sucked a bit more. Finally, she lowered her lips a bit, then began pulling his erection out from between them, still sucking as she went, getting every last drop.

"Ah! Oh my fucking-holy shit, Ellen!" he gasped, panting.

Gabe fell onto his back as she finished with him.

"Told you," she said.

"That was, by several magnitudes, the best blowjob I've ever had in my entire fucking life," he whispered, staring at the ceiling.

"And we haven't even fucked yet," she replied, getting to her feet.

He couldn't think of a real response to that, either.

Ellen stepped into his bathroom. He heard plastic

tearing and a lid unscrewing and gargling and spitting, then running water and a bit more of the same.

"I hope you don't take offense to that," she said as she came back.

"What? No," he replied.

"Okay, good. I just *really* like the kissing with you. You're an excellent kisser."

"Really?" he asked as she sat on the bed beside him.

"Yes! Fuck me and kiss me," she said, reaching out and gently teasing his cock with the tip of her finger.

He was at about half mast right now, but he immediately started stiffening up again as she touched him.

"On your back, spread your legs," he replied.

"You're a lot more take-charge in bed than I thought you'd be," she said as she did just that.

"Good thing?" he asked as he got onto the bed and took a moment to look at her.

She really did looked like a lounging goddess.

"Good thing," she murmured.

Then he was moving forward, his lust and desire for her so overwhelming and intense that it overrode everything else. He *had* to be on her, in her. She spread her legs out wider for him, exposing herself even more.

As he got in between those huge thighs of hers, he looked up at her, his eyes moving slowly along her long, luxurious body, over her huge breasts, and then up to her face…

She looked surprisingly vulnerable.

"You good?" he asked.

"Yes," she replied, smiling a little more easily.

"Now quit teasing and put it in me."

His whole body practically writhed with anticipation as she said that, and he did just that. Settling in between her thighs, he gripped himself and rested his head at the entrance of her glistening wet pussy. She shivered as he made contact and he could hear her breathing more heavily.

Placing his other hand on her hip, he began pushing his way into her.

She accepted him smoothly, and that moment as he slid into her, experiencing the perfect bliss that was Ellen Campbell, seemed to stretch out in time.

Everything else truly fell away as he pushed his way carefully into her.

She was so fantastically slick and hot inside. A loud groan escaped him at the same time it did her. He pulled back, then pushed in deeper, making her cry out.

He did it again, this time pushing all the way in.

Gabe rested there for a moment, looking down, seeing himself completely inside of her. He shifted, as she'd raised her legs for him. Resting on his knees now, he grabbed her hips and began fucking her. She moaned loudly, panting rapidly, and her breasts began to sway with the rhythm of their sex as he stroked into her.

"Oh fuck, that's good," she whispered. "Gabe, that's so good...harder," she moaned.

He tightened his grip a little, sinking in his fingertips, and started going harder and faster.

The pleasure of fucking her hot, perfect pussy was eating him alive, burning into him. It wasn't just overwhelming, it was utterly overpowering, rising over his senses like a tsunami darkening the land as it crested the horizon.

For that moment in time, he lived in the eclipse of their lovemaking as she darkened the skies of his personal world with her sheer, raw sexuality.

He reached forward, shifting his hands to her big breasts and groping them as he continued screwing her, stroking smoothly in and out of her sweet perfection. Her huge, pillowy breasts were so soft and smooth and hot, and he could feel her nipples poking into the palms of his hands.

At some point she grasped his wrist and tugged impatiently at him, and he took her meaning immediately, laying down against her. There was a height difference between them, but they could just manage to kiss as they made love.

The kiss was immediately deep and passionate. Her tongue probed his mouth almost furiously, and he moved his own forward. They met and twisted and danced together, and her taste again flooded his mouth.

He felt incoherent, not just with the physical pleasure of their coupling, but with the intimacy of the encounter, and the fact that it was *her*.

This woman he had dreamed of for four long years.

This woman who had left the strongest impression on him of any in his entire life.

Gabe broke the kiss at some point and found himself moaning her name again and again. Her smile was broad and satisfied, and she looked utterly lost in the moment, just like him.

At some point it came to him that he wasn't going to last much longer.

The pleasure of her perfect pussy was too much.

"Ellen," he gasped.

"What?" she replied. "What is it?"

"I'm going to come. Really soon. Do you want me to pull out?"

Her smile changed from sheer joy to something a bit more promiscuous, and he felt her shift beneath him.

"Don't you dare," she growled, and he realized she was wrapping her long, long legs around him.

He didn't last much longer.

Gabe went faster and harder, careening headlong towards his climax, and when it came, it was the strongest he ever remembered having. He cried out and pressed his hips forward. Faintly, he heard her gasp, then moan, and he could feel her hands on his sweat-slicked back.

"That's it, Gabe," she moaned, "give it all to me."

He was coming inside of her and the ecstasy was blinding.

He had never enjoyed this particular pleasure before.

Gabe could feel his seed leaving him in hard, furious contractions, pumping her full and filling her up. She squeezed him with her legs, pressing him just a bit deeper, as he released everything he had into her.

The orgasm lasted for a long time.

And then it was over, and he was left floating, weightless, high on a sea of pink, post-coital bliss, and he knew nothing but happiness as he laid there, naked and sweaty atop her, panting.

CHAPTER TEN

Neither of them spoke for a long time.

In fact, the first thing to break the silence was not either of them, but the steady staccato tapping of rain at the windows.

Ellen spoke first. "Mmm...it's raining, Gabe. It feels perfect."

He managed to generate a response. "That was my first time going raw."

She shifted beneath him. "Are you serious?"

"Yes. Dead serious."

"Holy shit. That's..." she laughed suddenly. "Oh boy, you're gonna fucking fall for me."

"What?" he asked, a little startled, though only mildly. It seemed as though he was encased in a shell of pleasant passivity, like he was stoned.

"Don't you know? Boys *always* fall for the girls who let them hit it raw first." She giggled, sounding highly amused.

"Uh..." That was all he could think to say in response.

"Oh Gabe," she murmured, and he shivered and groaned as she ran her fingernails gently down his back. "I'm really glad it could be with me."

"Really?" he murmured.

"Yes. You know, I've been thinking about this exact thing almost since we met."

"*Really?*" he repeated, raising his head now and looking at her.

She looked incredibly relaxed, sedated almost, and immensely satisfied.

"Really," she replied with that smile of hers. "When I saw you in the break room that first time, my first real thought was, 'oh he's *so* damn cute'. And it didn't take long for the sexual fantasies to start coming...mmm, if I'd been single at the time..."

"You'd what?" he asked.

"I'd have taken you for a spin," Ellen replied. "I would have asked you for a date, and if you didn't turn into a complete jackass, I probably would have taken you back to my apartment and fucked your brains out."

"I find that extremely difficult to believe."

She snorted. "Why? I honestly had been kind of worried I'd been a little too obvious. Then again, I guess you were a little lost whenever I came into the room. I saw the way you eye-fucked me every time you saw me."

"I, uh...sorry about that."

"Don't be. I'm not. From the right person, it can be...very nice. Honestly, I felt bad. I don't cheat. And my relationship was stable, and monogamous. It's why I tried hard not to lead you on. But then I kept thinking about it more and more, and..." she trailed off, looking uncomfortable now.

"And what?" he asked.

"Just remembering that there was a time there I was fantasizing about you a lot. Thinking about you, perhaps when I shouldn't have been...of course looking back on it now, I don't feel guilty about that at all."

"Wait, are you saying you were thinking about me during sex?" he asked.

She laughed and blew an errant strand of hair from her face. "Yes, Gabe."

"I also find that incredibly hard to believe."

She was silent for a moment, then she shifted again beneath him. "I need a shower. You blew a *huge* load in me."

"Oh, yeah. Sorry," he muttered as he pulled out of her and got off her.

Ellen laughed as she cupped a hand over her vagina and got to her feet. "Why? I've always heard there's something of a correlation between load size and satisfaction."

"Well...not always, but yeah. Also, it's been a while since I've jerked off."

"That would help," she said, and headed for the bathroom.

He laid there for a moment longer, staring at the ceiling now, still feeling like he was in a daze. None of this seemed real.

He'd had sex before. He'd lost his virginity over eight years ago now, and he'd had a few girlfriends since then.

But the sex had never been like that.

Thoughts were slowly beginning to penetrate his skull again, the world working its dark, relentless way back into his brain as the orgasmic high wore off. He heard the shower start up and the curtain slide one way, then another.

Gabe got to his feet and walked over to the bathroom. She had left the bathroom door open a few inches. He knocked on it.

"You care if I come in?" he asked.

"No," she replied. She giggled. "I already let you come in."

He chuckled and stepped in, then closed the door behind him, though suddenly wondered why he bothered. It was just the two of them here. Force of habit, he supposed.

"Can I, uh, join you?" he asked.

"If you want to. It'll be a tight fit, but...I don't

really mind that right now," she replied, her voice still a bit sultry and mildly demure.

He pulled back the curtain and stared at her for a moment, again struck by her intense beauty. She reminded him of an actress, or a model.

"You just gonna stare?" she asked, grinning at him.

She had his showerhead down between her thighs, aimed right at her crotch.

"Sorry," he murmured as he got in and closed the curtain behind him.

She was right, there really wasn't much room in here. But he found that he agreed with her: he didn't might the close confines.

For a moment, they just stared at each other. Then Ellen let out a little sound and shook her head. She replaced the showerhead.

"Don't take this the wrong way, but you...are kinda weird," she murmured.

"Why do you say that?" he replied.

"Most guys get awkward and jumpy leading up to the sex, and then they get all calm and confident after. It's sorta the opposite with you. Why are you so nervous?" she asked.

"I guess...I have a lot of questions. And I suppose you could say my reality feels particularly fragile right now? It's not just that what just happened was, by far, the best sex of my entire life, but it's that it was *you* laying me."

Ellen frowned slightly, still staring at him intently. She almost looked a little worried now. "Okay, let's just...slow down a bit. I was hoping the bliss phase would last a little longer...what are your questions?"

He tried to think of which one to ask first when,

abruptly, a new one leaped to the front of the line.

"Oh shit. Did I...I didn't take advantage of you, did I?"

She let out a surprised burst of laughter. "What!? How could you possibly think that?! I invited you every step of the way, Gabe! For Christ's sake, I thought I was going to have to just jump you. You were sure taking your sweet time."

"First of all, I was savoring it," he replied.

"Okay...fair."

"Second of all...I mean, you just got cheated on, your life just blew up, people don't always make the best decisions-it's just, how many stories do you hear about ill-advised hookups that begin with 'I did something really stupid'? You know what I mean?"

"Oh, Gabe." She stepped forward and hugged him to her wet, nude, voluptuous body. "This wasn't done out of a spur of the moment decision. I very much decided I wanted to have sex with you this morning. I had *hours* to consider it, and to not let it happen if I decided against it. I didn't. I very much wanted this." She paused. "God, you *did* want this, right? Ah shit, I didn't pressure *you* or anything, did I?"

"No," he replied immediately. "Not at all. I'd say I wanted that more than anything."

She let out a small sigh of relief, then a little laugh and pulled back, staring at him. "So you're telling me that if someone offered you a million bucks *or* you could fuck me, you'd choose me?"

"Oh yeah, in a heartbeat," he replied. She raised an eyebrow. "I'm serious!"

"I just...okay. Next question."

"What...is this? What's going to happen? I know that's an insane question to ask so quickly after a first hookup, but I just, I gotta know."

"Um, well." She paused, losing her smile. Then she chewed on her lower lip for a moment. "I...don't know," she admitted. She laughed awkwardly. "I'm not used to this. Usually I'm a lot more certain about things. I do know that I don't want that to be the only time we have sex."

"That's definitely something we can agree on. I haven't even had a chance to go down on you yet," he replied.

"Oh. That was...on the table?" she murmured.

"Uh, yeah. Definitely. I want to make you feel fucking *good*, Ellen."

"I. Oh."

"Are you blushing?"

"No! It's just...the shower got hot. I would very much appreciate some oral sex," she replied, smiling broadly. "If I'd known...mmm, maybe I would've been a little more patient."

"Well," he said, reaching out and rubbing his thumb gently across one of her nipples, making her shudder, "that's the fun of getting to know each other."

She laughed. "Okay, you haven't lost *all* your confidence, clearly." She began to say something else but her stomach growled. "Jesus, I'm fucking starving all of a sudden. Here, you can have the shower."

They maneuvered carefully around each other, and she stepped out, closing the curtain behind her. As he started cleaning up, he heard her drying herself off, and then suddenly she stopped and sighed heavily.

"Something wrong?" he asked, peering out.

The curtain was almost see-through. She was standing in front of the mirror, and now was looking down at herself.

"This really doesn't bother you?" she murmured.

"Your body? Your *amazingly* hot body? It bothers me in that it kept me awake at night and horny for four years," he replied, attempting to derail this particular train of thought.

"Yeah but I was definitely a lot hotter when we first met," she replied.

"I think you're hotter now."

"Oh come on, Gabe," she said, annoyance immediately obviously in her voice, "you don't have to patronize me. I mean, I get that you're into me, but you don't need outright lie to me."

He pulled back the shower curtain and stared at her. "Ellen," he said firmly, and she looked over at him, into his eyes. "I'm not lying to you. I'm not exaggerating. I'm being honest."

Ellen stared at him for a long moment, her lips pursed. "Are you a chubby chaser or something?" she asked finally.

He sighed heavily and pushed the curtain back.

"I'm sorry," she said immediately. "I don't know why I said that. Just-I'm sorry. I'm being difficult. It's just hard to accept. I got fat, and my fiance–" she heaved an angry sigh, "–*ex*-fiance–was always on me about it. Telling me I should really start going to the gym, or commenting on like every fucking meal, or like, pinching my thighs or my stomach, and I *know* I should've tried harder to keep the weight off but–"

"Ellen, what the *fuck!?* He sounds like a fucking asshole! I mean, he *is* an asshole, he cheated on you and then blew up at you when he got caught but, like, fucking hell! Was this recent?"

"No, it's been going for about two years now," she replied.

"That's so fucked."

"I mean, he wasn't completely out of line–"

Gabe yanked back the shower curtain again, incredulous. Were they seriously having this conversation?

"Ellen, are *actually* defending your ex-fiance calling you fat and teasing you like a cruel douchebag for years?!" She stared at him, looking a little lost. He relaxed suddenly. "Shit, now *I'm* sorry. I was-I didn't mean to...fuck, nevermind. I'm sorry."

He put the curtain back.

"No...you're right," she murmured. "Why the hell am I defending him? But...I don't want to be one of those women who's all 'you have to love me forever no matter *what* I look like', you know?"

"Ellen, I get that relationships can change, and that people aren't obligated to be attracted to each other, but you can *absolutely* have an adult conversation about it without acting like it's fucking middle school," he replied, then sighed. "I'm sorry if-no, you know that? I'm not sorry. I don't care if I'm out of line, he's a fuckhead and you didn't deserve that."

A long moment of silence passed. Gabe finished washing up and turned off the water. He pulled the shower curtain back, worried that he'd pissed her off when she still hadn't said anything in response. She was still standing there, now looking concerned.

"Ellen...are you okay?" he asked.

"I'm just thinking. About my relationship. How did I not notice that he was an asshole? Because it wasn't like there was this sudden nosedive in the relationship."

Gabe frowned, then grabbed a towel and started drying himself off. "Ellen, if there's anything I've learned about relationships, it's that they're complicated. I'm not giving you shit. Okay?"

She slowly nodded. "Yeah. All right." Her stomach growled again. "We should eat."

He took her towel when she finished drying off and hung it up for her. "Yeah," he agreed. "Let's figure something out."

Ellen left the bathroom and he took a few extra minutes to finish drying himself, his mind still drifting, though in a somewhat less pleasant manner now.

CHAPTER ELEVEN

As Gabe began preparing the oven for the frozen fish and shrimp they'd decided to heat up, he still felt very adrift.

What was messing with him now was that he wasn't completely sure where he stood with Ellen.

He felt like he had whiplash in terms of how familiar he was with her. On the one hand, they'd had months of frequent, in depth, even personal conversations. He felt like they'd truly gotten to know each other and developed a bond while working together.

On the other hand, that was four years ago.

On the *other* hand, she seemed to agree with his assessment on the bonding.

And, on top of that all, he'd now seen her naked and had sex with her.

"Was that seriously your first time going raw?"

He finished setting the temperature and initiated the heat up, then turned to face her. She was wearing a fresh pair of panties and a tanktop that did little to hide her huge breasts, her nipples obvious through the thin fabric.

"Yeah," he replied, "is that really so unbelievable?"

"It's just...how many girlfriends have you had?"

"Three," he replied, walking over and sitting with her on the loveseat. "And yes, I slept with each of them. The first was practical: we didn't have reliable access to birth control and neither of us trusted pulling out all that much. The second one was just *super* paranoid about getting pregnant. The third...I never fully trusted her, I guess. There was always this voice in the back of my mind telling me to use protection. Even though she offered to go raw."

"Smart, given what happened...you said she tried to stab you?"

He nodded. "Yes. And yeah, I'm sure it was smart. I wouldn't be surprised at all to learn she was hiding an STD or lying about being on birth control."

"Jeez, yeah. Baby-trapping. That's gotta be a fucking nightmare," she muttered. She looked over at something on the floor nearby and a deep frown came to her face abruptly. "Ugh."

"What?" he asked.

"Just...realizing that I have to face reality sooner or later." He realized she was looking at her purse. She sighed and got up, grabbed it, then sat back down. "It was a lot easier to forget everything after last night. I mean, the flirtation and the sexual tension and the teasing all helped enormously but...I did mean what I said, Gabe: I feel safe here. With you."

Gabe reached out and took her hand. She smiled and gave his hand a small squeeze. "I'm glad, Ellen. I want you to feel safe. I want to help you."

"That's really sweet. Also..." she giggled suddenly. "So I have a small confession. You must've noticed I was acting a little weird this morning, right?"

"Yeah, I didn't want to say anything," he replied.

"I appreciate it. I was a little freaked out because...I had a wet dream last night."

"Wet dream as in–"

"Yep. As in I had a little orgasm and made a small mess in my shorts. And...it was about you. When I woke up, for a few seconds, I thought it was real. I thought I'd come onto you in the middle of the night and we'd fucked like rabbits, and I woke up wanting more *so* bad. Then I realized it had been a dream and I was sitting there with fucking...orgasm in my shorts. Then I masturbated in your shower. And after that, I decided, 'you know what? I'm going to fuck him today. I am absolutely going to seduce and fuck him today'."

"I'm so glad you decided that," he said.

"Honestly, I thought you'd be more timid."

"So did I. I...am trying to be more confident."

"Well," she said, giving his hand another squeeze, "it's working. Just so you know." She lost her smile when she looked at her purse again. "But, unfortunately, I need to figure out precisely what I'm going to do. Because the disaster that my life has become is still ongoing. I have decisions to make, things to do, situations to deal with. One of which I am *not* looking forward to."

"What?" he asked.

"I have to go back to my apartment and get my shit. Not, like, furniture or anything, I don't care about the furniture, but there are some things I need. And I hate to admit it, but I'm scared to go alone. And...I realized it'd be a huge imposition to ask you to come with me, but–"

"I'll go with you," Gabe said.

She looked at him for a long moment, her eyes vulnerable again. "Are you sure? You really don't have to."

"I'm sure."

Her relief was obvious. "Thank you. I really appreciate it. And if worse seriously comes to worse I have mace and I know some self defense moves."

"Really?"

"Oh yeah. My first boyfriend got...handsy with me when I didn't want him to and it escalated and I broke a finger. I kind of panicked, grabbed his finger and snapped it. After that experience I decided I wanted to learn to defend myself a little better," she replied.

"Wow. It's hard to imagine anyone wanting to get violent with you."

"Because I'm so tall?" she asked.

"That's one of the reasons."

Behind him, the oven beeped. He got up and slid the tray in, then set the timer. Turning back around, Gabe saw that Ellen was staring unhappily at her phone. She hadn't activated the screen yet, the rectangle of technology sitting dark and dead in her long-fingered hand.

Suddenly, she seemed to come to a decision. "Fuck this," she said, putting the phone back in her purse, "I can deal with it later. I'm not ready to put up with this stupid bullshit yet."

Gabe sat back down beside her. "Whenever you're ready, I'll help how I can."

"You're a little too nice for your own good, I think," she said.

"Why do you think that?"

"Just...I don't know. A feeling."

"You're probably right, after what happened with my last girlfriend."

"What *did* happen?"

He laughed softly and shook his head. "We'd been dating for six months, and she'd always been a little, uh...off-kilter. Prone to emotional outbursts, she liked to fight, and drink. She never had her shit together..."

"God, why were you dating her?"

"I mean, I was desperately lonely. And she had amazing lips...and tits."

Ellen laughed. "I guess that's fair...although it's hard to imagine you being desperately lonely."

"I...are you serious?"

"Yeah."

"...why? I figured that'd be an incredibly easy thing to imagine."

"No, you seemed a little shy but I..." She paused. "I guess I always imagined you were doing well on the girlfriend front. Was I wrong?"

"Uh, yes. Very. I've had three girlfriends in my entire life. I've spent long, long periods of time alone. The fact that you're attracted to me is weird. Appreciated, but weird."

She looked at him for a long moment, then shook her head. "To be continued. Tell me about the stabbing."

"All right. Well, she'd been getting worse over the past few weeks before our relationship came to an end. She was getting paranoid, over everything. She thought I'd taken some money out of her purse. She thought I'd flattened one of her tires. She thought I was trying to get her fired at work. Every fucking time I had to fight tooth and nail to prove myself. She'd misplaced the money, she'd run over a nail, she was just generally shitty at her job.

"And then, finally, one night, the *last* night, as a matter of fact, she shows up at my apartment. Drunk, I thought. But it quickly became obvious that she was fucked up on something more serious than booze. I still don't know what it was, but she was angry. My roommate's girlfriend had just been leaving when my girlfriend got there and she just assumed I was cheating on her. She lost her fucking mind, came at me with a switchblade."

"Jesus, that must've been terrifying."

"Yeah, it was. But she was a lot smaller than me and uncoordinated. I managed to get the knife away from her and got her onto the couch. While I was debating about what the fuck to do, she passed out. My roommate wanted to just throw her out but I wasn't going to do that. He finally just gave up and went over to his girlfriend's apartment and I finally just went to bed and locked the door. The next morning I woke up before she did.

"She finally got up after like fourteen hours of sleeping and had very little idea of what had happened. She remembered we had a fight, but not what it was about. I didn't really care though. I told her what happened, she didn't believe me, I told her 'I don't care what you believe, we're broken up. I'm breaking up with you. Now. Get out, don't come back.' And...we fought some more but finally she left."

"I'm sorry, that sounds really awful."

"It was."

They fell silent again, then he sighed as his stomach growled.

"How can I be this hungry? We just ate like two hours ago," he muttered.

"Good sex burns a lot of calories," she replied with that sexy smile that came so easily to her. "And given that was the best sex of your life…"

"Fair point," he said. "You don't question that?"

"No. It was pretty obvious how absolutely mind-blowing it was for you."

"And for you?" he asked.

"Mmm...would you actually believe me if I told you it was the best sex I've ever had?" she replied.

"Probably not," he admitted.

She laughed. "Well, it's true. You...are good. But

it's a combination of things. I mean, I've been thinking about you...fantasizing about you, for years. And you were playing me like an instrument. With the fingers and the tongue and just...I'm very excited to see what round two looks like. My pussy really wants to be eaten."

"And I really want to eat your pussy," he replied. He looked at her for a long moment, considering what she'd just said.

Then the timer began to go off. He sighed and got up, heading for the kitchen again.

"What?" she asked.

"Just...I don't know. Nothing."

"No, come on, what? You've obviously got something on the mind."

"What I have to say is very...not confident. And confident seems to be working on you."

She laughed. "It's not 'working on me', Gabe. You aren't convincing me to sleep with you, you know."

"I...yeah," he replied, still unsure of how to say it.

He took the opportunity to transfer all the fish fillets and popcorn shrimp to one big plate.

"Uh, what condiment do you want?"

"That tartar sauce we got," she replied.

He poured some of that on one side of the plate, and then some ketchup for himself on the other, then brought it and a few cans of soda over.

"Thank you," she said.

"You're welcome."

Before eating, she turned fully to face him, her expression serious. "Gabe...I don't know right now where this...where we, are going, but I do want to say that regardless, I want something to remain true between us."

"What's that?" he asked.

"We don't bullshit each other. That was something I always loved about you, about our talks. If you don't want to talk about something, I can respect that, but I'd like for our answers to remain honest. If you have something to say...I want to hear it."

Gabe looked at her, into her eyes, and saw what he'd always seen there: a person he could trust. Or, at the very least, a person he did trust. And she was right, they'd always been honest with each other in the past.

"All right," he said. "The idea that you are attracted enough to me to have fantasized about me and had actual sex with me is basically science fiction to me. I've never felt attractive in my life and you are so far out of my league it's absurd. So you'll understand if I'm having some trouble adjusting to this idea."

"That's...okay, I guess I can understand that. I'm just having some trouble of my own adjusting to this. You seemed to have, I guess, a more quiet confidence? I don't know. Maybe I was just projecting onto you because I liked you so much. But...that's gotta feel good, right?"

"Oh yes. Without question that feels *great*. Some part of me is taking what you're telling me at face value, and that part is happy. Very happy. But the rest of me is just...wondering what I'm missing? If that makes sense?"

"It does." She took a moment to eat a few pieces of shrimp, then sighed softly and sat back in the loveseat. "Everything is really...up in the air right now. I guess we should probably just let things settle a bit more. Also…" She reached a placed a hand on his thigh. "We should definitely be enjoying these 'early in the relationship' chemicals."

"I'm not disagreeing but is this a relationship?" he replied.

Ellen pursed her lips once more. "…I don't know what I want right now, beyond the fact that I don't want to stop what we've started. Can we try again tomorrow?"

"Yes," he replied, and she regained her smile.

"Thank you. I appreciate it."

They ate in silence for a few moments, and already his mind was wandering. There were things he needed to do. He *had* to finish that third assignment and he fully intended to finish the fourth one because he wanted the bonus, even if it was just an extra ten. And then he really wanted to continue work on his new erotica series…

But more and more he thought only of being with her.

Of what she looked like naked.

Of how she sounded when she moaned in sexual ecstasy.

What it felt like to be inside of her…

"You're thinking about having sex with me right now, aren't you?" she murmured.

"What? Uh…yeah," he replied. "If we're being honest."

She giggled. "I'm thinking about having sex with you, too…" She chewed on her lower lip for a moment, then sighed. "We both have things to do, though. You still have work, right?"

"I do," he replied. "But…I could put it off."

"No. As someone who has been working for about twenty years straight, let me pass on some wisdom: if you have an important thing you need to get done, and you can do it, go do it. Now. Take a short break if you must, but don't let it linger. Just get it done. It's miserable sometimes, but it's the responsible thing to do. I can't tell you how much more productive I've seen people get once they actually implement this."

He sighed heavily. "Yeah, you're right. That's kind of what I've been doing. Although," he reached out and ran a hand across one smooth, thick thigh, "I've never had such an alluring distraction before."

"Never?" she replied. "I'm sure you've had horny girls around before when you were trying to work."

"I haven't actually, because I've been single for as long as I've been taking writing seriously. But even if that wasn't true, I've never in my life dated a woman like you before."

"And what kind of woman is that exactly?"

"An apex predator."

She let out a surprised laugh. "A *what?* Why do you say that?"

"If you look at human socializing and dating as a natural environment, then you are an apex predator. You are the woman most other women fear, with your raw power...are you blushing?"

"No! Shut up! I'm not blushing," she replied.

"You are!"

"Oh whatever," she growled, unable to keep a smile from her reddening face. She made a visible effort to compose herself and cleared her throat, looking at him again with her intense gaze. "So what does that make you then?"

"Lucky, lucky prey," he replied.

"Hmm. I don't think so."

"No?"

"No. I think you're another apex predator."

"Well...I suppose I don't want to disillusion you from that idea."

"Hey, you're the one who said he's trying to be more confident."

"I think there's a canyon of difference between being a bit more confident and turning into an asshole who thinks so very highly of himself."

"You're right, there is. But somewhere in that canyon there is a Gabe who is rather confident in himself and how he acts and presents himself, but who is still as patient, kind, and caring as you are now," she replied. "And besides, if railing me isn't going to get you more confidence, what will?"

"Okay, that's a good point. I will consider that...as I work on the part of my job I don't like."

"It's very nice that you have parts of your job that you *do* like," Ellen murmured. She shook her head and grabbed her laptop. "I should probably at least pretend to care about my job while I'm still on the clock, see if they sent anything to me."

"Good luck," he replied, finishing off his meal.

He rinsed his plate, set it in the sink, and then settled down at his own laptop.

CHAPTER TWELVE

The day vanished and night fell before Gabe even realized it.

He was deeply grateful that he'd gone ahead and gotten his work out of the way when it occurred to him just how fast the time was slipping by. He'd gotten both of his jobs done, and made some progress on the next one that was due tomorrow night, and then got a little bit written for his next erotica story.

But the siren call of spending time with Ellen became too much.

He kept looking at her, and most of the time he caught her looking at him. She would smile and sometimes blush a little and go back to what she was doing on her laptop. He sat at his desk and she sat on the loveseat.

She was right.

He felt high on early relationship chemicals.

Buzzed on her.

But worries kept creeping back into his mind. *Was* this a relationship? Were they together now or was this just…

What? A fling? Rebound?

Casual hookup?

It didn't feel like any of that. It felt serious. It felt intense.

It felt very intimate.

Especially when he gave up on work and came over to sit beside her.

"Hey, you finished writing sexy things?" she asked.

"Evidently. My focus is spent…" She put her long, glorious legs in his lap. She was still wearing only a tanktop and panties. "...no thanks to you."

She laughed. "Am I truly so distracting?"

"Ellen...yes. Good lord, you are distracting," he muttered as he ran his hands up and down one of her thick, smooth thighs.

He then moved his hand up until he reached her panties. He pulled them aside, stealing a look at her bare pussy.

"*Gabe,*" she whispered, blushing intensely.

"What?" he replied.

"...nothing."

He was being careful to check her body language. He'd read more than one frustrated post about guys who got too comfortable and too handsy, assuming too much after the first sexual encounter. But Ellen was more inviting than ever.

"So, what do we do now?" he asked.

"Eat dinner and watch something?" she replied, a very light teasing smile on her face now.

"Nothing else you want to do?" he replied.

"Well...there's other things I want to do. But I think they can wait."

"Can they now?"

"Yes. Things that we really enjoy doing are most enjoyable when they're...savored. Waiting helps with that."

"All right. How do you feel about breakfast for dinner then? I want to make some bacon and eggs and those hashbrowns we got," he said, patting her legs.

She pulled them back. "That sounds great."

He leaned in and kissed her. She slipped her hand over the back of his neck, deepening and lengthening the kiss. After flicking her tongue quickly into his mouth, she released him. He lingered for a moment, looking at her stunningly beautiful face, then got to his feet.

"You're a good kisser," he said as he moved over to the kitchen.

"So are you," she replied. "You want any help?"

"I don't mind doing it," he said as he got everything out and turned on the stovetop.

"All right then...mmm, been a really, really long time since I've had a meal made for me and not the other way around." She paused. He glanced back at her. She had a sour look on her face. "Been a long time for a lot of things," she muttered.

"Want to talk about it?" he replied.

She hesitated for a second. "Yeah, I do. You sure you want to listen to me bitch?"

"I'd like to listen to you talk about yourself and your life and your grievances," he replied.

"Why?" she asked. He glanced back at her again. She looked and sounded genuinely curious.

He went back to laying the bacon in the pan. "It's kind? I like you? I want you to feel better? It's what humans do?"

"It is *not* what humans do, in my experience."

"All right, I'll give you that. It seems like we've both ended up with the shit end of the stick when it comes to interacting with other humans, but it's what we're *supposed* to do for the people we care about. And however you feel about what's happening between us, I would like to think that you and I are friends."

"We are," she replied. "In fact, you are my best friend in the whole world right now."

"Seriously?"

"Yes. Seriously. I really did spend a long time hunting for someone I could think of to go to, to help me out. Somewhere I could feel safe, or at least somewhere I could be without getting blasted for fucking up another relationship."

"You didn't fuck up the–"

"I know. But people...enjoy placing the blame on who like least."

"People like you *least?*"

She sighed and stood up suddenly, then walked over to the kitchen and leaned against the counter.

"I'm not crowding you, am I?" she asked. "I just want to be near you…"

He grinned and kissed her. "I want to be near you too."

She let out a little laugh. "Good. Um. So, yes, I trust you the most, Gabe. Anyway...I guess, I don't know, I'm sort of getting mad at myself. How did I miss it? Only then I realize I *didn't* miss it. I was paranoid, and for a good reason! And I should've known better, it's happened before…"

"Fucking hell, Ellen. I'm so sorry," he said, and hugged her suddenly. She wrapped her arms around him, held him against her. "I can't imagine anyone wanting to cheat on you, but there are a lot of stupid fucks out there."

"There are," she agreed, releasing him as he stepped back and moved over to the stove. He flipped the bacon over. "I guess what's really bothering me is all the shit I took. What you said to me in the bathroom, about how up fucked up it was that he was saying these things to me-you were right. It *is* fucked up, and I don't know why I was taking it. I guess I felt–"

He looked at her again. She had crossed her arms, hugging herself almost, looking down at the floor.

"You can tell me," Gabe said.

She sighed softly. "I hate talking about this but...I haven't had anyone I could really *talk* to. If I'm being brutally fucking honest here: I felt guilty about getting fat."

"You aren't fat, Ellen."

"Fine. Putting on weight. I gained like thirty pounds while working from home. Probably closer to forty now. And, fuck, I don't know...I worked so damned hard watching my goddamned figure. I just...wanted a break. I wanted to fucking enjoy myself for once. But that's an easy mindset to slip right into and never quite get out of. I don't know. I'm just embarrassed. About all of it. There's a part of me that feels like I brought it on myself, but there's another part of me that knows that's bullshit."

"I think that's true for a lot of us," Gabe murmured. She looked over at him now, slowly uncrossing her arms. "Too many of us have that fucking voice in our heads, telling us all the awful, sadistic things we fear about ourselves. Our insecurities. And we just have to learn how to not listen to that bullshit."

She nodded. "Yeah, that's right."

Ellen fell silent for a long time, looking across the room at, he assumed, one of the rectangular windows high in the wall.

Their only view into the outside world, and all it showed was a concrete pit filled with trash and brittle leaves and a sliver of gray sky.

Gabe continued tending to the bacon and now the hashbrowns he had going, letting her think. She looked like she wanted to ponder but she didn't really want to be alone again either. He almost had to break the silence when it occurred to him to ask how she liked her bacon, but then he remembered a tidbit of one of their old conversations, on them agreeing that they both liked really crispy bacon. So he went with that and only pulled the bacon out when it was properly crisp.

Once he had it on a plate, he cracked a few eggs into the sizzling bacon grease and set about preparing them as well.

He realized quickly that they'd never discussed eggs.

"Hey, I remember that you like your bacon crispy, but what about your eggs?" he asked.

She lost her faraway look and focused on him. "You remembered that?"

"Yeah."

"Shit, that was years ago...um, over easy."

"Awesome, same," he said.

"How the hell do you remember this stuff? Seriously, I'm an accountant, I have to remember things as my job, and I'm pretty sure I would've forgotten that."

"I'm not sure," he replied. "I guess it's just that our conversations were a real highlight of my day." He paused. "If we're maintaining the truth: highlight of my life."

"Come on, I can't be *that* interesting to talk to."

"You were, and are, to me. Plus, I mean, a part of it was definitely 'holy shit a perfect ten older woman is having a real conversation with me'. And also we just clicked really well."

"Gabe, I have *never* been a perfect ten."

"You're a perfect ten *right now,*" he replied.

"No I'm not, and I'm not that much older than you."

"I know. I mean you're, what, thirty four now? To my twenty six. But years lived isn't so important as life lived. You're more mature than most fifty somethings I've had to work alongside. You just seem a lot more mature than me."

"Not *that* much more mature," she said. "Although I guess you have a point. I didn't really have a choice, though...you don't have to flatter me, you know. You've already successfully gotten into my pants, and you will again tonight and tomorrow and certainly the day after that."

"I'm not flattering you or trying to fuck you." He paused as he flipped the eggs over and tended to the hashbrowns, considering it. "I know it sounds hyperbolic, but I'm telling the truth. You're a ten to me. You're the woman who has become a yardstick against which I subconsciously judge other women, though I try not to. Mostly because it's not a healthy habit to judge people like that, but also because it's such an unfair contest...you're blushing again."

"I'm not!" she replied, unable to keep from smiling. "It's just...hot in here."

"Right."

She sighed. "Can we open up the windows?"

"No. Believe me, I really want to, but they warned me not to during rain. They'll leak, badly."

"Ugh, that sucks," she muttered, "I love being inside and listening to the rain and feeling the cool breeze come in."

"Same," he agreed. "Maybe someday, when I've put together enough money not to live in a shitty basement apartment."

"I still think it's pretty nice for a basement apartment."

"I *did* get lucky in that regard. The carpet's basically intact and not outright awful quality, the walls are painted pretty much evenly, all the fixtures aren't in terrible condition. Though there's that big dent in the washing machine. Pretty sure someone kicked it at some point in the past. But it all works, it all looks decent. I just wish I had a bigger place because while it's cozy for one, I imagine it's a bit cramped for you, and not what you're used to."

"Don't feel bad on my behalf," she replied, heading over to the fridge. "Right now, I like cozy. And right now, I'm sick to death of what I'm used to. That's what's been bothering me...you want some milk?"

"Yes, thank you."

While he got the food ready, she poured two glasses of milk.

"What has?" he asked.

"Everything I'm 'used to'. My relationships specifically. I don't know, I'm just looking back over them and wondering what the hell happened? I think of myself as...tough, like I won't take any shit from who I'm with. But don't most women think that? I can be ruthless when the situation calls for it, but how the fuck do I keep getting into these relationships where it all goes to hell and at the end I look back over the past few months, or even the last year of the relationship and realize that I *did* take shit? A lot of shit. How am I blind to it when it's happening?"

Gabe was silent as they finished getting the meal together. They moved back over to the loveseat and sat down.

"I think..." he hesitated, unsure if he could, or should, say it.

"Tell me," Ellen said. "I want to know what you think."

"Well...I think that relationships have a lot of potential for cognitive dissonance. Where you believe two opposing things at the same time. You believe you don't take any shit, but you also think 'maybe he has a point' when they give you shit after a while. Because despite how much the culture has shifted to 'ew that's toxic cut them out of your life *right now*', most people aren't willing to blow up a whole relationship over one, individual comment. Even when it's repeated over the course of months or years. And your brain just doesn't like thinking about the fact that maybe you are, in fact, taking shit, so it just sort of pushes the thought away."

"Hmm." She ate in silence for a few moments. "That makes sense. I just feel stupid. Like, how do I fall for the same shit so many other women do? I can't tell you how many wild ass stories I've read online and thought to myself 'I'd never put up with that', only apparently I would. I mean, not all of it, but it's just so...insidious. It's stupid but almost feels like one of those dramatic revelation sequences in movies, where we see a series of seemingly innocuous flashbacks that, in the new context, suddenly reveal the twist. The twist being: he was an asshole the whole time. I'm looking back and realizing I was putting up with stupid shit for months."

"We are a lonely species," Gabe murmured.

"What?" she replied, sounding almost a little startled.

"Humans. We're lonely by design. So we built a civilization formed around being with other people. And then somewhere along the way assholes realized they could monetize loneliness, so they engineered society to not just make us crave relationships and companionship even more, but penalized us for wanting to be single, or just for being single or alone.

And our specific corner of society knew that it needed an infinite supply of desperate, uneducated workers, so they twisted the social engineering a bit further and emphasized coupling.

"I know it sounds like a ridiculous conspiracy theory but they're barely even hiding it anymore. The politicians and the corporate shitbags all conspiring together." He sighed. "Now *I'm* ranting. But my point is a side effect of this is that we have been conditioned, pretty much from birth, to seek love and marriage and living together, and most of us don't even realize it."

"Well...I can't argue with that. Having a somewhat deeper view into modern economics, yeah, I can't deny that rich people are trying to fuck the rest of us over for their own benefit. To a fucking ridiculous degree now." She sighed heavily. "But that's what's on my mind. I thought I was a bad bitch, but really I'm just like everyone else."

"You *are* a bad bitch. You put your trust in someone and they abused it. That isn't *your* fault. And the moment it became obvious that he was fucking you over, you walked out."

"...I guess so," she murmured. Then she looked at him and laughed softly. "This has to be weird for you. You have this...obviously intensely overstated view of me, and it must be strange to find out I'm actually pathetic and riddled with insecurity."

"You aren't pathetic, Ellen. And this is...it's a little surprising. I mean, as I've said, it's *extremely* surprising that someone cheated on you, but it's not that weird that you have insecurities and vulnerabilities. It's a little surprising that you're as comfortable letting down your guard around me as you are. Not that I think you're wrong to, it's just...I didn't know you felt, uh, that way about me."

She laughed. "I guess I didn't either until I really thought about it. I actually wanted to keep talking, you know? I would have kept our friendship going, except that some part of me realized it wasn't...safe."

"Safe?"

"Maybe not the perfect word, but safe in the sense that...I would have been sorely tempted to jump you. And I don't cheat. I haven't and I won't. Honestly, it wasn't really a problem I'd run into all that often. I can get past it most of the time. Not with you, though."

"So wait, are you saying that…" He put his hand on her thigh again. "You were unable to resist me?"

She giggled a little awkward, blushing again, then cleared her throat. "...yes, that's what I'm saying," she murmured.

"That's amazing."

"I'm glad you're so pleased." She cleared her throat once more and shifted on the loveseat. "Let's watch something."

"All right. You want to find another fantasy thing?"

"No, let's watch something you want to. You know, take turns. There must be some horror thing you've been meaning to watch."

"All right then. Let me see what I can find."

CHAPTER THIRTEEN

"Hey, so...I won't be mad if you decide you don't want to do this," Ellen said as she laid on her back.

"Oh. All right, good to know," he replied, tossing his shirt aside and undoing his button and zipper. He paused. "Wait, is that a way of saying you aren't into it?"

"Oh no! God no. I'm *very* into it. I just-you know, sex is a thing. A big complicated thing. And I know people can get weird about it. And I just...I want you to feel like you can tell me no. But speaking for myself: I *really* want this."

"Good. I do, too. And I want you to feel the same way," Gabe replied, getting his pants and boxers off and kicking them aside.

"I appreciate that, and I do. Also..." She looked at him a little curiously.

"What?" he asked, suddenly paranoid.

He was actually a lot more relaxed about getting naked in front of her the second time around, but all at once his paranoia came rushing back.

"Nothing bad. Just...it just occurred to me that you never tried to take a pic of me."

"Do you want me to?" he asked.

"Do *you* want to? I don't mind. You can if you want."

"All right." He went to find his phone. "It honestly never occurred to me, but I guess I stopped thinking about it after my second girlfriend. The first was cool with it, but my second was extremely uncomfortable in front of the camera and *hated* having her picture taken. Nude pics were so utterly off the table I guess I stopped considering it."

"It seems really common nowadays," Ellen said as he came back over.

He fired up his camera and then paused. "Take your shirt off."

She smiled and he was very glad to see that she didn't hesitate as her tanktop came off. She wasn't wearing a bra or anything beneath it, and her huge, bountiful breasts came out and bounced amazingly as she tossed the shirt aside.

"Fucking Jesus," he muttered as he aimed the camera at her.

She just smiled and propped herself up on her elbows, shifting so that he breasts were a little more on display. His heart was already pumping hard but it sped up a little as he snapped the photo. He had a picture of Ellen, naked save for a pair of white panties, laying in his bed, smiling at him.

He wondered what else he could photograph her doing.

Well, that was for later, if at all. Though she did seem comfortable with it. But he wanted to enjoy his time with her here and now, in the flesh, instead of obsess over capturing evidence of it. This was going to live on his head forever.

"All right," he said as he set his phone down on the nightstand and then got onto the bed with her.

He gripped her panties and pulled them down her long legs, exposing her smooth, bare vagina. She was chewing slowly on her lower lip, watching him. Gabe took a moment to enjoy the sight of her completely naked and exposed to him, and also took the opportunity to recall everything he knew about eating pussy.

He'd done it often enough with three girlfriends, but it had been a while since the last time he'd done it, and Ellen was…

Well, possibly hard to please, given what she'd told him.

No time like the present, he thought and laid down in between her spread open legs.

He leaned in and kissed her inner thigh.

"AH! *Gabe!*" she cried, giggling.

"What? I thought women liked it when you kissed their thighs," he replied.

"I don't, I'm ticklish! And also, despite what men everywhere believe, tickling me will *not* lead to sex. It will lead to me accidentally hurting you because I absolutely lose my shit when I'm tickled," she replied.

"No tickling and no thigh kissing," he said.

"Thank you. I don't want to accidentally crush your head between my thighs."

He ran his hand along her smooth, soft skin. "There are worse ways to die."

She laughed and shook her head. "Focus, Gabe."

"Yes ma'am," he replied, which made her giggle again.

She lost her smile as he settled into place and carefully parted the lips of her pussy with his thumbs, exposing the nub of her clit. Leaning in, he exhaled slowly and felt a strong shiver ripple through her body as she groaned softly.

Good start.

He leaned in and began teasing her, very gently caressing her clit with the tip of his tongue. She let out a sharp moan and shivered again.

"Gabe…" she moaned.

"Yeah?" he replied.

"Just...mmm...keep going."

He kept going.

Gabe tried to gauge her reactions against his actions. Something he'd learned was women tended to like to be eased into sexual situations, and that most definitely included oral sex. But 'go slow' wasn't a sexual skeleton key.

They had difference tolerances for the teasing and easing in.

His second girlfriend was a very impatient lover. Much as she loved oral, she wanted him to get to the hard and heavy tonguing quickly, and if he didn't, she got pissed. And he really didn't want to have Ellen pissed at him.

After another half minute or so of gradually increasing teasing, he could sense a shift in her mood. She wanted more. So he gave her more, applying noticeably more pressure and picking up the speed a little bit while also using more of his tongue.

"Oh, *fuck,*" she moaned. "Oh, that's-ah!"

Her hips bucked a little and he couldn't help but smile at that. This was going really well. He kept going, gradually building and sometimes pulling back the speed and pressure. As he kept going, he decided to bring her to the next level and, hopefully, to climax. He slipped a finger inside of her wet, warm opening.

"Oh shit *Gabe!*" she cried as he pressed, fucking her with his finger.

Her hips bucked again and he had to fight a little to keep going. She was panting furiously now, moaning loudly, grabbing at the blanket beneath her. He kept going, using more of his tongue, pressing harder as he massaged her clit with it, and then he began using his lower lip. He worked her pussy as best he could, and then…

"Okay stop!" she gasped and he pulled back,

momentarily confused, and then he saw her begin to orgasm.

Her hips bucked wildly now and hot spray of feminine sex juices escaped her, staining the blanket as she cried out, her voice very loud. She managed to get a hand over her mouth, her whole body trembling as she came and moaned and yelled.

The orgasm seemed to go on for quite a while.

When it had passed, she went slack, her hand falling away, panting furiously, her eyes closed.

"Gabe," she whispered.

"Yeah?" he replied.

"That was the best oral I've ever had. Holy fucking God, Gabe." She took a deep breath and let it out slowly as she began fanning herself with one hand. She was slicked with a light sheen of sweat now. "Seriously, Gabe. Fuck. I just–"

She was interrupted by a hard shiver that ran through her body and turned her next word into an inarticulate noise of pleasure. Ellen seemed to take a moment to get herself under control, a broad smile coming onto her face.

"That good, huh?" he asked.

She laughed softly. "Yes. That fucking good. Oh my lord. I know some of it is that it's been *for-fucking-ever* since I've been eaten, but you are *very* good with your tongue and your lips and your fingers." She sat up, her bare breasts shifting and shaking pleasantly. A slightly guilty look came onto her face. "Can I be...a little selfish?"

"If you want to be, although I guess it really depends on what it is," he replied.

"When we have sex, can I be on top?" she asked, her expression becoming oddly shy.

"What? Yeah, definitely," he replied. "...how is

that being selfish? Unless we have two different definitions of 'on top'? You want to ride my dick, right?"

"Yes," she replied, shifting almost eagerly now to the side and motioning for him to take her place, then pausing when she saw the big dark spot on the blanket. "Fuck," she whispered, "I keep forgetting to put a damned towel down. This hasn't been a problem in ages."

"Really?" he asked as they got up and removed the blanket, then the sheets beneath it.

She sighed heavily as she saw some of it had gotten through to the mattress below. "It looks like I pissed your fucking bed," she muttered, quickly shoving the blanket and sheets into the washer and starting a new load.

She grabbed the other blanket she'd had to wash earlier out of the dryer, then went and got a towel from the bathroom and put it over the wet spot, the blanket over that. Then she patted it eagerly. He laid back down in the middle of the bed and watched intently as she climbed on to join him.

"So, um, I've never had a partner comfortable with me being on top," she said uncomfortable, almost like she was worried that if she told him this, he would suddenly adopt that stance himself.

Not that there was any risk of that happening.

"I find that very hard to believe," he replied as she got closer to him.

"Trust me."

"I do, I just...why?"

"I thought it'd be incredibly obvious." She swung a leg over him and mounted him, smiling tentatively down at him for a moment.

"It isn't," he murmured, staring up at her and

feeling like he was being straddled by some kind of sex goddess.

She looked beyond amazing.

Ellen laughed and shook her head. "My size, Gabe," she murmured, lifting herself and reaching between them. Then she paused. "Oh, I was going to blow you for a little bit. Um...can I give you a full blowjob later? I *really* badly want this."

"I accept this offer," he replied.

"Thank you."

"Also, your size is like a *reason* for you to ride me. Fuck's sake, you look *incredible.*"

She began to reply, then sighed, her cheeks flushing, then she lowered herself, taking his erection into her sweet, fantastically wet pussy.

Both of them moaned in pure ecstasy as he got inside of her.

At first she just straddled him, sitting against him with him completely sheathed within her. Then she grinned fiercely at him, leaned forward, and gripped his shoulders tightly. Her massive breasts were just about right in his face.

"Let me know if I'm being too rough," she said, and then she began to fuck him.

His hands found her huge hips and he sank in his fingertips and groaning loudly as the pleasure hit him in waves. The raw rapturous bliss of their sex pulsed through him and he could feel himself throbbing in response to her.

This was another particular fantasy he had thought of many, many times.

Being ridden by Ellen, the six and a half foot Amazonian goddess. It was somehow even better than he had ever imagined. He could feel her vaginal muscles clenching and fluttering around him as she rode him. The pleasure was hot and wet and so wonderfully wild. It was intense, not just pushing him towards an orgasm but shoving him violently.

Gabe held on grimly. No way he was coming too early with her just the second time in. He hadn't lasted all that long during the first encounter and she hadn't said anything, but that didn't necessarily mean anything.

But *damn* was she fucking so good...

He kept finding his attention drawn forcibly to her breasts, hanging down in his face, rocking back and forth as she used her powerful hips, riding him faster now. Finally, he let go of her hips and reached up, groping her massive tits.

"Lick my nipples," she moaned, leaning forward a little more.

He responded immediately, laying his hands beneath her breasts, cupping them to keep them from moving too much, (and keep them in his hands), and then raising his head and licking across one of her nipples.

She moaned and shuddered hard. He switched to other after a moment, dragging his tongue across her beautiful pink nipple over and over.

"Gabe," she whispered.

"Yeah?" he panted.

"Take a picture of me fucking you."

"I, uh, shit, all right," he replied, groping blindly for his phone on the bedside table. He finally found it and got the camera going, then angled it up at her and snapped a picture.

"How do I look?" she murmured, her eyes closed again like she was focusing intently, her hips still going into overdrive as she fucked his dick like a porn star.

"Like an Amazonian goddess," he replied, setting his phone aside.

She laughed, then moaned. "Your dick feels *so* good! Ah...come on, Gabe," she whispered, her eyes snapping open suddenly. She took his hands and put them back on her big tits. "Come for me," she said, her voice almost a growl as she gripped his shoulders again.

"Ah...no...Ellen," he moaned. "I want to last longer..."

"I don't care," she whispered, grinning fiercely now. "I want you to come inside me, Gabe. I want you to come in my pussy and fill it up. I'm gonna make you."

"Ah fuck, Ellen..." he groaned loudly as she began going even faster.

She took his cock into her perfect, slick vagina, fucking him raw with the pleasure of paradise, and he groped her hot, pillowy breasts as she bounced up and down.

The pleasure was far too much.

With a loud, inarticulate half-groan, half-growl of bliss, Gabe began coming inside of her. She let out a satisfied gasp as he began shooting his seed into her. His hands found her hips again and he held them tightly, thrusting up into her and shoving himself as deep inside of her as he could get, continuing to release his seed in hard, furious contractions.

"Yes, Gabe! That's it! Oh shit, fucking come in me!" she cried.

He kept coming for what felt like a long time and at some point he became aware of the fact that his cock was dry-kicking, nothing left to give.

"Ooh...shit...off, please," he whispered. "Carefully."

"Yeah," she murmured, cautiously raising herself up until his softening dick fell out of her. She quickly got up and headed for the bathroom. "I didn't hurt you, did I?" she asked. "Was I too rough?"

"No, not that," he replied. "That was perfect. It's my dick. I came too hard and it's, like...sensitive now? Like painful to the touch sensitive."

"Oh! Yeah, that's why I had you stop when you were eating me. My clit gets too sensitive when I orgasm from oral. Sorry, should've warned you."

He heard the toilet flush a moment later and then she rejoined him, laying on the bed beside him, all smiles and joy and hot, messy hair.

"That was so good," he muttered after a moment of laying there together.

"Yes. Yes it was," she replied dreamily. She took his hand. "Gabe...I wanted to say that this meant a lot to me. Being on top is my favorite position, but I don't ever really get to enjoy it. And I *enjoyed* the fuck out of that. If I hadn't been so greedy in wanting to make you come and I'd let you last a little bit longer, I would've come again, I think."

"That would've been nice."

She laughed. "No, because then we'd be really fucked for blankets."

"Oh yeah. Oh well. Still would've been worth it."

Ellen rolled over suddenly and rested half her body on his own. He reached over and began running his hand across her back. She sighed contentedly.

"This is really, really nice," she whispered.

"Mmm-hmm," he replied. "Do you have work tomorrow?"

"No. I am thankfully off for traditional weekends."

"Good. I have a few jobs to complete, but we

should do things tomorrow."

"Things?" she murmured, running a finger along his leg.

"I mean, yes, those things, but also other things. There's a park near here I wanted to check out, take a walk in, and maybe we could do something like bowling or mini-golfing...although I don't really have the money for that."

"I told you," she said, grinning tiredly at him, "I am your sugar mama. Trust me, Gabe, I got money right now."

He considered again telling her just how dire his own financial situation was, but kept it to himself again. He felt so good right now, he didn't want to mess it up.

"All right then," he replied, and she laughed and kissed him.

"Good. And yes, I'd love to do all these things with you." She yawned suddenly. "That...made me very sleepy. Can we sleep now?"

"Let me take a piss and then we can sleep," he replied. She got off of him and he stood up. "So are you cool on the lo-fi?"

"Yeah, actually. It was soothing, and I liked it."

"Awesome."

He started up a playlist and then took a leak, then turned out the lights and returned to bed. Getting under the blanket with Ellen, he ended up against her warm, nude body again.

"Will you spoon me?" she asked quietly.

"Gladly," he replied.

She rolled away from him and he got up against her back. He draped an arm over her, pausing to give one of her breasts a quick, gentle squeeze and making her laugh softly.

"You really can't get enough of those, can you?" she murmured.

"I really can't," he agreed.

Gabe got settled and soon found himself falling asleep to the gentle sound of rain, lo-fi, and Ellen breathing softly and regularly.

He didn't think he'd ever been happier in his life.

CHAPTER FOURTEEN

When they awoke the next morning, Ellen wanted to ride again, and he happily let her.

It was a hell of a wonderful way to be woken up, being fucked like that, and after they both orgasmed he felt very awake.

When she was finished, Ellen looked down at him with her wild pale blonde hair and a satisfied expression, her hands on his shoulders. "You are doing everything right," she murmured.

"Am I now?" he replied, running his hands up along her thighs.

"Yes."

"So are you."

Her expression changed to something more serious and she got off of him and laid down beside him, then hugged him tightly. He hugged her back, held her, feeling a sense of almost desperate need radiating off of her.

"That really means a lot to hear right now, after everything that's happened," she said quietly. "After you get so much resistance and pushback amidst so many setbacks and failures, you start feeling like you can't fucking do anything right. I've worked my ass off for *twenty fucking years* and what has it gotten me? Divorced twice. Cheated on twice." She paused. "That I *know of,* at least."

"Ellen," he said, and she focused on him, "life hit you really hard. And you didn't deserve it. And it really hurts. And that's all right. But you aren't a failure."

She stared into his eyes for a long moment, then hugged him again, holding him tight against her.

"This would be so much harder without you," she whispered.

"Having someone to listen to you and talk with you helps," he replied.

"No, that isn't what I mean. I mean without *you*. As in you, specifically. The best I could really hope for from anyone else in my circle is 'men are pigs' commiseration over margaritas. Commiseration can be cathartic, but this is a lot more meaningful." She sighed heavily. "God, I'm fucking selfish. You've got an entire writing career and a new apartment to manage and I just barge into your life, begging for attention—"

"Ellen!" he cried, pulling out of her embrace again. "You aren't being selfish! You're giving me space, you're giving me time. You aren't being unreasonable at all. Here." He patted her hip gently. "Come on, get up, we're taking a shower and getting dressed and going for a walk in the park."

She laughed as they got out of bed. "You think we can just outrun misery? Not that I'm disagreeing with your plan."

Gabe considered that for a moment as they headed into the bathroom. "Misery and depression are like meteors, I think. They're gonna hit, nothing you can do about that, but you *can* lessen the damage of the impact. Sometimes massively."

"Really?" she asked after a moment.

"Yeah. I think so, at least. I guess another analogy is: depression can be like a runaway train. You can derail it. It'll still do damage but far less damage than if it kept on going and smashed into a town. Although...it doesn't always work. Sometimes the depression train is an unstoppable juggernaut that could survive a nuke." He paused. "Sorry, not trying to bring the mood down. I'm going to brush my teeth now."

"Would it weird you out if I pissed? I have to really bad," Ellen replied.

"I don't care," he replied.

"Cool. I don't care if you do it either. Just don't shit when I'm in here."

He laughed as he put some toothpaste on his brush. "Noted, and same."

After a few moments, the two of them ended up in the shower together. Ellen took the showerhead down and aimed it at her vagina, putting one leg carefully up on the side of the tub.

"God, you fucking come so much," she muttered.

"It's your fault, you fucking slut," he replied, then froze up. "Oh fuck, I'm sorry. I didn't mean that. It's just my last girlfriend *really* got me into the habit of dirty talk and–"

"Gabe, it's all right," she said, replacing the showerhead. She had a somewhat deviant smile now. "I don't mind if you say things like that to me."

"...seriously?"

"Yeah. I...like it. Just not when we're in public. When we're here, alone...especially while having sex, you know...I like it."

"Huh."

"What?"

"It's just, you *never* struck me as having any submissive habits," he replied.

She laughed. "I know. Everyone assumes that, and in truth, I can go both ways. In most aspects of my life I have to be dominant, and it kind of helps that I'm so tall and people just sort of expect me to be a raging bitch, because otherwise no one would fucking take me seriously."

"Really?" he asked.

"Yes. It's a huge problem. It's one of those 'fish swimming through water' problems. Here, will you get my back?"

"Yes I will," he replied happily, lathering up some soap and running his hands across her back and over her shoulders and down her sides. "I know some of what you're saying. It's one of those things that's so ridiculously common that it's baked into real life and no one notices it unless they're looking for it?"

"Basically, yes. There's been several studies done, all with pretty much the same results, where they take two people working in usually an office building or something similar–a man and a woman–and swap their email accounts. To be done right it has to be two people working on the same project. And obviously no one else knows that they're swapped. What happens every time is that the men, who are respected and 'get a lot done', suddenly find themselves being questioned and second-guessed over *everything,* their coworkers being rude or disrespectful to them. All because they think they're talking to a woman. Okay, that's good."

She turned back around and let the water run down her back.

He considered her words for a moment. "I believe it," he replied. "I had a coworker I became friends with when I worked at the gas station and she showed me her Ember account, the messages she got. There were a lot of them, but *so* many of them were *immediately* hostile or rude or outright threatening. It was fucking insane what guys are cool with saying."

"Here, your turn," Ellen said, and they carefully maneuvered to switch places. She looked at him contemplatively as he began washing.

"What?" he asked.

"Just...it's a trite thought, but I find myself thinking you aren't like other guys. I mean, not *all* of them, obviously, but the times I've brought that up, or something similar to it, it's exceedingly rare for the man I'm talking with to agree with me. They have to argue or they have to explain why that might be or find *some* solution that shifts the blame off other men being assholes. You just...agree. But not because you're intimidated by me."

"I'm intimidated by you," he replied.

She smiled. "I know. But you aren't letting it stop you. You sure didn't let it stop you yesterday. But I always felt like you agreed or disagreed with me authentically. I guess a better way to put it is: you may be intimidated, but you aren't scared."

"Mostly true."

"Mostly?"

"I'm scared of fucking up...whatever this is," he replied.

"Hmm." She frowned a little. "We should probably talk about that."

"I would like to."

"All right. How about we talk about it over breakfast? I saw a gas station down the street. We could see if they have anything decent," she replied.

"Sounds good."

She smiled suddenly. "Independent of anything else: would you like that blowjob now?" She looked down and raised her eyebrows a little. "Wow, you got hard, like, *immediately.*"

"I was already most of the way there from being in the presence of," he reached up and cupped her bare, wet breasts, "these."

She laughed. "You really love them, huh?"

"I love *all* of your body," he replied. "How fucking big are they?"

"Double e-cup. And a pain in my lower back. I would be *really* appreciative of another backrub tonight."

"I can and will deliver one happily," he replied.

She laughed. "Because you know I'll spread my legs for you after you do it?"

"Well...that's not the *only* reason. I also do like you and to do nice things for you."

"I know. I like you, too. Also, you're just a really nice person." She leaned in and kissed him. "And also thank you for letting me use your toothbrush. I should probably buy my own."

"If you want, I don't mind sharing if it's you," he replied.

She snorted and then got out of the shower. He finished washing up while she dried off.

. . .

"What are you smiling at?" Ellen murmured as she pulled out of the parking lot.

"Just, uh...it's a thing I like, seeing my girlf...well, seeing a woman I am intimate with wearing my clothes," he replied.

Ellen laughed softly. "I don't think that's going to be a common occurrence, I'm afraid. Though I do like wearing it."

It was colder out today, cold enough for a hoodie. Gabe had two, one of which was two sizes too large for him, and just big enough for Ellen to look very good in.

She sighed and lost her smile quickly, though. "So, we should talk about it. What this is. Where it's going. Um...I'm feeling really, I guess, vulnerable right now? I get the feeling that both of us are a little frightened of being the first one to talk about it openly and directly, because what we say might be the opposite of what the other person wants, and...that is very uncomfortable. But I am asking you if you would be the first one to say what you want."

Gabe took a deep breath and blew it out as a harsh exhale. "All right," he said, and steeled himself.

Because this could all go wrong.

Their time together so far had been not just fun, but amazing. It was everything he had been dreaming of and fantasizing about for years. If anything, it was better than that.

But what if she was about to tell him that it couldn't last?

That it wasn't going to work?

There were a lot of things she could say that could ruin not just his day, but probably his next year. Because despite what people said about how it was better to have loved and lost than not loved at all...

Well...

Sometimes it might be far more torturous to have been given a taste of Heaven, only to be told shortly into your stay that there's been a mistake, and it's time for you to leave.

But Gabe had decided to be more confident, braver in this new life he was trying to make for himself.

And so he was.

"I want to date you, Ellen. I want to date you in a serious capacity. I want the past two days to continue on like this into the future, because you are the most amazing woman I have ever met."

Despite how vulnerable and worried she was

feeling, Ellen smiled broadly as he said that. She pulled into the parking lot of a rundown gas station and parked at the end of a row of cars. She killed the engine and then looked at him.

"I want to talk more in depth about this with just you and I, but also not necessarily in the parking lot of a gas station. So, just so that I don't leave you hanging, dying from anticipation: I want to date and live with you, too. But there are things we need to discuss."

Now he was smiling broadly, his chest fluttering and stomach flipping in excited.

Ellen wanted to be with him.

That didn't seem real.

"Gabe...are you all right?" she murmured with a little laugh.

"Uh...what?" he managed.

She laughed louder. "I'm glad you're so happy, Gabe. Let's get breakfast."

"...what?"

"Gabe!" She leaned in and kissed him quickly on the mouth, then took his chin gently between her thumb and finger and turned his head slightly. "Focus, dear."

"Uh...yeah. Yes. Breakfast. Focus." He nodded, blinked a few times.

"Oh my God," she whispered, unable to keep from smiling, then she giggled. "You're making me into a giddy high school girl again," she muttered, and then got out of the car.

"Is that so bad?" he replied, getting out as well.

The cold, wet air helped ground him back to reality a little.

"It's...unbecoming of a woman of my...stature," she replied, though he couldn't tell if she was being serious or not.

"Unbecoming? Really? Are you a proper lady from the Victorian Era? Would you like a hand fan and a fainting couch?"

"Oh shut up...I guess there are worse things than being reduced to a giggling teenager swooning over a boy I like."

"Far worse things," he agreed.

CHAPTER FIFTEEN

They headed inside and poked around for a while.

Ellen found herself a cheap toothbrush, some deodorant, and a brush. They both got donuts and milk, then headed back to the car. Once they were in, Ellen began backing out of the lot.

"Where's this park?" she asked.

"Follow this street for about four blocks and turn left. You should be able to see it from this street," he replied.

"Perfect. All right, so...us. As I said, I also want to keep this going. I'm in turmoil right now, but at the same time, I'm...not? Maybe it sounds crazy, but I think I knew this was coming."

"Us?" he asked.

"No. That was more hope on my part. I knew my relationship was dying. Or already dead even. But I didn't know it on the surface level?"

"You knew it subconsciously."

"Yes. I think I've been slowly adjusting to the fact that my relationship wasn't going to work out without my realizing it over the past several months. Maybe longer. So many little things I'm realizing now. It still hurts. A lot. And it's going to. But it isn't the same as last time. And part of what's making me do this is that everything that's happened since I've come to you, all we've done, it just feels...*right*. It feels like this is where I am supposed to be. And it hasn't ever completely felt like this before."

"What do you think that means?" he asked.

She was silent for a few moments. "Turn here?" she asked as they approached one of the stoplights.

"Yeah, here."

She turned when the light changed and he pointed. "There, there's the park."

"Cool."

She remained silent, staring out the windows at the gray city, until she pulled into the parking lot and parked in one of the spaces. They shared the lot with just two other cars and the place looked pretty much deserted.

It wasn't a particularly large park. Just a spot among a collection of trees with a track running through it, a creek near the back, an old brick bathroom, and some weathered playground equipment. In the gray light of day, it looked a bit depressing.

"Pass me my donut," she said, grabbing her bottle of milk and opening it up.

He gave her the donut and took his own. Careful of crumbs, he started to eat.

"I've compromised a lot in my life," Ellen said finally, after eating half her donut. "A *lot.* The more I look back over everything, the more I realize that I've put up with so much shit and compromised on so many things. And I don't want to do that anymore." She paused, then sighed softly. "That's not entirely true. I know that relationships take compromise, and I'm willing to do that. But I don't want unreasonable compromises."

"I think that's fair," Gabe replied.

"I figured you would. You've always been very reasonable, Gabe. Which is why I think this is going to work out in the long term...come on, let's start walking. I want to be outside and moving," she said.

He nodded and they got out. After throwing away their trash, they started walking together along the trail that ran around the outer part of the park, their pace slow.

"It sounds kind of obvious, but I've had to learn the hard way that often, you should state obvious things, because they might not be so obvious to everyone, or you and I may have different ideas on a given subject, but...this policy that we have of telling each other the truth. I want it to continue. I want it to be our policy going forward, if we're going to be dating seriously."

"I do, too. What does that look like to you?" he replied.

"It looks like...well, the obvious stuff. Don't lie, don't hide things from me, don't do things that you think you might have to hide. If you do something bad, own it. And this cuts both ways. Everything I'm asking of you, I'm committing to myself. If I ask you to do it, I will do it. But it also looks like...hmm. Telling each other stuff when we might not think it's worth it."

"Ah. You're talking about the little things. I should tell you if you're bugging me, you should tell me if I'm doing something seemingly inconsequential that's pissing you off or irritating you. This is how huge fights happen," Gabe said.

"Exactly. We're both going to be stressed from real life as it is, and then if we're getting irritated at home by each other, but we don't want to say anything because we don't want to seem petty or we're trying to keep the peace, that builds up until finally you lose your shit and throw your dinner against the wall because I'm chewing too loud."

"That...sounds very specific," he said.

She laughed softly and shook her head. "Yeah, not something I want to relive. So yes, I want to be open and honest with each other, but also, I want it to be okay *not* to talk about something, too. We don't have to tell each other everything. I'm a believer in couples maintaining their lives separate from each other in addition to building a life together. I don't want to be couple who needs to do fucking *everything* together, you know?"

"Yeah, I get that. We're allowed some measure of privacy, even from each other," he replied.

"Yes. God. Why are you so reasonable?" she muttered. "I'm-to be clear, I'm not complaining. Just...it's really weird. In a pleasantly surprising kind of way."

He shrugged. "I don't know. I guess it's just how I am?"

"Which is very good for both of us...so, anything you want to say?"

"Uh, yeah," he replied, pausing as they reached the rear of the park. He looked down the short hill there that let onto the forest and the creek. "Want to go down there?"

"Sure."

They moved down the incline, careful not to slip in the wet, dead leaves, and came to stand beside the creek. They both stared into the chilled water as it trickled by. A few tiny fish were swimming along between the rocks, prospecting for food.

Gabe dropped into a crouch, staring into the water. "So. I have no money."

"Like...at all?" she asked.

"Yes. I actually have negative money right now. I'm, like, five hundred dollars in the hole at my bank. When I was telling you about how desperate I suddenly got and began taking my writing seriously, I didn't really emphasis just *how* desperate I was. I was desperate to get my writing going, to be sure, but mostly I just wanted my own place."

He paused and reconsidered that. "Well, I guess the emphasis wasn't on me living there and no one else, because I am *ecstatic* about you living with me, but more just a place that I had more control over. And didn't fucking reek. Or was insanely filthy. Anyway. I spent more money than I had getting that apartment. So...yeah. I don't think I'm *terrible* with money, but I do have some debt beyond that." He paused. "Okay, maybe I am kind of bad with money, but I'm getting better."

"I know it's a sensitive subject, but...how much debt?"

"Lemme think. I still owe like three grand on my car," he said, considering it unhappily, "and I maxed out my only credit card at like two fucking grand. And I've also got medical debt from the time my appendix nearly burst. I needed emergency surgery. We had insurance but not good insurance. I was twenty, so I was still technically covered by my parent's insurance. But it's like eight or nine thousand dollars I still owe or something."

"All right, that's not too terrible," Ellen said. "I can probably help with some of it. I'm almost positive I can help with the medical debt. So much of medical bills is basically just them bullshitting the ever-loving fuck out of you and hoping you won't call them on it. If you do, they make some of it disappear immediately.

"And, well, to be honest, I'm not fantastic with money either. I used to be a lot better, but at a certain point I just kept getting pissed off because I was so fucking sick of denying myself things. So I started spending more, and that more became even more, and that became credit card debt. I just set it to pay the minimum like six months ago and just...stopped thinking about it?"

She sighed and shook her head. "I know, it's fucking stupid, and I should know better given my job, but I had so much other shit going on and everything's gotten so fucking expensive...I *have* money, though. Honestly, I could pay it all off right now, and I was actually going to next month, but suddenly I find myself in need of a surplus of money given my...life change."

"So, how do you feel about it?" he asked. "I know money is the number one reason couples break up. I'm not great at penny pinching, like at all. But I'm trying to get better. I mean, I've *had* to. But then you showed up and decided to be my sugar mama."

She chuckled. "Yes. And I wasn't being coy. I...kind of like that arrangement." She crouched down beside him, her leg touching his. "So, money. I know it's a difficult subject that has been...intensely gendered. I know you've been having some difficulty with my paying for things, but I appreciate that you aren't making a huge deal out of it."

"Well, it's not like I have much choice. And it's not like I don't appreciate you buying things for me. It's nice. Just..."

"Uncomfortable."

"Yeah."

"Because it makes you feel bad that you aren't the one paying."

"Yes."

"I appreciate that. For now, let's just say...that we'll work together on issues of money, and we won't try to hide things from each other. All right?"

"Deal," he replied.

"Good. Uh...anything else? Do you have any kids out there?" she asked.

"No." He paused. "I mean, I'd better not. As I said, I fucking wrapped it up every time I had sex. I'd hate to think that was all for nothing. But as far as I know: no, no children anywhere."

"Good. Same, obviously. Hmm. What else? Oh, you won't be meeting my parents. Or any of my family. I've cut them off. All of them."

"Basically same," he replied.

"Well, that makes it easier, at least." She paused. "Do you *want* kids?"

"I don't know," he admitted. "I mean, not now. Not anytime soon. Maybe never. I could live with never. The idea of being a parent frightens me."

"Me too, honestly. I...don't want to be pregnant."

"Oh. Well, I guess that solves it, then."

"Not necessarily. We could adopt. Or..."

"Or what?" he asked, looking at her. She looked oddly pensive.

"So, there's one other big thing I wanted to talk about. I am bisexual. But, practically speaking, it's never really made much difference in my life. Beyond making out with and groping girls at parties when the opportunity arrives, and one memorable night where I traded oral sex with a friend of mine not long after high school, I haven't done anything. I haven't really been with a woman. And now that I'm looking back on everything, I finally know why."

"Because you're into men more than women?" he asked.

"No. Well...I mean, yes. Sort of. That's some of it. I tend to prefer men. Though that has been...changing." She paused. She was looking at the water but here she looked directly at him. "To be clear, I'm very into you. *Very.* But honestly, I've been finding myself looking at ladies more than men over the past year."

"Okay, so...what are you saying, exactly?"

"I'm say that I would like to...experiment. With women. I mean, I've always wanted to, but the reason that I haven't, which I've finally pieced together, is that I've never really trusted any of the men I've ever dated before. Not with bringing another woman into bed. And clearly I was right at least a few times. But I trust you. When I imagine you and I going to bed with another woman, I don't get jealous, I get...horny."

"I...seriously? You're being serious right now?" he asked.

"Yes."

He was silent for a moment, then he grunted and slowly got back to his feet, his knees popping. Ellen did the same. She groaned and then twisted herself, first one way, then another. Something popped loudly in her back.

"Ah! God. I need another one of those massages," she muttered.

"I will give it to you when we get home if you want," he replied. "So you're saying you want to have a threesome with another woman?"

"Yes. And I want you to be involved. How do you feel about that?" she asked.

"Uh, like you're getting the shit end of the stick, kind of. I'm all 'sorry, I'm a penniless starving artist who's in debt and not much to look at', and you're like 'let's fuck other women together and I'll pay for everything!'. It doesn't feel fair to you."

"I mean I *want* to fuck other women with you," she replied. "And you're quite a lot to look at, you know," she murmured, reaching out and running her fingers through his hair, a small smile coming onto her face. "I know you're having trouble with it, but believe me, you're really fucking cute. And you can *fuck*, Jesus can you fuck. And eat pussy. Trust me, Gabe, I'm *very* happy to be in this relationship."

"All right, I trust you. And yes, I would be *really* happy to have threesomes with you and another woman." He paused for a long moment, running the conversation back through his mind for a moment. "But...wait. Hold on. This particular point came up following a talk about pregnancy. Unless I'm really fucking something up...was your point that I could get *another woman* pregnant?"

"Yes."

He looked at her for a long moment, trying to determine if she was fucking with him or not. But she looked completely serious. "You would be okay with it if I impregnated another woman?"

"...under certain conditions, yes."

"Those conditions being?"

"The next thing we should talk about. I'll need more time to think about it and obviously I'll want to ease into it, but I want you to know going forward: I am not opposed to dating another woman. Or two."

"To *me* dating other women or us?"

"Either."

He again fell into silence, staring at her. She stared back, her expression still a little pensive. "To be totally clear about this: you would be *okay* with a second woman living in our apartment, house, wherever, and her being my girlfriend, and having sex with me?"

"Probably, yes."

"So you aren't sure."

"No. I'm not sure because I haven't tried it yet, because I haven't ever felt...safe enough? To try it. If that makes sense. And I do with you. And just so that we're on the same page here, this isn't just a free pass to go out and bring some random chick home to fuck. Not that I think you'd do that, but I just want to clarify. If we were to involve another woman in our lives, even just sexually, it would need to be something we discussed in depth beforehand."

"That makes sense…"

"You still look nervous."

He sighed. "Well, this is obviously something I'd like to do. I mean, who wouldn't want to date or at least fuck two hot women? Or more? But from where I stand right now...I'm just gonna say it: I won't be willing to share you with another guy. I'm just...I can't see it happening and me being okay with it. It's not fair, I know, but it's the situation."

She considered that for a moment. "All right. I accept that."

"Just like that?"

"Yes. From where I'm standing right now, besides you, I'm done with guys. I'm tired of them. I'm tried of the bullshit, and I'll expand on that a bit more soon. But for now: I am okay with this arrangement."

"And if that changes in the future? Five, ten, twenty years down the road?" he asked.

"Then we'll discuss it again in the future," she replied. "Though to be clear, I'm a very loyal woman."

"Cross that bridge when we come to it, huh?" She nodded. "All right. Um. Hmm." He looked back up the incline. "Let's keep walking."

"Okay."

They got back onto the path and resumed walking. A cold wind gusted through the park, rattling the dead branches and stirring up the dead leaves.

"This all sounds good to me," he said after a bit.

"Good! It sounds really great to me. Hmm. I'm trying to think if there's anything else I should mention...oh, well, I'm lazy."

"What? That can't be true."

"It is. I work very hard at my job...well, I used to. I guess I still do, but it's not quite the same, knowing I'm going to get fired. But I'm shit for housekeeping. I hate doing dishes. I hate doing laundry. I *will* do it, but I don't like it at all."

He laughed. "Well, maybe we'll balance each other out. I'm kind of a neat freak and I like keeping things organized and cleaning up."

"Seriously? Because I will absolutely trade sexual favors for not having to clean."

"Will you now?" he asked.

"Oh yes I will," she replied with a smirk. She began losing it again as they approached the car. "Let's sit for a bit more. I have one other thing to discuss."

"All right."

They got into the car and sat together. For a moment Ellen simply stared out the windshield at the park beyond.

Finally, she let out a weary sigh. "Something I need for you to do is, mmm, how do I put this? Help me not fight with you."

"How can I do that?" he replied.

"I'm not completely sure, is the problem. I've become aware of something slowly over my life. I began to grasp it sometime in college. It's basically that there's something about me, and I'm positive it's my height, that causes men to fight with me. Over fucking everything. And I hate talking about it, because of that saying: if everyone you run into is an asshole, then you are the asshole. It feels like those douche-bros who keep ruining their relationships with obvious dickish behavior, but claim every single girlfriend they've had was a psycho."

"Well...I mean, I can see it," Gabe replied.

She looked over at him now. "So you believe me?"

"Yeah, I don't think you'd just lie to me. And it makes sense. Humans are...paradoxically simultaneously complicated and stupidly simple. We're genetically programmed for certain things. One of those things is viewing tall people as authority figures. That's why so many people in positions of power are tall.

"Given men tend to be taller than women, men have gotten used to other men being the tall ones. And then someone like you comes along, a really fucking hot woman who towers over them. It puts them on edge, makes them feel like they're being challenged, which doubly pisses them off if they're a douchebag who thinks women should 'know their place'. And then to complicate matters, you are also fierce and competent. You aren't very submissive. Which would just piss them off more."

"Yeah...that makes sense. And it's all stuff I've thought about. You pretty much hit the nail on the head...you really fucking get me, don't you?"

"I'd say so."

"I like that. It's so nice to be understood...I hope I get you as much as you get me."

Gabe shrugged. "In truth, there's not a whole lot

to get. I want to pay my bills writing books. I keep a neat home. I'm horny a lot."

She laughed and shook her head. "There's a lot more than that."

They both looked forward as they heard the unmistakable sound of sudden rainfall. It was light but it fell from the slate gray skies and the distant boom of thunder promised more. Ellen started up the car and began backing out of the space.

"Let's go home. I love being inside and snuggling and watching something when it rains."

CHAPTER SIXTEEN

"Hey, so...there is *one* other thing I wanted to talk about," Ellen said as Gabe began to get up off the loveseat.

"What's that?" he replied, gathering up the remains of their meal.

After coming back from the park, they'd pretty much just sat on the sofa and watched things, taking a break to fire up a frozen pizza for lunch, then they'd talked for a few hours, mostly about easier things.

Favorite books, favorite movies, music, stuff like that.

Safer things.

As happy as the conversation in the park had made him, it had also been emotionally draining. It was a lot to take in all at once.

And he was still worried it was going to go wrong somehow, or he was missing something crucial.

"Sex stuff," Ellen said.

Gabe finished throwing away the trash and then looked at her from across the room. She was staring at him with that smile she got.

The one he was coming to associate with the best of times.

"What about it?" he asked, coming back and sitting down beside her.

He took a moment to admire her. She looked so fantastically good, just wearing a white tanktop and a pair of panties. It seemed to be her favorite thing to wear.

Her smile widened a little. "Well, I think it best if we talk about our...preferences. And I thought it might be important to let you know that I...want to try something new with you."

"Oh really?"

She giggled. "That perked you right up. Yes. In much the same way that I'm finding myself contemplating my bisexuality, I also finally feel comfortable enough to really explore my submissive side. As I've mentioned before, I can go back and forth between dom and sub, but you strike me as someone who likes to be in charge...if I'm wrong, though, please tell me."

"No, you aren't wrong. I mean I'm okay with you taking charge of the encounter...when you *made* me orgasm that was...uh, pretty great. And not just because of the orgasm. But in general, yes, I'm not submissive."

"What I thought. So, uh...I would enjoy being...submissive. To you."

"What does that look like, exactly?" he asked, reaching out and running the backs of his fingers gently across her cheek.

Her smile widened a bit and she shivered. "I guess that's something we'd have to find out. That's what exploration is all about."

He grew a bit more serious. "I appreciate the innuendo, but I do think we should really talk about boundaries. I don't want to completely fuck up the mood by trying or suggesting something that's just a really hard no for you."

"That's really fair, actually. And appreciated. Um...okay, the only thing that comes out of you that I want on or around me at all is, you know, your cum. I don't mind if you want to shoot it on my face or my back or my tits or whatever, that's fine. But nothing else."

"Fair. And same."

She chuckled. "Okay, sweet. Um...call me what you will during sex, and I, uh...like slapping."

"You like slap*ping* or *being* slapped?" he asked.

"Being," she murmured.

"Interesting."

"I know. It's one of those things I'm not really comfortable that I like, but...well, I trust you not to mock me for it."

"I wouldn't do that," he agreed. "How do you feel about anal?"

"I'll do it," she replied, smiling again.

"You like it or you'll do it?"

"I sorta like it, but I'll do it if you want. Which I imagine you want to. You seem really obsessed with my ass."

"I'm obsessed with all of you, but yes, I would really, really like that. That's another thing I haven't done," he replied.

"For real?" He nodded. "Wow, I get several firsts with you. Lucky me. And you. Okay, um, let's see...no choking. I don't like being choked...were you hoping to?" she asked, noticing his expression change.

"Kind of, but that isn't what I was thinking of. You just reminded me of my crazy ex. She outright refused to do doggystyle, because she said it was demeaning to her in particular and women in general, but she really wanted to be choked."

"...how the *fuck* does that work!?" Ellen replied. "She *is* crazy."

He laughed. "Well, I think her logic was choking was okay because she was the one who wanted it, and doggystyle wasn't, because I was the one who wanted it, and she didn't. And, you know, I'm not into pressuring women to do things in bed they don't want to, but I always thought it was weird. Maybe she didn't think 'I don't want to' was a valid enough excuse? I don't know, but I fucking miss doggystyle."

"Well, I love it. A lot. So we can have a lot of sex in that position...is that your favorite?"

"Position? No. Missionary is mine."

"Really?" She got a little smile on her face, looking amused. "Missionary?"

"I know. Super vanilla. But yeah, I love it."

"I think it's sweet, actually. It's definitely the most...intimate position. And you seem to like intimacy."

"I really do...is there anything else?" he asked.

"Probably, but we've discussed enough," she replied.

"Well..." He leaned back into the loveseat and shifted. "In that case, I would really enjoy that blowjob now."

Ellen grinned broadly. "Say no more."

She stood up and moved the coffee table out of the way to give her some room, then she grabbed a hair tie out of her purse and arranged her hair in a simple ponytail. She knelt down before him and began unzipping his jeans.

"Take your shirt off," he said.

"Yes, sir," she murmured, pausing to strip off her tanktop.

As he she tossed it beside him on the loveseat and resumed undoing his pants, he suddenly became aware of his phone in his pocket. He had always been somewhat ambiguous on the subject of taking naked pictures of his girlfriend.

Nude pics were nice to have, but they always seemed like a risk. And one big thing he faced was that he did *not* feel comfortable taking a picture of his dick or without his clothes on. So it seemed a little unfair to ask to take pictures of his girlfriends without their clothes on. And that had pretty much been put aside after his second girlfriend.

But Ellen seemed into it, and he had to admit, the thought was really enticing.

It would mean there would exist photographic evidence of his dick, though. Unless he photographed it a certain way, or more specifically, at a certain moment.

"You look distracted," she murmured as she freed his erection from his boxers.

"I kinda want to take a picture of you sucking my dick," he replied.

"I'm okay with this."

"You seem really into my taking pictures of you naked," he murmured as he turned on the camera.

"Are you complaining?" she replied, raising an eyebrow.

"Nope, not at all."

She laughed. "Thought not."

Ellen began licking across his head, sending sparks of bliss into him. After a bit, she slipped his cock into her mouth and he put his hand over the back of her head. She let him, actually looking a little happy with the change, so he brought her as close to him as he could and held her there. He could feel his cock hitting the back of her throat.

He took a picture and damn if it didn't look hot.

"All right, keep sucking," he said, setting his phone aside.

"Yes, sir," she murmured demurely and started bobbing her head.

...

Gabe came awake in the darkness.

He laid there, very still, listening, trying to get a sense of the environment around him. Something was wrong, but he wasn't sure what.

Something had woken him up, and he had the impression he'd just been dozing.

He was on his side, facing away from Ellen, towards his dresser, where his lo-fi was playing at a barely audible level, and behind him he could hear the gentle rainfall.

Slowly, he rolled over and saw that Ellen was facing away from him, and for some reason he had the distinct impression that she was awake as well.

He considered that for a moment. He didn't know her sleeping habits. Was she a heavy sleeper or a light one? Was her laying awake, trying to get to sleep, normal?

For just a moment he was tired enough that he considered going back to sleep, but there was just something, he really didn't know what because she was saying nothing and he couldn't see her face or even her body language, but *something* was telling him she was upset.

"Ellen, you awake?" he murmured.

"Yes," she replied.

"...are you all right?" She was silent for a few seconds. "I'm here to talk if you want to talk," he added.

She sighed softly, still facing away from him. "You should sleep."

Okay, something was definitely wrong. He sat up and put his hand on her arm. "I'd rather talk with you if you're upset or worried about something."

"Are you sure?"

"I'm positive."

Another moment of uncertainty passed, and then he took his hand away as she began shifting and rolling over. She looked unhappy. She didn't meet his eyes in the faint light of the moon and the streetlights filtering in through the small windows.

"I feel kind of mixed up," she said, and after another long moment, she looked at him. "Is this too formal? Our relationship? That's part of it. Today almost felt like...a contract in some parts. We just outright say everything we want and what we don't want. Like I'm asking you to sign terms and conditions for dating me. Part of it feels...I don't know, not romantic?"

"Not every single part of a relationship is going to be romantic," he replied, and that seemed to put her at least a little at ease. "And to be honest Ellen, even if it is like a contract or a business transaction, I'd so much rather do this than not."

"Really?"

"Really. There are some things that, yes, I think it's better to sort of tease them out organically, learn things about each other. But there are other things, the things we talked about today, that I absolutely think we should just discuss plainly. Relationships are so fucked today because no one talks to each other, not plainly. It's like you were telling me, about how we should tell each other bluntly if we're pissing each other off, otherwise we'll just let it fester and then it'll explode someday. That isn't healthy. Communicating is."

"You don't think it robs the relationship of romance?"

He reached out and took her hand.

"Communication is romance and consent is hot. And I think you and I get to decide what's romantic."

She smiled now, looking deeply relieved. "That's...really good. Really, really good. Thank you." She sighed suddenly and let out a growl. "I hate how fucking insecure I am now."

"It's a reasonable time to be insecure," he said, rubbing her hand with his thumb.

"I guess so."

A moment passed in the gloom.

"There's something else," he said.

She laughed softly. "You're really good at reading me."

"I guess I am. What's wrong?"

"Well...there's a part of me that's worried I'm doing this *way* too fast. I got cheated on and then hooked up with you less than twenty four hours later. And now we're officially dating and living together barely twenty four hours after *that.* And some part of me is going 'what the fuck are you doing!? This is insane! Maybe this is why you have such an awful track record with relationships!', you know?"

"That's a reasonable thought," he murmured.

"Yeah, but there's this other part of me that's thinking 'He is *perfect* for you and haven't you been wanting for this for years!? And now you're both in a perfect position to get together and he's so great and kind and caring and you would regret it for the rest of your life if you walked away from this! And besides, where the fuck would you even go!?'.'"

"All right, yeah, that's...I can see why you can't sleep."

"And I'm fucking terrified of talking with you about it because how fucked up is it to talk with the guy I just started dating about the fact that I'm not sure if dating is even a good idea or not!?"

"But we are talking about it. And I'm not angry, or yelling at you, or shutting you down."

"No...you aren't," she murmured. "And that means more to me than I can say. And honestly really makes me lean further in the direction of 'this is what I need, this relationship is what I need'. But I also don't know if that's just my stupid desperate need to feel validated by having a significant other. Being single feels like a failure and I *know* that's stupid, but I can't shake that thought."

"Oh I know all about that," he murmured. "Ellen, listen...obviously I'm going to give a biased answer, because in truth, I have wanted nothing more in my entire life than a relationship with you. So I'm in Heaven right now. But I couldn't stand the thought of you feeling trapped. So I want to talk about these things."

She didn't say anything for what felt like a long time. She just looked at him in the gloom of what was now their bedroom.

Suddenly she shifted closer beneath the blankets, closing the distance between them, and hugged him tightly.

"You're a really nice person," she murmured.

"I'm, uh...glad you think so," he replied.

She chuckled softly. "I really do. Honestly that helps settle a lot of my worry. I need more time to really get everything sorted out, but...this helps a lot." She yawned. "I should actually sleep now. We both should."

"Nothing else you want to talk about?" he asked.

"Nothing right now...although there is one thing I want to ask."

"Yeah?"

"Can I spoon you?"

"Yeah, sure."

They shared a kiss and then he rolled over. She got up against him and he could feel her big, bare breasts pressing against his back.

"This is nice," he murmured.

"Because of my tits?" she asked.

"That's a big reason, yes."

"I can think of another reason why it's good that I'm spooning you."

"What's that?"

"I can do this."

She slipped her hand down into his boxers and wrapped around his cock, which was mostly erect already. He made a strange sound and shuddered with pure lust.

"I know what will help you sleep..." she whispered in his ear, making a fist around his cock.

He tried to say something but the words failed him as she started jacking him off. Gabe started breathing more heavily. They'd had sex before going to sleep and that had been amazing but he was rediscovering the fact that, once activated, he had an overactive sexdrive. He could feel her breathing harder and faster as she jacked him off.

"You've been a very good boy today," she whispered in his ear, "and it's time for your reward."

"Oh my fucking God, Ellen, that's...holy shit that's so good," he panted.

"I'm going to make you come so fucking-oh!"

He groaned as he started letting off.

"That's right," she whispered as she kept stroking his cock as it pulsed and twitched in her grasp, his seed getting all over her hand, "come all over me."

He groaned, his whole body twitching as he came, and then it was over and he was left adrift in the pink sea of post-orgasmic bliss.

"Oh fuck," he groaned.

"Wow Gabe, you came a *lot,*" she murmured, slowly extracting her hand from his boxers and getting up. "It's *all* over my hand, you bad boy."

"Thought you said I was a good boy," he replied dreamily as she headed for the bathroom.

She giggled. "Yes, I did say that."

She washed her hand and then came back to bed.

"Sorry I didn't last very long." he said, then yawned.

"Gabe," she replied, getting back up against him and spooning him again, "to be completely honest, when it comes to handjobs and blowjobs, I would much rather you come sooner rather than later. It keeps my hand or jaw from cramping up. Plus it feels good, knowing I got you off that fast. As for sex...well, as long as I orgasm at least once, I'd also rather it be too short than too long."

"Really?" he asked.

"Yes. I love sex, and I especially am loving it with you, but after a certain point it's just exercise. Fun exercise, don't get me wrong, but...well, that's how I feel about it."

"I'll keep that in mind."

"Don't worry. I'm sure I'm going to fuck you so much you'll build up a tolerance to my vagina."

"I highly doubt that."

She giggled again and held him closer to her. "Let's find out together."

"Deal."

"Goodnight, Gabe."

"Goodnight, Ellen."

CHAPTER SEVENTEEN

Gabe sat at his laptop and felt conflicting emotions.

Sunday had gone well. After their late night talk, he and Ellen had woken up late the next morning and pretty much just fucked around the apartment all day. Mostly figuratively, but twice literally. And then again before going to bed.

And that was…

Beyond nice.

When he had awoken this morning, though, he'd found her on the couch, working, in a clearly unhappy mood. He'd tried to talk to her about it, but she'd told him she was just in a shit mood and needed some time alone.

So he'd respected that and gone about his day.

He'd gotten another pair of assignments done and out of the way, and after a quick lunch, he'd settled back in to take a look over the state of his career as a smut author.

At present, he had a grand total of twelve short stories up, most averaging between five and seven thousand words. Not a whole lot apiece, but they were basically glorified sex scenes. He was nearing completion of the thirteenth title, what would be the second one in his new series that was going to be a four parter.

The one about Ellen.

He still didn't have a handle on how to tell her, or even if he should. And that was causing problems. Really, he should have had this one finished by now, but the fact that he might need to just toss it all and move on to another project instead and just give up on the whole thing was bogging him down, mentally.

He *should* tell her, he knew that, but he wasn't sure how to phrase it and now, to complicate matters more, she was clearly upset about something. So it wasn't a great time. And honestly, he would just give up and take the first one down, except that it was his longest and bestselling individual title.

Right now, he had earned five hundred dollars for the month off of a dozen short smut stories. A full one hundred of that came from that one title.

And people wanted more.

Barely half of the titles actually had any reviews with words, mostly people just submitted a starred rating if they did anything at all. But his latest one had a dozen written reviews, over half of which really wanted to know what happened next.

It wasn't going to make any bestseller lists, but it was clearly a step in the right direction...

Gabe sighed softly and decided he should probably try to push a little and help Ellen. He knew they were supposed to give each other space if they wanted it, but he also had the idea that maybe she leaned too heavily into that, and might actually be in the headspace of wanting him to push, at least a little.

It was weird, but he knew exactly what it felt like.

He turned away from his laptop and looked at her. She was sitting on the couch, leaned back from her own laptop, staring intently at her phone, which was perched on the armrest. Her expression was sour.

"Ellen," he said, standing up.

She blinked and looked over at him. "Yes?"

"...I really want to help you with whatever is wrong," he said.

She looked at him for a moment, and he was

worried he might have crossed over into the territory of pissing her off.

But then she relaxed, her shoulders slumping a little, and she let out a little sigh of her own.

"I appreciate that...and I guess I could use some help. At least someone to talk with."

Gabe resisted the urge to sigh in relief as he got up and walked over to her. Sitting down next to her, he took her hand, and she responded by grasping him warmly. Then, after a moment's hesitation, she set her phone on the coffee table, face down, and put her head in his lap, her legs dangling over the armrest.

She looked up at him a little mournfully.

"What's wrong, beautiful woman?" he asked, running his fingers through her pale blonde hair.

She laughed and blushed. "Stop," she whispered. "You're making me blush."

"Is that so bad?"

"...whatever." She sighed heavily. "So, my problem...ugh. Sorry. I know we just had the whole talk about 'we really need to be open with each other', but I just...do *not* want to talk about it. But I should, because we *need* to deal with it. My stupid fucking bitch shitface ex. Whom I fucking hate. I'm going to have to get my shit this week. I can't put it off longer than that. There's a chance he's already done something stupid, but...we'll see."

"I'm still down to go," Gabe replied. "I didn't mention it before, because I didn't want to set your expectations too high, but...I *do* know how to throw a punch. And dodge one. Mostly."

"Holy shit, seriously?"

"Yeah. I had a roommate for a few months who was a boxer and once she realized I wasn't–"

"She?"

"Yeah."

"A lady boxer?"

"Yep."

"...did you fuck her?"

"God I wish I had. She was so hot. She was cut. But I was with my second girlfriend at the time and she was just clearly not into me. But once she realized I was actually a safe guy to live with, we got to know each other a bit more and she taught me a few things. I practice when I can remember to. So I'm not *completely* defenseless."

"All right then, good to know," she replied. Her eyes slipped over to her phone again. "I should probably at the very least deal with my phone."

"What about it, specifically?"

"I've got voicemails and missed calls and text messages from a *lot* of people." She paused. "Well, probably it's more I've got a *lot* of them from a few people, but still, I have to deal with them. And I don't want to even go through the process of deleting them."

"I can understand that...so I'm curious, do you *really* have no one you can trust in your life besides me?"

"Almost," she said after considering it for a moment. "My best friend in the world moved away years ago, chasing someone she really shouldn't have. We still keep in touch and I still love her, but we've drifted apart. I'd trust her. I guess I probably would've reached out to her eventually. And there's one other woman who was my best friend's other best friend. We hung out for a while after my best friend moved away and for a bit I used to go to parties with her, because that was kind of her thing, but eventually I stopped."

"Any particular reason?" he asked.

She sighed. "Two. The first was that the guy I was with at the time started getting really jealous and didn't want me going to parties by myself, and also he didn't want to go that often. But also, I don't know, something never felt completely right. Like I wasn't fitting in right. I don't know. It was better when he went with me, but it still was weird...hmm."

"What?"

"Now I'm wondering what it would be like if you and I went to a party together. That just feels...right. Good. Comfortable." She stopped looking at her phone and returned her gaze to him, scrutinizing him closely. "That's something I always feel around you. Comfortable."

"I'm glad," he said, grinning down at her and running a hand over her head.

"Would you like that? To go to a party with me?" she asked suddenly.

"Well...what kind of parties are we talking about here? Are they the screaming crazy type of parties where people are doing meth and fighting each other?"

She cocked an eyebrow. "What the fuck kind of parties were you going to?"

"Unhappy ones where fun is measured in how many people get seriously injured over the course of the night. I was also forced to help host a few such parties when I found what I thought was an excellent rental deal. I got a room and half a bathroom for two hundred bucks a month at this rundown house some dude's dad owned."

"What happened to make you walk away from two hundred a month?" she asked.

He laughed bitterly. "They kept having parties.

Crazy ones. Mostly I didn't want to be involved because the people were fucking insane and interestingly they all somehow managed to understand 'don't fucking go in that dude's room'. I think they thought I was psycho or something, which was fine by me. But I finally moved out when a bullet went through my door and right over my fucking head while I was trying to sleep."

"Holy shit."

"Yeah. Sucked. I was out a few days later."

"You've lived kind of a crazy life so far."

"Not by consent. I'd much prefer to live a quiet life."

"Oh yeah?" she asked, grinning. "So I guess I shouldn't be so noisy when you're railing me?"

He chuckled. "I don't mind that noise." Gabe glanced up. "Although I wonder about the neighbors."

"Yeah...I'm trying to keep it under control, but you just fuck me *so* good."

He looked at her for a moment. "I don't know how to respond to that," he said finally.

She laughed. "That's all right, Gabe." She paused and lost her smile slowly, returning her gaze sourly to her phone. "Probably a good time for me to actually deal with this bullshit…"

Ellen grabbed her phone and sat up. She turned it on and groaned unhappily.

"Fucking...*fifty six* missed calls. Almost a hundred fucking texts, *Christ*. Thirty voicemails. Most of them from my dumb fucking asshole ex. Why does he suddenly want me? Months and months of neglect and then actual cheating, but now all of a sudden he wants me back?" she growled as she looked through the texts.

"He's selfish and greedy," Gabe replied. She looked over at him. "He had an *amazing* woman at home and whoever else on the side. And he wanted to maintain that. He doesn't care about you, he hates your absence because you were a useful tool to him."

She growled. "...you're right. Fuck. I'm so fucking angry I'm going to vomit again. How the fuck did I ever let myself get in this situation!? Why the fuck–"

Ellen cut off mid-sentence as her phone started to ring. They both started at the screen, which was flaring **BLAKE**.

"I shouldn't answer this," she muttered. Then, suddenly, "Fuck it." She answered the phone and put it to her ear. "What? What do you want?"

Gabe waited, trying to make out the response, but it was too indistinct. Whatever the guy was saying, Ellen cut him off.

"No, Blake. I don't want to hear it-*no!* I don't want to fucking hear it! You *cheated on me.* For a fucking *month!* You told me it was my fucking fault, Blake! You told me I suck in bed, you told me I'm getting fat and ugly, you told me a lot of fucking things! You can't take that back!"

She paused for breath and he immediately heard a reply launch off. Ellen waited, listening, scowling deeply, and then grit her teeth.

"Where I am is none of your fucking business." More talking. Ellen suddenly locked eyes with Gabe. "So fucking what if I might be at some other guy's house?! We're broken up!"

She looked like she was wrestling with something, but then her expression changed to one of abject rage. "Well if I *am* at another man's house, then he definitely has a bigger dick than you and he fucks *way* better and he actually make me fucking come!" she screamed, and then disconnected.

Almost immediately the phone started to ring again and she growled, rejected the call, then rapidly navigated the menus for a moment.

She hit something and then set her phone back down. "Fucking blocked," she muttered, then she groaned as she looked at Gabe. "I know! That was ridiculously fucking petty and immature but I don't give a fuck right now! He called me a stupid whore and just-*ugh! Fuck!*"

Gabe waited for a moment, then gently took her hand. "You want to go lay down? Maybe have a backrub?"

"Yes," she replied after a moment.

He stood up and she did as well, and she let him guide her over to the bed. He took a moment to get her shirt off, then had her lay down flat on her stomach.

Gabe considered how best to do this, then straddled her, pretty much resting on his knees and sitting on her generous ass. He started pushing his thumbs into her the muscles on either side of her lower spine and she immediately let out a moan and twitched.

"You are *really* tense," he murmured.

"Fuck yes I am," she replied. "I'm angry and I feel so fucking stupid for having ever dated that asshole, let alone got engaged to him! Goddamnit. This isn't even the first time I was cheated on. How do I keep-ugh, God, I'm so fucking stupid."

"You aren't stupid," Gabe said, and then pressed into her back, making something pop loudly.

"Ah! Oh...shit. That's a lot better. But I'm still–"

"You aren't stupid, Ellen, you were lonely, and

obviously they were hiding what douchebags they were. That's how abusive relationships tend to go, from what I understand. Everything starts out great and sweet and fun, and then, little by little, the narcissism slips in. It's like...cancer. It's growing in hidden places, and for a while you don't even know it's there. And even when it shows up, its initial symptoms are seemingly innocuous, disconnected things that, on their own, appear to pose no real threat. And even if you suspect, you find yourself making excuses, telling yourself it isn't real, because the idea of it happening to you is fucking terrifying."

"I still feel stupid," she muttered. She sniffed. "And angry. And bitter. And ugly." She sniffed again.

"Here, give me a hug, Ellen," he said, getting off her and laying down beside her.

She immediately turned to face him and hugged him tightly against her. She started to say something, stopped, and then started crying. It happened all at once and it was intense. He held her, ended up hugging her head against his chest as she grasped him and cried into his shirt. He felt awful for her and hated that she was feeling like this.

She didn't deserve this.

He tried to think of things to say to her, but in the end murmured generic platitudes along the lines of 'It's going to be okay'.

Ultimately, he thought that it more mattered that he was there, holding her, making the attempt to soothe her, than it did he said the right thing.

Maybe there was no right thing.

At some point her crying began to taper off, and then she stopped completely, but she still held onto him for several minutes, and so he kept holding her, running one hand along the back of her head, trying to help somehow.

Finally, she moved to disengage herself from him and he let go of her.

She sniffed heavily as she sat up, then she looked at his shirt, then sniffed again. "Ugh, gross," she muttered. "I fucking got snot all over your shirt."

"It happens," he replied.

"I'm...going to go wash my face. I'll be right back."

"All right."

She seemed calm, if still miserable, as she headed into the bathroom. Gabe got up and took off his shirt, then tossed it into the pile of dirty clothes. He was looking for a replacement when she stepped out of the bathroom, looking at least somewhat refreshed.

Ellen stared at him.

"What?" he asked.

"Would it be too much to ask that you keep your shirt off?" she replied.

He laughed. "No, I guess not. How about you?"

She smiled despite herself and then made her breasts sway back and forth. "Yeah, I can."

She lost her smile quickly and then sat down on the foot of the bed. He sat beside her and took her hand. She laced their fingers together.

"I feel so dumb," she muttered.

"Why?"

"Everything I said, but also now I just break down crying like a little girl and–"

"There's nothing dumb about crying, Ellen. You're upset, you cried, it's natural. We're *supposed* to cry," he replied.

"It feels like a failure," she murmured.

"I know but it isn't."

Ellen stared at the floor for another long moment and he waited there with her, holding her hand, hoping she was at least feeling somewhat better.

Finally, she let out a long, heavy sigh. "I can't put off going to get my stuff much longer," she murmured. "Can we do it tomorrow? Over lunch? I know when the best time to do it should be, and ideally he won't be there."

"Yeah, we can do it tomorrow," he replied.

Ellen turned to him abruptly. "Thank you," she said, hugging him again, "for helping me. And being nice to me. And putting up with me."

"You're welcome, and I don't consider it putting up with you. You're my friend, and my girlfriend, and you're going through a really difficult time, and I want to be here for you to help you through it," he replied.

She pursed her lips. "There's something really different about you."

"Different how?" he replied.

"It's just that I've heard this kind of stuff before. And there was always this little part of me that was resistant to what I was being told, thinking 'yeah okay dude, sure'. And I always thought that it was the part of me that was so fiercely independent and hated the idea of relying on anyone for anything. But now I'm thinking it's something else, because that's not happening at all with you. I believe you, and evidently so does that part of me."

"Obviously I think that's a good thing, but why do you think that is?"

She stared at him for a moment longer, then shook her head. "I don't know. Thinking is not easy right now. All I know is that I like it. It feels...like a relief. It feels kind of like I've had low level chronic pain somewhere in my body for years, maybe for my whole life, and now, suddenly, it's gone."

"That's good." She nodded. "All right, so do you want to do anything? Is there anything I can do to make you happy or more at least less unhappy?"

"...yes, actually. There *is* something I've been meaning to ask and it would probably be a great distraction right now. Can I read some of your erotica?" she asked.

Gabe considered hedging, but only for an instant. He stood up. "Yeah, let me get you a flashdrive with some of the stories on it."

"Thanks. I'm deeply curious about your writing."

He laughed awkwardly as he sat at his desk. "Well...don't set your hopes too high. I'm not that good a writer."

"I doubt that," she said, getting up and moving back over to the loveseat.

"Guess we'll find out."

He put the first five individual shorts on a flashdrive and then gave it to Ellen.

"Now what?" he asked.

"I imagine you have work to do. You should tend to that while I read your smut," she replied.

"All right then." He leaned down and gave her a kiss. "You'll let me know if you need or want anything?"

"I will. I promise...thank you, again."

"You're welcome, Ellen."

Gabe went back to his laptop and tried to resume his work.

CHAPTER EIGHTEEN

"How nervous are you?" Ellen asked as she navigated the city.

"Fairly," Gabe admitted, shifting in the passenger's seat. "But I'm okay."

"It's okay to not be okay," she said after a moment.

"I know, just...I'll be okay," he replied.

They both fell silent again as she rolled to a stop at a red light.

Yesterday had been...well, productive, at least. Gabe ended up switching back over to his less desirable jobs and got into a sort of masochistic groove where he just kept on pushing and working his way through them. He'd ended up getting the rough draft versions done for five more assignments and three shorts.

Ellen seemed to have lost herself in reading for most of the rest of the night, and evidently reading his smut had led her online to other smut and it seemed to have worked because when they went to bed she rode him until she came twice.

He'd needed a shower afterwards but they'd at least remembered to put a towel down this time.

They'd awoken early this morning and had tried to do things, to get to work on their jobs, share a meal, watch something, but neither could really focus because of the big event coming up.

And now, finally, it had arrived.

They were driving back to her old place.

"God*damn* you lived in a nice part of town," he muttered as he looked around.

There were a lot of high-rise condos and fancy

restaurants and expensive shops lining the roads, which were themselves in much better condition than he was used to. He knew the 'rich' side of town existed, but he pretty much never had a reason or even excuse to go there.

"It's not as great as it seems," Ellen replied.

He didn't reply, just stared out the window as she kept driving. The skies were gray once again, though it hadn't rained yet. He kept hoping for it, kept waiting for that unmistakable sound of rainfall to drift into his awareness.

A thought that had been hanging around came back to him again and this time he voiced it.

"Hey, Ellen...was it true what you said yesterday to your ex on the phone?" he asked.

"What, that you can fuck better and make me come? Uh, fuck yes it's true," she replied.

"No, the other thing."

"The other-oh. Mmm. Yes, that's true. You have a bigger dick. But...*please* do not go down that road. Because probably one of the most common complaints I've heard from women who have actually been with well-endowed guys is that they're fucking lazy. They really think jackhammering with a big dick is not just enough to satisfy a woman, but *more* than enough. Your dick feels *very* good inside me, Gabe, but not because it's huge."

"I see."

A few seconds of silence passed and she sighed. "I'm sorry if that seemed insensitive. I know it's a whole thing with guys, but I'm just...*sick* of it. And I'm not even trying to make the point that your skill with your tongue and fingers evens out your dick. You are doing *fine* in all departments. You finger good, you eat pussy *fantastically,* and you fuck good.

Really good."

"...all right," he said.

"You're upset."

"No, I'm...you know, just ignore me. I'm feeling insecure and it's stupid and I shouldn't have even brought it up."

"Gabe, just because you have no reason to feel insecure doesn't mean you won't. Like, I get it, okay? I really do. I know you guys have been just *bombarded* with fucking big dick propaganda your whole lives, and that sucks shit. It really does. I can kind of sympathize because they give us the same business about our tits and I *know*, I have huge tits, but when I was developing I spent a period of time there terrified that I was going to have small boobs and no guy was ever going to want to get with me. So I understand. But I'm saying you're fine. Honestly, if anything, you're just a little bit above average. And that's a huge win."

"You think so?" he asked.

"Yes! I don't just think so, I *know* so. It's a huge win for me personally at least. Like, too small I can work with. Too big? That shit just hurts. I've actually heard guys lamenting that their dick is too big," she said.

"You know, there's a part of me that wants to be all 'oh no what a fucking awful problem to have!', but for real? Yeah, that would suck if I couldn't have sex with you without hurting you."

"Exactly! Gabe, I want to believe me on this: I *love* your cock. Okay?"

He laughed. "Okay, yes, I believe you...and do I even need to say it?"

"You don't have to but I'd like you to."

"Fair enough. I fucking *love* your vagina."

She laughed and shook her head. "It sounds so weird hearing that. It sounds so...I don't know, clinical? You're the only guy I've ever met who actually uses the word."

"Is it bad weird?"

"Not really. It's kind of funny..." She lost her smile and exhaled sharply, then pulled off the road into the parking lot of one of those high-rise condo buildings. "Okay, this is it."

She drove around for a bit, clearly looking for something, and then parked.

"See anything interesting?" he asked.

"No. His car isn't here. Okay," she killed the engine and turned to look at him as she undid her seatbelt, "here's the plan: we're going to go in and you're going to follow me around and take whatever stuff I give you. I just need to do a once-over of the apartment. I know where a backpack I can use is and a suitcase. That should be enough to grab all the shit I actually care about. We get in, we get out, ten minutes tops."

"I'm ready," he replied.

"All right." She looked up through the windshield at the towering structure. Took a few quick breaths. Gripped the steering wheel tightly. "Let's get this over with."

They both got out of the car and headed for the front door. For some reason Gabe found himself expecting a doorman, but there was none, just a digital pad that Ellen punched a code into. Just another way to save money, he supposed.

The lobby was plush as hell. It all looked slick and fancy and *really* expensive. Exactly how much had Ellen been making? Or maybe he should be wondering how much Blake was making. That uneasy feeling only got worse as they rode the elevator up, and then it got a whole lot worse when they came into the actual apartment.

The couch alone probably cost more than two months' rent for him.

And the TV was probably three.

And she had walked away from this?

In a fit of rage, he reminded himself. Gabe tried not to get too panicky about it, but it was hard not to. People tended to get used to their lives as they got better. She had gone from an upscale condo that probably contained a hundred grand worth of stuff, to an apartment that possibly contained two grand worth of stuff.

He hoped to be well off at some point, but that was years away, longer probably...

"Fucking dipshit," Ellen muttered suddenly.

"What?" he asked, snapped forcibly back to the situation at hand.

"My ring is there," she replied, pointing, "and half his fuck texts are asking where it's at. He dropped like five grand on it. If I was a lot pettier I'd just fucking take it...come on."

She led him out of the living room, down a hall, and into what he realized must be her home office. Nice desk, nice swivel chair, nice bookshelves.

Shit.

"Perfect," she muttered as she went to the far side of the desk and came up with a backpack. She walked over to the bookshelf and began putting several books into it. "In the desk drawer there, the top one, will you grab the silver flashdrive?"

"Sure," he replied, going over and opening it up. He found it after some digging near the back, among a lot of office supplies. "What's on it?" he asked, bringing it to her.

"My porn," she replied.

"*Your* porn?"

She laughed. "No, not porn of me, porn I've found that I've liked. I watch a lot of lesbian porn and I save my favorites. And there's some hentai on there…" She paused as she slipped it into her purse and looked at him with a grin. "You wanna make some porn?"

"…I'm not sure," he admitted.

"Well," she said, going back to perusing her bookshelf, "if you feel the need, I wouldn't be against it. Maybe we can film ourselves fucking and then fuck to it? Or is that conceited?"

"I…don't know," he replied. "I actually don't have an answer. But…that could be really interesting."

"Exactly," she whispered with that same sly grin.

She tossed one more book into the backpack and then walked quickly over to the desk. Opening the drawers, she rummaged around in them for a minute, occasionally coming up with something: an expensive-looking calculator, a little notebook, a fancy pen, and tossed it all in.

Then she zipped it up and passed it to him.

"Come on," she said, stalking out and heading deeper into the apartment.

He followed and then hesitated, looking back down the hallway. He could just see the front door. It was still shut, but what if he was coming up right now? How badly would that go for them?

What if–

"Gabe, come on. Keep up," she called from the bedroom.

"Sorry," he replied, joining her. "Just…distracted."

"I know, but focus, we're almost done," she replied.

He nodded. She headed into a walk-in closet and told him to wait there. Gabe waited, slowly looking around the room. It felt very strange being there, and not at all in a good way. He was inside of her old life.

The life that had been hers less than a week ago.

He tried to be useful, pushing away at the thoughts and hoping to maybe point out something she may have overlooked, but it was too difficult. His mind kept wandering to dark places. He peered into the closet, saw her crouched in front of a dresser.

That walk-in closet was as big as his bathroom. Maybe even a little bigger.

"All right," she muttered, shoving something into a duffel bag and then zipping it up. She stood. "That's it, that's all of it. I got most of it first time around. But this is what I forgot because I was so fucking pissed." She emerged from the closet. "Let's go."

"Gladly," he replied.

They headed back down the hallway, and Gabe ended up in front as he was particularly eager to get out.

"Wait," she said suddenly.

"What?" he asked, pausing by the door.

"There's something in the kitchen," she replied, heading for the open doorway that led into the no doubt extremely expensive, fancy, and well-stocked kitchen, "I just want to grab—"

They both froze up as they heard a key to the door, and before either of them could do anything, it was pushed open and Blake walked in.

He froze up two steps in as he saw Gabe.

"Who the *fuck* are you and what the fuck do you think you're doing in my condo!?" he snapped, balling his fists up as Gabe tried to think of a response.

"He's with me," Ellen said, take a few steps closer to Gabe. "I just came to get the rest of my things."

A long, tense moment passed with all the ease of a kidney stone as he looked from Gabe to Ellen, then back to Gabe, his expression growing more sour all the time.

He looked about how Gabe expected him to look: tall, tanned, dressed sharply in nice business clothes, clean-shaven, his hair styled.

"You have got to be fucking shitting me," he replied finally. "*This* little pussy? This little bitch is who you ran to? You are fucking pathetic. Get the fuck out of my condo, you giraffe bitch, and take your fucking simp with you."

Gabe felt something twitch, hard, in his head. It was like he'd been doused in a cold wave anger. "Hey *fuck you,* asshole," he replied before he even realized he was replying.

"Go fuck yourself, you stupid arrogant shit stain!" Ellen snapped, her face reddening immediately. "I'm here to get my shit and leave with a fucking real man who actually fucking eats pussy!"

That hit a nerve.

Gabe saw the change in Blake's stance and face immediately. He was clearly a lot more pissed at Ellen, but Gabe was closer. So he raised his fist and came right for him.

"Blake, *don't–*" Ellen began.

Gabe reacted almost faster than he thought he could. He jerked his head back as Blake swung on him and then popped him right in the mouth. Blake let out a half-formed shout of pure shock, stumbled backwards, and then landed heavily on his ass.

For a few seconds, he just stared at the two of them, a look of total shock on his face. It didn't last though, and it twisted back into rage as he hurriedly got back to his feet.

"You fuckin–"

"Blake, back the fuck off," Ellen growled, her hand coming up out of her purse with a tazer. "I will fucking taze your ass. You *know* I will."

That seemed to put a little bit of sense back in the idiot, and he took a step back. "Just get the fuck out of here!" he snapped.

"Come on, Gabe," Ellen said, her voice low.

They began to head for the door, wary to keep a safe distance from him as he stood there, fuming as he stared at them.

"Wait," he said suddenly. "Where's the fucking ring!? No fucking way I'm letting you walk out of here with that!"

"Jesus fucking-Blake! How fucking stupid are you?! I fucking *told you* already, it's here, in the goddamned condo!"

"Where!?" he demanded.

She pointed across the room to their dining table. "There, you fucking dipshit!"

He looked at it, then marched over to it and snatched it up. As he was studying it, Gabe and Ellen walked back out into the hallway.

"Come on," Ellen muttered, hurrying him a bit.

They had almost made it to the elevators when he suddenly heard Blake call out: "Enjoy that used pussy, you fucking beta bitch!"

And then he slammed their door shut.

"Fucking baby," Ellen muttered as she punched the call button.

CHAPTER NINETEEN

Neither of them said anything as they got into Ellen's car and put their stuff in the backseat.

He felt kind of dazed and his wrist and knuckles were hurting a little. He put on his seatbelt with the kind of glazed automation that came from shock. At some point he became aware of the fact that they weren't moving.

He looked over and saw Ellen gripping the steering wheel. Her hands were shaking a little.

"Are you all right?" he asked.

She looked over at him. "Yes. I'm all right," she murmured. Then she blinked a few times and gave her head a little shake, and seemed to come back to herself. "Are *you* all right?"

"Uh...yeah, I think so," he muttered.

"Gabe!"

"What?!"

"You fucking punched him in the face!" she cried, breaking into a broad grin.

"Uh...yeah. Yes I did. That was probably stupid," he muttered, gripping his wrist and giving it an experimental squeeze. Besides a minor ache, it seemed fine.

"No, it was *amazing,*" she replied.

He looked back over at her. "Seriously?"

"Yes! I...fuck, hold on," she muttered, turning her key, which she'd put into the ignition but not actually activated. The engine hummed to life and, after a few quick breaths, she began backing out of the spot and then started driving them home. "That went perfectly!"

"I thought perfectly was he didn't come home,"

Gabe replied.

"No, I mean, yeah, okay, that would have been more perfect. But honestly? I kind of prefer this."

"I've never actually hit anyone before…"

"I'm sorry it came to that, and okay, yes, I probably shouldn't be reinforcing violence as a solution, but you know what?! Fuck that! Fuck that and fuck him! He fucking *deserved* that. He was going to swing on you, Gabe. I was going to taze his ass, but I don't think I could've gotten there in time, before he got to you. He absolutely would have punched you. But you fucking dodged it! I didn't know you could do *that!*"

"Neither did I, to be honest. It just kinda...happened? I guess that training was actually pretty useful."

"Gabe, trust me, he fucking deserved it so hard. Now he's got a fat lip to remind him what his stupid ass brought on himself for the next few weeks."

"I've never seen you so fucking angry before. I guess except when you were talking to him on the phone."

She sighed heavily, losing her smile. "I know it was fucking petty, what I said, but I wouldn't have said it if he hadn't called me a fucking giraffe. He *knows* that fucks with me! It was an intentional cheap shot and you know what? Fuck the 'moral high ground', if he wants to take a cheap shot, I can take one right back at him."

Ellen was quiet for a moment, then let out a long sigh. "But whatever, we did it. We're fucking through the worst of it. We got my shit and I never need to go back there for anything! I never need to put up with his stupid ass ever again!...are you okay, for real, Gabe? I know that was intense."

"I think I'll be all right," he replied. His heart was still thumping harder than usual and his stomach was churning, but…

He was actually feeling better. Almost good.

"Hey, you won your first fight," she said, regaining her grin.

"I don't know if that counts," he replied.

"He swung on you, you dodged, and you fucking one-shotted him. One solid punch to the mouth! It was a fight and you won."

"To be fair, you pulled a tazer on him."

She sighed. "Just enjoy the victory. I know it's not a path I particularly want to go down and for the love of God, don't go around picking fights, but it's really nice to know you *can* do it if it comes down to it. And it was *so* nice to see my man put my stupid fucking ex in his place in a way that he actually understands."

"I guess I can't argue with that," he murmured. "What got to him *so* much about the pussy-eating comment?"

"He used to do it but then he always tried getting out of it and I'm not really comfortable trying to make people do things, especially sex things, but I did keep asking for it. And it became this thing between us. For a while I finally just let it go, but then about a year ago I overheard him talking to one of his loser friends on the phone going on and on about how 'only beta bitches eat pussy' and 'real men don't eat pussy, they make women suck their dick', and like...how the fuck can you have that opinion and still be someone I want to fucking get married to!? It caused a massive fight and the super ironic thing was, he did actually feel guilty about not doing it."

"Why didn't he just fucking do it then, for fuck's

sake?" Gabe replied.

"Because he really believed that shit. He honestly believed that he was less of a man if he went down on his girlfriend. I thought we'd got it sorted, because he managed to reframe it as he just didn't like performing oral, and, you know what? Fine. I can accept that. I don't *like it,* but I can accept it. But that sort of kicked off...I don't know, a sort of relationship cold war? That was the first real crack in the foundation. And I could tell it bothered him, and I tried not to bring it up anymore, because believe it or not, I'm not a conniving bitch who enjoys torturing men.

"But it kept coming up in arguments later on. Ugh, whatever. It was only a few weeks ago that I started overhear him talking about how fucking 'alpha' he was and Jesus Christ, *please* never go down that fucking alpha beta whatever road, because nothing dries my pussy up faster." She paused. "Okay, I mean, there are worse things, but seriously, it's so fucking embarrassing."

"I fully intend to never go down that road," he replied. "Honestly, I've never really understood it? Like...how do these guys not understand that if you need to exclaim that you are an alpha, that means you *aren't* one? It seems like a painfully simple idea."

"It is. They're just fucking stupid. No surprise there."

They kept driving for a few moments, heading back towards the less financially gifted side of town, and Gabe found himself slipping back into that worry.

"Gabe!" she cried suddenly, shattering his thoughts.

"What?!" he replied, twisting his seat.

"We should get high!"

"...what? Did I hear that right?"

"Yes! Gabe! Weed is legal now, we should smoke some weed! Or get some edibles? Unless you don't want to? That's totally cool...unless you have a problem with me doing it?"

"No, um...no, I don't have a problem with it. It's just...I *never* thought you'd want to get high, Ellen. You seemed kinda straightedge."

"I guess I was, but only because I had to be. I mean, it's been a while since I've toked, but I do like to get drunk every now and then...so, what do you say? Get high?...get laid?" she murmured demurely, grinning more slyly at him. "Being high makes me *so* horny."

"Uh fuck yes, let's do that," he replied, and she laughed loudly.

. . .

"So, we're *completely* sure about all this?" Gabe murmured as they pulled into the parking lot of a fairly nondescript stripmall, one of the buildings sporting a sign that read **HIGHLY ENLIGHTENED**.

"I am," Ellen replied, finding a spot and parking. "Are you? We can just not do this if you're uncomfortable."

"I'm more just wanting to be sure we're...safe. That this is actually fully legal."

"Yeah, it is." She paused. "So, technically it's still not legal at a federal level, but basically we're good."

He looked up at the building for a moment. It felt so weird. He was going to just straight up walk in and buy something that people went to jail for like a year ago. Gabe took a moment to look around. Everything seemed so...normal. He wasn't sure what he was expecting, but at least from the outside the place had the same vibe as a convenience store.

Though the place lacked windows, and the door looked a bit heavier than all the others.

Well, this *would* be a target for robbery, given what they were selling and how much money they were no doubt making.

"I'm good, let's do this," he said, figuring why the fuck not?

Getting stoned and fucking Ellen sounded absolutely incredible, and after today...shit, after the past month, he could use something to take the edge off.

Ellen's expression brightened again. "Come on!"

She took his hand and led him over to the front door. The door opened on what looked like a waiting room, a simple room with a lot of chairs, at least half of them actually comfortable looking, and a huge beanbag. A bored receptionist with several piercings and tattoos waited behind a counter, and beside her were a pair of doors that led deeper into the building.

They walked up to the desk.

"IDs?" she asked.

"Oh, right," Ellen murmured, going into her purse.

Gabe felt a twinge of anxiety about that. They were going to have his ID on file? Well...what the fuck wasn't on file nowadays? He produced his own driver's license and the woman took both and scanned each of them, then passed them back.

"All right. Have a seat and we'll be with you in a minute," she said.

"Thank you," Ellen replied.

As he turned back, he saw several people were staring at Ellen. They quickly went back to whatever they were doing as they crossed the room and sat down beside each other.

"So," Ellen said after a moment, her voice quiet, "got any good stories about getting stoned?"

He thought about it, then grunted. "Not really. I've only done it like five times in my life. The only interesting thing that actually happened was, uh, sex stuff."

"Oh *really?*" she asked, leaning a bit closer. "Tell me about it."

He laughed awkwardly. "Really?"

"Yes."

He looked around, then lowered his voice a bit more. "Well, this was between my second and third girlfriends, and there was a party at my roommate's girlfriend's house for her birthday, I think. I didn't really assume anything was going to happen, sexually speaking, and I think that helped? I met a girl and I wasn't trying to hook up with her because it seemed hopeless, she was definitely too hot, and then we split a joint and then she kissed me."

"It's what I would've done," Ellen murmured. "And then what?"

"Well, we made out and I got under her clothes and fingered her for a while, and then she blew me," he replied, then chuckled awkwardly. "It feels weird talking with you about this."

"I like hearing about it," Ellen replied with a shrug. She began to speak again when the door opened and an attractive woman with dyed blue hair poked her head out.

"Ellen? Gabe?"

"That's us," Ellen said, standing.

Gabe got up and they followed the woman back through the door into the other half of the building where they had a lot of shelves behind long, glass-fronted display cabinets. There were a few other people behind the displays talking with a few customers.

"Hello, I'm Colleen, I'll be your server today," she said, leading them over to one of the cash registers and stepping behind it. "Is this your first time here?"

"Yes. Honestly, first time in a place like this at all and I haven't personally gotten stoned in over a decade," Ellen replied.

"More or less same for me," Gabe said.

"Nice! Well, I can help you find what you need. First thing to help narrow it down is, are you looking to smoke, eat, or drink?"

"Hmm...I have always kind of hated smoking," Ellen murmured. "I guess let's try eat and drink? Gabe?"

"Fine by me," he replied.

"Perfect. Next, are you looking for more energy or less energy?" Colleen asked.

"Wait, there's weed that makes you hyper?" Gabe replied.

"Sort of."

"We're looking for something to take the edge off and chill us out," Ellen said.

"Perfect. Here, let me grab a few things," Colleen replied, ducking down behind the counter. She came up a moment later with a plastic container and what looked like a can of soda. "Okay, this," she said, tapping the top of the container with her fingernail, "holds a dozen ten milligram gummies. This," she tapped the can, "is, more or less, weed soda, thirty milligrams altogether. This strain will take the edge off and should make you tired."

"What do you think, babe?" Ellen murmured, picking up the can and studying it.

For an instant he was thrown out of the moment as it occurred to him that this may be the first time she'd ever called him something besides his name.

"Sounds good to me," he replied, studying the container.

"All right! We'll take these then."

"Okay then. We only do cash right now. Let me just ring this up…"

"Any advice?" Gabe asked as she scanned both items and then put them in a little bag.

"Yes, actually. First, the biggest one: be patient. I'd say you two should split one gummy and then let time pass. Like an hour, maybe even two. If it doesn't do anything, then split one more. Everyone has different tolerances and potentially different reactions. I made the classic mistake when I first got into it."

"The mistake where you take too much?" Ellen asked with a little smile.

Colleen laughed. "Yes. I ate a gummy, got impatient after like fifteen minutes, ate another. Still wasn't feeling anything after another half an hour and ate a third. And, um...I was fucking *stoned* out of my *mind* after that. I was at home, luckily. I slept through the night and most of the day and woke up still stoned. I didn't feel right again until the day after that...all right, that'll be fifty two dollars."

"Oh wow," Gabe murmured as Ellen began fishing around in her purse.

"Yeah, it's a lot, but it's worth it. I think you two are going to have a lot of fun."

Ellen grinned, handing over the money and then running a hand lovingly down Gabe's cheek. "I think we are definitely going to have a lot of fun," she murmured.

Colleen laughed and handed them their receipt and the bag. "If you like it, we've got a lot more."

"I'm pretty sure we'll be back at some point," Ellen replied.

Gabe took the bag and began following Ellen back outside.

CHAPTER TWENTY

It began to rain lightly as they pulled into the apartment parking lot.

They had already swung by to drop off Ellen's things, so the only thing they had to bring in was their weed. Ellen was already giggly as they headed downstairs and he got the door unlocked.

"I should get you a key," he murmured, then paused. "Oh shit, I didn't even tell my landlord that you're here…"

"Oh, right. Uh…shit. Is that going to be a problem?" she asked as they walked into the apartment.

Gabe shut and locked the door against the world once more. It felt so much better to do now that he had Ellen in here with him.

"I have no idea," he replied. "What happens if they say no?"

"Then we say 'fuck you' and move," she replied, setting the bag down on the coffee table and then began getting out of her hoodie.

"Really?" he asked.

Ellen turned to look at him, suddenly serious. She tossed the hoodie aside and then began unbuttoning her jeans. "Gabe, I've been pining after you for years. I'm not giving you up."

He stared at her as her pants came off and she kicked them aside, in the general direction of the bedroom area.

"…really?" he repeated finally.

She laughed and walked over to him, put her hands on his shoulders and looked down into his eyes. God was she so tall. She had a solid six inches on him and when you were already nearing six feet, that seemed like a *lot*.

"Gabe," she said, more serious than ever, "I know this is hard for you to understand, because you clearly have put me so very high up, and I'm finally getting the idea that you look at me the same way cliché high school nerds look at the captain of the cheer squad, but something I want you to believe is that how you feel about me is the exact same way I feel about you."

Then she leaned down and pressed her lips to his. She hugged him and deepened the kiss, and it was a long, wonderful kiss.

"Uh..." he murmured as she finally came awake. "That's, um...you kiss good."

She laughed again. "Oh Gabe, we haven't even had any edibles yet and you're stoned," she murmured. She kissed him once more, then walked over and sat down heavily on the loveseat. "Come on," she sat, patting it, "sit down with me and get stoned."

"All right," he replied, kicking his shoes off and then taking his pants off.

After a moment's hesitation, he grabbed her discarded hoodie and hung it up next to his own on the rack by the front door.

"Sorry," she said, "I guess I should get better about that..."

"It's fine, I don't really care that much," he replied. "So...which should we do?"

"What she said," Ellen replied, tearing off the plastic that sealed the top of the little container holding their gummies, "we'll split one. Actually, you should probably put that can in the fridge while I...wrestle with this fucking thing," she muttered, struggling with the plastic.

He did that, staring at the can for a moment before putting it in. It was going to take some getting used to. For a while he had sort of prided himself on the fact that he didn't have any seriously bad habits. No drinking, no drugs, no smoking, no gambling. But it also occurred to him that he often had a difficult time coping with his miserable life.

Maybe some weed a few nights a week would help him.

"Got it!" Ellen said as he rejoined her.

She popped the top off and pulled out a square blue gummy. Studying it for a moment, she shrugged and then bit it in half, then passed what remained to Gabe, who ate it after sniffing it.

"Oh, God," she groaned after swallowing. "Ugh, that taste. Not nice."

"Fuck...yeah. Gross. It's like...an old ashtray that's been lightly sprayed by a skunk...here hold on."

He got up and grabbed a bag of potato chips and a can of soda from the fridge, then came back. They both dug in, passing the can back and forth and between eating handfuls of chips. Then they sat back against the couch and didn't say anything for a moment.

"Do I really make you that happy?" he asked, breaking the silence.

"Yes," she replied.

"Huh...why?"

She shrugged. "I don't know, Gabe. I mean, well, I know *some* of the reasons. You're kind, you're funny, you're creative. Responsible. Handsome. You–and I can't emphasize this enough–eat pussy *so* fucking well. But also, you don't...hmm. How to put this last one...you don't pressure me into things. You don't try to make me do things."

"There isn't a damn thing I could *make* you do, Ellen," he replied.

She laughed. "You'd be surprised. But...there's more to it. A lot more. I don't know. You just make me happy...hmm, what should we do?"

"I know what I want to do," he murmured, reaching out and fondling one of her breasts, so very visible through the tanktop she had on.

She giggled. "Not yet. I want to be noticeably stoned first...okay, I have something. I'm already in a pretty good mood, and I feel sort of...bulletproof right now."

"Bulletproof?"

"Like, emotionally. Let's talk about insecurities."

"Oh wow, really?" he asked.

"Yeah! It's something I wish I'd talked about earlier in my past relationships." She paused. "Ugh, actually, no, I don't. They just used it as ammunition when they were mad at me, as you saw today. But I trust you. Like, *really* trust you. I feel like you wouldn't hurt me."

"I wouldn't. Ever," he murmured, taking her hand and giving it a gentle squeeze.

"I know." She smiled lovingly at him and then gave him another kiss. "So, come on, insecurities. Or, better yet, I'll go first. I made you go first last time it was something serious...unless you really don't want to do this."

He sighed and shook his head. "No, we should if you want to. I mean, you're right: it's a good idea to know up front, and I trust you, too. It's important we know this stuff so we don't accidentally hurt each other."

"Okay, sweet. So, well, you know I'm insecure

about my weight. I don't know if I really got it across to you before, but I'm pretty insecure about my height. Like...it can really bother me. What's this look?" she asked.

"Well, it's just that...um..."

"Come on, tell me," she said, smirking.

"I love how tall you are."

She studied him for a long moment. "Are you sure you don't just really like *me* and you're just tolerating the fact that I tower over you?"

"I'm positive," he replied. "I really, really like how tall you are."

"Hmm." She pursed her lips. "So you'd be happy if I wore high heels? Brought my six foot five ass all the way up to six foot seven or eight?"

"Oh my fucking God yes," he replied immediately. "I'd be *thrilled.* That would be *amazing.*"

She continued scrutinizing him. "In public?"

"Hell yes," he replied.

"You're being serious right now..."

"I'm being dead serious, Ellen."

"Well, all right then. I'll have to call that bluff sometime."

"I'm not bluffing!"

She giggled. "I...believe you. It's just weird. I don't know. I know there are guys out there who like really tall women, but I never seem to actually meet any. I've actually had dates from my brief forays into online dating where the guy showed up, saw me, and was pretty much like 'this isn't going to work'."

"...for fucking real?"

"For fucking real," she said, rolling her eyes. "I mean, on the one hand, I appreciate that they're being up front about it. On the other hand, like...is it really that big a deal? So you can see why I'm sensitive about it. Plus I was relentlessly teased about it through middle and high school. I was six foot in seventh grade."

"Holy shit."

"Yeah. Only got worse from there. I was one fucking weird-looking, awkward, gangling teen until I finally evened out near the end of high school. Okay, so, what else? Um...I'm insecure about my hips, I guess. I know I said earlier that I liked what my weight has done for them, but then sometimes I see myself in the mirror and they're just...too big."

"No way," he said, reaching out and putting a hand on her hip. "Not too big. Too sexy is more like it."

"Oh my God, Gabe, shut up," she muttered, rolling her eyes again and starting to redden.

"I mean it." He hesitated. "Also, like...I don't want to tell you how you should feel about your body, but I also want to reassure you that I find you insanely fucking hot...but I also don't want you think that it's all that matters to me."

"Trust me, I don't. And I do appreciate it...okay, your turn. I've given you some."

Gabe shifted in his seat. "All right, fair. I'm insecure about...a lot. The obvious one: my dick isn't big enough. I'm not attractive. I'm not good at sex. I'm not strong enough. Plus, with the typical 'guy insecurities' bundle, I get the bonus of 'writer insecurities' bundle. I'm not a good writer, I'm not smart enough...I'm boring."

"How are you boring? I mean, all that is bullshit anyway." She hesitated, then sighed and winced slightly. "Sorry, not trying to say your feelings are bullshit. It's just...it's not true. Any of it! I mean, I've told you how I felt...how you make me feel. And you aren't boring, you're a writer! Who is actually pursuing your passion! If anything I'm the one who's worried about being boring and vapid. All I've ever done is work and consume media."

"Ellen, we never had a dull conversation," Gabe replied. "You aren't vapid. You're really interesting. And from what I've been able to tell, you're something of a workaholic. You don't really give yourself time to do much more than work, sleep, and consume media. But even with that, you're an interesting person."

"Well...I hope you're right. Oh, also! I have been reading your stuff and you are *not* a bad writer. You are a skilled, engaging writer."

"You sure you aren't just being nice?" he asked.

"Yes, Gabe. It...did what it was supposed to do."

"And what's that?"

"Make me horny, obviously. And-ooh."

"What?"

She closed her eyes for a moment, then smiled a bit wider. "I...feel it. It's coming on. I guess I'm pretty sensitive to it."

"What's it feel like?" Gabe asked.

"...my head is sort of, like, swimmy? I feel kind of dizzy, but it's a good kind of dizzy. It's not too different from being buzzed from wine." She giggled. "It's nice. It feels nice. Ooh!" Her eyes popped open. "Let's watch hentai!"

"Really?" he asked as she got up.

"Yeah!" She dropped down into a crouch and rifled through her purse. "Um...fuck, where is it?" she muttered. "Ah!" Standing back up, Ellen looked at the TV, then at his game console. "Can that thing take a USB?"

"Yeah, definitely. The slot's on the front," he replied. "Also...uh, how do you feel about the fact that I play video games?"

"Fine," she replied, crouching down in front of the console and hunting around for a moment. She found the slot and pushed the flashdrive in. "...should I not? You asked that hesitantly."

"No, I mean, it's great. I'm happy. It's just...I've had some women not react well to the fact that I play games. I don't do it a *lot,* but...usually I do it at least once a day. And despite the fact that we live in a world where celebrities brag about the games they're playing and games are more common than ever before and literal grandmothers are gaming, there are still women who take serious issue with it and think it's immature."

"Well there's also men who think only pussies eat pussy. There's a lot of morons in the world," Ellen replied, walking back over and sitting beside him. "But Gabe, please don't ever suppress yourself or your interests for me. I want you to have fun and to be able to relax the way you want to. Fuck, I'll watch you play games."

"Seriously? Because that would be the coolest fucking thing in the world," he replied.

She laughed, then started giggling, then kept giggling. Finally, she brought herself under control. "That's...funny. Or no, sorry, that's the weed making me laugh. I'm happy that you're happy." She giggled again and shook her head, sighing. "Fuck, now I can't stop laughing."

"Probably gonna be hard to watch porn then," he replied.

"I only collect the ones that aren't a joke," she said. "There's so many just ridiculous plots out there.

But really my biggest complaint is that they're all so short! They have the gall to call something with *two* twenty five minute episodes a 'series'."

Gabe turned on the controller and the console, then navigated to the media player.

"When was the last time you watched porn?" she asked suddenly.

"Uh...man, like...six months ago?"

"Are you fucking with me right now?"

"No. Honestly I don't really watch porn. I mean I went through a phase when I was in my teens where I did a lot more, but it just fell off."

"Any reason?"

He thought about it, then shrugged. "I don't really know. I guess at a certain point I had this realization, sort of all at once: why am I watching other people having sex when I'm not? So I just stopped for the most part."

"...that makes a lot of sense actually," she said. "So do you not want to watch it?"

"No I'll totally watch it with you, because I've always wanted to watch porn with my girlfriend. Because when we get horny, we can totally just have sex," he replied.

"Okay, sweet."

"So what are we watching?" he asked, seeing she had a few different folders. He selected the one that said hentai.

"Open up I'll Take Care of You. It's got three episodes, but they're short, like not even twenty minutes apiece. The plot is like an alien girl ends up stranded on Earth and a guy takes her into his apartment, and of course she doesn't look like an alien, she looks like a super hot chick with cat ears and a tail. And of course they fuck."

"You seem *really* blasé about this," he said.

"Yeah, I don't mean to, it's just, the plot is really cliché. I've watched a *ton* of these. But the difference is that it's done really well. Great animation, great dialogue, *really* hot sex. So hot."

"Fair enough. Although…"

"What?"

"It just seems kind of, um, sweet? I guess? I was expecting something a lot raunchier."

She giggled. "What, like, 'I'm Going To Wreck Your Vagina'?"

He laughed. "Yeah, something like that."

"There's a lot out there like that, and I go for that sometimes, but mostly I go for fluffier, sweeter stuff. At heart I'm a sweet romantic who wants to love and be loved, care for my man and be taken care of by him."

"I'll take care you," he said, putting a hand on her thigh.

She laughed awkwardly and began blushing.

"Hit a nerve?" he murmured.

"Shut up," she replied.

"You're blushing."

"I'm not! Dammit!"

"You are. You're so cute when you're like this."

"Oh my God shut up you fucking dork!"

He started laughing. "Wow, Ellen, this is like a textbook case of girls just devolving into giggling and blushing and fake anger when confronted with the boy they like."

"It is not!"

"Denial, Ellen…"

"Shut up and put on the porn or you aren't getting any pussy!"

Gabe tried not to smile and failed. Instead, he sat

back and put his feet up on the coffee table. "Okay, Ellen."

"...are you calling my bluff?" she asked, staring at him intently.

"Definitely not," he replied.

"Because you'd better not be."

"Hush and do as you're told, dear," he replied.

She continued staring at him. "Where is this coming from!? Are you fucking with me right now!?"

"No, you're being paranoid. That's just the weed," he replied, and he almost managed not to laugh and to keep a smile off his face. But a quick glance at her wild expression caused him to fail. He laughed and broke into a broad grin.

"You teasing fuck!" she cried. "Is this because of the weed?"

"I dunno," he replied, "but I thought you wanted to submit to me."

"I do, just...this is so wild. It's so strange to actually hear it coming out of your mouth."

"Are you going to do as you're told?" he asked. For a moment, she didn't answer, just looking at him, chewing slowly on her lower lip. "If it isn't working I'll stop," he said.

"No, don't stop," she replied. "I'll do as I'm told."

"Good. Get settled and be quiet," he replied.

In truth, he'd never really been in a dom-sub relationship before, and the idea that he was entering into one with Ellen, where *he* was the dom, was crazy to him. He wasn't sure if he was doing it right, so he was kind of going by feel alone. But she seemed to be enjoying it.

She sat down against him and he put an arm around her waist, holding her tight against him, then hit play.

CHAPTER TWENTY ONE

They got through one episode, and right as the credits hit, so did everything else.

"Uh...whoa," Gabe muttered. He'd been in the process of sitting up and now he fell back against the loveseat.

"What?" Ellen asked, amused.

"Uh...it's hitting." He chuckled.

"What is? The weed or the horny?" she asked, then giggled.

"Uh...both."

"What's it feel like?"

"Well...I'm dizzy. But you're right, it feels good. It's calming. But I also feel horny. It's...different, though. More powerful. More intense."

"You *do* have a steel hard-on right now," Ellen murmured, laying her hand on his boxers.

"Yeah." He paused for a moment. "Um...we should fuck."

She laughed. "Should we now?"

"We really should. Are you horny?"

"Very," she murmured.

She began to say something else and instead abruptly leaned in and kissed him. As her lips met his, he felt his whole body light up with desire. He'd been wanting her ever since they'd gotten back home, the yearning growing slowly as they spent time together, but it had been a gradually growing fire, being stoked slowly, swelling by degrees.

But this was like dumping gasoline on the flame.

Her lips were soft and warm and wonderful, and as he reached up and put his hand over the back of her neck, she moaned and tilted her head, leaning in

207

closer. She pushed her tongue in, deepening the kiss, and he moved his own to meet hers, to have them twist and dance together.

And he tasted her wonderful taste.

Their kiss seemed stretch out, a moment in time lengthening longer than it should have.

Finally, she broke the kiss and fell back, panting a little.

They stared at each other.

"Oh my God," she whispered finally, her voice intense, "that was an amazing kiss. Just...wow. That felt *good*. We *have* to have sex right now!"

She leaped up off the couch and then cried out as she almost fell over. She stumbled, caught herself against the wall, laughing as she did.

Gabe shot to his feet, worried she might have hurt herself, and then tripped over the coffee table and sprawled onto the floor. He grunted as he landed and rolled over onto his back, laughing.

"Oh no, are you all right!?" Ellen asked, hurrying over to him.

"I'm fine-*oof!*" he grunted as she tripped and landed half on him.

"Oh shit, I'm sorry!" she cried, and then both of them were laughing.

His hands went wandering as the lust again overcame the giddiness and he lifted up her tanktop, freeing her huge breasts.

"Oh my fucking God," he whispered as he began groping them.

She giggled, then let out a little moan. "Oh that's...that feels nice."

Ellen climbed on top of him and tossed her shirt aside, then leaned down and started kissing him again. Their hands went all over each other as they kissed, and then her hand was pulling his boxers down, freeing his erection.

"Shouldn't we get on the-oh fuck…" he groaned as she mounted him, pulled aside her panties, and slipped him inside of herself.

"Holy fucking-*ah yes!*" she cried as she began riding him.

"Ellen, fuck, you're so wet!"

"Gabe, this feels *so* good!"

He lost all track of time inside of her.

It was definitely different. More intense. Overwhelming didn't seem like a strong enough word. All-encompassing, maybe. Being beneath her, ridden by her, pleasured by her was like standing beneath a tsunami during an eclipse.

Their lovemaking seemed to go on for a very long time.

When it was over, he was very sticky around his midsection.

"Oh…oh…" Ellen whispered, panting, her mouth hanging open. "Oh my God, Gabe, I made such a mess," she murmured.

"Me too I think," he said.

"Oh-ho yeah," she replied. "You definitely did…we need a shower. Oh! I bet a shower would feel amazing!"

"Why is it this fucking powerful?" he asked as they got up off the floor and headed for the bathroom.

"I think it's because A) we're probably both kind of lightweights, which is great, and B) it's been a long time for both of us. Also, from what I understand, edibles hit different than smoked stuff."

She turned on the shower and they got in. She immediately moaned and shuddered.

"A shower also feels fantastic…I love weed."

He laughed. "Me too. That sex was...really something else."

"Yes-oh! Gabe! We should order...food! Something-uh...tacos! There's this great taco place that delivers! I'm so fucking doing this."

"I want a burrito," he replied. He paused for a long moment. "Uh...shit, wasn't there stuff you were supposed to be doing? Your job?"

"I'm done with my work for the day and if I have more it can wait, although I really doubt there's more," she said. "And whatever, we need some time to ourselves."

Gabe nodded in agreement and then hugged her. She laughed softly and hugged him back, and they stayed like that for a long while.

...

"Hey...I got a question," Ellen murmured.

"Shoot," Gabe replied.

They were laying together in bed, naked after another shower.

It had been a long, exceedingly pleasant night.

After eating tacos and watching some cartoons, they'd ended up splitting another gummy, which might not have been the best idea, because after that everything became a little hazy. Less in the sense that they didn't remember it, more in the sense that time lost meaning.

They were finally coming back down to lower, more reasonable levels of stoned.

They'd had sex twice more.

"There was something you said to me, on the first night. You said everyone at the store was nice to me, but it was the way you said it. Like you were trying to make a point, but then we got derailed, and I keep wondering what you meant."

Gabe thought for a moment. "Oh," he said.

"...oh? That's it?"

"Well...you know, it's one of those things. I don't know...I don't want to seem petty."

"Tell me, I want to know. I won't get mad."

"All right. Basically...I have my own kind of 'fish in water' problem. Or, no, I mean, *you* are having that problem, for one of my issues. It's kind of a broader issue, and it's basically...I hate using this word now, because people have ran it into the fucking ground and now it's meaningless, but it still functions as it's supposed to, or it can: you have a position of privilege, in that if you're even a somewhat attractive woman, you get used to just about everyone trying to interact with you."

"That is *not* a privilege," she muttered.

"No, like, I get that you have guys hitting on you all the time and making it weird, I'm more talking about the everything else. I imagine it isn't hard for you to get people's attention, or you probably have people offering to give you things or help you with things so much that you don't even realize it's so common. It's your default. Unless you're a *really* attractive guy, people are way more likely to ignore guys, or be jerks."

He shrugged. "It's just, that was my point: everyone's nice to you. Or, well, not everyone, but it's way more common. Most people seem like they, at best, tolerate me."

"Gabe, you don't think that's a little ridiculous?" she asked.

He sat up and looked at her. "You don't think that's just brushing off everything I said?"

She frowned. "You're right, I'm sorry. I-it's harder to think when I'm stoned. I'm sorry, that was rude. But what I mean is, I think your view of the world might be tainted by bad feelings. In truth, I think what you're saying about me having niceness privilege makes sense. But I also think, most of the time, people just...aren't even thinking about most other people they see in passing or casually. I mean, do you? How much of your own shit do you have going on?"

"...you might have a point," he admitted after thinking about it. "It's hard to gauge. But yeah, that's what I was saying."

"Well, it's probably true, but honestly, there are sometimes where I just want to be left alone. Something you might not have considered is that a lot of the attention I get is people kind of just staring. I'm such a rarity that people just stare." She sat up suddenly. "Did you know I'm in like the ninety nine point ninth percentile for tall women in the US given that I'm six five?"

"Seriously? It's that rare?"

"Yep. I looked it up one day."

"Well...lucky me," he murmured, reaching out and cupping one of her breasts.

She laughed. "I'm beginning to suspect you like strange women. Like...you'd fuck a nine foot giantess wouldn't you?"

"Yeah, definitely."

"And a mermaid?"

"Oh yeah. Hard yes."

"Knew it. So you are what they call a monster fucker."

"They *do* call it that," he agreed, "and I guess yeah. I mean not really though because monsters aren't real."

"Yeah, it's too bad. Be absolutely wild to have a threesome with some kind of wild demon chick, or a dryad nymph? Any in particular you'd want?"

"A dragoness," he replied immediately.

She looked over at him. "...you've definitely thought about this."

"A not-insignificant amount of the porn I did look at involved monster girls, so yes."

She giggled. "A dragoness, huh? Are we talking about those girls who have scales and tails and maybe horns? Or a full on dragon like we understand them dragoness?"

"Either or. I mean, as long as the dragon is sentient, female, and we're able to actually meaningfully have sex, I'm down."

"I'm glad sentient was first on that list," she said, then suddenly yawned. "Oh, my. I'm...tired all of a sudden. Like *hardcore* tired."

"Same," he said. "Let's sleep."

They began shifting around, getting under the blanket and then, once that had been achieved, curling up together.

Gabe was asleep before he even began to think about it.

CHAPTER TWENTY TWO

Gabe came awake slowly, gradually returning to consciousness.

It was light. He heard rain. Everything seemed far away.

Except for the urge to piss. That was right there and almost painful.

With a groan, he threw the blanket back and got unsteadily to his feet. He had a vague fogginess around his head and his senses. The world was strangely distant. He headed into the bathroom and took a long, long piss.

It occurred to him that he was naked.

He normally didn't sleep naked. Had he taken his boxers off in the night or something? He finished and flushed, then headed back to his bed.

That was when he saw Ellen asleep, laying on her back, her breasts bare and out, the blanket pulled down to show them off. Her mouth hung open and she was snoring faintly.

"Right," he muttered.

For just an instant, he'd forgotten that he'd gone to bed with her. Let alone that they were dating. He sighed and rubbed at his eyes, trying to remember what else he might be forgetting. There was something, but he wasn't sure what.

Apparently edibles fucked him up.

He couldn't really complain, though. The sex had been fucking amazing. Honestly, all of it had. Even just sitting around with Ellen doing not much had been amazing. He could see why people were so obsessed with drugs.

Even just weed took the edge off...well, reality.

Ellen was out, and Gabe wanted to be there again. He couldn't tell the time of day by the quality of the gray light filtering in through his windows, but he couldn't think of anything that needed his immediate attention, so he climbed back into bed.

He fell asleep almost immediately.

Some time later, he opened his eyes again, feeling more awake and aware. Behind him, he could feel Ellen stirring.

"Shit," he heard her mutter.

"You all right, babe?" he asked.

She was silent for a moment, then laughed softly. "I love hearing that from you."

"What?"

"You calling me 'babe', I wanted it a lot...and I think I will be okay after a shower and taking a *massive* piss."

"I need a shower too," he murmured.

For a moment, they just laid there, and then finally Ellen got up and headed for the bathroom. He waited until he heard the shower start up before joining her. He started brushing his teeth.

"Oh...yeah. Tooth. Teeth brush. Um, can you bring my toothbrush and the toothpaste in here for me? I forgot," she asked.

"Sure."

He finished up, then did as she asked and joined her in the shower. She brushed her teeth while he just stood there and soaked in the steam from the hot water, slowly coming more awake.

"I'm still kinda stoned," Ellen said after she'd rinsed and spat. She set the toothbrush and paste aside on one of the few small ledges sticking out of the wall.

"Me too...hmm."

"What?"

"Something's bugging me, but I'm not sure what. Like I'm forgetting something."

"Do you have any jobs due today?"

He paused. "I don't think so, but I should double check...oh! Shit. *Your* job. It has to be late."

"Oh, don't worry, I called in sick."

"I'm surprised you don't feel weirder about calling in sick because you're high," he replied.

"If this was a year ago, I wouldn't have done it, but I'd have been sorely tempted. If this was five years ago, I wouldn't get high on a weeknight and even if I was feeling like this, I would've powered through it relentlessly."

"What changed?" he asked.

"My slow, gradual realization that everything the bitter cynics say about corporations is true. They don't give even a single fuck about me. If anything, those who employ me are actively disdainful of me a lot of the time. They hate that they can't just have slave labor. They hate whenever we have pathetic human needs like 'childbirth' and 'getting cancer' and 'a death in the family'. At some point I realized hard work is rewarded with more hard work and nothing else.

"Maybe you're too young to remember, but they always told us that hard work pays off. That if you really bust your ass in a job, go above and beyond, really shine and show a great work ethic, you'll get your reward of raises and promotions and bonuses. That was true at some point, maybe when I was growing up. But it's absolute bullshit now. You take on extra responsibilities now? They think 'oh hey here is a person I can exploit and give extra work for no extra pay!' and they laugh in their offices over the stupid ass millennials."

"Jeez, I don't think I really grasped just how much you hate your job," Gabe murmured after a moment.

"I do. I hate it. I bet you thought I love working, right?"

"Kinda, yeah. I mean, during our time apart."

"I don't. I mean, sometimes I like it in a sort of masochistic way? Sort of testing myself against something I hate, pushing myself, seeing how well I can do. But I don't. I hate it. I've been busting my fucking ass for twenty years now. Two decades. And what the fuck do I have to show for it?"

"Twenty...wait, you started work when you were fourteen?" he asked.

She sighed heavily. "Yes. I did. My parents owned this little crap hole in the wall restaurant and pretty much as soon as I started high school they had me work there. Off the books, of course. I'd wake up at six in the morning to prepare for the day, go to class by seven thirty, get out at two thirty, home for perhaps an hour at most, and then right to the restaurant until it closed. I usually got home at eleven. I had enough time for a shower and whatever homework I could get done. I worked Saturdays, too. Twelve hour shift."

"Jesus fucking Christ, that's straight up abuse, Ellen!"

"I know that now. I didn't then. My parents always laid on the guilt any time I complained that I had no life of my own. No friends outside of class. I did that for four fucking years. I have no idea how I survived, but I did. My parents were always telling me how they needed me, how I was so fucking ungrateful because I was so lucky to have parents who were so involved in her life. They could kick me out if they really wanted to. They tried to keep me from college, but I said fuck that and just got the hell out of there."

"I'm so sorry, Ellen."

She sighed heavily. "Yeah, so am I. It's whatever, though...how are you for parents? You didn't really talk about them."

"No contact. They can fuck off and die. My mom always screamed at me and told me how fucking stupid I was when she wasn't blackout drunk. My dad was really controlling. Always pressuring me into everything he felt like I should do and screaming at me and smacking me around if the mood took him. When I was younger, like still in elementary school, I got really fucking angry one day. I wanted to do something, he didn't want me to.

"He was already mad over something, I don't know what. But we had an argument and he told me to go to my room. I did, slammed the door, and then all of a sudden I hear his footsteps stomping closer really fast, and he throws the door open, and he shoves me into my chair, and he goes to my closet. He pulls out my suitcase and starts throwing my clothes in it. I kept asking him what he was doing and he didn't say anything.

"And finally he just points and in this really dead calm voice says 'Get in the fucking car, Gabe'. It was his 'don't argue with me or I'll absolutely lose my fucking shit' tone, so I did what he told me. My mom was passed out at this point. I got in the car and I started asking again where we were going and he told me he'd had enough, he was going to give me to the government for adoption, and I really lost my shit. Just started crying and begging and pleading. I'd never been afraid like that before and he drove for what felt like a really, really long time.

"Honestly, it couldn't have been more than twenty, twenty five minutes, but it felt like hours and hours, saying absolutely nothing beyond 'I've had enough of your shit'. And then finally he stops at this building and parks and gets out and opens my door. Looking back at it now, it was just like an abandoned factory or warehouse or something, but at the time it looked like the gates of hell. He told me 'get out, I warned you, now you can't come home ever again', and I started begging again and he stood there staring at me for what seemed like a really long time, and finally he shut the door and got back in the driver's seat.

"And he looked at me and said 'I'll take you back if you promise to stop acting up forever', still in that really angry voice. And I did, of course. Promise. And we went back home and every time I started 'acting up', as he liked to put it, after that he'd remind me of that little incident. Stupidest fucking thing is I brought it up when I was twenty, that was around the time I stopped even trying to be around my parents, and he started yelling at me, telling me I was lying, he'd never do something like that, like I'd just dreamed the whole thing."

As Gabe fell silent, he realized Ellen just staring at him.

A long moment passed.

"Uh...sorry if I brought the mood down," he said awkwardly.

Ellen stepped up to him suddenly and wrapped him in a hug, then kissed the top of his head a few times.

"Gabe," she murmured, "that's the most fucked

up thing I've ever heard. That's so fucking insane. Just...oh my God, Gabe, I want to just hold you and make you feel better."

"It's all right, Ellen," he replied, hugging her. "It's a really shitty thing that happened, and sometimes I still get nightmares about it, but I've pretty much buried it."

"Are you sure?" She paused. "Is *this* what's been bothering you since yesterday?"

"What? No. I haven't thought about it for a while."

"...something's bothering you, though." She pulled back and looked at him intently. "I thought it was the thing with Blake, and if it is, that's fine. I just-I have this feeling, this really strong feeling, something's bothering you."

"...oh."

"So there *is* something else bothering you."

"Yeah. Man, you're *really* good at reading people."

"Mostly I'm good at reading you, Gabe," she replied. "Will you tell me what it is, please? I want to help."

"I...don't know if you can, but I also don't want to be pretending like nothing's wrong and you being unhappy about it, so I'll tell you. It's...embarrassing."

"I don't care," she replied, then paused and sighed. "Sorry, that came out wrong. I mean, I want to help you even if you feel embarrassed, and I won't mock you."

"I know, it's just...it sucks to talk about. Let's, uh, finish showering."

"All right."

She still looked worried but they continued their shower, washing and then drying. Once their morning routines were tended to, they pulled on some underwear and then went and sat down on the loveseat together.

"I guess I should just get it out of the way," Gabe muttered. He sighed. "So, put bluntly: I'm feeling really insecure after going to your place."

"Why?"

"Your place was fucking amazing, Ellen. It had the most amazing view of the city, and it all looked brand fucking new, and your couch alone was worth more by itself than everything in this apartment combined. You are very clearly used to such a better lifestyle, with expensive things, and it's not that I think you're a mindless consumer whore or something, obsessed with money and appearances, but I can't deny that this is fucking poverty," he said, sweeping his hand to encompassing the apartment.

"Gabe...first of all, this isn't poverty," Ellen said, sitting up straighter.

"Your bedroom was almost bigger than this entire apartment," he replied.

"I know, but it doesn't matter." She shifted around in her seat for a moment, frowning. "How to put this? I'm not going to try and bullshit you: yes, it is taking some adjustment to change from my old life to my new one, and yes, at least some small portion of that is going from a midtown condo to a studio apartment. But Gabe," she took his hands, "I want to emphasize this: I don't care."

"I mean yeah, right *now* you don't. We're in the beginning of the relationship and everything feels great and–"

"Gabe," she interrupted, "you aren't hearing me. I appreciate what you're saying, I fully comprehend it, but you're wrong. Yes, I *am* extremely happy right now because of what you and I have going and the fact that it just started. But I really do mean it: *I don't care*. Yes, when given the chance, I intend to buy a nicer, larger couch. A bigger bed. A dresser for myself. But I've been chasing stuff my entire life, all right?

"And it doesn't make me happy. I know, it's incredibly trite and cliché: stuff doesn't buy happiness and all that bullshit. It's not completely true. I'd be unhappy if all we had was a shitty box spring on bare concrete, and I'd be happier if we had a king size with memory foam. But it's secondary to my relationship with you. Stuff is nice to have, but I am not making the same mistake I've been making for the past twenty years."

"Which is?"

"Chasing better stuff. I want a house, Gabe, a house in good condition that I can be happy in, and yes, I want stuff in it, and yeah, I'd prefer sturdier, nicer-looking stuff, but I got into retail therapy, as they call it, and it's horseshit. It's a never-ending chase for a temporary high designed to drain us of cash. All that stuff didn't make me happy beyond a certain point. That's my meaning. I want stuff and a place to put it, but I want experiences with you a whole lot more than that. And that isn't going to change...all right?"

He looked at her for a silent moment, then slowly nodded. "I believe you."

"Good...feel better?"

He considered it. "I do, actually. Yeah." He blinked a few times. "Still feel like I've got a mild hangover, though. Nothing really hurts, but everything's sorta...slow?"

"Yeah, same." She looked to the kitchen. "How

about we make breakfast and watch a movie or something? Or maybe I can watch you play something."

"That sounds like a really perfect day," he replied.

She laughed and kissed him, and they headed for the kitchen.

CHAPTER TWENTY THREE

"*Gabe.*"

He jumped in his seat, turning around in his swivel chair to face Ellen. She was sitting on the loveseat, a look of immense amusement on her face. Her face was reddened. Her eyes were wide and the smile she had was huge.

"...what?" he asked.

It was Thursday now. They'd spent the rest of yesterday doing basically jack shit, just lounging around and relaxing.

Having Ellen watch him play games was absolutely surreal. The last thing he'd been playing was a spacebound horror shooter called Deep Dark that he'd only just started before moving, so it was a simple enough thing to just restart so she could get the full benefit of the intro level.

All in all, a really good day.

Today had been back to business, both of them going back to work. Gabe had an assignment that had slipped his mind and he'd just managed to get it under the wire.

"You wrote porn about me!"

He continued staring at her, for a moment unsure of what she was talking about. And then, all at once, the penny dropped.

"Oh," he said.

"Yeah oh," she replied, looking more amused than ever. "When were you going to tell me about this!?"

"Uh...tomorrow, actually," he said. "I...how'd you find out?"

"Well after you gave me those initial erotic titles,

I burned through them pretty fast and I wanted more. I considered asking you for the files, but then I thought: He is my boyfriend and I should support my boyfriend. So I bought the rest of your library. I actually bought all of them, even the ones I read already. And I just now got to the most recent one and, like, a six foot six blonde with huge tits!? Obviously me. And the protagonist is obviously you."

"Uh...yeah. Are you mad?"

"Do I look mad?"

"No."

"Exactly! It's fantastic! And hot! I just..." She giggled suddenly. "I kind of can't believe I'm in a porn. Erotica...where's the next one?"

"Done, actually. I was going to tell you before I published it. Well, I wanted to know if it bothered you. I feel like...I don't know, casting someone in an erotica novelette series that I'm writing and profiting off of might be a little weird. Even wrong, maybe."

"It's not a bad instinct," she replied with a shrug, "but I think if you don't use specifics beyond basic physical characteristics or personality traits in it, then it's fair."

"Really?"

"Yeah. I mean, pretty much everyone masturbates to other people. Celebrities, coworkers, friends, absolute strangers we saw on the streets. Some of those people write smut. It makes sense that we'd write...well, fan fics about people who make us horny. Real or not. Especially those that left an impression."

Gabe chuckled. "Well, you certainly did that. Like, *intensely.*"

"Obviously," she murmured. "I'm not dumping on the previous work, but honestly? The most recent work starring me is noticeably higher quality, in terms of prose and pacing. And it's longer, too."

"Yeah. I just...had more ideas. The stories I've been writing averaged five to seven thousand words. When I started writing the trilogies, they edged closer to nine to ten thousand. The first episode of Tall, Blonde, and Beautiful ended up being fifteen thousand words, and I actually cut it."

"There was more?" she asked.

"No, more like, the first episode was going to end after another two or three scenes, but when I realized how long it was, I decided those scenes would make a decent enough intro for the next title that I just shifted it."

"You *have* to let me read it. It's done?"

"Yeah, it's done. If you're okay with it, I'm going to publish it."

"Yes! Publish it! Get it out there! I saw the reviews for it and people want to know what comes next for us!"

He laughed. "Us?"

"Obviously it's a fantasy about what would've happened if I was single and you worked up the courage to hit on me when we were working together. And...you nailed it. In that I totally would've let you fucking nail me. Which I believe I have proved adequately."

"Well...mostly," he replied.

"Mostly!? How much more do I need to fuck you?!"

"Probably a lot more," Gabe replied.

She laughed. "Uh-huh...well, I will definitely get on that. In a moment. There's another thing I wanted to talk to you about. Don't worry, not bad."

"I'm listening."

"So, do you remember me telling you I had two best friends at one point that are the only two people beyond you I may still trust?" He nodded. "Well, the one who's still here, Emily, uh...apparently I texted her while we were fucking torched. When she responded, I reexamined my memories of her and realized that the main reason I was reluctant to talk to her again was because, uh...we had a huge fight."

"Over?" he asked.

"Something fucking stupid. In the sense that she was pointing out that Blake was a douchebag, and, naturally, I didn't take kindly to that. We were both a little tipsy and...yeah, it was ugly. We've been texting, though, and I apologized for being such a moron, especially in light of recent events, and she was very forgiving. And, basically, uh...she wants us to come over for dinner tonight. So...you down for that?"

"Hmm. What's she like?" he asked.

"These days? I'm not completely sure. But back when I knew her a few years ago? Think trashy party girl who survived her trashy party girl phase completely intact and was going legit. The last time we saw each other, she was taking night courses and working as a stripper, and had moved in with this other woman who was a lawyer. She was...intense. We've been sort of tentatively texting and she seems like she wants things to be like how they were, and she misses me. And I think it'd be nice to be a little social and hang out with her."

She grinned suddenly. "And who knows? Maybe she'd be down to fuck."

"Seriously?" he asked.

"Yeah. She's really hot. I'd absolutely go to bed with you and her, or let her go to bed with you," she replied.

"I...yeah, we should hang out with her."

Ellen laughed. "I thought that would get your attention. She wants us over at her house for dinner tonight, four hours from now. I can tell her we'll be there?"

"Yes," he replied. Gabe stood up. "I'm going to go publish Tall, Blonde, and Beautiful Two and get to work on the next one."

"Ooh! Wait!" She held out the flashdrive he'd given her. "First, give it to me."

"You got it," he replied, grabbing it and heading for his laptop.

Once he had it passed back to her, he sat down and eagerly began publishing the next title.

...

"You nervous?" Ellen asked.

"Yeah, honestly. I haven't been social in any kind of official capacity for...a very long time. It's always been casual, or situations that were just thrust on me against my will. Roommates bringing crazy idiots into our place of residence." He sighed.

"This will be different. In a good way," she assured him.

"I know. That's what worries me. Your friends are all over thirty. We're a different species. I'm still a twenty-something, scraping a life together, trying to keep my head above water. And you guys are all established with nice houses and cars that are paid off and good credit scores–"

"Gabe, calm down," she said. "Honestly, I feel more like you than you think. I don't have any of that. Except for a car that's paid off. My credit score is embarrassing right now. And I have the impression that she probably got her shit together, while my entire life fell apart. But you know? I'm not scared."

"Really?"

"Yes."

"Why?"

"I have you."

He looked over at her. She was smiling as she drove them through the dark city. "Come on, really?"

"Yes! I mean it."

"Well, I feel the same way, so I guess I can't argue."

She giggled. "Good."

"I just hope I don't embarrass you," he muttered, flipping down the sunvisor and looking at himself in the mirror. He frowned, tilting his head and studying himself. "Are you sure I shouldn't have clean shaved? I mean I like the stubble look but, I don't know, isn't it looked down on high society?"

"Gabe!" She laughed. "Come on, fuck high society. And it's not like they're high society, whatever that even means. And I want you to look kind of scruffy. You're a writer, Gabe. People make a lot of allowances for writers. You look...kind of rugged. Tall, dark, and handsome. Besides, while I appreciate basic grooming and hygiene, I'd rather you didn't obsess over your appearance."

"Big relief," he muttered, running a hand through his hair.

He'd fussed over himself for a while, and then Ellen had come in and he'd put himself in her hands. He'd buzzed his facial hair down to stubble and she'd taken a moment to trim up his hair a bit, then mess it up just the right amount. He was wearing his only nice clothes: black jeans and a crisp, button-down black long-sleeve that she'd left unbuttoned, the plain black t-shirt he wore underneath visible.

"Trust me," she said when he kept looking at himself in the mirror. "It's a good look for you, Gabe. Black hair and black clothes against the pale skin. It's...striking. And turning me on."

"Maybe we should head back and fuck," he said, putting a hand on her thigh.

"Gabe, no," she said, smacking his hand and then laughing. "Bad boy. Not while I'm driving. And we don't have time. That would add another hour at the very least. We'll just have to hold onto it."

"That's going to be hard. You are...oh so tempting," he replied.

"I'm wearing jeans and a t-shirt and your hoodie," she said.

"Exactly...what?" She had started to frown.

"Does it bother you that I don't really wear makeup or do anything with my hair? I sort of gave up on it at some point last year and...I don't know. I know so many guys are just used to it..."

"I don't care, Ellen," he replied. "If you want to do it, I support and appreciate that. If you don't want to do it, I also fully support that."

"You're really that chill about it?"

"Yeah. I mean, I beyond really basic stuff, I don't put much effort into my appearance. I can't give you shit if you don't either. I mean, I wouldn't anyway, but yeah, I'd rather you be happy and comfortable."

"That...means a lot." She looked around as they pulled onto a residential street. "Wow, okay, maybe you were right about the high society thing. Jesus. These houses all look like not a single one of them goes for less than half a mil. Like, man."

"Your friend seems to have done well for herself," Gabe agreed.

Every house they drove past was three stories, new, and fancy. Every driveway had a minimum of two cars, all of them expensive and clean. They paid attention to the addresses and drove until they found the one they were looking for.

"Wow," Ellen whispered as they parked in the driveway behind a sleek black four door that looked like it had come off the lot yesterday.

"Sure you aren't feeling outclassed?" he asked.

"I mean I am, but I'm still happy that I'm with you...come on, let's do this."

They got out and walked up the driveway, then along a path that was lit by small blue lights planted in the ground to either side. They got to the front door and Ellen hit the doorbell. A moment later, the door opened up and a woman with two sleeves of tattoos curling along her arms and up her slim neck, bright green eyes, and black hair pulled into a simple bun greeted them.

"Ellen! Shit. It's been forever and you are still...an absolute presence," she said, and as she spoke that statement, Gabe found himself relaxing.

His limited experience with people from the upper class or even just upper middle class had rarely gone well. They often seemed to affect a kind of patronizing kindness, a manner of speaking that conveyed a sense of smug superiority, all while maintaining the plausible deniability of a veneer of false kindness.

Emily had none of that. Her warmth was authentic, her smile genuine, and Ellen's reaction seemed to convey a similar release of tension as they hugged.

"You still have a real way with words, Emily," she replied as they parted. "This is my boyfriend, Gabe."

"The writer," Emily replied, sounding at once both amused and intrigued as she offered her hand.

He took and shook it. "Guilty as charged. Nice to meet you."

"You as well. Come in, please. Abby and I are very close to finishing dinner."

"Don't think I didn't notice that ring," Ellen said as she and Gabe took off their shoes and hoodies.

"Oh, yes." Emily's eyes fell to the wedding ring on her finger and she shifted awkwardly. "I, uh, would've invited you. I was going to. But it was such a small gathering, and–"

"Emily...we should probably settle this here and now, so the rest of the evening isn't awkward," Ellen said. "I'm sorry I flipped my shit and screamed at you. You were right about Blake, obviously. I'm sorry."

"I forgive you, Ellen. And I kind of deserved it. I was...I could've worded it *a lot* better, and I didn't mean for it to be, but it was kind of an attack. I was just dealing with some other shit and I took it out on you, and I'm sorry, too."

"Well, I also forgive you, and I'm glad we're hanging out again. And congratulations on, uh, everything," she said, briefly looking around the house.

It was as nice on the inside as it seemed from the outside. They had come into an entryway that opened up into several other rooms and had a stairway. He saw a living room with an absolutely huge screen mounted on the wall to his left, a dining room with walls covered in book-packed shelves. From somewhere deeper in the house, he could hear what sounded like rock music playing.

Emily chuckled awkwardly. "Yes, we've gotten rather lucky. Why don't you two sit down and we'll bring dinner out. It's almost ready."

"All right," Ellen replied.

She and Gabe did just that, heading into the big dining room and having a seat. He tried to keep calm but he was getting awkward flashbacks to his older life. When he was growing up, his family sometimes went over to his uncle's place, and unlike his father, his uncle had been very successful. Doing what, he wasn't ever sure, but it afforded him a nice house and a nice car and a lot of expensive things.

There was always an air of tension whenever they visited, usually for what they laughingly referred to as a 'family dinner'. It was obvious that his father resented his uncle, and he soon came to fear those dinners greatly. Because afterward, his father would get piss drunk and angry. He'd usually break something and ended up ranting about one thing or another, whatever had earned his ire, whatever was the reason he wasn't as successful as his brother.

But there was enough distance between himself and that past, and he had spent enough time at least trying to sort out his emotions, that he could recognize he was just projecting those old echoes onto his present situation.

His father wasn't a part of his life anymore. This was not his uncle's house.

Ellen wouldn't flip her shit when they got home...ideally. He believed her, that she was happy with him, but he also still harbored his own paranoid anxiety about their current situation. His mind kept going back to just how fucking nice her condo was.

Everything was going to be fine.
Probably.
"All right, dinner's coming!" Emily called.

CHAPTER TWENTY FOUR

Dinner turned out to be homemade tacos and burritos, and tasted amazing.

He'd been envisioning some fancy and expensive yet probably bad-tasting meal that he'd have to suffer through when he'd been coming over, but good lord was this a relief.

The atmosphere only grew happier and calmer as they began eating dinner.

Emily's wife, Abby, turned out to be a mousy, petite blonde who would look like something of a pushover if she didn't have eyes of cold steel and a brisk proficiency to everything she did.

"So, you two...catch me up," Ellen said. "We last parted ways when you two were just getting serious enough to move in together."

"A lot happened," Emily replied. "Back then, Abby took me in as a, uh, fixer-upper girlfriend. Lots of potential but boy was I trashy."

"Oh my God, Em," Abby muttered, rolling her eyes before taking another bite from her taco.

Emily laughed. "Don't let her try to spin it some other way. She couldn't explain to herself why she was so turned on by me, but she was, and when it became obvious that I was at least trying to get my shit together and I was very, very interested in all she had to offer, she decided to take me under her wing and try to let me blossom."

"And here I thought you were just looking for a sugar mama and a free ride," Abby murmured.

"You would've given me one, if I'd asked," Emily replied, smirking into her glass of wine as she took a drink.

"Yeah, I would've," Abby admitted. "But we wouldn't have gotten married."

"True. As you know, I was trying to get my shit together. Only it wasn't so easy. But it got a lot easier when my sugar mama let me move in and offered to pay all my bills while I sorted my life out."

Ellen nodded. "Right, you were going to night school for...uh…"

"Accounting, actually. You inspired me. Only I found out that I hated accounting. After that I thought maybe I might want to be a computer expert, get into IT work. Only that didn't work out either. Finally, after another three failures, about a year ago I got into stocks, and discovered I have some kind of bizarre savant knack for it. We have this house because of my stock trading."

"Holy shit, seriously?" Gabe asked.

She laughed. "Yup."

"Allowed me to quit my job," Abby said.

"You're not a lawyer anymore?" Ellen asked.

"I am not. I am now a 'legal consultant'. What that amounts to is that I offer legal advice to people on the internet. I cover my ass with some protective clauses basically saying you can't sue me if you fuck it all up, but yeah, I've got a good rep now. A solid website. Charge a fee to answer questions. I have a reputation for being able to cut through the bullshit and give you not only an accurate answer, but one the average person can understand."

"That's awesome," Gabe said.

"It sure is. It's *so* much easier than my old job. I clock maybe a dozen hours a week of actual work. I'm making perhaps half my previous income, but with her stocks, it doesn't really matter. Hell, we just got back from a trip to the Bahamas last month." She paused. "...shit, am I bragging? I'm sorry, I'm not trying to."

"No, congrats," Ellen said. "For real. You and Em always struck me as a really good couple...what are you smirking at, Emily?"

"Nothing," Emily replied, taking another drink of her wine.

"No, I know that smirk. Come on, what is it?"

"It's just...I have something mean to say, but I don't want to be mean."

"I can take it," Ellen said.

"Maybe not the best idea right now," Abby murmured, vaguely uncomfortable.

"Really, I promise not to get pissed," Ellen said. "I mean, unless you're actually trying to hurt me."

"No! I'm not, it's just...okay fine. Look, Ellen, I love you but you always had the absolute shittiest taste in men. Every guy you ever dated was a Grade A asshole. And I always found myself thinking 'she'd be so much happier with the opposite kind of guy, like a writer or something'. And now...here you are, with a writer, who seems like a reasonable, chill, kind guy."

Ellen let out an explosive sigh. "Yes, fine, you are right. You bitch. I don't know what my problem was, but...yes, I'm with Gabe now, and it's so amazing, and I'm so happy."

"You do seem to be aglow with joy," Abby said, smiling a little.

"How did you two actually meet?" Emily asked, looking at Gabe now.

"We worked together for a few months several years back," he replied. "We took breaks together. Got to talking. Got along well."

"Interesting, so...I'm guessing you worked at

whichever accounting firm she was working at?" Emily asked.

"Oh no, this was when I was working for that grocery store," Ellen replied.

"Really?" Abby asked. "When did you work for a grocery store?"

"That was like four years ago," Emily murmured.

"Let me just get ahead of this," Ellen said, "our relationship is just going to seem weird. I had been laid off at the end of twenty nineteen, and out of a bit of anxiety I took a job running the money for a little grocery store. Gabe and I happened to take breaks at the same time in the same room, and we hit it off. Only reason we didn't start dating then was because I was already with Blake. We fell off after I left the job and then reconnected last week after my life collapsed into a smoldering heap."

"...oh," Emily murmured. "I didn't realize it was quite that bad."

"What actually happened? If you don't mind talking about it?" Abby asked.

She sighed and took a deep drink of the red wine she'd poured for herself, then paused. "Gabe, you cool to be my designated driver? If you say yes, I will *so* fucking drunk suck you when we get back to the apartment."

"*Wow,* Ellen," Emily said.

"Uh...yeah, sure," he replied.

"Blake cheated on me. For a month at least. And then called me a fat ugly whore when I found out about it and confronted him. I'm also probably going to get fired because my boss can't tolerate it when a woman actually stands up to him." She finished off the rest of her wine and began pouring more for herself.

"...oh," Abby murmured.

"Jesus, Ellen, I'm sorry. I didn't know it was that bad."

"Yeah, well, it sucks but what can I do about it? I'm doing my best to rise from the ashes. Honestly, I'm surprised with how well it's going. But a lot of that is admittedly largely thanks to Gabe. He's got real knight-in-shining-armor status."

"Do I now?" he asked.

She laughed. "Clearly. I dropped in on him, pretty much a crying mess, on the day that he moved into a new apartment, alone I might add, and he basically took care of me all night and the next day. Really, he's been taking care of me since then." She smirked suddenly. "I guess I've been taking care of him, too."

"*Ellen,*" Emily said, her amusement obvious, "you are...a lot different than I remember."

"A lot more unrestrained," Abby agreed.

"I'm sick and fucking tired of being restrained and buttoned down. I want...something different. And that's what's happening with Gabe," Ellen replied. "I'm tired of doing what I'm supposed to do all the time. It's never made me happy." She paused. "Sorry, this is getting heavy."

"I can relate deeply," Abby said.

"You can?"

"Yes. It took everything I had to become a lawyer. It nearly broke me. More than once. There were times I was positive I wasn't going to make it. But somehow I did. And even after I made it, it was still so much. Just so much all the time. The amount of times I have completely broken down sobbing in Emily's arms is honestly embarrassing. By the time the opportunity arrived to really quit, I was pretty burned out."

"Were you afraid?" Ellen asked.

"Oh God yes. Terrified. I was sick over it, sleepless, miserable. I was so scared that I was throwing away over a decade of work. *Hard* work. And I would lose everything I'd gotten. And that I would never be able to get a comparable job again. I'd lose my home, my health...yeah, I was terrified."

"It was worth it, I imagine."

"I'd say it was beyond worth it and more into the truly necessary territory. It saved my sanity."

"Huh." Ellen looked down at her drink for a long moment. She shook her head suddenly. "Anyway, ignore me. I'm here to eat tacos and have fun."

"And get drunk, apparently," Emily murmured into her own wineglass.

"Yes! Emily! I am! What of it? Or should I bring up that time you literally p–"

"Don't you dare!" Emily snapped, then giggled. "I will end you. I have a knife within my grasp."

"Mmm-hmm," Ellen replied, smirking back at her.

"So the time she what?" Abby asked, a small smile on her face.

"You aren't allowed to know!" Emily snapped.

"I'm your wife. Yes I am. Tell me, Ellen."

"No!" Emily yelled, trying very hard to look stern, and then completely ruining the effect by snorting and smiling. She sighed heavily. "*I* will tell you, if you *must* know."

"I must know," Abby replied with a shrug.

"Fine. A long time ago–and I want to emphasize it was a *long* time ago–I got really shitfaced and laughed so hard I pissed myself. But it only happened once."

Ellen snorted. "Right. Once."

"Shut the fuck up!"

Abby sighed. "Is that it? God, we've all done that, babe."

"Have we all done that?" Gabe asked, looking at Ellen.

She immediately reddened in the face. "No!"

"Oh don't *even* try to lie after you fucking dragged that out of me!" Emily snapped. "She *absolutely* has fucking pissed–"

"Shut it!" Ellen yelled, then started laughing. Emily kept staring at her with a huge grin on her face. She sighed. "Fine, yes. Just a few times."

"I have to say, I'm impressed, Gabe," Abby said.

"What? With what?" he replied.

"I can't imagine this is what you thought would pass for dinner conversation when you got invited over here. You're young, what...twenty two? Twenty three? And you're hanging out with us in our mid-thirties, reminiscing over getting shitfaced and embarrassing ourselves. You don't look uncomfortable at all. Most boys seem to have trouble keeping up."

"I'm twenty six," was all he could think to say to that.

They all laughed.

"Gabe is...different," Ellen said.

"How am I different?" he asked.

"You're a shitload more mature than we were at your age, and a lot more mature than most men in general. In my experience, at least," she replied.

"My experience, too," Emily muttered.

"I'm very glad I don't share any of your experiences," Abby said.

"Emily's bisexual, like myself, and used to date

men more than women," Ellen murmured. "And Abby is full lesbian."

"Well...ninety eight percent," Abby said, taking another bite of her food.

"What? What's that mean?" Ellen asked. "You told me–"

"I know. That was...before. I've never been with a guy, even casually, but let's just say that there have been some who have...tickled my fancy, as it were, and I haven't ruled out the possibility of at least giving it a shot."

"By it she means getting fucking railed by a flesh-and-blood dick," Emily said.

"...wait so how do *you* feel about that, Em? I mean, you two are married," Ellen replied.

"Yes, we're married. Happily so. That doesn't mean we're completely off the idea of inviting someone into our bed. I know it would make Em quite happy if I found the right man for some...fun. And come on, Ellen, how many high-powered lawyer type women have you known in the circles you moved in? You know we're absolute fucking freaks. I mean, fuck, looked who I married."

"Fuck you!" Emily cried.

"Later, sweetheart," Abby replied, patting her hand.

"Maybe we should talk about something...safer," Emily said after a moment of trying to compose herself. "Gabe, Ellen tells me you're a writer, what do you write?"

Ellen immediately began laughing and coughing into her drink, and Gabe did as well.

"Now what?" Emily asked.

"It's something freaky, isn't it?" Abby asked.

Gabe looked at Ellen. She finished wiping her

mouth off and cleared her throat. "It's up to you tell them whatever or however much you want, babe."

"Oh man, what the fuck are *you* into?" Emily asked. "I've got to know."

He chuckled awkwardly. "Well, I write erotica. But, just to temper your expectations now, it isn't anything crazy fucked up. It's basically just short stories about a guy hooking up with a woman. Sometimes two women. Really basic."

"It isn't basic," Ellen whispered.

"It's spicy, then?" Abby asked, an eyebrow raised.

"It's, uh...maybe a jalapeno," Gabe replied.

"It's a ghost pepper," Ellen replied.

"I *really* should read this," Emily said.

"I think Ellen might be a little biased because we are having sex with each other," Gabe replied. "It's, you know, pretty standard stuff."

"You're blushing," Abby said.

"Ha!" Ellen cried. "Not so fun, is it?"

"Has Ellen been doing a lot of blushing around you?" Emily asked.

"No," Ellen replied immediately.

"She really has," Gabe said.

"Shut the fuck up!"

"All the time. Especially when I'm pulling her panties–"

"*Gabe!*"

"Hey, *you're* the one who's all 'chill out, loosen up, talk about sex!', babe," he replied.

"She's blushing now!" Emily cried, laughing.

"I hate all of you," Ellen growled.

"Don't dish it if you can't take it, I thought you'd know that much," Abby murmured. "What's so spicy about your erotica, Gabe?"

He shrugged. "I really do think that Ellen's biased. Full disclosure: I've only recently started writing seriously. I've got a dozen short stories up on Ignition. They're selling all right, but nothing crazy, and the responses aren't particularly strong."

"That doesn't necessarily mean much," Abby replied. "People tend to not want it to be known that they're reading erotica, so they don't leave reviews on their public account. And Ignition only lets you have one account. So the same freaks that are reading and reviewing the Clean Christian Romance are also reading 'Slut Fuckers Five' and 'Gang Banged In Europe' and obviously don't want anyone to know that."

"Sounds like you have some personal experience with that," Ellen said.

Abby shrugged. "I read a lot of fucked up smut. So did all the freaky chicks I worked with. Guys watch porn, women read it. I care less about who knows what I'm up to, so I make sure to review, but yeah, keep that in mind. Also, you're just getting started. Few people blow up all at once. That you're getting a response and making money at all is a testament to your skill. Ellen is probably biased, but less so than you'd think. And who knows, maybe she isn't. Maybe you really are that good. I'd have to read it for myself."

He sighed. "Great, another person reading the fuck stories I'm writing and I get to feel really weird about that."

"You don't want women reading your erotica?" she asked.

"I didn't say that. It's just...weirder when I have to meet with the person face to face, in the real world, and we both know about my...job."

"Making women horny for a living is a really good job," Abby said. "Especially if you're effective at it."

"He's effective," Ellen murmured. "So very effective."

"I don't remember wine making you this horny," Emily said.

Ellen laughed. "I'm not horny!"

"That's a bald-faced lie if I've ever seen one," Abby replied.

"I...whatever. Let's just eat."

"Might as well. I was hoping to get a fire going outside, sit around for a bit."

"Oh, yes!" Ellen replied, perking up. "I haven't done that in forever. You ever do that Gabe?"

"Not really. I've never been around someone who had an outside fireplace."

"Fire pit is more technical, but yeah, it's cool. Very relaxing. You'll love it."

CHAPTER TWENTY FIVE

They finished dinner, and Gabe helped Emily clean up while Abby and Ellen went out back to get the fire started.

Abby said she didn't trust Emily to do, to which Emily had told her to go fuck herself, to which Abby had responded 'not while I've got you to do it for me'.

"So...you and Ellen seem *really* close," Emily said as they cleaned up the kitchen.

"I'd say that's accurate," Gabe replied.

"It's just...I don't know. I thought I would've heard more about you."

"Didn't you two stop talking two years ago?" he asked.

"Yeah, but before that. You said it was when she was working at the grocery store. That was four years ago. We were still talking pretty regularly back then. She *did* mention you, and I remember thinking that you sounded really nice. So different from the idiots she normally dated. And I say that with a lot of love. I think Ellen is a really, really great person. It's just weird that she knew someone like you for two years and just...never brought you up?"

He considered it, thought about what she'd told him. "She had her reasons," he replied. "We sort of cut contact after she got her new job. We hadn't talked in years before last week."

"So...she really just showed up out of the blue and you just...let her in and took care of her? Just like that?"

"Yeah."

"Why?"

"I trusted her, and she was my friend, and she trusted me, and clearly she was in a really, really bad situation. I just...wanted to help her and make her feel better."

"That's really sweet."

They finished getting the dishes washed and put in the washer and the food put away. Gabe looked out the window. There was a huge backyard out there, with a nice deck and, beyond that, a big fire pit that was now aflame with Ellen and Abby sitting by it, talking.

Emily came to stand beside him, looking out the window as well.

"I used to be scared of Ellen," she murmured softly.

"Seriously?" he replied, looking at her.

"Yeah! I mean look at her! She's this six foot six blonde goddess with *massive* tits and the face of a fucking movie star. She's hot in a way that it makes even straight girls question their sexuality. I knew she could take my girlfriend or my boyfriend from me if she wanted."

"Ellen would never do that."

"I know, but..." She sighed and turned around, leaning against the counter. She held up her wineglass and swirled around what was left inside, looking at it intently. "You never *know,* you know? I trust her, I always have, but...you never *know.* You can't. No one can. We can only simply trust and hope. There was a part of me that was relieved when she left my life after that big fight we had...sometimes I ask myself if I had that fight on purpose."

"Did you?" he murmured, surprised by her intense honesty.

She sighed, long and weary. "...no," she said

finally. "Maybe I was more reckless in how far I took it, but it came from the heart. Blake was a shithead. I hated him. Some women just aren't keyed to red flags, you know? But I am. You know...mostly. It's a lot easier to see bad habits and dark behaviors in people when you aren't dating them. Ellen was perfect in every way, I thought...and still do, honestly, except for her taste in men."

She smiled suddenly and looked at him. "But you seem to have finally broken her of that."

"You think I'm a good guy?" he asked.

"Oh yes. I'm very confident in that. You're just so different, and you've got good vibes. You seem like a good mix of chill and kind. I think Abby..." she hesitated.

"What?" he asked.

"Nothing," she said, and he was curious to find her blushing a little.

"Obviously it's something."

"No, it's...for a later time, maybe. Forget it."

"...all right."

She looked relieved. "Thank you. Come on, let's go join them."

As they headed outside, pausing to pull on some heavier clothes and shoes, Gabe couldn't help but reflect on how different this was turning out compared to what he'd expected. He wasn't sure he'd ever met anyone like Emily and Abby, and he wondered how much of that had to do with their age. They just seemed a lot less reserved, but at the same time their cavalier attitude didn't really come off as mean or careless.

If anything, it had been a pretty fun night so far.

They were more relaxed, and Ellen seemed to be as well, and that was nice to see.

It was cold out, and Gabe thought there might be more rain on the way, but that could just be wishful thinking. He ended up sitting next to Ellen, who took his hand as soon as he sat down. Emily sat down next to Abby and for a moment, then the four of them just sat there, staring at the fire.

"Hey, Abby," Ellen said, and she sounded a lot more subdued now.

"Yeah?"

"What made you quit? I mean, what *really* made you quit? I know we didn't know each other that well back then, but you kind of struck me as the woman who would be working her ass off even if she won the lottery. Also, I'm not judging. I'm really happy to see both this happening and it working out. I'm just...curious."

"I understand," Abby replied. "And I get it. I *was* that person. Honestly, I'd still be going, maybe with a lighter workload, save for one thing. It was really one thing that pushed me out, that made me walk away without regret."

"What?"

"The people. Specifically, the people above me. Except for my immediate boss, she was a good person. A bit of a hardass, but you have to be in that profession. But no, the other people. I mean, several of my colleagues to be sure, there's a reason the whole 'lawyers are trash humans' thing is a trope, but truly, the trashiest of humans were the ones at the top. It just became obvious that it wasn't *just* that they were after money at any cost, it was the...the *disdain* that they had for anyone they perceived as below them.

"The arrogance. The pettiness. The need to lord their social power over everyone they could. It blinded them. I saw forty year veterans of the industry making the dumbest mistakes or the cruelest statements just to let everyone else 'know who was in charge'. The abuse of power, and for what? Just to make some poor intern feel like shit. And God the sexism I had to endure. The 'jokes'. It was always 'jokes' with them.

"They'd never miss an opportunity to tell me I was wasted as a lesbian, I just hadn't tried the right dick, I hadn't been with a 'real man'. And HR? HR was *with them*. HR was there to protect *them*. It was a fucking joke to them. A newer lawyer who signed on caught the bad side of some of their 'jokes' and I happened to overhear the *actual* response from HR, which was, 'Hey Maggie, it's a joke, not a dick, so don't take it so hard, yeah?'. That sounds like bullshit, but it's what I heard."

"Jesus Christ," Gabe muttered.

"Yeah. I'd had a lot of practice getting vicious, so I got vicious with that shithead. I'd seen him flirting with one of the secretaries and I knew he was engaged and I figured there was a decent chance he had done something stupid with her at least once. So that was when I walked in, stepped up to his desk, and told him that he didn't do his fucking job or if I ever heard him say something like that again, I'd be calling his fiance and telling her about his little secretary on the side."

"Holy shit, what'd he do?" Ellen asked.

"Blew up, started screaming at me, getting red in the face. It caused a lot of fuss, people came in to see what the fuck was going on, and one of the higher ups pulled him aside because they had to at least pretend they were maintaining decorum. But that was just one of a hundred stories I could tell. I got a lot more savage as time went on. Gave a guy a black eye after he grabbed my ass at work. Honestly, a lot better than filing a report. Also 'accidentally' spilled coffee in his lap when he kept muttering slurs whenever I was nearby. Taught him to shut his fucking mouth.

"So yeah, it was the people. It was the realization that for a lot of them, money is a side effect of what they're really after. What they're *really* after is power, and the ability to abuse that power, to abuse people and get away with it. Bosses are evil, and anyone who says otherwise is naive, delusional, or a bootlicker."

"Man, that's intense," Gabe murmured.

"Am I wrong?" she asked.

"No. You aren't. I wish you were. But that's been my experience."

She sighed heavily. "That's been a lot of people's experience. And most of the population has to fucking put up with it because everything costs too much, and the majority of us are one paycheck away from literal homelessness. Oh, but it's a fair system and anyone can be rich if they just try hard enough!" She shook her head. "We were lucky enough to get out."

A long moment of silence passed.

She sighed and took a drink from her glass. "Sorry, not trying to bring the mood down."

"Hey, I know something to bring it back up," Emily said, perking up. "Ellen, Gabe, you two want to come to a party tomorrow? A friend of ours has a campsite rented out in the woods like a few miles from here. Everyone's getting together to just, you know, vibe out in the forest."

"Gabe?" Ellen asked.

"Yeah, that sounds cool," he replied. "Be nice to

go to a party that isn't insane."

"Yes. We would really enjoy that," Ellen said.

"Sweet. I'll text you the details. It should be around six tomorrow night, but it'll be pretty casual. If you wanna be popular bring some beers or maybe some weed," Emily replied.

Ellen chuckled. "We could probably do that. Sharing is caring. With the right people."

"We don't really hang out with the wrong people anymore," Abby replied. "Cutting negative shitheads out of your life is...health. And sanity."

"Big yes," Ellen muttered.

"Uh-huh," Gabe agreed immediately.

"You been doing some pruning of your own lately?" Abby asked.

"Something like that."

Ellen ended up shifting around until she was leaning against him, hugging one of his arms and resting her head on his shoulder.

"You two are a *very* cute couple," Emily murmured.

"Yeah?" Ellen replied. She yawned. "You sure the whole amazon giantess thing doesn't ruin the picture a little?"

"I'm sure, Ellen," Emily said, her tone growing more serious. Then she laughed softly. "I would've been *all* over you if I thought you were into me back in the day."

"Same, actually," Abby said. "...hopefully that's not weird for you, Gabe."

"Nope. It's a really nice thought to consider," he replied.

"If I'd been single...eh, I'd probably have still been scared of fucking up the friendship. It *is* a pleasant thought, though," she agreed.

Gabe felt a tension come into the general social atmosphere, saw Abby and Emily glance at each other meaningfully, and Ellen was looking at them too, then she looked at him. He kept expecting one of them to speak up, and Ellen looked like she was just about to…

But she didn't. No one did.

The moment passed and the tension released.

He thought about what it might be like to take Abby or Emily to bed with Ellen. Or both of them. A foursome with all three of them…

He let the thought go, or tried to. Probably wasn't the best time.

The four of them kept sitting there for a while, staring into the fire beneath the stars in the chill October night air.

…

"Hey, um...I didn't embarrass you tonight, did I?" Ellen asked.

"What? No," Gabe replied, glancing briefly at her.

It was hard to tell, but he thought she was still pretty buzzed. They were driving home now, and he was getting used to driving her car. It was a very smooth ride.

"Are you sure? You can tell me, you don't have to be nice."

"No, I'm not lying. That was really fun, actually. They're really cool. I enjoyed that. And you sure seemed to, for the most part."

"I did," she replied, then smiled a little. "I'm glad you had fun."

"What's wrong? Something's wrong."

"Eh, just...you know, a few different things. Probably shouldn't have gotten drunk. I get a little stupid when I'm drunk." She paused for a long moment, twisting her lips. "I feel kinda bad. I...cock-blocked you tonight."

"What? How?"

"...Abby floated the idea of a threesome with you, me, and Emily. I told her not tonight, but I'd think about it." She waited for a moment. "You mad?"

"No, I'm not mad," he replied. "It was a good call."

"Seriously?"

"Yeah. All three of you were varying levels of drunk. It's not really a decision that should be made while drunk. It's also...kind of early in the relationship. I mean, don't get me wrong, that'd be fucking awesome, but we...are figuring things out. And if you three still feel like...letting me fuck Emily in the future, well, there'll be more chances, I imagine."

Ellen looked over at him for another long moment of silence.

"What are you?" she muttered finally.

"What?" he replied. "What kind of question is that?"

"Sorry." She laughed suddenly. "I'm still tipsly, uh, tipsy. This is absolutely wild to me. If I had told what I just told you to *any* of the other guys I've ever been with, they'd be alternating between screaming at me for cock-blocking them and begging me to talk her into it. And you are...way too reasonable. Mmm. I just-you're so nice. I want to do nice things for you."

"And I appreciate that. But I want our relationship to work more than I want to fuck other women," he replied.

"You sure about that?" she asked. He glanced at her. "Sorry, that was rude. I was joking, mostly. It's just...weird. Appreciated, don't get me wrong, but weird...do you *want* to be monogamous? Shit, I never really considered that. I just assumed you'd want to bring other women into our bedroom..."

"Trust me, I *really* want to fuck other women," Gabe replied. "Especially if they're Emily or Abby. They were both really hot."

"Okay. Good. There's definitely a part of me what wants to watch you doing it with Emily." She grinned broadly, but then slowly lost it. "You sure you want to go to the party tomorrow?"

"I'm sure, Ellen. Why are you so worried all of a sudden?"

She sighed. "I'm kind of a bulldozer. Like I said earlier, I don't get taken seriously by too many people. And I learned I needed to be kind of a hardass to get respect. And after twenty years, it resulted in me...well, being kind of pushy without realizing it. And I don't want to be pushy with you. And when I'm drunk I get, uh, really emotional. And insecure. Which makes me wonder why the fuck I get drunk in the first place."

"You gonna be okay?" he asked.

"Yeah, I'll be fine. Also I lied a little, I know exactly why I get drunk. It unwinds me at first and also it makes me really horny. And I want to fuck you into a coma when we get home," she replied.

"And you're sure you're feeling okay?" he asked.

"Positive."

"Then let's get home."

CHAPTER TWENTY SIX

Gabe felt weird.

He sat behind the wheel of Ellen's car, navigating a dark, chilly cityscape, Ellen beside him, studying herself in the sunvisor mirror and touching up her makeup...and he felt weird.

Sort of dislocated.

"Are you all right?" she asked, giving herself one more look in the mirror before flipping it shut. "You're really quiet all of a sudden."

"I feel kind of off," he replied.

"Why? If you don't want to do this, I won't be mad," she said.

"No, I want to do this, mostly. I don't know, it's not bad off, just...weird off. I don't really do this kind of stuff. I never really have. The parties that I went to before, I mean, they mostly came to me, to be honest. They were inflicted upon me, because people had them at my place. I pretty rarely actually went to any. And when I did, it never went well."

"Why?" she asked.

"I'm shy, awkward, and weird looking," he replied. "I do not belong at a party, except to be fucked with and made fun of."

"I'm sorry, babe," she said, a little uncomfortably.

He glanced at her. "Are *you* all right?"

"Yeah, it's just...I'm not good with handling...stuff like this. I'm trying, it's just...honestly I'm really not used to men just saying stuff like that."

"Should I stop?" he asked.

"No!" she replied immediately. "Don't stop. It's-this is important. Us being honest with each other.

Honesty is sometimes uncomfortable and sometimes it's downright ugly, but that's a price I am very happy to pay if it means I have a healthy relationship. Because I am learning that the alternative, where me and the guy I'm dating never actually are vulnerable with each other or talk about our feelings results in a profoundly unhappy relationship that's very surface level. I don't *want* surface level with you. I want deep and meaningful. I want to take care of you like how you take care of me."

"I appreciate it," he replied, then laughed a little awkwardly. "To be honest, I'm not completely sure how to respond either."

"I guess we'll learn together...what I can offer right now is that I understand how you feel. I've had a lot of jokes at my expense, usually with how tall I am, and that just...really fucks my mood up. Guys can be stupid shitheads, but girls...can be fucking *vicious*. Especially if they feel threatened by you. But this should be a nice party. I trust Em and Abby. But if you feel weird about it, if you want to leave for any reason, just tell me, and I will leave with you, and not give you shit."

"You won't be annoyed?" he asked.

"No. You're more important to me than a party," she replied.

"Hmm."

"What?"

"I don't know, just...feels like a potentially bad road to go down."

"How?"

"You were telling me that you stopped going to parties because of an ex who didn't want to go and so didn't want you going. I'm just thinking about what it might look like if I decide I don't really like parties, and so I stop going, and you keep going, but maybe you feel weird about going by yourself, or maybe I feel weird about being left home by myself, and-it just seems like something that might build resentment. I dunno."

"You think ahead a lot, don't you?" Ellen replied after a moment.

"Yes. Curse of being a writer, I guess. You start learning to follow something through to its logical ends, likeliest course it'll take, worst case scenarios…"

"That must suck."

"It's useful, but yeah. But don't worry about me, I'll be all right," he replied.

"You sure?"

"Yeah. I just need to chill. I think I'll be doing better once we actually get there and I integrate into the atmosphere."

"You'll tell me if you want to go home?" she pressed.

"Yes, I promise. And you promise the same?" he replied.

"Yes," she said. "I promise." She stared at him for a moment longer, then settled back into her seat. Then she sighed and flipped down the sunvisor again, studying herself.

"Something wrong?" Gabe asked.

"It's just been a long time since I've really worn makeup beyond the bare minimum, and I'm paranoid I look stupid or I fucked it up."

"You look amazing," he replied.

She laughed softly and then flipped the sunvisor shut again. "I think you're a little biased."

"Definitely, but that doesn't charge the reality that you're an absolute fucking apex predator of beauty."

She sighed explosively and shifted in her seat. "Gabe," she muttered.

"Someone's blushing," he murmured, giving her a sidelong glance.

"No I'm not! Eyes on the road!"

He chuckled. "You get so touchy about blushing."

"So do you."

"Yeah but guys aren't supposed to blush. Society is a lot more forgiving when women do it."

She considered it. "Yeah, that's fair. Still annoying, though."

"I think maybe it's something else."

"What?" she asked, her tone a little provocative as she looked at him. She was in a certain mood tonight.

So was he, apparently.

"I think you're so used to fighting for dominance in every type of relationship that you've had that now that you've found someone you want to submit to, you're finding that it's a bit more difficult to submit than you thought."

"Oh really?" she asked, her tone even more combative now.

"Really. You'll put your foot down and I'll respect it, and you know that. But you're having some trouble with the fact that I could tell you to do something and you'd do it."

"Someone's awfully confident all of a sudden," she said, crossing her arms.

"As you so firmly pointed out: railing you should give me a hell of a confidence boost. So...touch yourself."

"*What?*" she replied.

"You heard me. Unzip your jeans and put her hand in your panties and rub your clit," Gabe replied. She stared at him for a long moment. They rolled to a stop at a red light. He looked over at her. She was staring at him, blushing fiercely now, breathing heavily. "Now, Ellen. Do as you're told."

She swallowed, then started shifting around in her seat and unbuttoned and unzipped her bluejeans. She shifted some more, then slipped her hand down into her white panties. She gasped loudly, then moaned and began squirming around in her as she started touching herself.

"Oh fuck," she whispered, breathing heavily, "I've never done this before."

"Keep going," he replied.

She moaned in response. He watched her for a moment, then turned his attention back to the road. The light turned green a moment later and he started driving again. The atmosphere inside the car had turned to pure sex as she kept fingering herself, moaning quietly and squirming in her chair.

"Gabe..." she moaned after a few moments. "I have to stop."

"No. Keep going," he replied.

"Please...Gabe, I'm gonna come!"

"Is that so bad?"

"Gabe! I'll make a mess in my pants! Please! *Ah!*" she cried, and he was fascinated by the fact that she didn't just stop.

"All right, you can stop," he replied, and she went slack in her chair, panting furiously.

"You fucker," she whispered.

"You could've stopped at any moment," he replied. "Why didn't you?"

"I..." She was silent for a moment, then zipped

herself back up and shifted in her seat, sitting up straighter. "I don't know," she admitted, laughing awkwardly, still blushing fiercely. She hunted around in her glove compartment for a moment until she came up with an individual wet wipe. Tearing it open, she wiped her hand down. "That was really fucking hot," she whispered.

"It really was," he agreed.

"I seriously don't get you sometimes."

"Why?"

"You talk about how you lack confidence, but that was probably the strongest display of confidence I've ever seen from you. You were *so* good at it. You just...made me do that. I don't know, I...I really wanted to do what you told me."

"That's pretty awesome."

She laughed. "Yeah, it is." A moment of silence went by. "Not to spoil the mood, but I did want to say thank you, for last night."

"What about it?"

"I know I was pretty drunk by the time we got home, but I still remember it. I know I was...annoying. And kind of argumentative. And you were trying to take care of me. I know that the only reason I don't have a real hangover today is because you made me drink water. I...am going to have to work on letting you take care of me."

"I think it would be nice if you did that, but I also think you thanked me adequately last night."

She laughed. "I give really good sloppy drunk head, don't I?"

"Yes you do. That was really, *really* nice."

"I'll have to think of something else to help make up for last night, though. I don't think I did an adequate job," she murmured demurely.

He glanced at her. She had that look again. That submissive look that held just the right amount of deviancy and playfulness.

"Yeah, I think you'll have to," he agreed.

Gabe had to admit, he never thought he'd really be participating in this role of domination in a relationship. He never thought he'd be doing it in a relationship with a noticeably older woman. He *especially* never thought he'd be doing it with Ellen.

Or that she would be into it.

Or, strangest of all, that it would feel so *natural*.

"I will be a good girl and find something for you," she murmured.

"You'd better," he replied, then followed their GPS and turned onto a gravel road that led into the forest on the north side of the city.

He had mixed feelings as he closed the distance between himself and a party.

The closest he'd ever come to a good experience was getting blown by that chick at a party years ago. Which was certainly a good experience. But besides that, it was just a whole lot of irritation, annoyance, and awkwardness.

He figured there was a very good chance that this would at the very least go neutrally, because he had Ellen with him, and he did pretty much trust Em and Abby. They both gave very good vibes. Although he wasn't sure how he'd react to their presence again now knowing for a fact that Abby had offered her wife up for a threesome.

Good lord did he want to fuck Emily, though.

He really had a thing for women with tattoos, and he'd be lying if he said he'd never fantasizing about having sex with a married woman.

For a moment he felt his mind drift back to his

responsibilities, trying to remember if he'd forgotten anything. It had been a busy day. Ellen had woken with a small hangover and he'd done his best to take care of her between doing more work on his assignments. He'd wrapped up what he had to do and gotten just a little bit of writing done for the third novelette in his Tall, Blonde, and Beautiful series. So far the numbers weren't in yet for the sequel, but he had some hopes.

Through all that, though, or perhaps beneath it, he'd been detecting something going on with Ellen. She seemed distracted. It was faint and subtle, and he'd dismissed it at first. But as the day had worn on into night, it not just persisted, but grew.

He thought she might be distracted by the thought of him and Emily hooking up. Was she regretting even bringing it up? Realizing she'd actually be very hurt and jealous if something happened between them?

Well, they could talk about it after the party if she wanted to. That was no doubt still a ways off.

No, he just needed to clear his head and try to enjoy himself. It had been a very busy, very stressful week. Or had it been, truly? He supposed not that much had actually happened, but that whole thing with Blake had sort of eclipsed the rest of the week and made it all seem stressful.

"There, number seven," Ellen said, pointing.

Gabe turned onto another gravel road and drove until he found a small parking lot where just shy of a dozen cars had already gathered. He could see a few dozen people spread out across a clearing in the forest where a bonfire was blazing.

"We ready?" Ellen asked.

"Yep," Gabe replied.

Ellen grabbed the bottle of wine and Gabe got the twelve pack they'd bought on the way over. He figured it was probably worth at least a few social points to help provide some booze. Or, at the very least, nice.

As they got out and headed past the collection of cars into the clearing, he began to get a feel for the party, and as he did that, he began to relax.

Emily and Abby seemed to be correct in their assessment. It was a very chill atmosphere. No one was yelling. No one was arguing. No one was fucking loudly somewhere nearby. As he looked around at the people gathered there in small clusters, talking to each other, he realized that just about everyone seemed to be around Ellen's age or older.

That had to be the difference. He'd been going to parties that twenty-somethings threw, and those always seemed to have the psychotic tempo of frat parties in bad teen comedy movies. Everyone seemed to feel like if you went to a party, you *needed* to get shitfaced, get fucked up, and find someone to hook up, very loudly, with. Also, getting into a fight and breaking some shit also seemed mandatory half the time.

It had never felt like his scene.

They walked over to a big picnic table that was covered in snack trays, a few coolers, and a pair of kegs, as well as a lot of plastic cups, silverware, and paper plates. They set their contributions on the table and then turned towards the rest of the clearing.

"All right," Ellen said, "let's find Em and Abby."

CHAPTER TWENTY SEVEN

They found Emily and Abby standing around the fire with a few other people.

They both smiled as they came up and Abby leaned over and whispered something in Emily's ear, which caused her to immediately blush intensely and whisper 'shut *up!*' hurriedly back to her. Abby just laughed.

"Everyone, you probably all remember Ellen," Abby said, "we're hanging out again. And this is Gabe, her boyfriend."

Gabe found himself being introduced to half a dozen people, trying to keep up with their names. He had never been particularly good with names.

"He's a writer," Emily added.

That got several interested responses.

"What do you write?"

"Are you published?"

"How much are you making?"

"Let me just temper expectations now," Gabe replied, raising his hands. "I'm full on indie, I've only recently started getting actually serious about my writing, and I don't have a whole lot to show for my efforts right now."

One of the guys, shit, was his name Brad? Something with a B, asked, "What does indie actually mean?"

"It means I do everything completely on my own at this point."

"Wait, like, everything?" one of the women, Margo, asked.

"Yeah, everything. Editing, formatting, cover art, marketing. Well, not marketing, that just doesn't get done. And really, right now, I've only got a dozen short stories out."

"What do you publish through?" she asked.

"Ignition."

"What do you write?" someone else asked.

"Uh...romance," he replied, and Ellen, Abby, and Emily all laughed.

"So obviously not quite romance," Margo said.

Gabe looked around, considering the situation.

"You don't have to tell if you don't want to," Ellen murmured.

"Eh, fuck it," he replied. He'd spent a long time hiding a lot of aspects of his writing, especially the fact that he'd spent a long time writing fan fiction. "I write smut. Erotica."

"Whoa, nice," Margo said. "That takes guts. Especially as a man."

"Why do you say that?" one of the guys asked.

"Writing and reading novels is largely a woman's place, especially romance and erotica. It's mostly written by women and read by women. Although," she paused and looked at him, "are you using a female pen name?"

"No," he replied. "Though I was advised to."

"It'd make sense," she said. "But also, well, society tends to shit on guys writing romance, let alone guys writing erotica. So, bravo."

"Thanks," Gabe replied. "Although it won't really matter if it doesn't take off."

"You'll still have done it," she said with a shrug. "But I can understand the sentiment."

"How did you two meet?" someone asked. "From what I remember, Ellen tends to date, uh..."

"Douchebags?" Emily murmured into her drink.

"Em!" Abby whispered.

"I am *never* going to live that down, huh?" Ellen asked, rolling her eyes. "Yes, I had shit taste in men before. As for my amazing lover here, Gabe, we met at a grocery store…"

…

Time passed in the dark forest clearing lit by flickering firelight.

Gabe talked with a dozen different people and found himself slowly relaxing. He'd been tensed and kind of wound up in the very beginning, but something he was finding was that pretty much all these people were pretty chill and reasonable. Except for one guy who seemed intent on getting loud and drunk, and his wife had apologized after a while and they ended up leaving.

After a few hours, Gabe found himself sitting on the hood of Ellen's car with Margo, the woman who'd been asking about his books. She'd found her way back to him, evidently interested, though it became obvious why after she revealed she was a struggling author as well.

"So…I've got a blunt question for you. Don't answer if you don't want to. But how much have you earned this month?" she asked.

"About six hundred," he replied. He'd finally given in and checked his sales through his phone during the party.

"Shit, really? Off a dozen short smut stories?" she asked, incredulous.

"Well, baker's dozen now. I just published another one really recently. But yeah. Why?"

"Shit, man. Fuck. I've written four novels so far. I got started late last year, pulled two of my trunk novels, cleaned them up, put them out there. I'm thirty six now. I gave it a serious go about a decade ago, you know, getting published the traditional way. I even had an agent. But nothing ever happened. I tried for years, finally gave up. I don't really know what made me try again last year...I guess desperation. I hate my job so fucking much."

She sighed heavily and reached into hoodie pocket, fished out a cigarette and lighter. "You mind? You want one?" she asked as she stuck it between her lips.

"No on both accounts, but thanks," he replied.

She grunted and fired it up, sighed heavily and blew out a puff of smoke. "I've written two more books this year, but I'm lucky if I string together a hundred bucks in a month. You must be good."

He shook his head. "I don't think I am, really. I mean, I can't tell, but I think it's more just that people love reading erotica. I think there's this huge need for it. But also I did my research beforehand. There was a lot of practical advice I managed to soak up."

"Like what?"

"Markets. Markets are everything. It's something no writer really wants to hear, but that's only because they hear 'you need to sell out and write what's popular', but that isn't really true. Not completely."

"What does it mean then?"

He sighed, considering how to articulate the idea. "It's more like...you need to find the type of narrative you enjoy telling, and, ideally, your favorite genre, but maybe your top three, then study the shit out of it. What covers are dominating the charts. What types of narratives are selling. Is first or third person doing better? How long is the typical work? How long between releases? Cover art is a big one, though.

"I think I could be doing a lot better, but I don't have money for more proper cover art. Basically...from what I've heard, you want to find out the primary thing that people show up for in a given sub-genre. You really want a sub-genre to operate in. Fantasy is too big a genre. But gaslamp fantasy? Steampunk fantasy? Dark fantasy? Much more manageable, although even still, expect stiff competition."

"After all that, then what?" she asked.

"Write and write hard. And fast. People want good books, but all the old hands I've asked or seen interviewed say they want faster more than they want better..." He paused, realizing that Emily was staring at him intently from across the clearing, a strange smile on her face.

Looking around, he saw Ellen talking to Abby not too far away. Both of them saw him looking at them and they each flashed him the same devilish smile.

Now what the fuck were they up to?

"And that's it?" she asked.

He shook his head. "No," he replied, coming back to the conversation. "It's also persistence and luck. A lot of luck. But, you want my most practical advice?"

"Yes."

"Figure out what type of smut you find hottest, make sure it doesn't break any rules, and start writing the shit out of it. If you've been writing for years and years, you should be good enough to make at least *some* money from erotica."

"Huh...all right." She hesitated for a moment. "Sorry if I just like railroaded you with that conversation. I'm...kinda desperate."

"It's fine. Honestly, I am too, so I really get it."

"Emily *really* looks like she wants to talk to you. I should probably make room. Thanks for talking with me."

"Not a problem. Good luck."

"You too."

As soon as she stood up and walked away, Emily began walking over. She was swaying her hips a little more than seemed natural and her smile was very...friendly wasn't quite the right word, but he took it as a positive thing.

"Hey you," she said.

"Hello," he replied. "What's up? Everything all right?"

"Everything's fine," she murmured, running her finger around the rim of her cup. "So...you've been eye-fucking me all night."

After a slight pause, Gabe relied: "I could say the same about you."

He wasn't sure if that was true, but it sounded like the kind of thing he should say. Or, anyway, it sounded like something someone more confident than him would say. It seemed to work. She just smirked into her cup.

"Maybe," she said finally.

"Are you drunk?"

"No. I'm a little buzzed. Why?"

"Just...curious."

"Hmm." She reached out suddenly a traced a finger across the back of his hand. "You're pretty cute, you know?"

"Evidently," he replied.

"What do you think of me?"

"That you're hot as hell, but I thought that'd be obvious. Your tattoos are *so* fucking hot."

Her smile broadened. "You like my tattoos?"

"I love them," he replied. "They look so kickass and hot."

She giggled and shifted around a little. "A lot of guys tell me my tattoos are trashy or ugly."

"They're idiots. And rude."

"I thought so, too." She hesitated. "You wanna fool around in my car?"

"I would *love* to do that, but I need to speak with Ellen about this first." He paused. "Is this authentic?" he asked suddenly.

"What do you mean?"

"It's just...you told me yesterday that you were once scared of Ellen being able to steal anyone you were dating. Does this have anything to do with that, or are you really into me?"

"Man, Ellen was right: you're pretty sharp. Yes, I'm really into you. I'm not doing this to piss Ellen off. God, that'd be so fucking stupid. Besides the fact that I'm still kind of scared of her, Abby would kick my ass. She respects Ellen a lot. No, I just really think you're a cutie and it's been a really long time since I've done anything with a guy and you...really do it for me. And Abby said she was cool with us, you know, fooling around. Ellen seemed cool with it, so..."

"All right, if you're sure," he said, raising one hand and motioning to Ellen, who was still watching him with Abby.

"I'm sure," she replied.

Ellen just smirked at him and mouthed *make me.*

Gabe felt himself flush with abrupt, frustrated lust. This was going to become a thing with them. It was absolutely going to become a thing.

"Get the fuck over here right now if you know

what's good for you," he said in a low voice, staring right at her.

He wasn't sure if she could read his lips, but he imagined she got the gist of it. Her smile broadened a bit more and she began walking over with Abby.

"Oh my God...how did she hear that?" Emily muttered. "And how did you get away with saying that to her?"

"Ellen...*really* likes me," he replied.

"Apparently, man. That's...hot."

"Glad you think so.

Ellen and Abby came to stand before him.

"What's *so* important?" Ellen asked.

"Keep it up, see what happens," he replied. Both Abby and Emily looked deeply amused. "Emily here would like to fool around with me. I want to know if you're okay with that."

"I'm okay with it...so long as I get to watch said fooling around," Ellen replied.

"Abby?" he asked.

"She wouldn't have done this without my permission, but I appreciate that you are seeking it. Yes, I've sanctioned this little...event," Abby replied.

"Well?" Emily asked.

"Let's go," Gabe replied.

"Perfect! Come on!" She took his hand and started guiding him back towards the cars.

"What exactly does 'fool around' actually mean?" Ellen asked.

"You know: some kissing, some groping. My tits are definitely coming out. And maybe...other things."

"What other things?" Ellen asked.

"Maybe I'd like to see what else I can do with my mouth."

"I think Gabe would also like to see what else

you can do with your mouth," Abby murmured.

"I know for a fact he wants to see that," Ellen said.

"Well then, let's get to the car."

CHAPTER TWENTY EIGHT

Gabe's heart was hammering now and his desire had turned into raw lust. He had a steel hard-on by the time they found Em's and Abby's car. It was a sleek dark blue van with, apparently, a lot of room in the back. The trunk popped open as Abby hit a button on her keyring and revealed they'd put the backseat down over the trunk space, giving them a lot of room to work with.

"You planned this?" he asked as they began climbing in.

"More like hoped," Abby replied.

"Why? Not that I'm complaining," he added quickly.

"Em has a crush on you and I don't mind sharing if it's purely physical. I've got a little bit of a thing for watching her with other people," Abby replied with a shrug.

"Can we also talk about that later?" Ellen asked.

"Yes, Ellen," Abby replied, pulling the trunk door shut behind them all.

Gabe tried not to freak out.

This was something he'd fantasized about a lot. Although it was safe to say that he'd fantasized 'a lot' about several different things. But this was really going to happen, right here, right now, and Ellen was here with him.

He glanced at her, trying to get a read on if she was actually uncomfortable and just doing this for his benefit or maybe even lying to herself about she really felt. But she looked pretty enthusiastic. And now that he had seen her drunk, he could tell she was pretty much sober.

"So, uh...how do we start? I've never, um, done this before," he asked, feeling the confidence he'd been trying to build tonight fading in the face of an actual woman wanting to do sexy things with him.

Emily giggled. "You've never made out with a chick before?"

"No, I mean, I've never done stuff with another woman while...my girlfriend was watching," he replied.

"Can I get a video of this?" Ellen murmured. "Or at least a pic?"

"Abby?" Emily asked.

"I don't care, just keep it to yourself," Abby replied.

"Don't worry, I know better. Gabe?"

"Yeah, go for it," he replied, rapidly becoming insanely distracted as Emily started pulling her hoodie off. She wore just a thin t-shirt beneath it, her nipples obvious through it, and then her t-shirt was coming off.

"Take yours off too," she murmured.

He began to say something, then stopped himself and began taking his shirt off. Emily had some really nice tits. Nice teardrop shape, pale, vividly pink nipples. She had a metallic flower tattooed partially onto her right breast.

"Holy crap," he said, setting his shirt aside.

She laughed. "You like them?"

"Duh."

"Boys are easy," Abby murmured.

"I can't really disagree. Tits kind of make everything better," he replied, reaching up and cupping them.

Emily let out an exhale of what seemed like satisfaction as he began feeling her up. She leaned in.

This was it. This was a thing that was really going to happen.

Her lips met his.

She tasted vaguely of alcohol, but mostly of something sweet and kind of fruity. It was a really good taste, and his mouth was flooded with it as she moaned and slipped her tongue in. He moved his forward to meet hers and then he was making out with her.

He was groping and making out with his girlfriend's hot married friend, in the back of a car at a party.

This definitely didn't seem real.

But he was lost in the moment. Lost in her sweet taste and soft breasts and wonderful lips and probing tongue…

They seemed to make out for a while, eventually hugging each other intently and then laying down on the floor of the van, rolling around a little as they kept kissing.

And then Emily came up for air, panting. She pushed some of her dark black hair out of her face and then thrust her hand back and said, "Hair tie."

"You going for it?" Ellen asked, passing her one.

"I'm going for it, girls," Emily replied, quickly and efficiently pulling her hair into a ponytail.

"Going for what?" Gabe asked.

"Putting your dick in my mouth," she murmured with that sultry smile of hers.

"Oh, wow, okay," he muttered as she began undoing his pants.

"Get settled," she said, laying down on her stomach. There was just enough room for her to do so in the back of the van. He sat down with his back to one of the front seats, watching her intently as she got his cock out.

He noticed, with highly distracted interest, that his anxiety wasn't really creeping up. Showing his cock to another woman, let alone two, while his girlfriend was watching, practically in public, *while being filmed*, should have made him extremely anxious.

But it didn't.

He was hard as a rock as she pulled him out of his boxers.

"It has been a while," she whispered, then licked up along the length of his shaft and dragged her tongue in a swirl around his head.

"Haaa….shit, you clearly haven't lost any skill with your tongue," he muttered.

"She really hasn't," Abby said. "She went down on me last night and oh my, the orgasms."

"Speaking of orgasms, can I come in your mouth?" he asked.

"Mmm-hmm," Emily replied.

"She said 'I'll suck him dry and swallow everything'," Abby said, laughing.

"Wow, you're such a slut, Emily," Ellen said. Emily flipped her off as she slipped his cock into her mouth. "Don't tempt me," Ellen murmured.

"Holy shit," Gabe muttered as she started bobbing her head, her lips slipping up over his head warmly and wetly again and again.

She lavished him in pleasure with her wonderful mouth and the experience became only more surreal as the seconds ticked by and disappeared into the void of bliss. He found himself putting his hand over the back of her head, and then gripping her ponytail.

"I do the same thing," Abby murmured.

"Fucking-ah man, this is *really* fucking good,"

Gabe panted as she kept going.

"Keep going, Em, you've pretty much got him," Ellen said.

Ellen had been learning to read him, too. He was really close and she could see it, either on his face or in his body language. And Emily was *so* good at what she was doing. The pleasure was building, washing through him.

She kept working him until he popped. It happened suddenly, powerfully, and he gripped the back of her head, a groan escaping him as he started to orgasm. She made a satisfied sound and kept on sucking, working his shaft with her fingers.

Emily did exactly was she'd said she would. She sucked him dry and swallowed everything, and it was a beyond captivating experience.

"Fuck!" Gabe gasped as he went slack and she finished up.

She laughed, wiping her mouth with the back of one hand while holding the other out. "Yep. I'm that good," she said.

"Here, babe," Abby said, passing her a cup.

"Thanks. The taste doesn't really agree with me," Emily murmured. She laughed after taking a drink. "My mouth seems to agree with you, though."

"So very much," Gabe murmured.

It occurred to him, suddenly, that his dick was still out and that there was now photographic evidence of its existence.

He found that he didn't care nearly as much as he had not all that long ago. He'd always thought of himself as an odd one out, because every guy seemed so damned eager to take a picture of their dick to send to some chick who didn't want it.

That particular urge still wasn't with him, but

after being with Ellen...

He did actually feel more confident.

"How'd it look?" he asked as he tucked himself away and began fixing his pants.

"Incredibly hot," she replied.

"Good then. Hopefully part two will look as good," he replied.

"What part two?" Emily asked.

"Take your pants off and I'll return the favor," Gabe replied.

"Oh shit, really!? Awesome." She quickly finished off her drink, then passed her cup back to Abby and began undoing her pants. "Let's fucking *go,* dude!"

...

"You look really happy," Ellen murmured, breaking the peaceful silence that had settled over them.

"I feel pretty damn happy," Gabe replied.

He waited for a moment, staring into the faint remnants of the fire, wondering if Ellen was going to speak up.

After he'd gone down on Emily, (which she had found very gratifying), they'd gotten back to the party, lest they be missed.

Though from some of the looks, at least a few people knew or at least guessed what they'd slipped off to do.

After that, there'd been another hour or so of conversation. Mostly people asking him about his writing or Ellen about her life. Neither he nor her seemed too keen to talk on either subject, for the most part. He still felt embarrassed that he had just barely a dozen short stories to his name, and Ellen was still grappling with everything that had happened.

Ultimately, they'd ended up in comfortable seats by the fire, chatting with each other for a while until they'd both fallen into a long silence. Almost everyone else had left at this point. There were just three cars remaining in the lot from what he could see, and one was Ellen's, and another was Emily's and Abby's.

The two of them were over talking to the only other remaining couple, hanging out in front of Ellen's car. He suddenly wondered if they were giving them space. Once they'd sat down together at the fire, no one had talked to them save to say goodbye.

Ellen didn't say anything. He felt a small worry that had been growing ever since his time with Emily grow a lot bigger.

Well, time to put that newfound confidence to use and actually speak up.

"What about you? You look...pensive," he added.

She smiled without looking at him, still staring at the dying flames. "Pensive, that's a good word." She paused for a bit, slowly losing her smile. "I'm...distracted," she admitted.

"By what?" he asked.

"I kind of want to wait until we get home to talk about it."

"...is it what I did with Emily?" he asked.

She looked at him suddenly, startled. "Oh shit," she said, sitting up straighter. "Fuck, it does seem like that, doesn't it? No, I'm totally cool with what happened between you and Em. Trust me. I'm not upset about that at all. It's...complicated. I'm not mad at you. It's-this is a me thing."

He felt a lot of relief flow into him as she said that, but it wasn't long lived.

"Are *you* all right, though?" he asked.

She smiled and reached out, taking his hand. "Yes. I'm all right...for the most part. Please try not to worry, Gabe. I'm happy. This was a really great night. I'm having fun."

"Me too," he agreed, deciding to just do what she wanted.

Whatever it was that was bothering her, she clearly wanted to wait to talk about it. He could live with that, and he understood the feeling of wanting to just put off a bad thing while you're still trying to enjoy yourself.

It was intruding on your enjoyment, but it would intrude a whole hell of a lot more if you actually had to talk about it.

They both looked over a moment later as they heard approaching footsteps. Emily and Abby were joining them and the couple they'd been talking to were driving away now.

"How are you two doing?" Emily asked.

"Sleepy, feeling good," Ellen replied and Gabe agreed.

"So..." Abby said. "You went down my wife...after she went down on you...how do you both feel about that now that some time has passed?"

"I'm still horny," Ellen replied, making them both laugh. "But for real, I'm all right with it. I'm happy. It looked pretty enjoyable."

"Oh my it was," Emily murmured.

"I'm the same. I feel kinda...I think I feel weird about it, but not on purpose, if that makes sense?"

"I think that's your brain freaking out a little because we've been conditioned by society to never do what we did in the back of that van," Ellen said.

"That's understandable. I thought it would be a good idea to check in with you both. Emily was actually low-key freaking out a little earlier," Abby replied.

"I was not!" Emily snapped.

"You so were."

"Why were you freaking out?" Gabe asked. "I didn't do anything stupid, did I?"

"No," Emily replied immediately. "God, this is exactly why I didn't want to say anything. No, Gabe, you were fantastic. I just feel guilty, for no fucking reason. My brain just is all like 'holy shit Em you just fucking cheated on your wife with some dude a party!', but the rest of my brain then responds, 'Yeah and she was fucking watching and consenting, why the fuck am I freaking out about this, it isn't cheating?' For real, though, that was fun."

"So we're all good then?" Gabe asked.

"Very good," Abby replied. "Believe me, I would not have let you even hold her hand if I had a problem with you eating her pussy. You're a good guy, Gabe. It seems like Ellen finally got it right." She paused, then a look of mild horror passed across her face. She sighed heavily as she glanced down into her cup. "I'm sorry, Ellen that was mean. I'm a little drunk."

"I thought you were the designed driver tonight," Ellen said.

"I was, but then I wanted to get drunk, so Em sobered up."

"Don't worry, I didn't drink that much and I've been cut off for about two hours now," she said.

"All right then...and it's fine, Abby. I mean, you aren't really wrong, it seems," Ellen replied.

"It was mean, regardless," Abby replied. "I just...was very frustrated with your relationship choices because I respect you so much and just...but it doesn't matter. I'm just glad you're happy."

"Me too." Ellen stood up. "We should probably be going. I feel like we're keeping your here."

"We were waiting on you," Emily replied. "Not going to leave you here alone."

"Same to you then," Ellen said. "Let's all get out of here."

Gabe got to his feet and they took a moment to put the fire out, then headed back to their cars. They hugged each other goodbye, and Emily gave him a kiss on the mouth, which he still wasn't a hundred percent on how to feel about, though he enjoyed it a lot, and then they got into their cars and began driving home.

CHAPTER TWENTY NINE

Gabe tried to contain his worry as they drove back to the apartment.

Ellen was clearly extremely distracted by something. She said nothing and looked out the window. She seemed worried. He was beginning to wonder if something had happened that he'd missed, but what?

He believed her about Emily, and he'd been with her basically the entire time. Maybe there'd been someone there who had upset her just by being there, someone she'd had a shit past with. Or maybe she was just in a bad mood because she'd been cheated on and her she was going to get fired. That was entirely possible.

Gabe was intimately familiar with the fact that sometimes bad moods just hit you, and sometimes in the strangest of places.

Somehow, though, they made it home.

They got out of the car and headed into the apartment. As soon as they were in, Ellen walked over to the bed and sat down on the foot of it, still frowning and looking down.

"Can we talk now?" he asked as he joined her.

"Yes," she replied, then said nothing for a few moments longer.

"Are you angry?"

"What? No. Gabe, I told you I wasn't," she replied, looking at him now.

"You said you weren't angry about Emily," he said. "Not necessarily that you weren't angry."

"Wha-Gabe! Come on, you said you trusted me to tell you if I was angry."

"I do, just...we're both humans. And humans are...rarely truly rational. I trust you, Ellen, it's just...I'm always preparing for the worst."

She sighed. "I guess I can't blame you for that. I do the same." She took a deep breath and let it out slowly. "Okay, so, I need to talk to you. About my...career."

"Uh, okay. I'm listening," he replied.

"I told you that I'm going to get fired soon. And so far, this week has just reconfirmed that notion. The amount of my work is less than before, and communication is almost nonexistent. Today, I tried logging into something I used to have regular access to, but it said my credentials had been revoked. They'll be locking me out of more stuff. I think I'll be lucky to last the rest of the month."

"All right," he said when she stopped speaking for a bit, "but we planned on this, right?"

"Yes. I was up front with you about this possibility. The thing that I haven't been up front about, to you or to myself, is that...I don't want to go looking for another job. I want to just be free of work, at least for a while. And I need to know how you feel about that."

Gabe wasn't sure what to say at first. So *this* is what had been upsetting her. He understood that. A relationship was an active process, and for it to function properly, the parties involved had actively try to maintain it.

He had heard *so* many stories of one person quitting their job, or getting laid off, or not having one when the relationship began and just never getting one despite promising to, and it had fucked up the relationship.

"Well," he said finally, "on a personal level, I'd

be okay with you not having a job...provided it feels like we're both still contributing to the relationship and, I guess, the household? What I'm trying to say is that I think there's ways other than earning a paycheck that meaningfully helps manage a life together. I mean, I'd be a huge hypocrite if I told you no, go out and get another job, when I'm here putting everything on the line to write stories about people fucking."

"That is a job, though," Ellen said.

"It's *trying* to be a job."

"My point, though, is that...I want time where I have little in the way of responsibilities. I'm fine with helping keep up the house, honestly. I can do chores. But I want...time to rest. I've been fucking going and going and going since I started high school and I'm just so fucking tired. And I know this isn't completely fair to just ask of you, especially putting it like this, because you'll probably feel like a huge asshole if you want something different, but I'm...kind of at the end of my rope."

"Ellen," he said, slipping an arm around her, "I understand. And I'm all right with this. You've been through a lot. And I want you to be able to rest and heal and enjoy yourself. I'm willing to work with you on this, to figure out a way to make it happen. My only real concern is...you're going to drain your bank account making that work. This place is twelve hundred a month, and that's just rent. We don't even know if they'll be okay with you living here yet. But I do want to say that I'd be okay with you not having a job."

"That's a really huge relief," she said, then laughed softly. "God, that's really what was bothering me so much. I just sort of realized all at once while we were at the party that the idea of going back to work, finding another job, putting up with more of the endless petty bullshit, was intolerable. I was talking with Abby, looking at what she had, what she and Emily had, and I realized I wanted that more than anything in the world with you."

"I want that, too," he replied.

"You really do? You really would be okay with having a girlfriend who doesn't have a source of income?"

"Yes, provided it's working. And I mean if I was making enough money from writing, why should you have to go work a job you fucking hate? Or even just find tolerable? We work so that we can live, we don't live so that we can work. At least not on fucking horseshit jobs. And so many people are looking for a way out, if you can actually find one, you should take it."

"And you really don't have any problem with my seeing a relationship with you as an out for working a job I hate?" she asked.

"Not so long as you're with me for *me*," he replied.

"I am. And I will be. I'd be with you even if I had to work a shit job for the rest of my life. I just want to be around you all the time. I want you to be a part of my life." She paused, a startled look coming across her face. "...I love you."

"You do?"

"Yes. I...I'm just realizing it...or maybe I'm just admitting it to myself. Ah man." She stood up suddenly and started pacing. "I'm sorry. I didn't mean for this to get this intense. I didn't even realize it, but I think I kind of did? I've been wanting you in my life for years now, missing you, and it never went away.

And this last week has been...a fucking fantasy for me. Amazing." She stopped and looked at him. "There's no question, and I'm sorry if it's a lot to throw at you right now, but I have to say it: I love you, Gabe."

He stared up at her.

She stared back at him.

The moment seemed to stretch out in time.

And then Gabe stood up and hugged her. "I love you too, Ellen."

She let out a half-laugh, half-sob and hugged him tightly. She squeezed him, holding him firmly against herself, and he did the same back to her.

It had occurred to Gabe at some point that he'd fallen in love with her during their conversations. It was a startling revelation. In his own way, he'd loved his first two girlfriends.

He'd...liked his third, for a while there.

But with Ellen, it had hit him hard and keen.

At first, he'd taken it for infatuation. Of course he was incredibly into her, she was amazing and so far out of his reach it was laughable.

But it had gone on, painfully, for a long time after she'd left his life. And the feelings had slowly faded, eventually, but they had never left him. It became a thing he tried not to think about, and that grew easier with the passage of time.

Easier, but never easy.

And when she had come back into his life, it was like dumping gasoline on a flame. The love had come back, strong as a hurricane.

It felt enormous in its power, and it felt different with her. He'd always felt a little disappointed and often guilty in his previous relationships. He said 'I love you' to them, but it seemed somehow lacking. It was passionate at times, but never in that way that people described in poetry. For a long time, he thought it just wasn't true, over-exaggerated.

And then he'd met Ellen.

And now, here in his apartment with her, saying it to her after hearing it from her, it felt like he imagined it would.

It was staggering, paralyzing, titanic in its power.

And he'd never felt anything more wonderful.

After some time they let go, stepping back a little and staring at each other. He saw that her eyes were wet. His were as well, he realized.

She laughed softly and sniffed, reaching up and brushing at her eyes. "Happy crying, at last," she murmured.

"It's pretty nice," he agreed, doing the same.

They looked at each other for a moment longer, kissed, and then sat down together again on the foot of the bed.

"So, we're in agreement then: we're in love and we want a life together," Ellen said.

"Yes," he replied. "Very much in love."

She giggled. "This feels really good."

"Yes it does." He grew more serious, some of the good cheer disappearing as he was hit by a cold splash of reality. "And as blissful as it is, we still need to face reality. We have to find a way to live, which is expensive."

"I know," Ellen replied, "and...I think I might have found something."

"When?"

"Today. I was...fantasizing about this, having a home with you, and it led me to look for homes in the city. Also just places to live in general, since I like having options in that regard. And I stumbled across something...strange."

"What?"

"There's an ad for a rental house, it just went up yesterday. It's a nice house. Small, but nice. The rent is listed as 'negotiable for the right man'."

"...huh. That sounds weirdly shady," he replied.

"Yeah, but also I've come across a lot of eccentric individuals in my time as an accountant. Nine times out of ten, if you're looking at something and you think it's shady, it is. However, sometimes, it's not shady, it's...unique. Strange. A one in a million opportunity. I've tried to train myself to look for these opportunities, and I've got a good feeling about this. I e-mailed the woman offering. Her name is Sadie. Beyond that, I don't know anything."

"Did she reply?" he asked.

"Not yet, no. But I think she will. Soon. And regardless, I have enough money to keep us afloat for at least three months."

"That's good..."

"You sound reluctant."

He sighed. "I hate not having money, and I still feel kind of uncomfortable being...dependent."

"I know. And I understand. But this is life, Gabe. Ideally, we will both carry each other. But sometimes I will carry you, and sometimes you will carry me. We have to accept that if this is going to work. And...you should let me carry you. I love you and I'm happy to do it."

"Honestly, I'm happy to be carried by you, I just...it feels like a failing. I love you and I think you're amazing and I just want to, you know, provide for you, take care of you."

"And I appreciate that. I think it's only fair that I'm allowed to feel the same way."

He nodded. "Yeah, that's fair."

She kissed the side of his head. "So, I'll take care of us until you make your writing work, and then you can take care of us. And then we'll settle into something more long-term, figuring out who does what best."

"That sounds like a plan to me," he said.

She yawned. "I'm very sleepy now." Ellen stood up and began taking her shirt off. "How about we consummate our love and then have a nice, long sleep?"

"That sounds very nice," Gabe replied, standing and starting to undress as well.

CHAPTER THIRTY

"Hey...are you annoyed about the house?" Ellen asked.

"...what?" Gabe replied, looking over at her from where he sat at his desk.

It had been a quiet day so far.

He'd woken up earlier than she had and had spent the time trying to get ahead on his work orders. He'd been feeding these little ten and twenty dollar payments into his bank account, whittling down that red number that glared at him whenever he logged in. So far, he'd managed to get it down to negative three hundred.

In a few days it was going to get worse because bills were due and he hadn't started publishing his erotica until early October, which meant he wouldn't get paid until the first of December, as the payout was on a one-month delay.

Though it really depended on how much Ellen took care of.

"I sort of found the house and e-mailed that woman about it without saying anything to you, and this is a pretty big thing that might affect both of us a lot. I'm realizing that I should've talked to you about it first," she replied.

He thought about it, then nodded. "Yeah, that makes sense. I'm not annoyed, though. But yeah, we should get into the habit of talking to each other about things."

"I'm not great at it," she murmured. "I agree with you, it's just...thanks to how I am and how most modern relationships tend to go, the division of labor was pretty sharp, and I ended up just doing things.

Either because it was expected, or because I hated arguing. But I'll try to readjust. Like I said, I got used to fighting over and for goddamn *everything*. But I...have to remember, it's going to be different with you."

"It's going to be different," Gabe replied, getting up and joining her on the couch. "It's going to be better."

"A lot better. God, it already is. This last week...oh my God, has it been a week? Only a week? Fuck. Feels like a month I've been here with you. But it's been amazing. And different. It feels different. It's better. Happier. Calmer. I mean, you make me feel excited and...bubbly, but I'm also at peace in a way I haven't really been. Or at least I don't remember feeling this way."

"I'm glad. Peace is good," he said.

Before Ellen could reply, her phone began to ring. She grabbed it and studied it with dread, then confusion, then realization.

"House lady," she said, and answered. "Hello, this is Ellen Campbell...yes, that's right." She paused. "Yes, I do...yes, he is...all right then. She wants to talk with you," she murmured as she typed something into her phone.

"All right, you're on speaker phone," Ellen said.

"Hello, my name is Sadie Hayes. You are the boyfriend?" came the voice.

She sounded...

Like an ice queen. A mature, sexy ice queen. With just a hint of guile.

"I am. My name is Gabe Harris."

"Gabe...what is your profession?"

For a moment, he paused, wondering not precisely if he should lie, but more if he should embellish the truth.

Something, he wasn't sure if it was something about Sadie, the fact that Ellen was there, or something inside himself, told him not to.

"I'm an independent erotica author."

Ellen looked up at him, mildly surprised, but said nothing.

Sadie paused for a long moment. "I see. Very interesting. How old are you?"

"...twenty six. Any particular reason?"

"Curiosity. Where are you at with your career?" she asked, sounding more invested now. A lot more invested.

"Honestly? Just starting out. I've been writing off and on for years now, but it wasn't until the past month or so that I got serious. I've got about a dozen shorts out now."

"I see."

"Can I ask a question now?" Ellen asked.

"Yes," Sadie replied.

"You said the pricing was negotiable, what does that actually mean?"

"It means that I am willing to accommodate you if I like you."

"So, by 'willing to accommodate', do you mean something less than say...five hundred a month in rent?" she asked.

"Yes," Sadie replied almost immediately.

Interesting, she didn't have to think about it. So either she'd set a price lower than five hundred dollars monthly, or she didn't really care about the income. But what the hell could she be after then? What could she care about that they had to offer?

"How do you know if you'll like this?" Gabe asked.

294

"After a face-to-face meeting, I believe," Sadie replied.

"Is there any way this could be done soon? We're on a bit of a timeline," Ellen asked.

"How tight?"

"We live in a month-to-month contract renewal apartment, so, four days including today."

"Hmm. All right. I will e-mail you an address. Meet me there in an hour. We can talk. Also...Gabe, please e-mail me what you consider to be your best erotic short, promptly."

"...uh, is this part of the rental agreement?" he asked. "Not that I'm complaining, just curious."

"Yes, it is," she replied.

"Okay. I'll send it over."

"Thank you. I'll see you two in an hour. I look forward to our meeting. Goodbye."

"Goodbye," Ellen said, and hung up. "So...that was really weird."

"Yeah. What is she actually after?"

"She responded strongly to you being a writer," Ellen murmured. "Maybe it has something to do with that. Or maybe it's just a bonus. Dunno, but we'll find out. We're absolutely doing this...right?"

"Oh yeah, I'm way too interested in what she's up to and also desperate to live somewhere less than five hundred a month," he replied.

"Same." Ellen smirked suddenly. "She sounded hot. Like a cougar. Maybe she's hoping to fuck you."

"She knows we're together," he replied.

"Yeah, but a girl can hope."

"Are you referring to her or yourself?"

Ellen shrugged. "Both."

He looked at her for a long moment. "So are you *really* cool with me having sex with other women? I feel a little stupid after last night. We had that whole talk about 'we should wait' just Thursday, and then literally the next day I put my dick in a married woman's mouth and then go down on her."

Ellen laughed. "I'm sure, Gabe. Last night was...definitely a test for myself. I was pretty sure I was going to be cool with it, and I thought Emily would be a safe test. No way she'll catch feelings for you, she's way too in love with Abby. I'm pretty confident you won't for her, either. And after reconnecting with the two of them, I trust them enough to watch you get intimate. And I was very cool with it. It was extremely arousing."

"You weren't jealous?" he asked.

"No. I thought I would be, I was afraid I'd be a little, but I wasn't. At all. I...don't really know why or how, but I wasn't. It was just a great experience. Also, I wasn't bullshitting you: it looked *really* hot. You getting head and also you eating pussy."

"That's good to know, at least," he murmured.

"You sound like you don't believe me."

"I just, uh...I dunno. I'm still wrestling with it." He stood up. "We should get ready. Will you send her the erotica?"

"Yeah," Ellen replied, grabbing her laptop and firing it up. "Which one?"

"Which one's best?"

She smirked. "Is it arrogant if I choose Tall, Blonde, and Beautiful?"

"I don't think so. You *are* amazing."

She sighed in that awkward way she did when he embarrassed her and reddened slightly. "Shut up," she muttered.

"You have no idea how to handle it when I compliment you, huh?" he asked as he shut down his own laptop.

"Yes, I do," she growled.

He laughed. "Telling me to shut up is an appropriate reaction to me telling you how beautiful you are?"

"Yes, it is. Now shut up."

He closed his laptop and stood up. Walked slowly over to her until he was standing directly in front of her, getting between her and her own laptop.

She looked up at him.

"Perhaps *you* should shut up," he said, staring at her. He put his hands on her shoulders and pushed her back against the loveseat with a bit firmness. "Or perhaps I should *make* you shut up."

She was breathing more heavily now, a bit more flushed. "That...is very tempting. But we really can't afford to miss this opportunity."

He sighed after a moment and stepped away. "You're right."

"Later," she said firmly.

"Later," he agreed.

She finished her work on the laptop, then shut it down and got to her feet. "All right. Let's go see this mysterious Sadie."

...

They quickly remembered that they were supposed to wait an hour, and the location was only about fifteen minutes away, on another side of town. They waited for as long as they could, but it soon became clear that hanging around was going to result in sex, so they headed out.

After getting some gas and then hanging out inside the gas station, browsing the shelves without really looking for anything, they had finally eaten up enough time to head over there.

They took Ellen's car, with her driving. Gabe was mildly surprised by the area. He'd expected it to be worse, maybe fearing that Sadie was a slumlord, though that did seem oddly unlikely. It wasn't incredibly upscale, not like where Ellen had lived, but it was nice, in a subdued sort of way.

The house itself was a nice little single story blue structure, with a neat yard, and a simple but sleek turquoise car parked in the driveway. As they parked beside it, the front door opened and a woman got out.

"Oh my, Gabe, she's a fucking *cougar,*" Ellen whispered as they killed the engine.

"Yeah...she is. But don't...distract me."

"All right." She laughed.

They got out and walked around to meet Sadie.

She was indeed very beautiful, aged like fine wine.

She had lightly tanned skin and stood maybe five and a half feet tall. She wore jeans and a simple sweater, both of which hinted at what the dating sites now referred to as 'a little extra'. Her hair was black and pulled into a simple bun, and her blue eyes almost glittering with energy and intellect. He'd guess that she was somewhere in her forties.

She looked up at Ellen with something like shock for just a second, and then got herself under control again.

"It's good to meet the two of you," she said.

"You too, Sadie," Ellen replied.

"Why don't we go inside and then I can ask a few more questions," she offered.

"Sounds good to me," Gabe replied.

They followed her up to the front door. He

couldn't help it: he checked out her ass. It looked pretty incredible in the jeans she was wearing.

She unlocked the door and led them into a living room that was a bit bigger than the one he had right now, although admittedly it was hard to tell given he didn't have so much a living room as an area that served as one.

"So you own this property?" Ellen asked.

"I do," Sadie replied, leading them to an open doorway to the left in the back wall. "I bought it earlier this year and had it renovated. The paint on the walls and the carpets are all new, as are most of the windows." The door led to a nice kitchen, definitely bigger than the one he had now. "Fridge is new, oven...is not ancient. It works fine, though. And it comes with a microwave. And over here..." She walked over to the far left corner that obviously sported a closet of some kind.

She opened up a door to reveal a small, cramped area the size of a large closet that held just barely enough space to walk in and a washer and dryer.

"Wow, very nice," Ellen murmured.

"Yep. Had these installed as well," Sadie said, and led them onward, to another open door that led into what seemed to be a little connecting room at the center of the house. Three more doors awaited them.

She showed them what waited in each. The one to the left was a bathroom of a decent size while the other two directly ahead featured empty rooms, one a bit larger than the other.

"And that's the house," she said as she brought them back into the living room.

"All right. It's a nice house, and we would like to negotiate," Ellen said. Gabe was very interested to see this side of her.

The business side. The serious side.

She drew herself up to her full six foot five height and her expression was calm but serious. Authoritative without being threatening.

"Very well. If you would indulge me: tell me your story," Sadie replied.

Ellen seemed to deflate a little. "Our story?"

"Yes. You two seem like you've been together for a while."

"Oh...uh," Gabe chuckled awkwardly. "Actually we haven't."

"Really?" Sadie asked, clearly more interested now.

"Yeah, we've just been dating for a week, but we've known each other for a few years now..."

They spent about half an hour detailing their relationship, before they'd started making love and after. Sadie asked a lot of questions, and given the nature of the situation, odd though it was, both of them found themselves being very open and honest about basically everything.

In a strange sort of way, it was freeing.

He thought that maybe he might hide the fact that he was an erotica author, but now...maybe not. Why should he?

"All right," Ellen said once they'd finished, "now that you have our life story, I have a question."

"Ask away," Sadie replied. She seemed even more receptive than before.

"What is it exactly that you're looking for? Because you're obviously looking for *something*."

"That's a fair question, and I suppose I've beat around the bush enough. I have not had...the happiest life. But I finally find myself in a position of comfort. Now that the money is here, I'm finding that it isn't doing as much for me as I'd hoped. In centuries past, artists and writers and poets and musicians sometimes had patrons.

"Wealthy people who had a great love of creativity would fund them financially so they were free to create art. This always appealed to me, this idea of being a patron of the arts. And now I'm in a position to do so. And you two strike me as very...authentic. Very in love. And Gabe, I read your short story before coming over here, and it was...quite good. I want to read more."

"Huh," Ellen murmured. "That...is not what I expected."

"What did you expect?" Sadie asked.

"I don't know, to be honest. That's why I was so stumped. But...all right. I'm game if you are, babe."

"Yeah, I'm game. What are your terms?" he asked.

"I have a contract drawn up that I need all of us to sign for the sake of safety on everyone's part. But there are two primary things I am asking for: the first is that you take care of the property, don't damage it, and the second is that, occasionally, I will request a custom erotic short to be written by Gabe for me. That second one will be...off the contract. And given that I know the creative process can be difficult, and that a working writer is a busy writer, I'm willing to work with you on a timeline. And, I suppose I don't want to make it a requirement, but I *do* want you seriously pursuing your passion," she said.

"That's fair, given this is a 'patron of the arts' kind of deal," Gabe replied.

"I'm glad we agree on that. In return for this, I will accept a flat three hundred dollar per month rent for living here."

"...seriously?" Ellen asked.

"Seriously. I will sign a legally binding document agreeing to this. I've done my research and I have two copies printed out in my car right now," Sadie replied.

"All right then," Gabe said. "If Ellen's good, I'm good."

"Yeah, I just need to see the documents, but this sounds good."

"Perfect, let's do it," Sadie said.

She led them back outside, locking the door behind them, and over to her car.

Getting in, she produced two pieces of paper. She gave one to each of them and they both read over them. To Gabe, it looked pretty simple and straightforward. They agreed to pay three hundred dollars a month and to keep the rental property in reasonable condition and not do any damage to it or do anything illegal in it, and in return she would let them live there for at least six months and she would fix anything that broke.

"This looks good," Ellen said.

"Yep," Gabe agreed. In truth, he trusted Ellen's judgment on this kind of thing more than his own. Though nothing here was ringing any warning bells for him.

"Excellent," Sadie replied.

They each signed both papers, and he and Ellen kept their copy. As he looked at Sadie, though, he had the distinct impression that she still had something she wanted to say. And like she was wrestling with whether or not to do it.

Finally, she cleared her throat. "Ellen...may I speak with you about something...unrelated? Privately?"

"Uh...sure," Ellen replied.

"Let's go back in the house," Sadie said.

"Okay. Be right back, love," Ellen said, kissing Gabe quickly and then following Sadie into the house.

Well...huh. What was this about?

Gabe watched them go back into the house and close the door, then went over to Ellen's car and leaned against the side. He waited, putting his hands in his hoodie pockets, wondering more intently with each passing moment.

Maybe she trusted Ellen more than she trusted him, which would make sense given how much more put-together and competent Ellen seemed and was. Maybe she still had some concerns about the whole thing.

Admittedly, he would.

Or maybe it was something else, but what the fuck could it be?

Whatever it was, he doubted Ellen would keep it from him...unless it had nothing to do with him. He thought about that for a bit. Something he remembered from his past relationships, *especially* his last one, was that apparently he was allowed no secrets. He had to tell them everything. It bothered him mainly because there were still aspects of his life that didn't involve his girlfriends. Namely, other people.

Gabe believed in keeping other people's secrets...up to a certain point.

He hoped never to be faced with something like learning someone had committed a murder.

While he was still considering the possibilities, the door opened up and they came back out. He studied their faces, trying to get a sense of the situation. They were both fairly composed, but not completely.

Ellen looked rather amused.

Sadie looked vaguely embarrassed.

Stranger still.

"Everything good?" Gabe asked uncertainly.

"Everything's great!" Ellen replied as she joined him. "We can start moving in now! And I want to. I want to rent a van and get all your stuff over here and sleep in this house tonight." She raised her hand as she came to stand before him, showing him a pair of keys. "Here. For the house."

"Nice," he said, taking one and adding it to his keyring as Ellen did the same.

"Ellen has my number if you need anything. I'll be in touch with my first...commission in the near future. It was nice to meet both of you," Sadie said.

"Nice to meet you as well, Sadie," Gabe replied a little awkwardly.

She looked at him for a long moment, then her eyes slipped over to Ellen, and then she simply nodded, got into her car, and drove off quickly.

"...so what the fuck was that about?" Gabe asked as they started getting into their own car.

"That...was a private conversation, I'm afraid," Ellen replied.

"For real?"

She started up the car. "Yes." She lost her smile and turned to face him. "Sadie had a question to ask me. She also asked me that I not tell you until it became relevant."

"So it relates to me then?"

"Yes. To us. But I promised Sadie that I wouldn't betray her confidence. And...trust me, dear, it's nothing bad. It's just...private."

"For the present."

"Yes."

"But not in the future."

"Correct."

He stared at her, weighing the options. He genuinely wasn't sure if he pressed her if she would tell him, but after considering that, he quickly decided it didn't matter. At least not right now. Hadn't he *just* been thinking about this?

"All right," he said, settling back in his seat and putting on his seatbelt, "I trust you."

"Thank you. I love you. And trust me, if it was something bad, I wouldn't be so eager to keep it in. But it's nothing bad. It's really good, actually. Just...thank you for trusting me. And respecting Sadie's privacy."

"You're welcome, and I do believe in that."

She let out a sigh of relief and pulled out her phone, then began typing on it rapidly. "Thank fucking Christ. Blake had to know fucking *everything* all the goddamned time and-mmm, no. I'm done talking about him. He's out of my life. Gone forever."

Gabe considered how to respond carefully. "He hurt you, Ellen," he said, and she looked over at him. "I don't want you to feel like you have to just shut up about what happened to you. I'll understand if you don't want to talk about it, but...I'm not sure it's the best idea to just try and bury everything."

"That's a good point," she replied. She smiled suddenly and took his hand. "Thank you."

"For what?"

"For having an actually fucking healthy relationship with me. For caring, and listening, and being there for me. It means a lot more than I can really say," she said.

"You're welcome, and thank you for the same thing," he replied.

She laughed and kissed him, then resumed typing on her phone. After a moment, she passed it to him. "Navigate me to the rental place."

CHAPTER THIRTY ONE

A sense of unreality had been haunting Gabe ever since he'd had that revelation late one night, smelling cat piss and seeing nothing but horror awaiting him in his future.

As he'd set his hand and his mind towards working his way into writing and out of despair, he had slipped in and out of a curious state where, at times, his world seem a little off. Sometimes it felt great, because it felt possible that he might actually be doing it. He might actually be meaningfully walking the writer's path to success.

Other times, it was terrifying and soul-crushing as he became certain that he was fooling himself and he would never escape poverty and depression.

That sense of unreality had ballooned to ridiculous proportions when Ellen had reentered his life and become his girlfriend.

He'd been slowly adjusting to it over the past week, riding the highs and lows like a roller-coaster, trying to maintain his sanity, his workload, and his relationship.

But as he drove a moving van for the second time that month through the streets of his city, following Ellen back home, that sense was higher than ever before. And yet, despite that, he also felt like he'd crossed some sort of threshold.

As he reflected on it, Gabe began to wonder if maybe some of that sense of fragility came from the fact that he really was gambling everything. If it didn't work out, he was pretty fucked. But now that frailness was lacking.

Despite his inherit mistrust of the world at large

and people in particular, Gabe trusted Sadie. He trusted that she was telling the truth, he believed what she'd told him. And he trusted Ellen. Maybe it was a terrible idea.

This was how people ended up homeless and fucked nine ways from Sunday.

They trusted the wrong people, often because desperation forced their hand or blinded them.

He knew he had a choice here, but the cold, perhaps sad truth of the matter was that Gabe would rather live in, and believe in, the world where he built a life with Ellen and Sadie was legit. And for better or for worse, he believed he had a chance here.

Whether or not that chance actually meant he figured out some way to get his writing career off the ground was indeterminate as of yet, but goddamn did idea that he had at least a semblance of a fair shot feel good.

Gabe pulled into the parking space next to Ellen and killed the engine. He checked his phone, bubbling with excited energy, wanting to get things *done*.

It was still relatively early in the day, almost two o'clock. They could definitely get themselves moved out of the apartment and into the house within a few hours. Six at the most, depending on if there were problems.

"You look really excited," Ellen said as he rejoined her and they headed for the building.

"I am extremely excited," he replied. "This feels...insane."

"I'll admit, this is pretty unlikely, but I think we've been handed something fantastic," Ellen agreed as they walked inside.

"Like a winning lottery ticket," he murmured.

"Right. But we have to remember that a lot of

people who win the lottery end up fucked again, or worse. Being lucky is just half the battle, we're going to have to take advantage of this. Although in truth, I still *really* want to take a break and relax."

"I'm still down for that plan," he replied, walking over to the only closet he had and opening it up.

He began pulling out the empty suitcases stacked in there. Three in total, two of his, one from Ellen. Ironically, they'd gone to the trouble of making room for her clothes earlier in the week and they should've just left them.

Oh well. It wasn't like it was a lot of work.

"I still really appreciate it," Ellen said as she grabbed her case. She paused and grinned at him, touching his leg. "I will show you exactly how much I appreciate it tonight."

"...oh yeah?"

"Yeah." She leaned in and kissed him, then moved over to the dresser, where she dropped into a crouch and began stuffing her clothes into her suitcase.

For a moment he was struck by the sight of her ass, her jeans pulled tight across it. Good fucking lord did she have a huge ass.

He made himself focus. There were things that needed to be done, and quickly.

. . .

The experience of moving to a new place was completely different when it was done so with a second person. Especially if that person was someone you loved and were just at the beginning of building a life together with.

It seemed to go a lot quicker.

He and Ellen got everything bagged and boxed up in about half an hour, then loaded the van up with the couch, the coffee table, Gabe's desk and computer chair, and the television. They drove it over, dropped it off, and then came back and did the same with the bed, the nightstand, and the entertainment center.

As he drove the van back to the rental place, he found himself marveling over how long his initial move seemed to take. He supposed it made enough sense that it went a lot slower when he was doing it alone, but that still didn't seem to cover the discrepancy.

Moving into the apartment felt like it had taken all damn day.

Even stranger was that it felt like he'd moved into his new apartment last month, not last week. And that kind of freaked him out. When people moved, they typically stayed where they were for at least a year, often longer. That he was moving out a week later had the feeling of wrongness, a sense that he thought everything was going well, but he was actually missing something *massively* important and fucking himself over.

He was probably just being paranoid, and he still felt good about the situational development, it was just...

What if he was missing something?

Good things tended to happen to other people, in his experience. Gabe Harris's place in life was to fail and suffer.

Success was alien and certainly he found himself not trusting it.

It really cut against his decision to be more confident, but it was hard to be confident when abject misery and crushing loneliness were the norm.

What really told him that something was different was that, despite these miserable assessments of himself, he still felt really good.

He parked the van in the lot beside Ellen and they went inside and finished returning it, then headed back to the apartment and started going over everything one more time, to make sure they hadn't missed anything.

"Huh," Gabe murmured as he stood in the center of the studio apartment and looked around.

"What? We miss something?" Ellen asked.

"No, just...probably should've bought a vacuum cleaner," he replied.

"The carpet looks fine, but yes, I would like to buy one. I intend to actually, that was something I wanted to speak with you about: we should do a big shopping trip. There's a mall on that side of town and there's a big furniture store. I want a real couch, and a dresser for myself. Maybe some lamps, too. And I'm sure some other things will leap out at us. And I will pay for it."

"Well, if it's happening, you'll have to," he said. "And you've got money...how much money do you actually have in your bank account?"

"Just over twelve thousand dollars," she replied.

"Wow."

"I know. It seems a like a lot, but it...goes faster than you'd think. Although it'll go a *lot* longer on three hundred a month. That flat fee means no utilities. Well, beyond our phones and the internet. Which we need to get set up, and soon."

"Oh...yeah." He sighed. "I'm bad at this stuff."

"A lot of people are. It's hard to keep track of everything."

"Yeah...are we going to have any trouble with

untangling your old life from this one?" he asked. "Was your name on the lease? Is his name on your car? Bank accounts?"

"You aren't *that* bad at this stuff. Ironically, no, we won't. Blake was...paranoid, and in truth, so was I. We were both fairly established when we met, and after that, we wanted to keep everything separate. It probably should've told me something that I was nervous about adding him to any legally binding document...but no, we're good. My car is mine. I wasn't on the lease to the condo. Our bank accounts were totally, a hundred percent separate."

"Thank God," he muttered.

"Yep. So, clean break. We're good. It's all Gabe and Ellen all the time now."

He couldn't help but grin, at least a little. "Well...with some 'also featuring' a hot chick every now and then, apparently."

Ellen smirked. "Yes. Very much that. If it had been a bit of a raunchier party, I would have suggested you have sex with Emily."

"Wow."

"Would you have?"

He thought about it. "...yeah, I would've. Whether or not that'd be a great idea upon further reflection is less certain, but yes. I would have fucked the shit out of her."

"It would've been fine. And *oh* so hot."

"If you say so."

"I do say so," Ellen replied. "Now," she said briskly, looking around, "let's finish cleaning the place up so we can at least try to get the security deposit back, and then go *home*."

"Our home," he said.

She smiled broadly. "Our home."

...

"A little more," Ellen said.

Gabe grunted as he shoved the bed a bit further. "There?"

"Yes, perfect," she replied, moving to the side and giving it a final inspection. "Yeah, there's enough room to roll out of bed or get up in the middle of the night for something."

"Good," he said, straightening up and rubbing his back with a groan.

"Maybe it's time I gave you a massage," she said.

"I would really like that," he replied.

"I will so totally give you a happy ending."

"I would like that even more."

She laughed. "First, though, let's go get something to eat. I saw a little burger and fries diner just two blocks away when we were moving stuff. It looks like it might be one of those weirdly amazing hole-in-the-wall restaurants."

Gabe considered it. He wanted to just sort of crash out here at their new home. But Ellen seemed invested in the idea, and he had to admit, he was curious, and he didn't want to make his own food right now.

"All right," he said.

"Thank you." She kissed him and began changing.

He smelled himself and frowned. Yeah, probably should at least try to freshen up. It was cold out, but all the moving and running around had worked up a bit of a sweat.

Fifteen minutes later, they were in Ellen's car,

driving down the darkened streets of their new neighborhood. It almost looked deserted, though they passed a few people walking along the side of the road, heading home or somewhere else.

"How's your work?" Ellen asked.

"I've got it done for today, but tomorrow something is due, and then three somethings are due after that," he replied. "I've got a dozen active orders altogether."

"You don't seem to like them," she said.

"I hate them, mostly. I mean, the short story commissions are okay, sometimes, but everything else is fucking awful."

"You could stop doing them."

Gabe began to respond negatively, as it was a thought that had sorely tempted him over the past few weeks, but he knew he couldn't stop. Only now he could.

He could stop.

"Shit, I guess so," he said finally. "Although my bank account is still negative."

"Would you let me write you a check?" she asked. "To get it out of the negative and give you some spending cash. I wouldn't want it back. I'm okay with us looking at our money as, you know, our money."

"Are you *sure?* Because that seems like a ridiculously tilted deal in my favor. I'm literally three hundred in the hole, and you have twelve fucking grand."

"Gabe...how can I put this?" she murmured as they pulled into the parking lot of the little diner, which was called Sherry's, and parked. For a moment she simply looked down at the steering wheel. Then, abruptly, she turned to look at him. "I don't really care about money. To be clear: I want it, but only for security. I want to be sure that I don't have to worry about bills, about food and gas, about some big, expensive thing happening. And I know, that's a big ask for a lot of people, but once we're secure...I don't care."

"Are you sure?" he replied after a moment. "Everyone cares about money."

"Not everyone," she said, "and I'm pretty sure. I know it's a really big deal and it causes a lot of breakups, and I'm not saying, for example, 'I don't care about money, so you can buy anything you want', I still want to have conversations about purchases, especially larger ones, and I want to be responsible with our resources, and to be comfortable, but I'm saying...there's more to how I want to view my life than how much money is coming in each month to the household."

"All right," Gabe said. "I'll take you at your word, and I want the same thing. I mean I want a lot of money, but yeah, mainly so that I can make problems and bills go away."

"Good...and yes, I also know that I have a conflict of interest, because of *course* I want to live in a household where money isn't the measure of value since I will soon lose my only source of income. But I don't always intend for it to be this way. I want to find *some* way of earning money. Shit, maybe I can be like Abby: offer accounting advice over the internet...so will you? Let me give you a check?"

"Yeah," he replied. "I feel weird about it but it makes sense and I only feel weird about it because emotions, ones that I shouldn't really listen to."

"Good! Come on, let's get food."

They got out of the car and headed inside. Sitting

at a window booth, they looked over as a waitress approached them.

And Gabe felt thunderstruck.

She might have been the most traditionally attractive woman he'd ever seen in the flesh. She was a pale redhead, probably less than five and a half feet, and trim but...

Busty. Trim but curvy, he saw from the size of her hips. She had one of those 'how in the fuck' bodies that a lot of porn stars and strippers seemed to manage.

Part of what made him realize she was so attractive was that she looked haggard, her hair pulled into a very rough ponytail, she wore a red apron over a simple t-shirt and some simple jeans that didn't do much to flatter her figure, and she didn't seem to be wearing any makeup at all, and despite all that, she still looked extremely alluring.

He made himself focus and looked briefly at Ellen, wondering if she'd noticed his obvious attraction to the waitress, and saw that she looked even more captivated than he did.

"Hello, welcome to Sherry's. I'm Holly, I'll be your waitress," she said, sounding tired but friendly. She set down a pair of plastic, single-sheet menus. "Can I get you something to drink?"

"Uh...yes," Ellen murmured, seeming to come back to herself. "...just a moment."

She looked at the menu and Gabe did the same. They both ordered soda and, since the selection was limited and they already had an idea of what they wanted, they each ordered burgers with all the fixings and fries.

Holly smiled winningly at them, took their menus, and promised to return with their drinks soon.

Gabe couldn't help it, he looked at her ass.

It was harder to tell, because her jeans were a little loose fitting, but it looked like she had one hell of an ass.

"Oh my God," Ellen whispered when they were alone again. "Gabe, oh my God, she is so hot."

"Yeah," he muttered. "Jeez. I was thinking things I was feeling a little guilty about."

"Don't be, I'm not," Ellen murmured with a smirk.

A look flicked across her face, one of guile, and then something seemed to change about her. She sat up a little straighter, but then leaned forward a bit more, showing off her big breasts. Her expression changed to something more friendly...and alluring.

As Holly came back with their drinks, Ellen focused that allure on her. "Thank you very much," she murmured, her voice holding just the right amount of sultry seduction.

Holly's gaze shifted to Ellen, lingered, hesitated, then flicked quickly to Gabe, who simply offered a friendly yet very slightly beguiling smile, then they shifted back to Ellen.

"Uh...you're welcome," she murmured, flushing a little and smiling just a bit, then she retreated back to the kitchen area.

"You're flirting with her," he said quietly.

"You want me to stop?" Ellen replied.

"No. You seem really good at it."

"Can you *imagine* a threesome with her?" she whispered, leaning forward excited. "She's a fucking goddess. She's a supermodel. Good lord, I don't think I've ever seen such a hot girl."

"She seems kinda young," he said.

"Early twenties, I think," Ellen replied, then

shrugged. "So long as we aren't doing anything fucked up and she's into it, I think she's fair game. If fifty plus dudes can date teenagers, then I can sleep with a young woman in her early twenties."

"Yeah that's fair," Gabe said after considering it. "Do you really think it'll work?"

"We'll see. I have to...feel it out. If you're happy with it, I can take charge on this. We'll go the slow route."

"Yeah, seduce away," he replied.

She smirked. "Good...this should be fun."

CHAPTER THIRTY TWO

It was interesting watching Ellen work.

And it seemed to be very effective on Holly. He wasn't fully convinced that she'd be into him. He also found it ridiculously hard to believe that she was single. And yet...there was a kind of innocence to her. An awkwardness, an uncertainty.

Ellen made little kind comments and remarks each time Holly came back, and she came back seemingly more times than a typical waitress would otherwise. She seemed a little caught, like she was really enjoying her interactions with Ellen, but wasn't sure if she should be.

Gabe wondered if something might come of it as he ate his burger, which turned out to be decent, but not amazing. But after they paid for their bill, Ellen flirted just a little more, gave her a nice tip, and then they headed out.

The slow game indeed.

"That went well," Ellen said as they got back into her car.

"Yeah?" he replied.

"Yes. She's very interested, but right now, she's going to tell herself it was fun, but a one time thing, she probably won't see us again. And then...we're going to come back. And she'll be excited. And we'll keep flirting, and..."

"And?" he prompted.

"And then she'll fucking ride your cock like a pogo stick," Ellen replied, starting up the car.

He laughed. "I'm sure."

"I think she will. But only time will tell. For now, let's relax."

They drove the short distance back home, and that sense of unreality came to him again as they walked up to the front door.

"Wow," he murmured as Ellen got it unlocked and they headed inside.

"What?" she replied.

"Just...this is so surreal. This is our house. I mean, we don't own it, but we live here. And it's our space. Our home. Officially now."

"Yep," she said. As they took off their shoes and hoodies, Ellen pointed to the bedroom. "And now you will go lay down in bed without any clothes on, and I will give you a massage."

"Yes ma'am," he replied.

They walked back through the house, *their* house, to the bedroom. He tossed his shirt into the laundry basket, then set aside his pants and began to crawl onto the bed.

"Ah-ah!" Ellen said, her own shirt coming off.

"What?" he asked.

"Naked."

"Completely?"

"Every scrap of clothing."

He laughed. "All right."

He tossed his socks and boxers into the basket as well and laid down on his stomach on the bed. Ellen rested on her knees over him, then he felt her shifting around, and then suddenly something soft and very warm and smooth began rubbing across his back.

"Are those...your tits?" he asked.

"Yep," she replied. "How does it feel?"

"Very nice. Goddamn your tits are soft," he muttered.

"That they are."

She did that for a while longer, then switched

over to the more traditional method of massaging, using her hands and fingers. He groaned as she started working his back, starting high and then going low.

"I guess I have some skill at this, too," Ellen murmured.

"You have strong hands."

"I have big hands," she said. "Which guys do not like, I have noticed."

"I like them."

"You like everything about me." She paused. "Do feet do anything for you? I've been told by several of my lady friends I could make *bank* as a foot fetishist."

"They don't, but I admittedly wish I was. You've got nice feet. But again, you have nice everything."

"If you say so..." She leaned into his back suddenly and something popped loudly.

"Ah! Fuck!" he cried.

"Hurt you?"

"No...yeah...sorta?" He chuckled. "It was good."

"Figured I'd give it a shot, return the favor."

"It is very appreciated."

She kept going, alternating between pressing her hands into his back, kneading his muscles, and running her hands across his skin. He suddenly understood why she'd been making noises like that. His back was apparently pretty sensitive and this felt amazing.

Ellen laughed softly.

"What?" he murmured.

"Something insane just occurred to me."

"What's that?"

"The life that I'm now actively trying to live...it's exactly what every other guy I've dated wanted or tried to get me to live. But I was so resistant to it every time. If they knew I'd made this change, that I was actively pursuing it, they'd be so enraged."

"What changed?" he asked.

"Trust. I trust you."

"Huh."

It seemed like there was a lot more to unpack from that short statement, but from the way she continued massaging him, and then popped his back again, he thought that maybe she didn't want to talk about it any longer.

And as she got off him and said, "Roll over", Gabe found that he didn't feel like talking about it any longer either.

. . .

Gabe awoke to the sound of rain and lo-fi, and the urgent need to piss.

It was so urgent that he got up and walked to the bathroom without really processing the fact that he was barely familiar with the place he'd awoken in. As he flushed the toilet and moved to the sink, looking at himself in the mirror, he finally put together that this was the first morning awakening in his new house.

House.

Not apartment.

Not his, really, but his enough. His and Ellen's home.

He quickly washed his hands and brushed his teeth, then stepped out of the bathroom into the central room that connected the whole house. There was a lot to do, and he had been feeling some excitement growing in him, but it died away like a flame being snuffed as the fully realization of the fact that they had successfully moved to a better place settled over him.

Gabe felt a quiet kind of awe.

He looked back into the bedroom. They had placed their bed beneath a window a bit high on the wall. Ellen slept, mostly hidden by the blanket they shared, and looked very peaceful. The rain beaded and ran on the windows, and the gray light put it somewhere before noon.

Gabe moved on, drifting over to the smaller bedroom that he'd claimed for himself, his office.

He had never in his life had a room that could be called an office.

It was pretty barren right now. Just a desk and a chair and nothing else. Something about that appealed to him.

He drifted further, into the living room. They would have a bigger couch soon. Today, hopefully. Some lamps. Ellen wanted to get a new coffee table, and he didn't blame her. This one was kind of shit, the glass filthy even after cleaning it, the table dented and dinged from a decade of use. He wasn't even sure where he'd gotten it.

The kitchen now. They'd make meals here together. Something about that appealed to him in a way he didn't fully comprehend. It seemed like such a simple thing, but there was something very wonderful about having a partner to prepare food with.

Maybe it was an old seed planted during the caveman days, still there in the more ancient parts of the human mind that told us boobs were awesome, clean water was great, and spiders were scary. Hmm. That thought sparked something, something that had been lingering, but he wasn't completely sure what.

Gabe moved back to the bedroom and prepared to gather up some clothes so he could dress after showering, but instead he stopped and lingered, looking at Ellen.

She looked ridiculously beautiful, and he wondered just how right she was about him putting her on a pedestal. She was correct, he had done that. But he knew it was possible that he'd elevated her to the status of godhood in his own mind, and she may let him down by being merely human. But that didn't seem to be happening.

He just felt love for her, flaws and all.

Ellen opened her eyes and looked at him after blinking a few times. A slow smile spread across her face. "If literally anyone else on this planet was staring at me when I woke up, I'd scream," she murmured, then stretched and yawned. "Why were you watching me sleep?"

"I was awestruck by your beauty and my love for you," he replied.

She stared at him. "I can't tell if you're intentionally being over the top or if that was an authentic answer."

"It was an authentic answer, babe," he replied, moving over to the dresser to gather his clothes.

"I'm so not used to this," she muttered, sitting up and stretched again, then popping her neck.

"What?" he asked.

"Being...I don't know, worshiped sounds like too strong a word, but like, just telling me how amazing you think I am. It seems like every guy nowadays is afraid of giving *any* ground and actually admitting to being in love with their girlfriend, or even just liking her, beyond the absolute bare basics."

"How does it make you feel?"

She pursed her lips, considering it. "I mean, good, to be clear. But also strange? Like I'm missing something? I know I'm not, it's just...weird." For another long moment they fell silent and just looked at each other. Finally, Ellen looked at the window. "It's raining."

"Yes it is. I take it as a good omen," he replied.

"We should shower."

"That's what I just about to do."

She got up and they headed for the bathroom. He started up the shower and got in while she brushed her teeth. When she joined him, she looked around appreciatively.

"This shower is bigger," she said.

"That's what I was thinking," he replied.

She smirked. "Good. When we finally snare that redhead, she can join us in here."

"You seem really confident. Also, that sounds so...devious," he said.

She laughed. "Sex isn't devious?"

"Imagine if it was me saying that. I don't think it'd go over so well."

Ellen considered it, then shrugged awkwardly. "You have a point, there's a lot of double-standards. I mean, I'd be okay with it if this conversation were swapped, but that's also because I know you aren't a predatory asshole. And it's not like we're going to hurt or lie to her. When we get her into our bed, it will be with her happy consent, and she will leave satisfied. And I *am* confident."

He laughed. "I hope you're right. She is...something else."

"She really is. It's hard to believe a girl that beautiful is working as a waitress at such a shit place."

"I wonder why she is."

Ellen shrugged. "Could be anything. Maybe she

likes it there, although I doubt it. Maybe she's doing someone a favor. Maybe she has no idea how overwhelmingly hot she is. Maybe she doesn't care. Maybe she was desperate."

Gabe finished washing up, rinsed off, then gave up the shower for Ellen.

"We really gonna buy a bunch of furniture today?" he asked.

"Yes," Ellen replied. "And have it delivered as soon as we can. Why don't you get ready? I'm honestly pretty impatient to get this process started."

"Well, yes ma'am," he replied, getting out.

"Don't sass me," she murmured.

"What are you gonna do about it?" he replied.

"I'll have to think of something...exciting."

"Uh-huh. You do that, love."

She yanked back the shower curtain and glared at him. He looked back at her and for a moment they simply stared at each other.

"Get back to your shower," he said.

She continued glaring at him for just a few seconds longer, then lowered her eyes and murmured, "Yes, sir," before slipping the curtain closed.

Gabe finished drying off.

This was shaping up to be his most interesting, and arousing, relationship ever.

CHAPTER THIRTY THREE

As they pulled into a parking spot in the vast lot outside the mall, Ellen's phone buzzed.

Before getting out, she pulled the phone out and checked it.

"...what the fuck?" she muttered.

"What is it?" Gabe asked. She showed him the screen. Just a simple text that ready: *Did you really think you could keep this from me?*

"You have no idea who that is?" he asked.

"No, I don't recognize the number at all," she muttered. She hesitated for a moment. "Maybe I should just block and delete..."

"You could ask who it is," he said.

She hesitated further. "Yeah...the area code is familiar," she replied. Finally, she sighed and fired off a response: *Who is this?*

A pause, then: *Duh, Krystal, how the fuck do you not know that?* Another pause and then, before she could reply: *Oh shit, I forgot, I never told you I got a new number.*

Ellen heaved a sigh of relief and rapidly began texting back. "This fucking bitch," she muttered. "Remember how I told you I had two best friends? And one moved away? This is one who moved away. Her name is Krystal and she's even hotter than Emily. Honestly, I think she's up there with Holly in terms of pure sex appeal. She's like an older, more filled out version of our favorite waitress, with a lot of tattoos."

"Oh man, I fucking love tattoos," Gabe said.

Ellen laughed. "Yeah, Em mentioned that. Big bonus on your part. She really loves compliments on her tats. So does Krystal...you wanna see Krystal's tits?" she asked suddenly.

"Did you mean to say tats?"

"No, I did not."

"Oh. Well, I mean is that even a question," he replied.

She laughed. "Fair point. I want to see them again, too."

"Is she the one you shared oral with?"

"Yes." Ellen paused. "Is that...a problem?" she asked suddenly. "Krystal is the closest I ever got to dating a woman. We fucked around a lot in our youth."

"No, it's not a problem," he replied.

"Okay, good. I didn't want to assume. So you want me to coax nudes out of her for us?"

"Yes. I mean, provided she's comfortable with that."

"She should be. Hold on...just telling her about you. She's also a writer."

"What kind?"

"Like you, although she's been at it for longer. She writes erotica and romance. Just not...very successfully, I think." She finished typing a moment later, then slipped her phone back into her purse. "All right, let's do this."

They got out and began walking towards the mall. The rain had slackened by now. It was just past noon and the rain was little more than a mist, falling from dreary gray skies. There was a surprisingly low amount of cars around, and Gabe figured most people must be taking this as a day to stay indoors. Fine by him.

There was something almost magical about going to big places that were normally packed during low tide times. Unfortunately the pandemic had killed a lot of that and no one was open twenty four hours a day anymore.

His favorite time to shop had usually been sometime around midnight.

They walked into the food court and found it almost empty. As they delved deeper into the vast mall, Gabe couldn't help but smile stupidly. Here he was, shopping with his girlfriend.

With Ellen.

She was getting looks again, but that was true of everywhere he was finding. She did really stand out. He thought of how much trouble she'd said she'd had dating. Were there really guys who'd just immediately give up if given a shot with a woman as hot as Ellen if she was tall? To him, it seemed impossible.

He'd be tripping over his own two feet trying to date a woman taller than him.

It was obvious that there existed a group of guys out there who were incredibly into that, but Gabe thought that he was in an even smaller group, as most men who were into women taller than them wanted to be dominated by them.

Gabe wanted to dominate.

And he was so fucking lucky Ellen was into that.

They found the furniture store not much later and started wandering around. As they stopped in the couch section, Ellen's phone buzzed again. She pulled it out and checked it.

"Whoa-ho, nice," she muttered, and showed Gabe.

"Holy shit," he whispered.

There was a picture of a pale, tattooed redhead who had her shirt pulled up, showing off some really fucking nice tits.

"*That* is Krystal?" he asked.

"Yep."

"Good fucking lord is she hot. Like *damn* those are some nice tits..." He looked at her awkwardly as he passed the phone back. "Is it weird, me drooling over other women like this?"

"No," she replied. "I mean, I'm the one showing you. And we can drool together. Krystal would one hundred percent hop into a threesome with us if she was single."

"So she's not single, huh?"

She laughed. "Disappointed?"

"Oh come on, of course I am."

"Me too, actually. No, she's not. She lives about three hours away and she's pretty steady with another chick named Liz. Who is also super fucking hot, but in a different way." Ellen fired off a response and then moved over to one couch that was of a pretty good size. She sat on it, then stretched out on it. It was just big enough to contain her great height.

"You like?" he asked.

"I do. Although I feel like it could be more comfortable...let's keep looking. Also, tell me if you see one you like," Ellen replied, getting up.

They kept searching, having to shoo off a sales associate twice, wanting to hunt on their own. There were a lot of couches, and Gabe kept trying not to freak out at the prices. The average couch was like five hundred dollars, and those were the low-end ones. Some of them were over two grand. And they passed one over three.

To a poverty-stricken twenty-something, this felt like the kind of place he shouldn't even be allowed entrance to.

Currency contained worlds.

Finally, they took turns trying out one that was almost eight hundred dollars, and Ellen decided this was the one she wanted. As she flagged down an associate and had them prepare it to be bought, he felt a different kind of anxiety settle over him. It only got worse as they moved deeper into the store, taking almost two hours to wander around, checking everything out.

In the end, they settled on another nightstand, a new coffee table, a tall but narrow dresser, and a bookshelf.

After taxes and a next-day delivery fee, it came to just shy of three grand.

Gabe tried not to have a panic attack. He kept it together as they headed out of the store and back into the mall.

"What's wrong?" Ellen asked.

"I'm having...difficulty," he replied.

"With? I know that was pretty expensive but honestly that's normal for furniture shopping."

"It's not quite that, it's...I don't know," he muttered. "Something I can't quite grasp. Something that's scaring the shit out of me."

She looked at him as they walked, then frowned. "Shit, you're really pale. All right, come on, let's get to the car and talk."

"Yeah," he managed.

It felt like a really goddamned long walk, but finally they were back in the vehicle.

"Okay, Gabe, try telling me what's going on," she said, sounding anxious.

He'd been thinking furiously on that all the way back, and thought he had something, something to grasp onto and tie to his present condition.

"I thought maybe it was just a bigger version of

the weird feeling I get when you spend money on me, given the amount. But that isn't it. This is different. I think it's...it's the fact that this is such an obvious and literal investment into...us."

"What do you mean? Why is that scary?" she asked.

"I guess it feels like a lot of pressure? I don't know. I think maybe I'm freaking out because you just invested three thousand dollars into our home and thus our life. Not *your* life, *our* life. I'm pretty sure three thousand dollars eclipses everything all my exes combined spent on me in total. And it's just-what if I'm not enough? What if I fuck all this up? How much are you going to piss away on a relationship that wasn't worth it?"

"Gabe," Ellen said, taking his hand, "I get it. It's all right."

He laughed a little wildly, shaking his head. "How is it all right, exactly?"

"Because I believe in what we're doing, Gabe. I believe in us, together. Living together, loving each other, building a life together. I trust you. And I'm scared, too. What if I fuck everything up? What if there *is* something wrong with me? Something that keeps making my relationships crash and burn? Because I have a shit track record. But I think that everything will work out because we both want it to, and we both trust each other and believe in each other. We're both working towards the same thing. It won't be perfect, but it doesn't have to be."

Gabe mulled over that, staring at the dashboard, and he felt some deep knot of tension slowly begin to release.

He nodded. "You're right," he murmured, then looked at her. "I'm sorry. I don't mean to be so fucking anxious all the time."

She laughed softly and gripped his hand. "I understand. I really, really do. Our lives are changing and even positive changes are stressful, *especially* when you've been fucked over by life so many times that you no longer trust positivity. You're waiting for the other shoe to drop. Waiting for life to shovel shit on you, because it's so much more painful if it's done right when you're enjoying something. I don't know what's coming, but I know that this is going well so far, and I know that for the first time in a very long time, I feel...confident in my relationship. I guess my point is, Gabe, that whatever happens, we'll be able to handle it together."

"You're right. At a certain point I need to stop worrying so much about what might be," he said, giving her hand a squeeze.

She smiled broadly and then leaned over, hugging him tightly. "I really do love you, Gabe," she murmured. "I want this to work, and I know you do, too. It's going to work."

"I love you too, Ellen...and you're right. We'll figure it out."

They parted and just smiled at each other for a long moment. Then, suddenly, a look came across Ellen's face. "Hey! I just realized, we're actually not that far from Becky's now. We should totally go there and do some shopping."

"Really?" he asked.

"Yes! It'll be wild to go back there...unless you don't want to. You seem reluctant."

"Yeah, it's just...I dunno. It's nothing."

"No come on, tell me."

He sighed. "You remember Sandy?"

"Ugh, yes. She was really all up in my business

when I worked there, always trying to hang out with me and help her out with things. Which wouldn't really bother me except that she was so obviously sucking up to me, just trying to get things from me...but what about her?"

"I asked her out a few weeks before I left and she fucking laughed in my face. And just so there was no confusion, she said, 'Wow, Gabe, really? You and *me?* Come on.', and then she walked away. That was definitely the most painful rejection I've ever had. Like, fuck."

"Jesus, that's cruel," Ellen muttered. "What's so fucking great about her that she thinks this? Fucking bitch, you know what? We're going."

"Why?"

"Because I bet she still works there and there might be a chance that she's working today and I will absolutely rub her fucking smug face in the fact that you and I are in love and you are fucking *pounding* me," she replied.

"I...all right," he said, laughing a little. "This is a strange side of you."

"I'm pissed," she replied, reaching for her keys. Then she paused. Another look came across her face. "Hey, Gabe, you drive."

"All right, any particular reason?"

"Yes."

"...would you care to share that reason with me?"

"You'll see."

"All right then."

They got out and switched seats. He fired up the car and began making his way out of the parking lot, heading for Becky's.

Ellen began texting on her phone and continued to do so for several minutes as Gabe navigated the streets. The gray city was largely empty today and it was a very pleasant experience. Honestly, this was paradise as far as Gabe was concerned: rainy, chilly, Ellen, no one else.

She began to put her hair into a ponytail.

"All right, Gabe, I'm going to touch you now," she said as they stopped at a red light.

"Uh...okay?" he replied.

She reached over and began unzipping his pants.

"Wait, what are you doing?"

"Road head," she replied. "Unless you don't want me to?"

"I...all right, go ahead."

She chuckled. "That's what I thought."

Ellen finished unzipping him and then dug him out of his boxers with dexterous fingers. He felt a flash of lust and anxiety as his cock, which was now fully erect, was exposed.

"Don't worry," she murmured, and then he groaned as he felt the hot, wet pleasure of her mouth began to envelop his erection.

Gabe almost missed it when the light turned green again. Gripping the steering wheel tightly, pressing his lips together in concentration, he forced himself to focus on the road and remember the way to where he was going.

He was almost there.

This was really stupid.

But holy fuck did it feel good.

Ellen was taking his whole dick into her mouth now. She held her head in place, his head partway down her throat, and she swallowed. He groaned louder as she did that, all those slick, hot throat muscles tightening around his most sensitive spot...

Gabe managed to make it into the parking lot and

parked before the orgasm came on. It was intense and he lost focus, groaning loudly, a hand settled on the back of Ellen's head as he came in her mouth, down her throat.

She kept swallowing, each time it sent a burst of absolute ecstasy roaring through him. She drained him, taking everything he had to give, and then sucked for a few moments more.

Gabe, at some point, had put his head back against the headrest and closed his eyes. When he opened them, he found himself looking at a woman. She worked for the store and obviously had been out collecting carts from the lot. She was openly staring at him. Her eyes widened a bit more when Ellen raised up, wiping her mouth on the back of her hand.

"What?" she asked, when she noticed him staring.

She followed his gaze and as soon as they were both looking at the pretty brunette, she suddenly looked away and hurried into the store.

"She totally saw that," Gabe said.

"So?" Ellen replied.

"Well...I guess it doesn't matter. Just...awkward," he muttered.

"Hot. She thought it was hot."

"How can you tell?"

"I know that look. Come on, I need a drink."

CHAPTER THIRTY FOUR

Gabe hadn't been back to Becky's in almost half a year.

During the last visit, in April, he'd come back for a reason he hadn't been able to name. Maybe nostalgia. But Sandy had been there, working one of the cash registers, and she sneered when she saw him.

Incredibly, as he walked back inside with Ellen and a cart, he was surprised to see that she was still here and working a register today.

The look of shock she had when she saw him and Ellen together was funny and somehow deeply satisfying.

"Yep, she saw us," Ellen muttered as they walked into the first aisle.

"Wonder if we'll run into that brunette. She looked really embarrassed," Gabe replied.

"And aroused. Maybe we can have some fun," Ellen said quietly.

"She did look pretty hot."

They began working their way through the store, tossing things into the cart as each caught their attention. Gabe tried to remind himself not to get used to this. They were going to have to get on a budget. Things were getting more expensive, and Ellen's money wouldn't last forever. He paused as he remembered something.

Pulling out his phone, he began writing a text message.

"Who you texting?" Ellen asked.

"Landlord," he replied. "Need to tell him I'm not renewing my lease. Hopefully there's no complications." He finished the text and replaced his phone in his pocket. As he did, Ellen's own phone chirped.

She sighed and pulled it out, then laughed softly as she checked it. "Krystal...is in a mood," she murmured.

"What kind of mood?" he asked.

"A horny kind of mood. I guess she has the green light from her girlfriend to full on flirt with us and share pics and vids. She wants something in return, though. Here, how about you send her that pic you took of me sucking your dick?"

"...all right," he replied.

Gabe took down her number carefully, as he didn't want to send this to the wrong number and, once he had it, texted the picture of Ellen, topless, his cock halfway down her throat, staring up at him with eyes like a succubus.

Krystal responded almost immediately: *LOL I fucking love that the first thing we ever communicate with is a picture of Ellen sucking your dick. I think we're gonna get along great. Also hi I am Krystal, Ellen's long-time friend from high school.*

Before he could respond, he saw a picture appear. One of her pulling a tanktop forward and revealing her bare breasts to the camera.

He fired off a quick response: *Fucking hell you are REALLY hot.*

"Watch where you're going," Ellen murmured as he almost walked into a display.

He sighed and almost put his phone away, but Krystal responded.

Thank you. From what Ellen says, so are you. I feel like I wouldn't be out of line to ask you for a proper photo?

He considered it, then responded: *All right, but*

let me finish shopping first.

One more response came back before he pocketed the phone again: *Okay but don't keep me waiting too long.*

He laughed. "Your friend is...interesting."

"Yeah. Krystal's a lot like Emily, though if anything she's even more prone to...impulsiveness. She's chilled out some now that she's made it into her thirties, but that girl is still a little nuts. I sometimes feel bad for Abby and Liz. Crazy is *very* fun in bed, less fun when you're trying to do adult things. Hmm..."

"What? That sounded like a somewhat devious 'hmm'," Gabe asked as he put some bread into the cart.

"Just wondering what it would take to get her up here...and if Liz would be cool with her fucking around with us. I genuinely can't remember if their relationship is open or not. I mean, it's gotta be some kind of open if she's cool swapping nude pics and vids. But I guess that's something to be considered in the future."

They pressed on, moving through the aisles and getting what needed to be gotten. They still had some food leftover from their initial run, but he'd known they would need more soon. Especially if they were intending to have someone over.

Was he really believing that something was going to happen with Holly?

That was certainly more hope than belief. She was way, *way* out of his league.

Then again, so was Ellen. And Emily.

As they drew close to the end of their little shopping run, Gabe found himself getting a little anxious actually confronting Sandy. Although he had to admit, after his confrontation with Blake, he felt a lot more confident about uncomfortable social situations. And thinking about that, he started to feel better about the whole thing as they approached the checkout lanes.

"Just let me handle it," Ellen murmured.

"You sure?" he replied.

"Yes. Don't worry, I'll be subtle."

"All right."

They walked up to Sandy's lane and started unloading the groceries onto the conveyor belt. Sandy had clearly been waiting for them.

Well, waiting for Ellen.

"Ellen! Hi! I'm sure you remember me," Sandy said with a bright and vaguely off-putting smile.

"Yes, I do. Hello, Sandy," Ellen replied with a very cool, cordial tone of voice.

"How have you been? I think I lost your social media info? I tried to keep in touch, but...uh, you want to get a drink sometime? I'm finally old enough," Sandy said, her voice getting just a little frantic.

"Well..." Ellen replied, then glanced down meaningfully at their groceries, which were piling up.

"Oh. Yeah. Right. Sorry," she said, and hurriedly began scanning and bagging them.

Ellen waited until she was through about half of it before she spoke again, and Gabe noted that Sandy kept shooting very uncomfortable and confused glances his way as she worked.

"Things haven't been great," Ellen said. "I found my fiance cheating on me last week."

"Oh my God! I'm so sorry," she replied quickly. "Maybe we could have a girls' night and talk about how lame boys are."

"Well, the thing is, I ended up getting with Gabe, and he's been helping me get past it. *Very* effectively," Ellen replied.

"I..." She looked startled by the statement, shooting another glance at Gabe, who was still waiting behind the cart. Sandy finished bagging the last of the groceries and Ellen was in the process of transferring them back to the cart. "What do you mean with?"

"I think you know what I mean, Sandy," Ellen replied.

"Uh...yeah. What do you mean by get past it?"

Ellen smirked and Gabe was honestly surprised that such a simple smile could convey so sexual a connotation. "How do *you* get over a bad breakup?"

Sandy seemed not to have an answer to that. Ellen finished bagging and paid, then made room for Gabe to come out. He began heading for the exit, but hesitated as he realized that Ellen wasn't with him. He looked back.

She was motioning to Sandy, who walked closer and leaned in. Ellen shot him a wicked smirk, then put her hand over Sandy's ear and whispered something. Sandy's eyes widened and she flushed as she looked directly at Gabe.

"Wh-what?" she managed as Ellen pulled back.

"You heard me, Sandy, don't act like you didn't," Ellen replied, walking away.

As soon as she joined him, Gabe started walking again. His curiosity was piqued intensely, but he managed to hold his tongue until they reached her car and popped the trunk.

"Okay, *what* did you say to her?" he asked.

Ellen smirked. "That you eat pussy like a demon and fuck like a porn star."

"*What!?* Ellen! How is that, in *any* sense of the word, subtle?!" he cried.

She laughed. "Fine, I've lost my subtle touch, but fuck that bitch! She laughed in your face, Gabe. You're *my* man now and I get a little fucking feral about that shit, but more than that, you're so nice! And good! And *great* in fucking bed! Like, she is *lucky* that you asked her out."

"I don't know," Gabe murmured as they got into the car after putting the cart away, "she's pretty hot."

Ellen turned to stare at him, her face now utterly bereft of amusement. "Gabe, you didn't really just say that."

"I mean...is she not?" he replied uncertainly.

"Gabe! That isn't the point! You literally just gave her a pass because she's hot! That's fucking horseshit!"

He considered it. "Huh...well, that wasn't quite my point. It was more that I was reaching out of my league."

"You weren't! I will fully admit to bias but I think you're about equal in terms of pure physical looks."

"Okay, now I know you're shitting me. I think less of her now, but I used to think she was a solid eight, maybe nine. There is no *way* I'm there. If I was, a lot more women would've hit on me."

"That's less true than you think. Much as a lot of us might rail against it, society has bred certain tendencies into us that we tend to follow subconsciously, and one of those is: women tend to want to be approached, instead of approaching. That usually only happens if you're like fucking famous male model hot. But that's besides the point: she's a bitch, and being a pretty, thin blonde doesn't let her off the hook."

"I agree, I mean I'm still pissed about it but whatever. It doesn't really matter." He stared the car and began driving them back home.

"Are you annoyed at what I did?" Ellen asked after a bit.

"No," he replied. "Honestly, it was pretty funny. And there's a part of me that's petty too. But honestly, looking back on it, we would've been a bad match."

"So you wouldn't fuck her if she offered today?" Ellen asked.

"No," he replied.

"Interesting. Why?"

"Besides the fact that she insulted me pretty badly? And the fact that we'd be a bad match? If she suddenly decided I was worth dating, or even just fucking, just because I have your approval? She can go fuck herself. I shouldn't need to be vetted by someone else for her to decide it's acceptable to like me. Either she likes me or she doesn't. If all she's considering is my social standing? She can fuck off," he explained firmly.

"Mmm. That's such a strong position," Ellen said.

"Well, it's how I feel."

"And I believe you, and I'm impressed. It's going to sound really, *painfully* cliché and edgy, but I don't like posers. That's why I never liked Sandy. She's a poser. She'll say whatever she has to to try and get in good with the people she thinks will make her more popular or get her what she wants. She has no convictions. She'd sell her soul if she thought it'd make her more popular. But that's part of why I love you. You're authentic. You want to be a writer so much you basically put everything on the line to make it work."

"I also seem to have caught a hugely lucky break," he replied.

"But you didn't know that was going to happen. You had literally no idea it was even possible. You're the real deal. And I massively respect that." She sighed suddenly. "God, if anything I'm the sellout. I worked my ass off for twenty years, hating almost all of it."

"What was the alternative?" Gabe asked.

"Trophy wife, housewife, mom," she replied with a shrug. "But that'd feel a whole hell of a lot worse, honestly." She laughed suddenly, bitterly. "And yet that's what I'm going to do as soon as I get fired. Be your fucking trophy girlfriend."

"Is that how you see the relationship?!"

"No," she replied quickly, sighing, "sorry. I don't-I'm sorry. That's not what I meant, Gabe. We're in love, and that's great, and I'm in heaven. It's just...I'm quitting my job to sleep in late, lounge around the house, and hang out with my boyfriend. Not for another job or a passion. Just to be lazy."

"You're not working so you can take a *break,* Ellen. That's reasonable. You feel guilty because we've been raised in a capitalist nightmare hellscape that keeps demanding more and more, not giving a single fuck about the humans it crushes along the way. You aren't a bad person for taking a break."

"What about after the break?" she murmured.

"You'll figure something out. You're too smart and motivated not to. Just...give yourself time to let your life readjust, to let the dust settle. God, you aren't even fired yet."

"...you're right. I'm sorry."

"It's all right."

They pulled into the driveway a moment later and began bringing the groceries in.

"Oh...so I was too distracted by thinking about what I was going to say to Sandy to ask, but: why did we get *this* much candy?" she asked.

"It's Halloween in like two days," Gabe replied.

"Oh...right." She smiled suddenly. "You wanna pass out candy?"

"Do you not?"

"No, I don't mind, I just...haven't really lived in a situation where that was a thing for years now. I'd forgotten, really. But yeah, I like the idea. It'll be fun. Hmm, maybe we should've bought some decorations or something..."

"I'm cool passing out candy," he replied.

"Yeah. Me too. Decorations always seem like a big pain in the ass to set up and I'm as much a fan of horror as the next girl, just...not *that* much of a fan. Okay, we'll pass out candy. Like a real couple," she said.

"We *are* a real couple."

"I mean like...I dunno, it's the kind of thing married couples who've been together for ten years or longer do, you know? It's not really something you do with the girl you started dating two weeks ago."

"Fair point." He paused, stared at her.

She smiled slightly. "It just occurred to you to ask me if we should talk about getting married, but then you got incredibly intimidated by that, because it's so early in the relationship, and because the last guy I agreed to marry cheated on me, so you figure it's a sore spot still, right?"

"Jesus Christ, yes," he replied. "How the fuck do you–"

"I'm just really keyed into you, and...let's save that talk for later. Okay? Let's just say, I'm not opposed to it. But I'd like to wait."

"Okay then."

They shared a kiss and resumed putting away the groceries.

. . .

Later that day, after he had reluctantly let Ellen take his picture to send to Krystal, for the first time Gabe entered his office with the intent to work.

It seemed bigger than he remembered as he came to stand at its center. For a moment, he felt stymied, unsure of what he was actually going to do. There were things to do, to be sure, but he felt caught.

After a moment, he became aware of rain. It had picked back up a little. He walked over to the pair of windows and opened them, looking out onto what was now his front yard. He looked out the window for a long moment, then turned back and walked over to his desk.

Turning on his laptop, he opened up his list of responsibilities.

He looked at the two columns. Several minutes passed.

He still had about a dozen responsibilities, all of them due within the next week.

Abruptly, Gabe made a decision.

He began opening up the sites where he freelanced and started changing his outgoing message, switching his status to closed. He would finish up his current responsibilities but Ellen was right.

It was time to go all in on his writing career.

CHAPTER THIRTY FIVE

"Oh my fucking God *yes,*" Gabe whispered harshly as accepted payment for the absolutely final assignment that he had agreed to take on.

And, with a lot of luck, the last one he'd ever take on.

For a long moment, Gabe simply leaned back in his chair. After a bit, he propped his feet up on the desk and cracked his knuckles, then his neck, relieving some of the tension. He needed a proper massage tonight.

It had been a very long week. Probably the longest he'd had as a writer.

While the week had been largely about finishing off his non-erotica assignments, he had also decided to go back over his old works after Ellen had found some errors while reading. She'd already ended up making corrections while reading the first collection he'd given her, and she happily agreed to do the same to the rest.

He also took the opportunity to invest in a new formatting program that would give him a little bit more leeway when it came to the presentation of the work. It was a hundred bucks, but Ellen was very happy to pay for it.

He still wasn't entirely convinced if it was worth it to spruce up a bunch of short erotica stories, but then it occurred to him that even if his works seemed to have a brief surge of sales that quickly burned off, people almost certainly would find his older works.

It made sense to try and make a good impression, and maybe it would make him stand out a bit more.

He'd also been finishing up Tall, Blonde, and

Beautiful Three. It was longer still than the last one and he'd again found himself having to cut off the end to save it for the next book. This one had reached about twenty thousand words. No longer a novelette but a short novella. It made the prospect of writing the next one, what was supposed to be the last one, a little daunting.

But that could wait.

He had earned a proper weekend, he thought, and it was here, Friday night.

The week seemed to have gone by quickly. The only real night he'd taken off was Halloween. He and Ellen had passed out candy and watched an old cartoon movie that she remembered from back in the nineties and he barely remembered seeing. It had been surprisingly creepy for being a PG cartoon, but horror was more than blood and jumpscares.

He'd managed to get internet installed and wrapped up affairs at his apartment. Surprise: he didn't get his security deposit back. But he didn't feel like fighting, just wanting to be free of any potential hassle.

On top of all this, he'd also gotten Sadie's first request.

They officially had each others' e-mails and phone numbers, and she sent him a surprisingly detailed message for her first erotic tale. She wanted him to write a sexual encounter between a woman who was clearly her from maybe twenty, possibly even thirty years ago, and it seemed like he was writing out a fan fiction for her if she'd left a relationship and had just gotten fucking smashed on the rebound by a character who, after a moment's consideration, he realized resembled him.

That was probably a coincidence, though.

He'd gotten some work done on that, but he intended to finish it next week before firing up what was probably the final Tall, Blonde, and Beautiful.

His phone buzzed. He grinned and grabbed it. Firing it up, he saw another text from Krystal.

Flirting with her had been an extremely bizarre experience. He'd never really seen the point in sexting or flirting online with a girl he didn't know, especially if there was no chance they were going to hook up.

Doing it with Krystal, though...

He could see the appeal, at least under certain conditions.

He knew she was the real deal: an actual woman actually flirting with him intentionally. She wasn't just sending him random pics on the internet she'd found of a hot chick and although he doubted he was actually going to get a chance to hook up with her, she'd hinted that it might not be out of the question.

And good fucking *lord* did he want to fuck her.

Besides being fun and flirty, she was *crazy* hot. Kind of like a thicker, tattooed Holly.

Speaking of Holly...well, one hot redhead at a time. His thoughts were drifting.

Okay dude, I finally gave some thought to what it's gonna take for me to give up that pussy pic. You gotta fuck Ellen raw, her laying at the edge of the bed, you standing, and you gotta film it, like close up of your dick just fucking ramming in there, then pull out and bust all over her pussy. Give me that hot vid and I'll give you what you want.

Gabe stared at the phone for a long moment, genuinely surprised.

And tempted.

Krystal was pretty free with what she showed

him. He had a very, very nice collection of her tits and her fantastic ass. She had a perfect ass. Big, shapely, and pale. He was honestly unsure if she was touching up her pics, but Ellen assured him she wasn't.

But he wanted to see her pussy.

He wasn't sure why. Maybe it was as simple as the fact that he hadn't yet, but he wanted to. He'd asked, and he could tell from her tone, inasmuch as one could be conveyed via text, that she knew she had something he really wanted, and wanted to tease him a little.

Not something he was particularly adverse to.

As he was considering it, he heard something, just barely at the edge of his perception, and got the notion that Ellen was standing right outside his closed office door. For some reason that worried him just a little.

Let me think about it, he texted back, and set his phone down.

Getting up, he moved over to the door. He heard retreating footsteps. Okay, so, she had been just standing outside his door. Why?

He opened it up, seeing her big backside as she retreated into the living room.

"Ellen?" he asked.

She stopped, hesitated, turned around, an awkward smile on her face. "Hey, babe."

"Were you...standing outside my office?" he asked.

She bit her lower lip, not quite meeting his eyes. "Yes."

"Why? If you wanted to talk you–"

"I know," she said, looking at once both uncomfortable and awkward. It didn't fit her at all. "I just...missed you."

"Oh. Sorry, honey," he said, walking over and hugging her. "I didn't mean to be locked up in there all day."

"It's all right," she replied, but there was definitely something in her voice.

He pulled back and looked up at her. "What's wrong? Something's wrong."

She was quiet for a long moment, then asked, "Are we...okay?"

"Yes, we're okay. We're definitely okay. Why are you asking?"

She still looked uncomfortable, if anything she looked like she was bordering on upset. "I just...you've been away from me so much this week, and I know you've been busy, like really busy, but then today, I don't know, I just get thoughts in my head and sometimes they just won't shut the fuck up and I think you're mad at me about something but you don't want to talk about it and you're shutting me out and I don't know how to handle that because I might be imagining the whole thing–"

"Ellen," he said, hugging her tightly again. "Oh my God, I'm so sorry, honey. Shit. I'm not mad at you, at all. In any way."

"Goddamnit, I knew it was nothing," she muttered.

"You should have talked to me about it but I should have been better about spending some more time with you. I...clearly got very used to just shutting myself up in a room all day long if the opportunity was available and if the inspiration struck, and it's been striking all week long. I'm sorry, Ellen."

"I forgive you," she said, sounding relieved, "and sorry for getting worked up. I'm just...adjusting to this and I still get bouts of terror over fucking it up. I'm happier with you than I've ever been in my life and I'm so fucking scared of losing that."

"Ellen," he said, pulling back again and looking directly at her, "if I have a problem, I *promise* I will speak with you directly about it. I promise that you won't just...wake up to find me leaving you or something. Even if it came to that, I would never do that to you. Trust me, you will know something is wrong *way* before we get to the breaking up stage."

She smiled broadly and kissed him hard on the mouth. "Thank you," she said. "That's another thing I could never talk about: breaking up. It was always 'we'll never break up, why are we even talking about it?'. Like talking about it means we're anywhere even close to doing it."

"It's something more people should talk about," he agreed. "So...feel better?"

"Yes. I do. Pretty much a complete one eighty...are you done in there?"

"I am done. I finished the last assignment. As in, cashed it in, and there are no more, and also Tall, Blonde, and Beautiful Three is published, and I am fucking *done* for the week."

"We should absolutely celebrate," she said, suddenly excited. "I think tonight's the night and we can so totally fucking seduce Holly into our bed."

"You're that sure?" he asked.

"Yes...but I want sex first," she replied.

"I do, too. And, speaking of that..."

"Yeah?"

"Krystal's willing to send me a picture of her vagina, but she's holding it hostage, apparently," he said.

"...for what? I'm *really* curious."

"She wants us...actually, I'll get it for you." He went back to his office, grabbed his phone, and called up the message again as he returned to her.

Ellen took the phone and looked over it. Her smile got bigger and bigger as she read it. "Oh my God, I am *so* down for this. Are you?"

"Surprisingly...yeah. I am."

"For real!? Holy shit, let's do it."

She passed his phone back and began hurrying off to the bedroom, shedding her shirt as she went. Gabe laughed as he followed her, turning on his camera function.

"You're really excited about this, huh?" he asked.

"Yes," she said simply, bending over and showing her big, bare ass as the loose shorts she was wearing came off.

Ellen had more or less given up on panties and bras since they began dating. Something he couldn't claim to dislike in the slightest.

A new text message popped up before he set his phone aside and got undressed.

So are you gonna do it?

He laughed and began replying. *Yes.*

"What?" Ellen asked.

"Krystal. She's pressing me for confirmation."

Another response: *HOLY SHIT ok don't be lame like so many other guys and be dead silent the whole time, like make some noise or something*

"She wants me to make noise," he said, setting the phone aside to get out of his shirt and undoing his pants. They dropped, pooling at his feet.

"She's right to ask, it's hot," Ellen said.

"Noted. Okay," he said, as nude as her now. He grabbed his phone and turned on the camera. "On your back, spread your legs like the slut you are."

"Are you recording?" she asked.

"Yes." She sighed. "If I'm showing my dick, you're showing your submissive side. And don't pretend like you don't want to."

"Yes, sir," she murmured after hesitating briefly.

She laid on her back and spread her legs, giving him access. The bed was at perfect fucking height. It was a little weird, maneuvering as he held the phone. He'd never actually filmed himself having sex before.

Gabe stepped up to her and rested his erection at the entrance to her pussy. He took a moment, phone in one hand, his cock in the other, and rubbed his head between her lips, making her moan and shudder.

He slipped inside of her, finding her wet and welcoming and an absolute pleasure to be in.

Right away, as he started fucking her, Gabe knew he wouldn't last long. This was turning him on enough that his stomach was roiling with wild lust and desire for Ellen. And Krystal. Knowing she was going to watch this and maybe even pleasure herself to it was a lot. It felt weird watching his erection disappearing into her Ellen's sweet pussy over and over, going faster as he grunted and groaned, trying to remember not to keep quiet.

At one point, when he knew he was on his way to an orgasm, he aimed the phone up at her huge tits, bouncing and jiggling with the rhythm of their lovemaking. Then he refocused on her pussy and started rubbing her clit with his thumb.

Most of her sounds had been incoherent moans and cries of pleasure, but now she screamed his name as she began to climax almost immediately. He groaned as a hot spray of her sex juices escaped from around his cock.

He fucked her until she'd finished orgasming, then pulled out at the last second and started coming. He did his best to get it all over her pussy as he jacked off, shooting thick spurts of his seed out and onto her bald vagina, and she twitched each time a fresh spurt landed.

In the end, he made a huge mess across her pussy and got some on her lower belly and her inner thighs. He ended the recording and tossed the phone onto the bed, knowing he'd drop it soon otherwise, and began to sit down on Ellen's other side.

"Wait, Gabe, get my shirt," she said. "I'm gonna fucking drip everywhere."

"Right," he replied, grabbing it and tossing it to her.

She caught it and pressed it over her crotch. "Gabe. So much. That was a *lot*."

"I was super fucking horny," he replied, still panting a little.

"Wow, you're sweaty...shit, I am, too. That was crazy hot. I came so fucking hard," she murmured. After a moment, she got up. "Okay, come on, we should shower, get ready. We've still got a hot redhead to bag. And don't forget to send that."

"Oh I won't," he replied.

"You really want that vag pic, huh?" Ellen asked, laughing as she walked out of the bedroom and into the bathroom.

"Yep," he said, sending the video and then getting up and following her.

They were in and out of the shower, clean and dry, in fifteen minutes. As they came back into the bedroom and began hunting for clothing, he checked his phone. He had a few messages. The first thing he noticed was the picture Krystal had sent.

"...wow," he muttered.

It was of her, on her back, completely naked with her legs spread open. The picture, which had to be taken by her girlfriend, showed everything.

"Holy shit, I forgot how seriously hot she is," Ellen said quietly when he showed her.

He then read the messages she'd sent.

DUDE

OMFG

WTF

WHY IS THIS SO HOT

I JUST FUCKING CAME THREE TIMES MASTURBATING TO THIS

While he was thinking of a response for that, another message and picture came.

Just in case that wasn't enough. You fucking earned it. You fucking OWN that tall bitch.

The next image was from the top down, a lot closer, of her bare pussy. She had a light dusting of red pubic hair.

"What now?" Ellen asked as she got into her jeans.

"Uh...you don't wanna know," he replied.

"What? Now I *have* to know."

He chuckled awkwardly as he showed her. She read it and her eyes widened. "Ooh that *bitch,*" she hissed, passing the phone back. "If I ever talk her into coming down here and fucking, promise me you will help me *dominate and destroy* that little slut."

"Okay, I promise," he replied.

Ellen looked indecisive for a moment, probably thinking about how she wanted to respond to Krystal's claim, (not that it was necessarily wrong), but finally just shook her head and sighed. "Come on, get dressed. It's time to see Holly."

CHAPTER THIRTY SIX

"You seem really confident about this," Gabe murmured as they pulled into the parking lot of the little diner they'd been frequenting this week.

Holly was apparently a very busy woman, because she'd been there every single time they'd driven by and then come in. He'd be a bit more worried about it not working or them coming off as creepy if it wasn't obvious that she was so damned into them.

Well, she was obviously into Ellen, but Ellen was positive she was more into him. He wasn't so sure, but he also did have a history of missing obvious tells.

"I am," Ellen replied, parking. She killed the engine. "You should be too."

"Why?" he asked.

"One: she's very into you. The way she looks at you-trust me. She wants your cock. Two: it's true what they say, women can sense insecurity. It's not a dealbreaker for a lot of us, but it weakens your position. Three: you already pretty much nailed the confidence thing. Just do what you normally do when you're feeling good. Also, to take the pressure off: if this fails, I'm pretty sure Em will lay you," she replied.

"Seriously?" he asked.

They hadn't really talked since they'd swapped oral, mostly because he'd been busy, and he suddenly wondered if he should have been trying to talk to her more.

"Seriously. We've been texting. She's horny for your dick and Abby is cool with it happening, so long as she gets to watch. Plus, you get to go raw: Emily got fixed like a decade ago. You can't knock her up and we're both clean."

"That...makes me really horny," Gabe muttered.

"Good. Let that motivate you. And just...be chill. And hey, you've got me with you."

"That I do," he agreed.

Ellen grinned and kissed him, then they got out and walked inside. It was officially November now, and it felt like the world knew it. It was colder now, and though it hadn't rained since, the skies were often overcast, and he could feel rain coming sometime soon.

Holly looked right at them as they walked in, and blushed and smiled that awkward, shy, and increasingly hopeful smile.

Good fucking *lord* did he want to have sex with her.

She was seriously famous actress hot.

They took a seat at their regular booth and she was right there with menus and a really sexy smile.

"Hello Ellen, Gabe," she said.

"Hi, Holly. It's really good to see you again. It's been a long week. Gabe's been working very hard," Ellen replied.

"Really?" she asked. "On your books?" She paused, flushed a little. "I mean, obvious-that was a dumb question. Sorry."

"It's fine," he replied. "On my latest book but also wrapping up the rest of my non-creative projects. Now it's all writing all the time."

"That must be really exciting," she murmured. She cleared her throat. "Uh, what can I get for you tonight?"

They ended up ordering their usual of burgers,

fries, and sodas, though Ellen substituted a baked potato instead of fries, and Holly wrote it down and hurried off, promising to get it to them soon.

"And now," Ellen whispered as she pulled out her phone and began navigating it, "my ace in the hole."

"So you *do* have something," he muttered.

"Yes. I do. When I lay this phone on the table, don't pick it up, just look at it."

"Check."

After a moment, she set the phone down between them on the table, pushed far enough back that while it was still visible from where Holly would be standing, it didn't seem incredibly obvious that she was meant to see it.

Gabe's eyes bulged slightly as he saw that it was a picture of Krystal's glorious pale tits.

"Are you crazy?" he whispered.

"No. Trust me. And Krystal consented to this."

"*Seriously?*"

"Seriously. She said if it helps get us lai-oop, shh. Look at it, casual," she murmured as Holly began coming back with their drinks.

"Here are your drinks—" She paused, her eyes widening as she set them down and caught sight of the perfect bare breasts on display. She stumbled socially for a moment, then straightened up and took a step back. "And I'll be back with your food shortly."

Holly turned around and walked away.

By God she had *such* a hot ass. She'd really dressed up today, or at least compared to normal. She was wearing some jeans that *really* showed off her figure, especially her ass and her hips, and her shirt was pretty low-cut, showing off some really nice tits.

He thought she even had on makeup. Was that seriously for them?

If she was trying to seduce them, it was working.

"So what did that accomplish?" he asked quietly.

"Now she's horny," Ellen replied. "She's gotta be bi, or at least questioning, because she looks down my shirt every chance she gets."

"To be fair, basically everyone loves boobs, even straight girls," he replied.

"Maybe, but I think she's bi. At the *very* least, I can get you laid."

"...you are the best girlfriend on the planet."

She just smirked and took a drink. "I know," she murmured.

A few minutes later, Holly came back with their food. She lingered for a moment, looking like she was trying to figure out what to say, but then some more people came in and she had to help them. She was definitely the hardest working person in the building. Or at least in the front part. And she *did* look a bit flushed, maybe a little sexually frustrated.

Gabe found himself feeling genuine excitement as they ate their meal.

This might actually work.

Up until now, it had basically been a fun fantasy, but now it seemed suddenly very real.

They'd come to visit every day this week, and Holly was always there to serve them. They flirted, she flirted back, though clearly she was more inexperienced. She was oddly shy for how heart-stoppingly attractive she was.

"Let me take the lead," Ellen whispered as they finished their meals.

"Check," he replied. She smiled and brushed her foot against his beneath the table.

Holly took a little bit longer than usual to come back with their check, and not because she was still busy. She seemed to be lingering around the kitchen. She did come back, though, holding their bill. She set it down cautiously on the table.

"So...Holly," Ellen murmured, running her finger around the rim of her glass and pausing just a few seconds before favoring her with a sultry smile.

"Yeah?" she asked tentatively.

"What time do you get off work?"

"Uh...about half an hour."

"Would you like to hang out with my boyfriend and I?" she asked. "We live really close. You could follow us back to our house."

"Oh wow, um, you mean like a..." she looked around the almost-empty diner, then leaned in and whispered, "like a date?"

"Something like that, yes," Ellen replied.

"With both of you?" she asked, her voice even softer.

Ellen looked at Gabe, and then so did Holly, almost like she was asking some kind of permission.

"If that's what you're into," he replied, and he was surprised at how casually and coolly that came out.

"Oh, yeah, I...uh...I am," she murmured. For a moment, she looked indecisive.

"If the answer's no, that's completely cool," Gabe said. "We won't be offended."

"That helps," Holly murmured. She looked uncertain for a few seconds longer, then abruptly came to a decision. "Yes."

"You wanna come?" he asked.

"Yes," she repeated.

"Oh sweetheart, I *promise* you will most

certainly come," Ellen murmured.

Holly blushed even more fiercely, looked down as Ellen laid a pair of twenties on the table. "Keep the change."

"Thanks...um...let me finish up my shift...you'll wait for me?" she asked.

"We'll wait for you," Gabe replied.

She nodded, then took the money and ticket and hurried off.

"I can't believe this is actually happening," Gabe muttered.

"Yep. Told you," Ellen replied.

"She might decide to call it off halfway through."

"And that would be disappointing, but I don't think she will. Relax, babe."

He slowly nodded, sitting back in his seat.

Ellen was right, he should relax.

This was going to go well.

...

Holly eventually disappeared into the kitchen and emerged about twenty minutes later. Her apron was missing and she was wearing a hot pink hoodie that looked exquisitely good on her. Gabe felt himself thrumming with excitement as she walked up to their booth.

"Okay, um...so I'm ready if you are," she said with a shy smile.

"We are so very ready, Holly," Ellen replied.

"Yep," Gabe agreed, both of them getting up. They led her outside to their car. "We live about two blocks down that road."

"All right. I'll follow you," she replied.

"Perfect."

They got into their cars and drove out of the parking lot.

"I told you…" Ellen teased.

"We got lucky," he replied. "And we haven't closed the deal yet."

"We pretty much have, and that wasn't luck, it was skill. You're better at this than you think you are," she said.

"…maybe. I guess we'll find out."

As they pulled into the driveway, Ellen grinned fiercely. "Are you excited, Gabe?"

"I mean yeah, of course I am," he replied. "I'm just...trying to temper my expectations." He paused. "Oh fuck."

"What?" she asked.

"I never bought any condoms," he replied.

"…oh. Well...I *think* I might've bought some and put them in my purse, but now I cannot fucking remember. Shit. Well, don't worry," she said, "if we can't find any, then I'll run out and grab some from Becky's. Give me a chance to fuck with Sandy again. Come on."

They got out while he was still processing that and he glanced back at Holly to see how she was doing. From her expression and body language, she seemed anxious but also excited. He wondered what her history was. She seemed so oddly shy.

"You guys have a nice house," she murmured as she approached them.

"We're really just renting," Ellen replied.

"Oh. I still think it's pretty nice."

"Thank you. I think you're pretty nice," she murmured.

"Oh. Um. Heh, thanks," she managed, blushing again.

Gabe got the door unlocked and they went inside. As he welcome them in, he looked around the living room. It definitely looked a lot better with a new coffee table, a lamp, an end table, and that couch. It really tied the room together.

"Oh wow, it's so nice and clean in here," Holly said as she hung up her hoodie. She paused. "Should I take my shoes off?"

"Considering what we're hoping to get up to, I'd say yes," Ellen replied, taking a seat on the sofa.

"Yeah, that makes sense," she murmured.

Getting out of her shoes, Holly lingered for a moment, standing there, looking a little lost. Then she walked over to the loveseat and sat down. For a moment, no one said anything.

Finally, she cleared her throat and spoke up again. "So, um, I just want to be, like, completely, one hundred percent sure that we're both on the same page...you both invited me here to have sex, right? Like, a threesome, with both of you?"

"That is correct," Ellen replied.

She let out a sigh of relief. "Oh thank God. Okay. Good." She was blushing more fiercely now and shifted around. "Well, uh, if you wanted I guess we could go back to the bedroom…"

"How about we take it slow?" Gabe suggested. "Get to know each other, ease in it. I want you to be really sure you want to do this."

"Like if I want to change my mind?" she asked.

"Yes," Ellen replied. "It's very important to us that you feel comfortable and safe. And just so we stay on the same page: if you change your mind at all, at any moment, just say so, and we'll stop."

"You won't be mad?" she asked quietly.

"No," Gabe replied. "Very disappointed,

admittedly, but not mad. Ellen is right, as much as we both want to have sex with you, don't feel like you have to. The whole idea of this is fun."

"I like that," she murmured. "I, uh...I have to admit, I've never done anything like this before. I'm...really inexperienced."

"Truly?" Ellen asked.

"Yeah."

"But you're…"

"What?" she asked.

"A supermodel?" Gabe offered.

She let out a surprised laugh. "What!? What do you mean?"

"You're a straight ten, Holly," Ellen said.

"I'm…" She glanced down at herself awkwardly. "Sweaty and dirty after a long shift. I've got bags under my eyes. I mean, I tried to touch myself up when I thought you two were, um...looking to hook up. I mean, I know I'm pretty, that's been made obvious to me, but come on, there's no way I'm a straight ten."

"You are," Gabe said. "Like *Jesus Christ* are you hot."

Holly stared at them for a bit in silence, then blinked and shook her head. "You know, I'll take it. I guess if you two are looking to have sex with me, I should be happy that you think I'm a supermodel. Um, as for your question, uh...do you really wanna know?"

"Yeah. If you're willing to talk about it, tell us about yourself," Ellen replied.

"Okay. There's not a lot to tell, I'm afraid. I grew up under the tyranny of shit ultra religious and conservative parents who hated sex and told me I'd get pregnant and die if I ever had extramarital sex and...all sorts of other lovely things. I got into college and stupidly convinced my high school sweetheart to move across the state with me so I could attend, even though he hated the idea. And then I let him talk me into quitting after a year.

"I tried making the relationship work for another two years but his severe, terrifying anger problems ultimately killed any positive feelings I had for him. I broke up with him eight months ago, hauled my meager worldly possessions back here, rented an apartment, got two jobs, and I've been furiously working to get my life together ever since and holy crap I am oversharing. Are you rethinking this whole thing now?"

"Not at all," Gabe replied.

"It sounds like you've been through a lot, Holly," Ellen said.

"Not really. I mean, he never hurt me...physically. I'm in debt but who isn't? I hate my job but who doesn't? And my inexperience, well...I never dated anyone until senior year. And that was him, my high school sweetheart...ugh, Scott."

"Wait," Ellen cut in, leaning forward and looking at her intently, "you're telling me you've only been with a single person in your life?"

"Yeah...is that bad?" she asked. "I always thought it was good? Because of the whole body count thing? Higher is better for guys but lower is better for girls?"

"First of all, body count is bullshit. Second of all, no, it's not bad, Holly. I wasn't judging at all. Just...surprised." She paused, considered something. "How was he in bed?"

"I used to think good," Holly replied, "but then I realized that he's the only person I've ever been with, so maybe he was awful?"

"Could be..." Ellen murmured with a small smile. "You'll certainly find out just how good Gabe is tonight." She paused. "Provided that is what you're looking for."

"Oh, um," she smiled and blushed, shifted around on the loveseat, "well, yes. I-yeah. What I'm looking for."

"What *are* you looking for, specifically?" Gabe asked.

"He's *very* eager to put his dick inside you," Ellen whispered loudly, making Holly giggle.

"Well, uh-so I mean, I just tell you, flat out, what I want?"

"Yes," Ellen replied. "I have found that when it comes to most things, it's best if you just say precisely what you mean. We are the ones who invited you into our house for sex, and you are the one who so graciously accepted, so I believe you should be the one to state your terms first."

"All right, uh, that makes sense. Yeah. Well...so the thing is, I'm bisexual, but I've never actually, um, done anything. With a girl. So, I guess, if we're being very up front about it: I'd like to make out with both of you, and I'd like to be gone-uh, I'd like you to go down on me, Ellen, and then I want to have sex with Gabe. Oh, also, um, I'll suck dick and, if you really want me to, I'll try eating pussy, too."

"That all sounds great to me," Gabe said.

Ellen laughed softly. "It sounds good to me, too. And, for the sake of continued responsibility, I'm afraid I need to ask: are you on birth control and do you know if you are clean from STDs or not?"

"Oh, right, yeah. Duh. I'm on birth control. I'm very good about taking it. And after I broke up with my boyfriend I kept thinking that maybe he might've cheated on me at some point. I don't have any proof but when I started reading about some of the most common signs and he did some of them, so I went and got a round of tests at a clinic. I came back clean for everything and I haven't even kissed anyone since. God, I haven't even held anyone's hand."

Gabe waited for a moment, then looked at Ellen. He was reluctant to speak, because he felt like it might be taken the wrong way if he were the one to suggest going raw. He saw a look of almost stern calculation and scrutiny on Ellen's face as she studied Holly.

"Did I say something wrong?" she murmured.

"No," Ellen replied, relaxing. "Not at all, Holly. Sorry. I was just...calculating, I guess. I've gotten really good at reading people. I feel like I can trust you. So I want to put an offer on the table that I *know* Gabe wants and honestly? I'd like it, too. But also want to emphasize that you can one hundred percent say no to this and it won't be a problem."

"...you're not gonna ask me to do, like, gross stuff, are you? Because I'm not really into that..."

Ellen laughed. "No, nothing like that. I'm going to ask if you would be willing to have unprotected sex with us."

"Oh." She considered it for a moment. "I'm guessing since you're offering, you both are positive that you're clean?"

"We are," Ellen replied. "Gabe and I both experienced...*very* unhappy breakups and, like you, were very paranoid. I knew for a fact my fiance was cheating on me. So we both got tested, and we're both clean."

"Oh my God, I'm sorry...holy shit, how insane

would someone have to be to cheat on *you?* And your *fiance?* Like...what the fuck? Did you kick his ass? Or her?"

Ellen laughed. "Him, and no...Gabe socked him in the mouth, though."

"Whoa, really?" Holly asked, looking to Gabe now.

"Yep, knocked him right on his ass!"

"To be fair, it wasn't quite so cut and dry," Gabe said.

"Don't listen to him, he's a total badass," Ellen replied. Gabe rolled his eyes. "Anyway...so how do you feel about that?"

"Well...yes. Yes, I want to go raw. I've never done it before."

Ellen's eyes widened. "Holy shit...that's amazing."

"It is?"

"Yes! Oh man, you're going to have *such* a good time tonight! Going raw is *amazing!* Gabe had never gone raw before either, and he did it with me for the first time, and, well, Gabe?"

"It's fucking incredible," he said. "Night and fucking day difference."

"Even for girls?" Holly asked. "I've heard that it's really just great for guys..."

"As a lady who has been fucked raw by Gabe *many* times over the past few weeks, I can assure you that it's fantastic," Ellen said.

"Oh, well, all right then!" She stood up suddenly. "Let's do this!"

CHAPTER THIRTY SEVEN

Something occurred to Gabe as he held Holly's soft, warm hand and led her into his and Ellen's bedroom.

Holly thought he was a confident person who knew what he was doing and had his shit together.

It didn't really matter that this wasn't true, she believed it. What felt so significant about this was that Gabe wasn't just observing this on an intellectual level, he understood it at some deeper, emotional level.

And that seemed to grant him some kind of strange but firm certainty.

As they headed into the bedroom, he considered it rationally. If what Holly said was true and he took her statements at face value, then she probably wasn't that experienced in bed. He knew he could satisfy Ellen, which went a hell of a long way towards being confident that he could satisfy Holly.

He felt his train of thought begin to derail intensely as Holly took off the shirt she was wearing and dropped it on the floor, revealing a lot of smooth, pale skin. She had on a sports bra underneath. She started unbuttoning her pants.

Well...

A lack of confidence wouldn't serve anyone here, and for once, he found that the anxiety wasn't being inflicted on him against his will.

Gabe took off his shirt and began undoing his own pants.

Ellen went and leaned against the dresser, watching the two of them with a big smile on her face.

"Ugh..." Holly groaned as she got down to her bra and panties.

"What?" Ellen asked.

"Just...I was hoping this would happen, but also I didn't really think it was going to. I should've shaved. I kinda just trimmed a little because I was feeling lazy," she said.

"I don't mind," Gabe said.

"You sure? I've heard that's like such a thing nowadays," Holly murmured uncertainly.

"I'm positive, and you should keep taking your clothes off," he replied. "Unless you want me to do it."

"I..." She smiled and turned fully to face him. "Yeah, I'd like that."

He was down to his boxers now. He prolonged putting them off as he stepped up to Holly. Good fucking lord was she beautiful. She looked like a porn star even more than before now. She had kind of ridiculous proportions.

He suddenly wondered if Ellen was going to feel self-conscious.

She seemed to be very happy right now, though, so he ignored the thought and began carefully working the bra up, lifting it up over her tits.

They tumbled out and for a moment he was struck stupid by them.

"Holy. Fuck."

"What?" she asked.

"Good *lord,*" Ellen whispered.

"*What?*" Holly asked, sounding a little worried now.

"Your tits. They are...fucking amazing. Lift your arms," Gabe replied, and got her bra off when she regained her smile and did as he said.

He tossed the sports bra aside and took a moment to simply admire her breasts. They were very pleasantly large, pale, with perfect pink nipples, a dusting of freckles over the top, near her collar bones and spilling down.

Gabe laid his hands across them, groping them gently, and she shivered as he did. They were incredibly soft and wonderfully hot. After a moment, he let go and crouched down. Grabbing her black panties, he pulled them down, revealing her pussy and her red pubic hair.

"You don't have a thing to worry about," he murmured, running his fingertip slowly up her inner thigh. She shivered hard in response.

He stood up and stepped closer to her, laying his hands on her bare hips. She looked up into his eyes, looking at once both excited and a little anxious. There was an obvious expectancy in her gaze, though, and he could tell right away that she not just expected him to lead, but she wanted it.

He could do that.

Gabe kissed her. The reaction was intense, she wrapped her arms around him and kiss him back, pushing her lips firmly against his own. He held her, feeling her big, bare breasts pushing against him, her nipples against his skin as their lips pressed together. And then he opened her mouth with his own and slipped his tongue in.

She moaned loudly and her taste flooded his mouth. Holly moaned again as he slipped a hand over the back of her neck and leaned in, deepening the kiss further. Her tongue eagerly met and danced with his own, and they made out for a good, long while.

When he pulled back, she was panting.

"Oh," she whispered.

"Oh?" he replied.

"I, um...I need a shower. I just-uh, I just realized." She blinked a few times, then giggled. "I've been running around all day, I should wash if Ellen's gonna...you know."

"That makes sense. How about we shower together?" he replied.

"Yeah, that's, um, yes. I can't believe how horny I am. It's fucking with me," she said.

"I know the feeling," Gabe replied. He took her hand and led her into the bathroom. Ellen followed and leaned against the sink now, watching them both. She still looked very pleased.

Gabe turned on the shower and then took his boxers off. He saw Holly's eyes dip down and she seemed immediately, visibly relieved.

"Oh thank God," she whispered.

"What?" he asked.

"It's just...I thought you had, like, a huge cock," she replied. Ellen started laughing softly.

"You...did?" he asked. "And you're relieved that I don't?"

"Yes. I just...Ellen's so, you know, tall. I thought maybe you had a huge-nevermind." She paused. "Oh shit, did I say something stupid? I'm sorry! I didn't mean anything bad!"

Gabe shared a look with Ellen and was very grateful to see that she was still amused.

"It's fine, Holly," Ellen said. "I can see why that would make sense."

"Okay, it's just...I always get kind of scared of it, like, hurting? Because it's too big. And, just-you know, nevermind. I should probably stop talking about it. I'm just, the last thing I'll say is that I'm *really* happy about its size," Holly replied.

"That's good to hear, Holly," Gabe said, trying not to laugh as he joined her in the shower.

"Hey, uh...so I have a question," Ellen said as he began pulling the curtain closed.

"Yeah?" he asked.

"Holly...would you consent to me filming this?" Gabe looked at Holly, who seemed to really be considering it. "No pressure. If the answer's no, that's fine."

"I...you know what? Yes. Do it. I've always wondered...you won't, like, show it to other people, will you?" she asked.

"No, Holly," Ellen replied, growing more serious. "We would never do that. And if you change your mind, we'll delete it. Okay?"

"All right. Thanks, it's-you guys are really nice," she replied.

"What we aim for," Ellen said, then regained her smile. "So, never gone raw, never been with a girl, never been filmed...you're really pure."

"Is that a bad thing?" she asked.

"Not at all. It means Gabe and I get the pleasure of...corrupting you."

"Oh." She smiled more broadly, reddening. "That's...it sounds nice. I like the idea."

"Good," Gabe said. "Now let's wash up."

He had lathered up soap and a washrag while they were talking, and he had Holly step out from under the water, trading places with her as Ellen pulled her phone out and started recording them. Gabe ran the soap over her slick naked body and her every reaction seemed pleased and even joyous. In fact, for a bit, he wondered if she was overacting as he ran the soaped rag across her back, her shoulders, down to her amazingly proportioned ass.

But then he remembered that she said she hadn't been with anyone for a long time. Maybe longer than he had, as unlikely as it seemed.

Had he been like this with Ellen?

Gabe pushed the thought aside and focused on taking care of Holly. He kept cleaning her until he moved around to the front, his chest against her back, and he began giving special attention to her breasts. He kissed the sides of her neck as he cleaned and massaged her breasts, her reactions intense and wonderful.

Then he moved lower, abandoning the washrag for the moment, and running his hands around her crotch, carefully caressing her with the tips of his fingers at first.

"Oh my," she whispered, shuddering hard.

"You still good?" he murmured in her ear.

"Ahhhh...yes," she replied softly, shivering again. "That's-mmm, this is great. Don't stop. Please."

Gabe responded by continuing to touch and caress her, working slowly inwards towards her clit until he touched it with his fingertip and began to massage it. She let out a cry of pleasure. She was extremely keyed up, and he learned just how much when, maybe fifteen seconds into the pleasuring, she orgasmed.

She orgasmed *hard*.

He had to hold her up to keep her from falling over as she began crying out, soon breaking down into full on screaming as she came.

"Oh my God," she panted when she was finished, "oh fuck. Oh fuck. I need to sit."

"Yeah, here," he said, carefully helping her down.

"Holy shit...holy shit..." she whispered, leaning against one wall, her eyes closed. Occasionally another quiver would run through her nude, wet body. "That was...oh my God. Too intense. I haven't orgasmed like that in...I can't remember. Fuck."

"That was incredible," Ellen murmured.

"I'm worried I looked stupid," Holly replied softly. "I couldn't control myself at all."

"That's what made it look so good," Ellen said. "Trust me, girl, you looked *amazing.*"

"Thanks," Holly replied. She looked up at him with a sultry smile, looking absurdly erotic with her red hair wet and plastered to her face. "Hey...since I'm down here..."

She reached out and wrapped her fingers around his erection. Gabe just turned to face her a little more by way of reaction and she took the meaning immediately, shifting so that she was sitting at the proper height and sticking her tongue out.

Gabe settled a hand over the back of her head as Holly started licking his erection. Hot pleasure jolted into him as her tongue went everywhere. She took her time licking, dragging her tongue all over his shaft and head, granting him a great deal of pleasure. When she slipped it into her mouth and started sucking him off, bobbing her head, he knew the temptation to blow off was going to be too much. Well, he could do it twice.

"Use your tits," Ellen said after a bit.

Holly took his dick from her mouth and grinned, taking the opportunity to push her hair back out of her face.

"All right," she said, grasping her big breasts and pressing them together with his erection between them. She began sliding them up and down.

The sight was incredibly erotic.

Right when he was about to ask her about taking his load, she asked, "Do you wanna come on my face or in my mouth?"

"Face," he replied immediately.

She grinned more broadly. "Okay. Just tell me when."

"Good girl," he replied, putting his hand over the back of her head again.

She took his meaning and put his dick back in her mouth, then began bobbing her head again. She definitely wasn't as skilled as Ellen at pleasuring dick with her mouth, but Gabe found that he did not mind at all. He was thoroughly enjoying what she was doing for him and glad that they seemed to be so sexually compatible.

Holly had him coming in less than half a minute after that. He gave her a quick warning and she fumbled it a little bit, seemingly surprised, but she got him out of her mouth and started jacking him off rapidly so that he began shooting his load right onto her face. He groaned as his seed came out of him and spurted across her beautiful, pale face.

She opened her mouth at some point and aimed his cock into it, letting him shoot the rest of his load inside. When he was finished, she put his dick in her mouth and sealed her lips around it, then sucked as she pulled her head slowly back, giving him an extra burst of pleasure.

"Oh fuck," he panted as she finished with him.

"Can I get some help? You came on my eyes," she said, her eyes shut firmly.

"Yeah," he replied, reaching up and getting the showerhead down. "Hold your breath."

She nodded and he washed her face off, cleaning

his seed from it. She reached up and ran her hands over her face several times, then opened her mouth, gargled and spat a few times, then he returned the showerhead and helped her up.

"So, did it look good?" she asked, grinning in a way that made it seem like she already knew the answer.

"Extremely," Ellen replied. "So fucking hot. Now, why don't the two of you finish washing up so that I can have my time to shine?"

CHAPTER THIRTY EIGHT

A few minutes later, Gabe found himself holding the cell phone and recording probably the most erotic, sexiest thing he'd ever seen in his life.

He was in the bedroom and both women were completely naked now. Holly was on her back with her legs spread wide and Ellen was knelt at the foot of the bed, her hands wrapped around Holly's thick, pale thighs and her face buried in Holly's crotch.

Their redheaded lover for the night was crying out in pure ecstasy as Ellen went to work on her.

Holly cried out as she ran her hands over and through Ellen's pale blonde hair, shuddering and jerking violently as the pleasure ate into her. Ellen really knew what she was doing, he saw, her tongue as skilled with Holly as it was with him.

He watched intently as Ellen licked at her clit, easing back sometimes and then piling on the pressure, going harder and faster. And then Holly let out a long, loud cry of bliss as Ellen slipped a finger into her and began fucking her with it.

She made her orgasm twice before she finally sat back and wiped her mouth with the back of her hand, grinning fiercely.

"Okay, your turn," she said, standing.

They switched places and Ellen took the phone. She continued recording as Gabe took up her spot, standing at the foot of the bed in between Holly's spread open legs. Her pussy was positively glistening with desire and she shuddered as an aftershock of ecstasy ran through her.

"Are you ready?" he asked, laying a hand on her thigh.

"Yes," she replied.

"Are you still comfortable going raw?" he asked.

"Yes," she moaned, "use me."

Gabe almost felt a shudder of pure lust run through him as she said that. He was erect again but that just made his whole body pulse with need, with intense want, and he stepped up against her and penetrated her without waiting any further.

Holly moaned loudly, her body trembling, breasts jiggling magnificently as she accepted his length, and oh good lord how *wet* she was inside. How fantastically hot. How she sheathed around him perfectly. He groaned and grabbed her hips as he worked his way inside of her.

"Oh *fuck!*" she cried, bringing her legs up, folding them, and spreading them wider. "Oh my fucking God it's *so good!*" she shrieked.

"Told you," Ellen said smugly.

Gabe grasped her big heaving breasts, feeling electrified with lust as he drove into her. Once he was comfortably inside of her and felt she could take him all, he really laid into her, stroking fast and hard, making her scream and shudder and writhe in pure ecstasy.

Her very quickly became lost in the encounter, aware of only Holly before him.

She opened her eyes at some point, staring intensely at him, panting, gasping almost. She placed her hands over the back of his and before long he took them and they held their hands together between them, fingers lacing, still staring at each other.

Something was definitely happening. His heart was racing, singing in his chest with lust and desire and something more.

At some point, the session became less sexual

and more intimate and he didn't know what to do about it or even how to stop it. Gabe found himself worrying that Ellen would get angry, get jealous, but she said nothing. A quick glance at her showed her face mostly hidden behind the phone. She didn't seem angry but he couldn't tell for sure.

And then Holly drew his attention back, forcefully, like magnetism. He locked eyes with her and then he leaned down, embracing her more, and she wrapped her legs around him. They kissed passionately and he felt her hands at his back, felt her writhing in pure rapture as he made love to her.

When he knew he was very close to finishing, he began to ask, "Can I–"

And she interrupted him with an immediate: "Yes."

And then it was like she was begging him to finish inside of her, begging with her body, and then he started to orgasm. Gabe had to hold himself up, letting go of her and pressing his hands into the mattress as he cried out and started to come inside of her. He released his seed into her waiting, willing pussy and she took everything he had, crying out as she squeezed him with her legs, forcing him deeper inside of her.

Gabe filled Holly up with every bit of his seed left in him and the pleasure was like a seismic event, like a tidal wave cresting his own personal horizon.

All he saw were her eyes.

It ended slowly, and he could feel his body jerking in fits and starts as the aftershocks of the orgasm ran through him. He came back to himself, sweaty and trembling a little, gasping for breath as he rested his head against Holly's, staring down at her.

Neither of them spoke as they recovered for a

moment, then they both moaned as he pulled carefully out of her. They continued to recover in silence as he sat down heavily on the bed beside her and flopped onto his back, staring at the ceiling, feeling dizzy.

At some point he became aware of Ellen walking, first out of the room, then back into it.

"Here Holly," she said, and he was so glad that he couldn't hear a trace of anger in her voice.

"What...oh...thank you," she murmured, accepting the toiletpaper and beginning to clean herself up. He'd made a huge mess inside of her.

"Are you okay, love?" Ellen asked, appearing in his field of vision and smiling down at him serenely.

"Yes...a little dizzy. Fuck," he whispered, still panting.

"That was extremely intense," Ellen replied.

"Yeah," they both murmured.

"So, was I right about going raw?" she asked.

"Fuck yes. Also about the other thing. Holy mother of God, I've *never* had sex like that. Or oral. You are...oh I don't even know. That oral was-I didn't know it could feel like that."

"You can see why being corrupted is a good thing," Ellen replied.

"Yes. Goodness." She shuddered again and made a sound deep in her throat. "Um...would it be absolutely rude to ask to spend the night? My legs are actually shaking so bad I don't even know if I could drive home safely..."

Ellen laughed, sounding genuinely amused. "I'm all right with it. Gabe?"

"Yeah, definitely. We could all fit in this bed," he replied.

"Oh, I meant, like, the couch out there, but...well,

if you'd let me, yeah I'd love to." She yawned suddenly, long and loud. "Oh wow I'm like *crazy* tired now, but I need another shower…"

"I'll help you," Gabe said.

"Thank you. You're both so nice."

It took him a bit, but Gabe managed to get up, and then he and Ellen both helped her back to the shower. She wasn't kidding about her legs, or about how tired she was. They took a quick, economical shower, her mostly cleaning up between her legs, and then he was helping her to bed. She was having trouble staying awake as he got her beneath the blankets.

"Are you sure I'm not imposing?" she murmured.

"We're sure, Holly. Do you work tomorrow?" Gabe replied.

"No…I'm off for tomorrow," she replied, then yawned again.

"Okay. Sleep long and well, we'll be here if you need anything," he said.

"Kiss me goodnight," she murmured as she got settled in the center of the bed beneath the blankets.

He laughed and kissed her. She kissed him back with a little burst of strength, then she fell back into the bed and before he and Ellen left the room, she was out like a light.

Gabe closed the door most of the way and then looked at Ellen. She was looking back at him and her expression worried him a little. She didn't seem angry, but she did seem…he wasn't sure. Intense, at the very least.

"Do we need to talk about that?" he asked quietly.

"Yes," Ellen replied, and nodded her head to the

living room.

He followed her and they sat down together on the sofa. Ellen continued staring at him in what almost seemed like wonder for a bit longer.

"So...are you angry?" he asked.

"No," she replied simply, shaking her head.

"All right, good start. What...how do you feel about what just happened?"

"Amazed," she replied.

"Seriously?"

"Yes." Another moment of silence played out between them and she finally gave her head a little shake and sat back and relaxed a bit. "Sorry, I'm not trying to freak you out. I'm...honestly really amazed."

"By what?"

"A few things. I mean, the first thing was how fucking *hot* that was. That was the hottest sex I've ever seen in my life. Fucking no contest. But also how intimate it got. You two...*really* connected."

"And that doesn't bother you?" he asked.

"Are you going to leave me for her?" Ellen replied.

He blinked, surprised by the bluntness of the question. "No," he said simply, knowing it to be true.

He *really* liked Holly, he could tell that already, and not just because she was a supermodel crossed with a porn star in terms of sheer sex appeal, or because she apparently loved fucking him as much as he loved fucking her. He imagined they would get along well, and while he imagined it was very possible that he could fall in love with Holly if they began dating, his love for Ellen felt...undeniable. Immutable. Eternal.

"And I believe you, so I'm not jealous," she replied. "If anything, I'm happy. That girl...is very lonely. I can just tell that. She's lonely and she's been through a lot and she's...lost. I think she might be like us, Gabe. She has so few other people she can count on, people she can actually trust. I want to just...take care of her. Don't you?"

"Yeah," he murmured. "I got that feeling too."

"And she wants to be taken care of. By us." She paused. "Maybe I'm wrong, maybe I'm going too fast with this, but I really don't think so. But, at the very least, we can afford to wait. Let some time pass, hang out with her more, get to know her better. But that isn't even the thing that has me so amazed."

"What is?"

"Seeing you with her, Gabe. The way you treated her, the way you talked with her. You were dominating and *hot,* to be sure, but more significantly, you were patient and kind and loving with her. She put herself in your hands, utterly, and every step of the way you were *so* good with her. That girl felt *loved* during that, I could see it in her eyes." She laughed softly, shaking her head. "It sounds insane, but seeing you fuck another woman made me love you more. But you were amazing with her. It just...I don't know, I guess it really threw into sharp focus for me how kind and loving you are."

"...I'm not sure what to say to this," Gabe murmured after a long moment.

"You don't have to say anything," she replied, leaning forward and kissing him. "Just know that I feel even better about our relationship, and about taking it in this direction. Maybe I'm jumping the gun, but...I don't think I am. I knew I at the very least wanted to attempt getting another woman involved in our relationship sexually. But seeing with you Holly...I can definitely see us dating her and living with her. It just-this feels so *right,* Gabe."

"I...feel the same way," he murmured. "But...it's hard to tell if I'm just absolutely psyched at the idea of fucking and dating two *insanely* hot women."

Ellen laughed. "I understand. I'm feeling the same way, if I'm being completely honest. And like I said, we'll take our time. We'll see how it plays out. But I think that's the direction we're headed in." She broke off and yawned. "Shit, I'm tired, too."

"Are you horny?" he asked.

"Duh."

"I don't think I could have sex again tonight, not after that, but I can definitely get you off," he said.

Ellen grinned broadly. "I love you so much."

"I love you too, Ellen. Now, spread your legs."

CHAPTER THIRTY NINE

Gabe had dreams that night, all of them good.

At some point, dream melted into reality when he came awake to Ellen pushing him onto his back.

"*Someone* has morning wood," he heard her murmur.

"Uh...what?" he managed, then groaned loudly as he felt her penetrate herself with his erection. She moaned as well, taking his length in as she pushed herself down, and fuck was she *wet*. Gabe groaned louder as she began to ride him and his hands found her hips.

"Oh man, you look so amazing, Ellen," Holly murmured.

Ellen rode him until she made herself orgasm, letting out a high-pitched cry of absolute bliss and making a little mess on his hips and thighs, and then she looked over at Holly. "You wanna finish him off?"

"Yes," Holly replied immediately and eagerly.

Ellen laughed. "Love you, sweetheart," she said, and then got off of him and headed out of the room.

Holly mounted him so eagerly that she almost fell off the bed, but then she was taking his erection into herself again and she moaned loudly. Then she was riding him with an intense speed, gasping and panting and moaning in sheer bliss as they fucked, her tits bouncing amazingly.

She kept going until she'd made herself orgasm and when she laid down against him, spent, Gabe rolled over so that she was beneath him and she screamed in pleasure as he began driving into her.

"Oh *yes! Gabe! YES!*" she shrieked and then he

cried out as he started coming inside of her again.

It wasn't as intense as last time, but it was especially gratifying given it was morning sex with a hot redhead he was still adjusting to sexually.

Like last time, they laid together for a while, her atop him, her huge tits pressing against his bare chest, both of them sweaty and breathing heavily.

They didn't move until he heard Ellen finish with her shower and emerge from the bathroom in a robe with her hair wrapped up in a towel.

"Shower's free, you two," she said.

"I do need another shower," Holly murmured.

"Same," Gabe agreed.

"Can I use your toothbrush?" she asked as they got up and headed for the bathroom. "I was so horny last night I wasn't really planning ahead."

"Yeah, you can," he replied.

He started up the shower and waited until she'd finished. While she climbed into the shower, he washed his toothbrush off and then brushed his own teeth. Stepping into the shower, he found her with the showerhead down, aimed up at her crotch.

"You come, like, a lot," she murmured, yawning.

"You're *really* hot," he replied.

She laughed, then slowly lost her smile as she finished up and replaced the showerhead. "So...Ellen's really cool with the fact that we full on fucked, right? I mean, I know she went down on me and everything, it's just...I've never done anything like this before. Not even close. I've never even seen people have sex, outside of a little porn and hearing people doing it at a party once at college..."

"Don't worry, Holly," Gabe replied, "Ellen's cool with what happened. Honestly, she's really happy. We stayed up and talked a little bit about it last night and she's really thrilled about it."

"Okay. That's good. I like you and Ellen, it's just...she's *really* intimidating. I'd be so scared if she got mad at me. And I've *never* seen a woman mad like a woman who caught her boyfriend fucking another woman."

"Trust me. Everything is very chill and happy right now," he replied.

"Good." She looked relieved, then she smiled and hugged him suddenly. "Thank you."

"For what?" he asked, hugging her.

"For being so nice. I've always wanted to do something like this, but I was always so scared to. And I know that a lot of it was my stupid religious parents trying to scare me, but some of it was legit. I mean, there's a lot of stories out there about hookups gone really wrong. And I thought that even if it did go decently, it'd be...not all great."

"How so?"

"I don't know, I guess I figured I'd be more...used?" She laughed. "I mean, I know I literally told you to use me, but it's like you can separate domination during sex and everything else. You can fuck me like a slut and still be nice to me, if that makes sense?"

"That makes a lot of sense," he replied, and kissed the top of her head.

She giggled and rubbed herself against him. "Yeah, it's just...nice. It feels *so* good. I haven't been touched in forever, even just a hug."

"Ellen and especially I will be so very glad to continue touching you, in a lot of ways," he replied. "If you're interested in that."

"Dear God *yes,* Gabe," she replied, stepping back and looking at him intently. "Last night was the best thing I've ever felt in my entire life. Without question. And I really, really, *really* want more."

"I do, too," he said, giving her bare ass a squeeze. "A lot more."

"Oh fuck, I just realized we haven't tried doggystyle yet. Ellen was *really* right about it feeling different and *so* much better raw. I mean it might have been your dick or how you fuck, but I think it was the lack of a condom. Just...*ah!* It was amazing." She shivered and grinned broadly.

"I do know how you feel about that. Fucking Ellen raw for the first time ever was mind-blowing. Night and day difference." He stepped under the shower and began washing his hair. "How about we finish up and I put together some breakfast?"

"Seriously?" She laughed. "I was gonna offer, actually."

"You've been working all week, and I don't mind," he replied. "Besides, I'm the host."

Her grin broadened a little and she giggled again. "All right...man, if Ellen didn't have you I don't think I'd leave until you agreed to be my boyfriend." She lost her smile suddenly. "Ah man, did I make it weird? I...don't really know what's okay in situations like these."

"I'll take it as a huge compliment," he replied, "and if I wasn't dating Ellen, I'd be very happy to date you."

"I...oh. Mmm. All right," she murmured, blushing now.

They finished cleaning up, got out, and dried off. When they got back into the bedroom, Holly frowned at her clothes, still discarded on the floor.

"Hmm...my clothes are still gross," she murmured.

"I could wash them," he replied.

"What'll I wear in the meantime?"

"You could wear nothing. I'd be pretty thrilled to have such a hot naked redhead in my house," he replied. "And so would Ellen."

"Okay then," she said with a shrug and a smile.

Gabe finished getting dressed and gathered up her clothes, tossed them in with his and Ellen's own, and then headed to the kitchen. He heard Ellen make appreciative sounds as Holly walked into the living room. He heard them start talking as he started up the laundry, then moved over to the oven and began preparing breakfast.

"We good with bacon and eggs?" he called.

Both women called back affirmatively and he got to it. From the sound of the conversation, it seemed like they were getting along very well. As he fried up the bacon, he found that he had his own concerns about the situation. He believed Ellen that she was happy about everything that had happened so far, but he couldn't shake the paranoia that she was going to realize she hated the fact that she'd invited another woman into their bed.

He'd been on the bad end of some hardcore jealousy and it had been extremely unpleasant.

But as he finished off the bacon and moved over to the eggs, he felt the fears slowly begin to dissolve. He trusted her, and more than that, he trusted her to know herself. They were still figuring things out, but Ellen seemed pretty confident, and so far she hadn't misled him, even unintentionally, on much of anything.

Gabe decided he was just going to enjoy this.

He had a hot, naked woman he'd just had sex with, twice, in his house, and she was chatting happily with his girlfriend, who he'd also had sex with, and if he couldn't enjoy that, then he wasn't really going to enjoy much of anything.

Finishing up, he brought the food out to the living room and sat down with them to enjoy breakfast and bask in the glow of the morning after.

"This is amazing," Holly said as she started eating. "Thanks for...everything. The sex and letting me spend the night and the breakfast and being so nice. Have you both really not done this before? Because this all feels so...handled, you know? Like you know *exactly* what you're doing."

"This is definitely the first time we've done something like this," Ellen replied. She paused. "Well...I guess that isn't completely true."

"Oh yeah?" she asked.

"Yep," Ellen said, picking up her phone and navigating it. "Last week we went to a little get together to reconnect with one of my oldest, and only, friends left. And...well, if you want, you can watch."

"Em said it's all right?" Gabe asked.

"Yep. She said I could show it to 'sexual conquests we trust'," Ellen replied.

"You both definitely conquered me last night...and this morning," Holly said, grinning. She accepted the phone and watched the video. "Oh...holy crap, she's *hot!* All those tattoos..."

"Her wife is watching her suck my dick," Gabe said.

"Whoa! That's-wow." She started breathing a little more heavily. "That's...really hot."

"It gets better in the second half," Gabe replied.

He kept eating as Holly kept watching the video, and before long Ellen leaned over and joined her. He soon heard Emily crying out.

"Okay, wow, yes. Crazy hot," Holly murmured.

"You look like you're getting pretty hot and bothered," Ellen said. "I'm pretty sure Gabe wouldn't mind a round three."

"I, uh…" She passed the phone back, flushed again. "Well…" She paused as a beep sounded from somewhere nearby. "Damn, that's my phone," she muttered, getting up and tracking down her purse. Gabe found himself with a great view of her well-padded ass as she dropped into a crouch and rifled through her purse.

Holly stood and turned to face them, navigating her phone. She paused and looked down at herself. "It's weird being naked around you both but...also not weird? I thought I'd be a lot more uncomfortable, but I'm not."

"Good, you shouldn't be, you look fantastic," Ellen said, leaning back and opening up her robe, exposing her long, nude body.

"So do you," she said, then sighed as she looked at her phone. "Shit, right. I forgot. I had responsibilities today."

"You can't blow it off?" Gabe asked.

"No, not really," she replied, sounding deflated. "But, I have to stay at least until the laundry is done and I have my clothes back."

"True," Ellen replied.

She rejoined them on the couch and they went back to eating.

They ended up talking for the remainder of their time together, mostly listening to Holly talk about herself and her life. The more they listened, the more it felt like she was one of them: a disillusioned, disenfranchised soul in the process of being slowly consumed by modern society. And the more it seemed like Ellen's assessment was correct.

In the end, Holly dressed and then slipped into the bathroom.

"Hey, would you both come in here for a minute?" she asked.

"Yeah," Gabe replied, and they joined her, finding her standing in front of the mirror, staring at herself. "What's up?"

"Could I have a favor?"

"Sure," Ellen replied.

"Would you both, like...pose with me for a picture? I kinda want to brag to my friends about the *amazing* hookup I had with the hot guy and the tall goddess and they will never believe me if I don't have evidence." She paused. "Unless that's weird? I mean, you don't have to."

"I'll do it," Ellen said.

"Yeah, definitely," Gabe agreed.

"Thank you!" She aimed her phone at the mirror and they took a moment to adjust themselves. Ellen still had her robe on. She shifted it so that it showed off a lot of her huge breasts and put off the most satisfied, seductive grin he'd seen her wear.

Holly snapped the picture. "Okay, that's awesome...could I get another, with you two kissing me on the cheeks?"

They both agreed and leaned in, kissing her on her cheeks until she snapped a second photo.

"These are so awesome, thank you! You guys are both so nice and fun," she said.

"You're pretty nice and fun yourself," Ellen replied as they walked back to the living room.

Holly pulled on her shoes and coat, then hesitated as she slipped her purse over her shoulder. She looked at them a little hesitantly. "So...can we do this again?

I don't really know the protocol."

"We don't really either. I think we should just be kind and say what we want. No bullshitting each other," Gabe replied, and Ellen nodded. "And I'd be very happy to do this again."

"So would I," Ellen said.

Gabe reached out and ran a finger slowly along Holly's jawline, down to her chin, and she closed her eyes and shivered, exhaling harshly. "You still need to be broken in," he said, and surprised himself by saying it. It just felt right, and apparently it was.

Holly smiled demurely. "I'd like to be broken in a lot more by both of you."

"Good. We're free most nights, so how about you let us know the next time you want to come over," Gabe suggested.

"I will," she said. Holly began to turn to leave, but stopped, turning back. "Can I have a kiss? From each?"

"Yes," Ellen said. She leaned in and gave her a long, lingering kiss. Gabe did the same, savoring the experience.

"Thanks," she murmured, hesitating for a moment. She began to say something else, stopped herself, laughed awkwardly. "Uh...okay, bye," she said, and headed outside.

They stood in the doorway, watching as she walked out into a gray world. It hadn't rained during the night, but he smelled it on the air and doubted it would be much longer before at least a light rain began to saturate the city once more.

Holly got into her car, started it up, then waved goodbye with a cheery smile before backing out and driving away.

They closed the door and sat back down on the

couch.

"That was amazing," Gabe said after a bit.

"Very," Ellen agreed.

They sat together for a bit longer until finally Gabe roused himself.

"What now?" Ellen asked.

"I'm actually feeling pretty inspired to write," he replied, "you okay with that?"

"Yeah, definitely. Go. Put that inspiration to use," Ellen said, grinning. "I've got to brag to Krystal about the *insanely* hot redhead we bedded."

He laughed and gave her a kiss, then headed to his office.

…

"Hey, babe...are you all right?" Ellen asked from behind him.

Gabe came out of his thoughts, realizing that he'd been staring at the video of a bonfire he'd called up for some time now. It was raining again.

"Yeah," he replied, distracted.

"You've been looking at that video a lot recently," Ellen said, walking into his office. He'd left his door open this time around. "Is there something significant about it?"

"Maybe," he replied. "I guess...mmm."

"Tell me what's on your mind."

"All right, might as well. Two things are on my mind. The more immediate one is that night at the party, looking at the fire after hooking up with Emily, it gave me this idea. Like a hint of an idea, like a spark, but I kind of rejected it because it seemed a little nuts. But it won't leave me alone, I keep thinking about it and even more than that, it keeps growing. New ideas are adding onto it."

"What is the idea?"

"I want to write, like, a stone age erotica? But that's stupid, right? I can't really find many other examples of it, beyond some famous romance novels that are stone age or stone age-adjacent and have sex scenes, or those weird time travel novels, where like a chick gets thrown back in time or a Viking or caveman or something gets thrown forward in time and then sex happens. I kinda just want to write about, you know, two stone age people meeting and banging and maybe falling in love?"

"So why not do it? Especially if there's not really any examples of it. Maybe it's a thing people want to read and you could fill that gap?" she suggested.

"Maybe. But sometimes a given niche isn't written about for a good reason, that reason being: no one wants to read about it," he replied.

"Perhaps...but aren't you in a position to find out?" she asked. He considered it. "I mean, we've got time. You could make this a side project, and if you're feeling it, you should do it."

He nodded after a moment. "Yeah, all right. You've got a point." Gabe laughed and shook his head, a little frustrated. "I feel like I hesitate over everything."

"Well, you're cautious. And that's not a bad quality or instinct. But...yeah, you could probably stand to be a little more decisive." She paused. "Although honestly, I feel like you're already headed in that direction. You've gotten more confident in the short time that I've known you, and it seems to be serving you well."

"Apparently," he muttered.

"What was the second thing?"

He frowned, then got up. "Come on. I want to talk about this where we can both sit down." She followed him into the living room and they sat together on the couch. He held up his phone. "I went through every single contact on my list and something just kind of hit me: I can't really trust or rely on just about anyone in my life, nor do I want to see them. And it really hit home what we were talking about earlier, how it seemed like, except just a tiny handful of people, there's really no one else we can trust but each other. So I deleted everyone in my phone but you, Holly, Krystal, Emily, and Sadie. It was almost three dozen numbers."

"I did that too, actually, earlier in the week," Ellen said.

"And it got me thinking about other things. Mainly about you and me, and our life together. Something feels different now. It's like...all my life, I've been waiting for something, or trying to get to something, reaching for something, some way of living that I want but can't just not get, but can't even figure out how to get *to*. And now, suddenly, it's like, I found the path. I found the way forward. Everything I've been doing ever since I made the decision to get serious about my writing, and especially since you came back into my life, just suddenly feels so much more meaningful and significant. And a lot of stuff is just colliding in all the right ways."

"So what are you thinking specifically?" she asked.

"I'm thinking...you and I should go our own way. Every job we've ever had is fucking bullshit. The bosses are bullshit, the wages are bullshit, the work is bullshit. So many people are fake or liars or trying to fuck us over somehow. Society is always trying to cram us into some stupid fucking box and demand that we conform and work ourselves to death and I've always hated it.

"I've always felt like every job I ever had was just a waste of my time, it never felt like it *meant* anything. But the writing, and the things I've done with you? It *means* something. I want to find some way to make our lives work with me writing independently, and you not working and figuring out what you want to do with your life, and we rely on ourselves and people we actually trust and no one else. I want to craft a life and a path of our own."

"I want that, too," Ellen said, getting more excited as he spoke. "That's *exactly* what I want, and everything you're saying, I've felt it too. All of this, everything we've done together, it finally feels *right*. It finally feels like I'm going in a direction that I want to go in." She paused, then held out her hand. "So, we're doing this?"

Gabe took her hand and squeezed it. "We're doing this."

ABOUT ME

I am Misty Vixen (not my real name obviously), and I imagine that if you're reading this, you want to know a bit more about me.

In the beginning (late 2014), I was an erotica author. I wrote about sex, specifically about human men banging hot inhuman women. Monster girls, alien ladies, paranormal babes. It was a lot of fun, but as the years went on, I realized that I was actually striving to be a harem author. This didn't truly occur to me until late 2019-early 2020. Once the realization fully hit, I began doing research on what it meant to be a harem author. I'm kind of a slow learner, so it's taken me a bit to figure it all out.

That being said, I'm now a harem author!

Just about everything I write nowadays is harem fiction: one man in loving, romantic, highly sexual relationships with several women.

I'd say beyond writing harems, I tend to have themes that I always explore in my fiction, and they encompass things like trust, communication, respect, honesty, dealing with emotional problems in a mature way...basically I like writing about functional and healthy relationships. Not every relationship is perfect, but I don't really do drama unless the story actually calls for it. In total honesty, I hate drama. I hate people lying to each other and I hate needless rom-com bullshit plots that could have been solved by two characters have a goddamned two minute conversation.

Check out my website
www.mistyvixen.com

Here, you can find some free fiction, a monthly
newsletter, alternate versions of my cover art where
the ladies are naked, and more!

Check out my twitter
www.twitter.com/Misty_Vixen

I update fairly regularly and I respond to pretty much
everyone, so feel free to say something!

Finally, if you want to talk to me directly, you can
send me an e-mail at my address:
mistyvixen@outlook.com

Thank you for reading my work! I hope you enjoyed
reading it as much as I enjoyed writing it!

-Misty